THE SAVIOR'S RISE

THE SAVIOR'S RISE

TALLI L. MORGAN

TLM Books

For Adam. Because you told me to, and also because you were right. I wasn't done.

This is the way the world ends
This is the way the world ends
This is the way the world ends
Not with a bang but a whimper.

— T.S. Eliot, "The Hollow Men"

PART I

I

TAJA

TAJA STOOD AT THE EDGE of Båthälla's town square and faced a crowd of at least two dozen former friends and neighbors all shouting praises to *Sawwia Setukkda*, but every pair of eyes was on Jekku.

He had expected this, to a degree. But it had been so easy to forget over the past few days that Båthälla was still painfully stuck in the past, and Taja remained an unwelcome outsider.

Beside him, Jekku shifted on his feet, betraying his unease. Taja started to reach for his hand, but stopped himself. *No, not anymore.* He tried to read Jekku's expression, but whatever he was feeling was uncharacteristically under wraps. His eyes darted from one side of the town square to the other, taking in the faces of Elshalans who had paused in the middle of their day to gawk at the returned Second Savior.

More shouts of "*Sawwia Setukkda!*" echoed across the square and then Taja saw the flicker of panic in Jekku's eyes. Anxiety stirred in his chest; hadn't Jekku expected this? They had talked about this. Taja had told Jekku to be ready to step back into the role of Second Savior until the two of them found a way to tell Båthälla the truth. Taja and Jekku had spent hours trying to imagine every feasible outcome of their return to Båthälla, and Jekku had insisted that he'd know what to do when the moment came.

But now it was here, and Jekku was frozen.

Apparently Taja was alone, after all.

It's fine, it's better this way. He was *Sawwia Setukkda*, not Jekku, and he could do the talking. He could face his own people.

These are the people I grew up with. Most of them were like family at some point. I have friends out there. I have relatives and neighbors and kind acquaintances. It wasn't as though they were strangers.

Taja took a deep breath and stepped forward. He had to force himself to keep his head up and shoulders straight; he could not afford to show a single hint of doubt or weakness. Yes, these people were once his friends and loved ones, but seven years was a long time to be apart from them. Especially since all Ebris had done for those seven years was stir up exaggerated lies about Taja's loyalty to Båthälla.

He stopped in the middle of the square. A few murmurs scattered around him, but mostly the lingering Elshalans just stared. Taja made himself meet their eyes. Most of them looked confused, some a little apprehensive. He could feel the more hostile glares boring into the back of his head, and told himself not to look. A few people quietly slipped away, moving on with their days.

Taja let them go, but he couldn't afford to lose any more attention. He looked around the square, then went to the giant brass bell that hung in its tower beside the temple. It was meant to be used only by the gods for important announcements, but...

This qualified.

Taja grabbed the rope and yanked it hard. The bell's shrill clang rattled his bones, but it did its job. Minutes later, dozens more people rushed toward the square. They scrambled with wide eyes and panicked expressions that visibly hardened when they saw Taja standing by the bell.

He went up the temple steps and waited for the crowd to settle. Now it was truly a crowd; at least a hundred people gathered before him, with more still coming from the farther reaches of the village. Taja ignored his thundering heart and cleared his throat.

"People of Båthälla." The crowd fell instantly silent. "I know I'm the last person you want to see here. I know we have a rocky history. But just for a minute, hear me out. The news I bring concerns every single one of us."

He paused and scanned the crowd. "Lord Ebris has Fallen."

An outburst of gasps and voices drowned out Taja's attempt to reassure them. The faces before him quickly turned from shock to rage; any hope Taja had that they'd listen to him was instantly snuffed out. He searched the gathering for any sign of lingering attention, and his heart seized as his eye caught on someone he hadn't thought of in years.

Oh, no.

Ellory Ives was famous in Båthälla for two things: being Lord Ebris's son, and not shutting up about it. They were nearly the spitting image of Ebris -- the only difference being their eyes, which, instead of honey gold, were mismatched: one blue and one green. But if something like arrogance and a general tendency to be insufferable were inheritable traits, Ellory had received a double helping of each.

To Taja, they were famous for being a lifelong thorn in his side.

Taja tracked them as they shoved through the crowd. Fury burned in their mismatched eyes, and Taja scrambled for something to say before Ellory could gain the first word and the upper hand; if he lost his audience to Ellory, he'd never get it back.

"Listen!" Taja pleaded, shouting over the increasingly angry voices surrounding him. "I know how it sounds! But give me a chance to explain and you'll understand that Ebris never had our best interests in mind. Only his own. There's a reason he Fell. Just give me—"

"*Enough!*" The square fell abruptly silent at Ellory's booming voice. They shoved their way out of the throng and up the steps, facing Taja. "*Traitor,*" they hissed, and Taja winced. "How *dare* you? First you turn your back on your own people to chase after a human girl, and now you have the audacity to come back here and claim that *Lord Ebris* is the one who betrayed us?" Ellory barked a mirthless laugh and looked over their shoulder at the gathered Elshalans. "Sounds to me like someone doesn't know how to let go of a grudge. Is this your *Sawwia Setukkda,* my friends?"

A unanimous cry of *No!* rang up from below.

Taja's hands began to shake. His instincts shouted at him to run, but what good would that do? He forced himself to hold Ellory's gaze, to not shrink under the glare of the one person who had *always,* without fail, found a way to dig deep under his skin.

Ellory's mouth twisted into a scowl. "You're a disgrace. Get out of my town."

Taja swallowed and struggled to keep his voice calm. "I have every right to be here that you do. Take *your* resentment out of here, Ellory."

They opened their mouth to retort, but Taja barreled on. "It's true I made a mistake, but that was *seven years* ago. Isn't it time to leave it in the past? Ebris found it in him to forgive me. You ought to learn to do the same. I am not your enemy. Ebris is."

The next seconds blurred. Ellory swept their hand through the air and Taja ducked, certain they were about to strike him but the blow never landed. He felt a burst of heat and caught a glimpse of gold flame, and then a deafening *CRACK* shook the ground. Taja stumbled on the stairs and looked up just as Jekku leapt in front of him, lightning crackling around his hands. Overhead, the sky turned inky black, casting the village in shadow.

Taja's heart pounded. The people gathered in the square had surged backwards, away from the temple. Silence reigned once more, and even Ellory –– who'd been forced back by Jekku's magic –– looked rattled. Taja felt a flicker of vindication.

"*Enough*," Jekku snapped. His voice dipped low as the rumble of thunder he cast. "We are not your enemies! This is a lot to take in, and we understand that, and we know you don't want to believe it. Neither do I, nor does Taja. Betrayal stings. But pain can heal, and denying the cause of it will only fester the wound."

He lowered his hands and let down his guard, just a little. The thunder faded and the sky began to brighten again. "I know you're angry. I know you haven't forgotten what Taja did, but like he said, he is not the same person he was seven years ago. Maybe it's time for all of you to forget your grudge."

Taja swallowed, face burning. Part of him was grateful that Jekku had stepped in, but the other half of him was mortified that he needed to be rescued at all. This was not the way to prove himself as a capable savior.

"You were willing to give me a chance before," Jekku went on. His voice was no longer dangerously low, but light and calm. "You welcomed me, a stranger, someone you'd never seen before and had no reason to trust. You accepted blindly that I was *Sawwia Setukkda* simply because Ebris said so. But you don't know me. You do, however, know him." Jekku gestured back at Taja. "If you're going to look up to either of us, it should be him."

Taja held his breath and watched his people exchange looks with each other. He saw their lips move in whispers he couldn't hear. Some of their expressions shifted from suspicion to shock as they realized what Jekku was implying. Then the murmurs grew louder.

Taja glanced at Ellory and his heart sank further. He'd hoped Jekku's words had gotten through to them, but if anything they looked angrier than before. Their eyes caught Taja's and they scowled, then turned on their heel and shouldered their way across the square.

Some of the tension bled from Taja's shoulders. With Ellory out of sight, at least he could breathe.

But then he heard the first murmur of *Sawwia Setukkda*, and his heart raced toward panic all over again.

And then it got worse.

"*Sawwia!*" A girl's voice cried over the mumble of voices. She raised her hands over the heads of the people around her, and began fighting her way forward as more and more Elshalans peeled away from the crowd and left. "Please, *Sawwia*, don't say this! Don't let the traitor fool you, too!" She broke her way out of the throng and fell to her knees in front of the temple steps. Tears streamed down her face.

A young man knelt down beside her, placing a hand on her shoulder. When he raised his head, Taja could only describe his glare as murderous. "*Sawwia Setukkda*, we ask your guidance. Please, the traitor cannot stay here. He only brings lies. He will bring about the fall of our village."

"All Death!" wailed the girl on her knees. "All Death reigns so long as he lives!"

"Unless the Savior protects us," soothed the man. His eyes found their way back up, settling on Jekku with all the reverence one would turn toward a god. "And you will, won't you?"

Taja couldn't move. Couldn't breathe. He felt like an iron hand had seized hold of his heart and lungs and intended to crush them to dust. People began shouting again, pleading with Jekku to save them. Their voices blurred together into insanity that left only two words ringing in Taja's ears: *Savior. Traitor.*

"Jekku." He could barely get the name past his lips. He couldn't take in a full breath. "Get us out of here."

Jekku swept his hand through the air and clenched his fist. Another *crack* of lightning webbed through the sky. Taja flinched instinctively, hit with a flashback of being struck by this very magic, but the bolt never touched the ground. When the accompanying thunder faded to a rumble, the village fell silent once more.

"I am not *Sawwia Setukkda*." Jekku's voice rang louder even than his magic. He stepped aside, turned to Taja, and met his eyes. Steady and confident and entirely at odds with the terror pounding through Taja's heart. Jekku gave a slight nod, then looked back at the village. "Taja is."

As soon as the words were out, Taja wished with everything in him that he could snatch them out of the air. He knew it had to be said, but—

What he wouldn't give to sink through the ground. Or run — as far from this town as he could possibly get. Suddenly everything he wanted to fight for fled from his heart, and he wished to every god he knew that this had not fallen on his shoulders. He should have let Jekku be the Savior. Should have just stayed in Båthälla and forgotten all about the Oracle Stone after he'd brought Jekku to Ebris. For exactly one heartbeat, Taja wished he'd never met Jekku at all.

He looked hopelessly at his people. They would never look at him the way they looked at Jekku. They would never trust him as their leader or their Savior. He was not the Peacebringer. He was not *Sawwia Setukkda*. Ellory Ives was right; Taja was and only ever would be the traitor.

"I'm sorry," he gasped. "I can't do anything for you."

"Taja..." The unmasked disappointment in Jekku's voice nearly tore Taja in two.

He shook his head and darted down the temple steps. He kept his head down, refusing to see the faces around him. He found the Sky Elk waiting at the edge of the town square and clambered onto its back, then coaxed it into a gallop that took him through the woods around the village. The trees blurred around him. He blinked hard, willing away the tears that stung his eyes, but he'd barely made it to his cottage before they spilled down his cheeks. He managed to keep it together until he was inside, then slammed the door behind him and slumped to the floor.

Ugly, painful sobs wracked his body. He choked them out, didn't bother to hold anything in. He buried his face in his hands and gave in to the weight on his chest, letting it sink him lower.

He couldn't do this. This was not what he was meant for. *Second Savior of the Elshala*. Hell, he'd barely been Elshalan for the past seven years. How could he have ever thought that was the path for him?

Behind him, the door rattled. Someone knocked.

Someone. As if he didn't know who it was.

Taja didn't move. He could not face Jekku right now.

"Taja." Jekku's voice, muffled and soft, came from the other side of the door. "I know you're there. Let me in."

Taja sighed and wiped his hands across his face, though he knew it was pointless to pretend he hadn't just had a breakdown. He dragged himself to his feet and reluctantly opened the door. Jekku looked up at him, biting his lip, and took a small step into the house.

Taja let the door fall shut and leaned back against it.

Jekku turned around to face him and lifted his hands. "What the hell."

Taja straightened. He had not expected Jekku to be upset. The obvious frustration in his expression sparked a flicker of anger in Taja, and before he could stop himself, he blurted, "Why did you do that to me?"

Jekku raised his eyebrows. "Do what? Defend you to your own people when you clearly weren't going to? Did you think I was just going to stand there and let them drag you through the mud?"

"We had a plan!" Taja snapped. "You were supposed to handle it from the beginning, but it was a disaster because *you* froze."

"*I* froze? I was giving you a window! A chance to stand up for yourself and try to win them over! It's not my fault that you couldn't do that."

Taja barreled on before Jekku could see how much that stung. "Do you have any idea what that was like for me? Do you understand *at all* what it's like for me to stand in front of people I've known my entire life and be rejected by them all over again? To be— To be ignored and brushed to the side while everyone fawns over *you* instead?"

"You had a chance to change that," Jekku said, not unkindly. "You could have led them to your side. You could've shown them that you are deserving of their respect."

Taja shook his head. "Their eyes were on you alone before I even opened my mouth, and for what? You're not even one of us! You don't belong here!"

Jekku shut his mouth. Taja watched his walls go up. The barest flicker of shock crossed his eyes, then he shuttered everything behind a blank, hard expression. He clenched his jaw, then shouldered past Taja and stormed toward the door.

Taja cursed under his breath. "Jekku—" He tried to catch him, but Jekku left without stopping.

The walls rattled when he slammed the door.

2

JEKKU

SO MAYBE JEKKU had been a little unfair. Maybe he could have been kinder and handled that conversation more gracefully. Maybe he could've been a touch more empathetic.

But what Taja had said to him was needlessly cruel.

You don't belong here. As if Jekku didn't know that. As if he didn't feel that right down to his bones. It'd be one thing if the gods flung those words at him, but to hear it from Taja, just days after Jekku had told him that he wanted to be with him wherever he went... Honestly, it would have hurt less if Taja had slapped him.

Jekku stormed away from Taja's cottage, but veered away from the main road up to the village. The last thing he needed were more needy Elshalans who refused to believe he wasn't their Savior. Instead he found his way down to the river and followed it until the forest's murmurs faded under the rush of water.

It was so easy to forget how *much* went into fully trusting another person. It wasn't all easy banter and not-so-subtle flirting; there was actual work required, and Jekku wasn't willing to pend that energy on just anyone. In fact, Taja was one of two. And the first one... Well, Jekku had clearly seen what he'd gotten out of trusting Leo.

He stopped walking and had to remember to breathe. The now-familiar ache weighing on his heart pressed down harder, as if his memories themselves threatened to suffocate him. It was too late to force them out of mind; he had to let them run their course. After six years of so much noise in his head, it was hard to drop one thought in favor of another. There was *nothing* in his head now, no stream of time threads or whispers of people's lives. It was quiet up there, and Jekku found himself annoyed that his thoughts didn't move fast enough. Instead, they lingered on the things Jekku preferred to forget.

Like Leo, and the sweet way he smiled at Jekku. And the kindness he'd extended to him when Jekku had first stumbled to the doors of the monastery. And the soft way he'd kissed him, the first time and every time after that.

On their own, those memories weren't the worst. It was what came next that choked the life out of him.

Jekku closed his eyes. *Stop. Think about something else. Yes, he betrayed you, yes he went behind your back for all that time. Who cares? It was never going to last, anyway. You left him. It doesn't matter if he—*

But it did matter, and nothing Jekku tried to tell himself would change that. He had loved Leo, against his better judgment, and denying it would not lessen the blow that each time Leo had said those words back to him had been a lie. Or maybe Leo had meant it, but clearly it wasn't enough to keep his eyes on one target. Jekku didn't know which was worse.

The memories of Leo loosened their hold. Jekku's mind drifted back to the present. He took a second to steady himself, taking deep breaths, and then continued along the river. He passed by the grove where he'd shot arrows with Taja and found himself smiling at *that* memory. Gods, that seemed like ages ago, but it couldn't have been more than a couple weeks. It was strange to think that in such a short time, Taja had become someone whose opinions and feelings mattered to Jekku.

You don't belong here.

Yeah, Jekku knew that. He just liked to fool himself by thinking it could be true, if not in a place then with a person.

But clearly that person didn't feel the same. Despite... literally everything.

A small voice in the back of Jekku's head reminded him that Taja was upset and angry when he'd said that, so he probably didn't mean it. That voice was probably right. But what if he did? Jekku himself was guilty of spilling things he'd otherwise never say when he was upset enough, so what if what Taja had said was just the truth of how he really felt?

When had this become so confusing? Jekku thought he knew how to read people, but apparently not. Apparently he was hopelessly blind to anything that lay under the surface.

Jekku came upon a heap of smooth boulders on the riverbank and paused. He listened to the rush and bubble of water rushing around the rocks, the gentle rustle of wind through the trees, the far-off chirp of birds hiding among the branches. Jekku closed his eyes and breathed in the scent of the earth, the air, the water, and though the winter sun was distant, it warmed his face when he tipped back his head.

One by one, his troubles sloughed off his shoulders. He shook off his anger at Taja. He shrugged off the anxiety that had stirred up when he'd returned to Båthälla. He brushed off the tangle of emotions surrounding Leo. He listened to the earth living and breathing and let the sounds calm him.

When he opened his eyes again, he wasn't alone.

Jekku nearly jumped out of his skin. Lady Nedra, the Elshalan Goddess of the Moon, stood beside Jekku on the riverbank. No, not on the bank, he realized; she stood up to her ankles in the water. The hem of her white gown flowed around her, tugged by the rushing stream.

Isn't that cold? Jekku wondered idly. Then he blinked and looked up at her. "Um. Hi."

A small smile tugged at the corner of her crimson-painted lips. She studied him curiously, as if confused as to why he was here, of all places. The feeling was mutual. And why hadn't Jekku realized she was here? Now that he was close to her, he could feel the overwhelming presence of her magic. It surrounded him like a dense fog, mingling with his own magic and making his skin tingle. Nedra's power zapped Jekku with a glimpse of what the Oracle Stone had felt like, and for a bare second, something within him longed for that power again.

He took a step back from Nedra and let his magic settle. "I, uh, didn't expect to see you out here."

"Likewise, *Sawwia Setukkda*. Of course, that's not who you really are, is it?"

Jekku looked down at the muddy riverbank. "No, Lady Nedra. I'm afraid... Lord Ebris was mistaken." He braced himself to be chastised for that comment, but Nedra snorted.

"Would not be the first time." A hint of annoyance edged her tone. "Why have you come back to Båthälla, then, Jekku Aj'ere? The last time we met, you were insistent that you did not belong here. What changed, now that you know you have no destiny with the Elshalan people?"

Oh, fantastic, this was precisely what he wanted to hear at the moment. He might not be the Second Savior, but something in Båthälla still called to him. He had history here, after all, that he had yet to fully explore.

He shrugged, then let his shoulders slump. "I came back for Taja," he told Nedra. "Only the two of us know the truth of what happened with Lord Ebris, the Oracle Stone, and the Royal Sorcerers. Our battle isn't over until everyone else knows the truth."

Nedra raised her sharp eyebrows. "I see. And what did happen at Gallien's Peak?"

Chaos. That's what happened. Utter chaos. Jekku fidgeted, twisting a strand of his hair around his fingers. "It's a long story."

"Understandable. Answer me this, then." She paused and waited for Jekku to look up, but he had trouble holding her intense gaze. It didn't help that she was also unreasonably beautiful. "Is Lord Ebris coming back?"

Jekku didn't know what to expect by answering this question, but, "No. He's not."

For a beat, Nedra simply held his gaze. A spark of fear shot through him. But then she said, "Good."

Jekku blinked. "What?"

"*Good*," Nedra repeated. She stepped out of the river and her dress dried instantly. "Ebris was going to drive Båthälla into the ground, Jekku. He was killing us. When you arrived, I had hope or the first time in decades that we'd be saved. But I knew it as much as you did: the Peacebringer's successor would not be an outsider."

She finally broke Jekku's gaze and looked out at the river instead. "Saevel knew, even back then, that Båthälla had problems. They knew the gods were the root of those problems. They fought so hard... It breaks my heart that someone still has to fight now, even after everything they sacrificed to win. But Ebris's grip on this village and on our people has never lessened. In fact, it has only grown stronger, and I have feared for a very long time that he would soon strangle us."

Nedra turned to Jekku again. "If someone was going to turn the tide and free us from Ebris's chokehold, it would be one of us."

Jekku nodded, understanding. "But you played along so Ebris wouldn't get suspicious."

Nedra lifted her chin. "That's the trick with my brother: he must be told what he wants to hear. He must see what he wishes to see. I was more than happy to dress you up and go along with his insistence that you were the one, but I am glad you escaped when you did. I could not watch him use you to destroy the world. I could not bear to let him do to you what he did to Saevel."

"Let's just be glad it didn't come to that." Jekku rubbed his hands up his arms. He wanted to think he wouldn't have been so easily manipulated that he would have needed Nedra to interfere, but then he remembered how convincing Ebris was. How, even when Jekku was certain he was not the Second Savior, Ebris had made him doubt his own logic. His power of persuasion was dangerous; Jekku was all the more relieved that he was out of the picture now.

He hoped to the gods it stayed that way.

"Come with me, Jekku." Nedra inclined her head in the direction of the village. "I want to show you something." She barely waited for his agreement before she started up the riverbank and into the woods. A knot of anxiety formed in Jekku's chest as they passed by Taja's cottage; Jekku darted a glance at it, but if Taja was still there, he hadn't lit any lanterns. Jekku hurried his pace and kept his head down, especially when he followed Nedra into the village proper.

Thankfully, the crowd from earlier had cleared. Most people had gone back to their routines, but a few lingered in the square chatting in pairs or passing through. It might have been Jekku's imagination, but he swore their conversations cut off abruptly when he and Nedra entered the square. He told himself it was because of Nedra's presence, and prayed no one would recognize him.

That prayer was rather hopeless, considering his distinctly not-Elshalan features. But luck was on his side, because no one called out to him and he heard barely a whisper as he followed Nedra up the temple stairs. Still, he didn't raise his head or release the tension in his shoulders until he was inside and out of sight.

"Here." Nedra went to the side wall to the right of the entrance and pulled back a curtain that concealed a closet set into the wall. It was packed with various sizes and lengths of the same green robe. She chose one and brought it to Jekku. "Put this on. I know you're not Elshalan, but it's a sign of respect."

Jekku hesitated. "Respect to Ebris?"

Nedra frowned. "No. To all of us, and also to the heavens and the universe that created us. Put it on." She turned on her heel and strode down the center of the long marble room without waiting for him.

Jekku shrugged on the robe and scrambled to catch up. He fussed with the braided cord that tightened the garment at his waist. It was a little big on him, sliding off his shoulders, and it felt wrong to wear it in this sanctuary of gods that weren't his. He was only half Elshalan, after all, and he wasn't getting the impression that that counted for anything here. He didn't know a thing about that side of his identity, and donning this robe almost felt like an insult. But Nedra had personally handed it to him with an order, and even if the Elshalan gods were not Jekku's gods, he supposed he should listen to them. He owed it to Nedra after swooping into town and declaring that Ebris was his enemy.

Nedra made no sound save for the gentle hush of her long skirt trailing over the marble floor. She paused in the back hallway of the temple, and Jekku felt loud and clumsy by comparison when he stopped abruptly and his shoes scuffed on the floor. At least there was no one else here to watch the false savior stumble his way through their temple.

"In here." Nedra opened a sliding door and ushered Jekku into a room that he recognized at once — and not just because of the thick scent of incense. This was the sanctuary where Ebris had shown Jekku the Prophecy of the Second Savior. There it was, inscribed in the marble on the back wall, and the gold urn still sat on its altar in front of it. What was different, however, was the glass dome beside the urn. Underneath it hovered a wilting flower. A lily, to be exact.

Jekku hovered by the sliding door, but Nedra went directly across the room to the altar. She placed her hand on the bell jar, and for a heartbeat the flower encased beneath it seemed to perk up. Some color rushed back to its petals, but in a blink, it sagged and curled up once more. A petal came loose and fell onto the stone table.

"Saevel and Taja mentioned something about a White Lily," Jekku said. "Is this it?"

Nedra nodded. "For generations, this flower was believed to be the life source of Elshalan magic. Ebris told our people that if the flower died, their magic and their connection to the gods would be severed forever. Losing one's magic is akin to losing a part of one's soul. Naturally, no one wishes for that fate. I would not wish it upon my worst enemy."

Jekku clenched his teeth. *But you let it happen to Taja.*

"Anyway, it was all a lie," Nedra continued, oblivious to Jekku's shift in mood. "Our magic thrived just fine on its own, but Ebris convinced our people that if they let our magic leave the confines of Båthälla, it would only kill the White Lily faster. Sharing Elshalan magic with humans became just as taboo as your practice of blood magic. And as I'm sure you know, given your friendship with Taja Ievisin, sharing magic is not an offense that is taken lightly."

Jekku eyed the dying flower. "Saevel said that the White Lily is dying because Ebris was smothering it — and your magic."

"Ebris attached our magic to the flower in the first place," Nedra said. "And then he suffocated it, slowly, to make it look like

omeone had to come to our rescue. When all along he planned
o be that hero himself." She shook her head. "It is the same story
now that it was nine hundred years ago. Different threat, same
goal. Back then, Saevel Balnorin was able to uncover the truth
nd fight back. I wonder if you and your *Sawwia Setukkda* will be
ble to do the same."

Jekku looked away. "Taja shouldn't have to do this. It's cruel.
Take away his magic and his dignity, banish and ignore him for
even years, let him be berated and disgraced by people he used
o call family... and then expect him to save your asses from your
own demise?" He met Nedra's eyes again and shook his head.
Why not just... take the lid off the flower? If Ebris fabricated
his entire situation, why do you need a legendary Savior at all?"

Nedra's gaze hardened. She stood up straighter, then lifted
he glass dome off the White Lily. At once it brightened and un-
urled. Petals that had shriveled on their stems now filled with
ife.

Jekku felt the rush of magic like a punch to the gut. He
gasped, head spinning, and had to grasp the wall so he didn't
collapse. It was the Oracle Stone all over again, but amplified a
housand times. It was the agonizing throb of a Royal Sorcerer's
power forcing the universe into his mind.

Jekku could barely gasp out a plead for Nedra to make it stop.

She replaced the dome, cutting off the storm of power, and
ekku sagged against the wall, panting.

"Let me ask you something, Jekku Aj'ere." Nedra stepped toward him and offered a hand to steady him, but he ignored it.
"What did the Oracle Stone feel like, when you held its power in
your hands?"

He took a second to catch his breath. "It was unbearable."

"And how was that rush of power you just felt?"

He just glared at her. His pulse throbbed in his head, and hi magic still burned in his palms. Båthälla might find itself be neath a thunderstorm if Jekku's magic didn't settle on its own.

"Mhm." Nedra quirked an eyebrow. "If I lift the shield and le the power contained in the White Lily rush back all at once, i would be... more than excruciating. It would be what you jus felt times a thousand. I fear it would damage my people's magi rather than refresh it. No, the White Lily must remain enclose until we find a way to free and exercise our magic gradually."

Jekku shook off the last of the effects from the Lily's magi and approached the flower. "Where I'm from, we conduct magi through song. The melodies harmonize with the earth's magic and it helps us control and direct it. I wonder... if there's a solu tion to be found there."

Nedra studied him. "All humans conduct magic throug song?"

"Well, no," Jekku said. "Only those who are taught here ir Doweth."

Nedra beamed a grin that might've outshone the sun. I spread to her eyes, creasing happy lines around the corners, anc she let out a soft laugh. She looked up at the prophecy on th wall and shook her head. "Oh, Saevel, you wonder."

Jekku wasn't following something. "Huh?"

"They didn't tell you?" Nedra looked amused. "Jekku, Saeve invented the way your people conduct magic to this very day They were the first to figure out that magic can be harmonize with music."

"*What?*" Jekku sputtered a laugh. "Wait, but... they told me *not* to rely on singing to control my affinity. They said it was too limiting."

Nedra shrugged. "Times change and so does magic. It evolves and grows just as we do. Perhaps over time, it has become calmer. Kinder. Of course, magic has never been ours to possess, but perhaps it's allowed itself to become domesticated." She laid her hand on the glass dome again. "And maybe that's the problem. Maybe it has forgotten how to survive on its own."

"Can a naturally-occurring power like that really just forget how to live?" Jekku asked. He'd always understood that magic was nature beyond humans — it existed despite and in spite of them. This was like hearing that the wind had forgotten how to blow without people fanning the air.

"If it's not allowed to thrive properly, it weakens," Nedra said. "Humans want to control things. It's in your nature. I'd say it's my kind's nature, too. We want to understand, to take apart and tinker and piece back together in a way that we can wrap our heads around. We want to unveil the secrets of the universe." Her eyes flicked toward Jekku. "Don't we?"

Jekku sighed and looked up at the prophecy. That name stared back at him, bold and harsh as the stone into which it was carved. His worst mistake, literally written in stone. Was that always who he was destined to become? The one who asked for too much? How long ago had this prophecy been written? How long had Jekku's future been cemented in the stars?

He wanted to believe that his life could have taken infinitely possible routes. During those four years in the dark, he had *needed* to believe that if he had made a different choice — just *one* different choice — he would not be there.

But it wasn't as though Riddler was a title like Peacebringer or *Sawwia Setukkda*. There was no one else that could be up on that wall. So apparently Firune's pet was who he was always going to become.

Jekku leaned on the stone altar, feeling like the whole temple's weight was on his shoulders. Was this really how the universe worked, in predetermined plans and destinies written in stone? No, no, it couldn't be. Jekku refused to believe it. He had seen the universe, and though those secrets had slipped from his memory as soon as Firune's curse was broken, he knew it in his bones that his life was his to command. No one — not even the universe itself — had the power to direct him on a path that wasn't his.

Leaving Ajaphere eight years ago was a choice. Agreeing to Firune's offer was a choice (even if it was a poor one). Escaping Gallien's Peak four years later instead of killing himself was a choice. Remaining at the monastery, leaving to find the Oracle Stone, and finally coming back to Båthälla with Taja were all Jekku's choices. No one had forged those paths for him. Firune and Ebris had both tried to guide Jekku in the directions each of them wanted him to go, but in the end, Jekku chose for himself. In spite of the gods who wished to control him.

If he could defy a Royal Sorcerer and a god, he could defy the stars.

He looked at Nedra. "There was a time when all I wanted was to know everything. I thought I deserved to see the universe's se-

rets. But now I know that there's nothing good to be found behind doors we're not meant to open."

Nedra smiled. "When we try to seize things too tightly, when
we yank the leash too hard, the very thing we wish to control
crumbles in our hands. We choke it to death. Magic is no different. It is a living, breathing thing that indeed is beyond human
control, but when millions of people across hundreds of years all
wish to seize the same power in the same way... well, wouldn't
you get tired, too?"

Jekku drummed his nails on the altar. "So what's the answer?"

A smirk touched the corner of Nedra's lips. "I don't know."

"But... you're a goddess." Jekku blinked. "Aren't you supposed
to be...?"

"Omnipotent?" She laughed. "Only sometimes. It's tiring to
see the entire breadth of time. But you know that."

"All too well."

Nedra drew her fingers through her silky hair. "I gave up
my omnipotence when I left the Sky Palace to walk among hu-
mankind. It was one of many divine privileges I sacrificed, but I
can't say I regret it. So no, Jekku, I do not know what to do about
your magic. But I trust, with the right allies, you might unearth a
solution."

Jekku glanced at the prophecy again, then let his gaze fall on
the White Lily. "I don't think there's a lot I can do. I'm just here
to support Taja. I play no real part in this. Why do you think I
can help you?"

"Jekku." Nedra set her hand on his shoulder, sending a burst
of magic through him. "You don't have to have your destiny writ-

ten in stone in order to play a part. Find your role, and let everything else fall into place."

Find his role? Here? Jekku didn't see how he could possibly have a place here, even if it was his father's hometown. He was still an outsider, still an *other*, and Taja had made that clear a day.

He was upset. He didn't mean it. Jekku really wanted to believe that, but the words sounded empty in his mind.

He sought Nedra's gaze. "I'm nervous for Taja. I don't know how to help him."

"You do," Nedra assured him. "And you will. Besides, you won't be alone. I'm on your side, Jekku, no matter what my people or the other gods say."

Jekku set his hand over hers. "Thank you." A goddess as an ally. That was a start.

Nedra inclined her head toward the sliding door. "Go talk to him. I heard your return to the village was... less than ideal."

Jekku grimaced. "Could have been better."

"He'll need you in the coming days," Nedra said. "He'll need every ally he can get, but... he values your companionship."

I think there's a bit more to it than that, Jekku thought, then shoved it away. He thanked Nedra, then quietly left the sanctuary.

He was barely two steps out of the temple when something heavy collided with his head and pain exploded through his skull. The world spun, and then blinked out.

3

TAJA

THE LAST PLACE Taja wished to go after the incident this morning was the temple, but he needed allies, and if any of the gods were going to help him, it would be Nedra. Besides, he couldn't stay holed up in his cottage forever. He'd had enough of that for one lifetime.

His temple robe was gone, lost somewhere between Båthälla and Westdenn or Aylesbury or one of the other handful of places he'd traveled with Jekku, Lilya, and Saevel, but the bright green garment would make him too conspicuous anyway. He opted for a gray hooded cloak instead and kept his head down until he was on the temple steps.

He looked up and pushed the hood back, only to come face to face with Ellory Ives.

His reaction must have shown on his face, because Ellory laughed. "Well, don't look so pleased to see me." Their two-tone eyes glanced over Taja. "Missing something?"

Taja crossed his arms over his chest and pulled his cloak

tighter. Leave it to Ellory to make him extra conscious of his absent temple robe. "I have to get a new one."

"Ohh, lost your robe, did you?" Ellory's voice dripped with fake sympathy. "What happened? Your little bedbug take it?"

Heat rushed to Taja's face. Ellory wasn't getting the satisfaction of a reply to that. He stormed past them, but halted again when they stepped into his path. "Come on now, Taja, I was only joking. I'm sure the robe got a bit faded and dusty in those seven years hanging in a closet, yeah? Bet you needed a new one anyway."

Taja ground his teeth. "Leave me alone, Ellory." He shouldered past them and stepped into the temple. Thankfully, they did not follow. Taja paused a second to steady himself. He knew that Ellory's intention was to rile him up and make him angry, and though Taja refused to let them see how much they got under his skin, it unfortunately worked. Sometimes he swore that bastard could read minds.

Taja shoved Ellory out of mind and went across the temple. He stared straight ahead, resisting the urge to meet the eyes of the people around him who he knew were staring at him. He forced his head up and walked like he knew he belonged here.

Even if he didn't. Even if everyone else here knew it, too. But maybe pretending would make him believe it.

Nedra was nowhere to be found in the main room of the temple, so Taja went down the back hallway and ducked into the private sanctuary that bore the Prophecy of the Second Savior on its wall. He was surprised to see the White Lily had been moved here as well, though it didn't look any better. It wilted and died before his eyes; another petal broke free and fell to the white marble altar as Taja approached. Taja lightly touched the top of the glass dome; only the barest flicker of power awakened within him.

He looked up at the wall. The prophecy stared back at him. His future, carved in harsh lines and crisp letters. His destiny, literally written in stone. The last time he had stood in this room, Ebris had told him he was his people's only hope for bringing the Second Savior to Båthälla. Well... now he knew that had not been entirely false. But it would have been so much easier if Tekku *was* the Savior.

"I hope you know it was never going to be easy."

Taja spun around, heart leaping into his throat. He nearly expected to find Lord Ebris standing behind him; he did not expect the Peacebringer.

"Saevel," Taja breathed.

They flickered a smile. "Hello, *Sawwia Setukkda*."

Saevel looked the same as when Taja had last seen them alive, right down to their loose-fitting white shirt and fitted trousers. They were barefoot and the sleeves on their shirt only reached their elbows, but if they were cold they didn't show it. Their white-blond hair fell in a long swoop down their shoulders, and there was an air of peace about them that hadn't been there before.

Taja moved closer to them, but stopped a couple feet away when he realized Saevel looked... ghostly. They appeared slightly transparent, a bit blurred around the edges.

Taja felt a stab of disappointment. "You're not really here, are you?"

Saevel shrugged. "I'm here enough."

"Did you come back to help?"

Saevel leaned back against the wall and crossed their arms. "What can I do that would truly help you, Taja?"

He stammered for an answer. *Something. Anything.*

"Look." Saevel sighed, shoulders slumping. "I'm sorry that didn't see it sooner. I regret that our time was cut short and tha even I fell into Ebris's trap. I'm sorry that I insisted Jekku wa *Sawwia Setukkda* even when he tried to tell me he wasn't. I shoul have realized, but there was more magic surrounding Jekku tha there was surrounding you, so my instincts told me it was him At any rate, should-haves won't get us anywhere. We know now that it's you. So the question is, what are you going to do?"

Taja shook his head. "I don't know. I can't do this alone Saevel."

"And you won't." Saevel came toward him and reached ou to touch his arm, but their hand passed through it and left Taja with a sudden chill. He drew back. Saevel frowned. "Sorry That's new. Anyway, you have allies, my friend. Find them. I'll be around, too, just in a... less corporeal way."

Taja studied them. "Where... are you?"

Saevel said something in reply, but their voice came out muf fled and garbled, as if they'd suddenly been submerged underwa ter.

Taja blinked. "Um... didn't catch that."

Saevel frowned. "Huh. Guess I can't talk about it here."

"But— Are you safe? Are you at peace? *He's* not there, is he?"

Saevel didn't have to ask who Taja meant. "No. Not with me anyway."

Good. "But are you alone?" Taja couldn't think of anything worse than spending eternity alone, no matter how peaceful it might be. Nine hundred years trapped in the Oracle Stone must have been torture.

To Taja's relief, Saevel shook their head. A small yet genuine smile curved across their face. "No. At last, I am not alone. Don't worry about me, Taja. For the first time in centuries, I am okay. I'm at peace, and I'm happier than I have been in a long time. I want this for you, too. But I'm afraid you'll have to fight for it first. My time has come to an end, but your battle isn't over."

Taja sighed. "I just wish…" He didn't even know how to articulate it. He wished it didn't have to be him, but saying that in front of the First Savior who had sacrificed everything for their people seemed a little… insensitive.

"I know." Saevel met Taja's eyes. "I didn't want it to be me, either. But I saw what had to be done, and I knew that if I didn't fight, no one else would. I had to step up and lead. I didn't trust anyone except my friends and allies to fight as hard as I would. Sometimes the world is placed in your hands, Taja, but other times, you pick it up and carry it of your own accord." Their eyes moved to a spot over Taja's shoulder, and they nodded once.

Taja followed their gaze to the prophecy on the wall behind him. *His* prophecy. "But I—"

But when he turned back to Saevel, they were gone. Only a faint scent of grass and mint remained in the room, mingling with the oppressive smell of incense.

Taja looked up at the prophecy once more. *Darkness falls and All Death reigns.* The threat was clear: if he did nothing, his people would die. They would fall into an age of chaos and darkness because of Taja's inaction. He couldn't let that happen. Ebris might be gone, but his influence survived, and the other gods were still here.

Taja let his gaze fall to the dying White Lily. Its message was clear, too. The only future for Båthälla was one free of the gods' iron grip.

But first he had to find them.

Taja read the prophecy once more. If this was supposed to portend his future, maybe there was something useful in these cryptic words. He'd never thought to read into it before.

In ages past, in years gone by
A Savior brought peace but was destined to die.

Easy enough: Saevel. They'd sacrificed themself to save Båthälla — and perhaps this whole country — from a time of chaos and oppression.

The First may rest but a Second will rise
To carry in scarred hand the Arcane
That shall deliver heavens to earth
And raise hells to the skies.

And now that Saevel was gone, it was Taja's turn to step in. Jekku was right; the reference to his hands — scarred from the ritual that took his magic — was so obvious, Taja didn't know how he hadn't realized it immediately. And he had carried Arcane Magic — the power wielded by the Royal Sorcerers — when he'd used the Oracle Stone to trap them once more.

Taja puzzled over those last two lines. The Oracle Stone's

power was certainly enough to rain heavens and hells upon the earth, but he didn't think the prophecy was that literal. Could heavens be referencing gods? Yes— that must be it. The stone had brought back the Royal Sorcerers, who were akin to gods at their full power. Not to mention the literal gods that hungered for the stone's power as well.

But *raise hells to the skies*... What else would have emerged if the stone had truly been allowed to live once more? Was that what the prophecy meant, or was Taja taking it too literally?

He didn't know what to think of this cryptic message.

He moved on.

No hero, no legend, no Savior shall he be
'Til those of his fathers awaken memory.
A wish shall make the Riddler see
A Fall shall set the Savior free.

This was where the words really got confusing, because even now Taja couldn't look at this stanza and say it *wasn't* about Jekku. He had no idea he was half Elshalan until Saevel showed him his parents' memories, and it was only then that he was able to get in touch with his affinity. It was partially thanks to Jekku's powerful magic that the four of them won that night at Gallien's Peak, and that had qualified him as a savior in Taja's book.

Then there was the next line: *a wish shall make the Riddler see.* That was undeniably about Jekku; that was the cruel nickname Firune had called him when Jekku was imprisoned at Gallien's Peak. That could not be anyone else. And hadn't Jekku said that

a wish — made toward the Master of Wishes himself — was wha
had gotten him cursed in the first place?

So even if Jekku wasn't *Sawwia Setukkda*, he was still in th
prophecy. Clearly he was meant to be here just as much as Taj
was, but Taja didn't like the implications of that. Was everything
in their lives really so predetermined?

Taja moved on to the next lines. *A Fall shall set the Savior free*
Well, that was obvious: Ebris's Fall had freed Taja from his influ
ence and control. Ebris's failure had given Taja the space to step
into his role as *Sawwia Setukkda*.

Maybe that was where Jekku came in. Would Taja have
known he was the Savior without Jekku telling him? He wanted
to think he would've figured it out, but he'd been so embarrass
ingly blinded by Ebris...

Wait. Jekku could see futures with his curse. Surely he must
have caught a glimpse of Taja's future somewhere along the way
A wish shall make the Riddler see. Had he seen that Taja was des
tined to become *Sawwia Setukkda*? Had that helped him put the
pieces together and call out Ebris's lies?

So that was Jekku's role: to be Taja's eyes when he'd been kept
in the dark.

Taja still didn't like that this was all written in stone, but he
admitted it was comforting that, one way or another, Jekku was
always going to be part of his life.

Suns rise, nights fall, eons stream by
But the Second shan't come till All Death is nigh
In flame, in thorn, in heart of stone,
Second Savior, awaken, find home.

Ebris was the sun. Oridite, the night. Eons streaming by... that could be another reference to Jekku's curse, or it could refer to Nokaldir, god of the universe and time itself. Or perhaps that line simply meant it would be many years before *Sawwia Setukkda* appeared. But Ebris's rise as patriarch of Båthälla and his recent hunger for more power was what would have brought about All Death. Maybe the first line had multiple meanings?

The next line puzzled Taja. Flame, thorn, heart of stone? What did these things symbolize that would lead Taja to understand and step into his role?

He'd come back to that one.

Yet should he stray
Should he be led another way
Darkness falls and All Death reigns
Until a Savior is born again.

Well... that was clear enough. If Taja failed to banish the gods, they'd cause a dark age of hopelessness and suffering. At least there was a glimmer of hope — the possibility of another Savior in the future — but that could be centuries from now. Båthälla couldn't wait that long.

It was up to Taja.

He turned to go, but first stopped to set his hand on the gold urn beside the White Lily. "Rest, *Sawwia*. Our people are in my hands."

Taja left the sanctuary but hesitated before he stepped into the main room of the temple. He scanned the few people still kneeling in prayer; Ellory was not one of them. *Good.* Taja didn't have the patience to deal with more of their childish taunts.

Just go. He should not be this anxious to walk through the temple he'd found solace in for most of his life. But Ellory's words this morning sank under his skin more than he'd like to admit. *You're a disgrace.*

Yeah, well, maybe he was. That was everyone else's problem.

Taja breathed a short laugh. He was starting to think like Jekku.

The thought of him made Taja's heart sink. Where was Jekku? Båthälla was a small village; unless he was literally hiding in the woods, he should be easy to find. Taja had searched around on his way from his cottage to the temple, but he'd seen no sign of him. Maybe he didn't want to be found yet. In that case, Taja should leave him be and give him space, but on the other hand, Taja didn't want to stew in his guilt until Jekku decided to forgive him. At the very least, he wanted to apologize. He certainly didn't deserve Jekku's immediate forgiveness, but he hated to leave that final note of a slammed door hanging in the air for too long.

Talk to the gods first. Then Jekku. Taja took a final glance around the temple in case Ellory had somehow snuck in. He wished there was a back door, but then he heard Saevel's voice in the back of his head, scolding him for being a coward. *These are your people, and you are the one who will save them. Make them see you.*

Saevel was right. About Taja being a coward, and also about him not being alone. He just had to figure out who his allies were.

That, too, would start with the gods.

4

JEKKU

JEKKU'S SENSES CRAWLED BACK TO HIM one by one. He heard garbled voices, smelled incense, felt a cold floor beneath him and a rough wall against his back. A faint ache throbbed through his wrists — were his hands tied? Where the hell was he? A single flickering torch on the opposite wall cast shadows across the small room; Jekku watched the flames dance as his vision slid back into focus.

He fully jolted awake when something foul-smelling violently filled his senses; he sneezed, eyes watering. He blinked and looked up, and then this all made sense. "You," he croaked.

"*You.*" The Elshalan who had confronted Taja in the square earlier drew back holding a tin of dried leaves. Jekku didn't know if it was actually possible, but this Elshalan looked so much like Ebris that they *had* to be related. Their brown skin was several shades lighter than Ebris's, and their eyes were blue and green instead of gold, but the thick black curls, the squared jaw, and rounded shape of their eyes mirrored the Fallen god exactly.

Even the irritated curl of their lip and hardness in their two-ton
eyes was reminiscent of Ebris.

"Who are you?" Jekku said. "You were there earlier in th
square. You turned everyone against Taja."

They drew themself up straighter. "Vaeltaja Ievisin is a traito
and a coward. He doesn't belong in Båthälla any more than yo
do." Jekku winced, but before he could say anything, they contin
ued in a softer tone. "But you already know that, and we're no
here to talk about Vaeltaja Ievisin."

"Then why are we here?" Jekku lifted his bound hands. "In th
right context, I'm into this as much as the next person, but usu
ally people don't do this when they just want to *talk*."

"Expect worse if you don't cooperate," snapped anothe
Elshalan whom Jekku hadn't noticed before. She hovered by th
door, one hand on the hilt of a dagger on her hip.

"Now, now." The one in front of Jekku waved a hand. "He'
right." They bent down and untied the silk cord around Jekku'
wrists. Jekku held their glare. They smiled. "This is no way t
treat our guest."

"You punched me in the face," Jekku retorted. He lifted
hand to rub his cheek, where a tender bruise was already form
ing. His fingers brushed a light scrape on his cheekbone, wher
one of the many rings on the Elshalan's fingers must have torr
the skin. "Gods, if you just wanted to talk, an invitation to te
would have sufficed." He scowled.

"Do you know who I am, false savior?"

"No. I recall asking that earlier and not getting an answer."

"How rude of me, to neglect to introduce myself." They stoo
up and brushed off the front of their green temple robe. "M

name is Ellory Ives, keeper of the Temple of the Sun. And I am the son of Lord Ebris."

Well... damn it. Jekku had suspected it, but he hadn't wanted to be right. "Ebris was your father, huh? That explains a lot."

"Ebris *is* my father," Ellory snapped. "And the reason you're here, heretic, is because I want to know what the hell you think you're doing, marching into Båthälla like it's your birthright. I don't know what lies you've been fed, but the traitor is *not Sawwia Setukkda*, and neither are you. Do you really think the Peacebringer would have chosen an outsider as our Savior?"

"No," Jekku said, "and that's why it's not me. It *is* Taja. Read the prophecy. It's undeniable. And Ebris knew it too." Jekku sat back against the wall and crossed his arms. "If anyone was feeding me lies, it was Ebris himself. He knew that Taja is the Savior, and he didn't want to believe it. He knew your people would react precisely how you did: with outrage and hate. He didn't want that anger directed at him when he announced that Taja was the Savior. He covered his own ass by directing everyone's attention to me and making Taja believe he was just a pawn. But I'm not going to let him be degraded like that. He *is Sawwia Setukkda* and was always meant to be. His place is here, among the people he wants to help. Why can't you accept that?"

Ellory narrowed their eyes. "Don't presume to know us. You're not one of us."

"I *know* that." Jekku tossed up his hands. "I'm not trying to be one of you. Trust me, I know I don't belong here." He swallowed as the sting of Taja's words sank in again. "All I want is for you to listen to Taja. I know you don't want—"

"Save it," Ellory snapped. "Lord Ebris has sacrificed more for this town than you will ever understand. He has provided all of us with comfort and protection, and we are fortunate to live in the palm of his hand. Båthälla is his beating heart. It is his treasure. But I do not expect you to understand that." Ellory moved a few steps backward. "Leave, false savior. Consider this a friendly warning. And be lucky that it's coming from me and not from Lord Ebris himself."

Jekku stared after them as they strode across the dark room and went to their companion. The two exchanged a few quiet words, then Ellory made to leave. "Ellory," Jekku called. "Lord Ebris isn't coming back. He Fell. He's gone."

Ellory's shoulders tensed. Slowly, they turned their head back toward Jekku. "No, he is not." They turned to their companion again. "Drop his heart rate."

The girl gasped. "What?"

Jekku stared at them. "What?"

"Ava, do it," snapped Ellory.

She flicked a glance at Jekku. "Ellory..."

"Wait—" Jekku started to stand, but a sharp pain in his chest forced him back down. He slumped against the wall and pressed a hand to his chest, as if that could stop the vise-like pressure around his heart. His head spun, his vision tunneled, and then—

Nothing.

***

Jekku? Jekku!

He jolted back to consciousness, gasping. For one horrifying beat he thought he was drowning; he couldn't get enough air in is lungs, and an odd pressure still squeezed his heart. His pulse thundered, yet he couldn't shake the feeling that his heart wasn't beating correctly.

"Jekku! Are you in there? Can you hear me?"

He blinked. That voice was real. Not in his head. Not a dream. He pulled his thoughts together. "I— Who's there?"

"Jekku! It's me." The voice drew closer and footsteps approached the door to this damp little room where Ellory had left him. A shadow appeared on the floor, obscuring the faint light that filtered beneath the door.

"Taja?" Guilt twisted in his stomach. Taja wasn't the first on Jekku's list of people he wished to see right now, but if he was Jekku's ticket out of this room, he could set aside his grudge.

For now.

That said nothing of forgiveness yet. Not until he got an apology.

The door rattled as Taja felt around, looking for a handle that apparently wasn't there. "I can't find... Can you open it from that side?"

Jekku shot him a look even though Taja couldn't see him. "Haven't exactly had a moment to try, seeing as how I've been knocked out twice now."

"You *what*?" Taja's shadow moved back and forth as he continued searching for a latch in the door. "How did you even get down here?"

"Take a guess." Jekku got up from the stone floor and rubbed his temples, where an ache steadily throbbed through his skull. What the hell kind of mage could stop someone's heart? A healer? Weren't they supposed to do the opposite of that?

"No. *Ellory?* They wouldn't."

"They would," Jekku said, "and they did."

Taja muttered a curse. "I can't believe— Anyway. They're
fire mage, so they couldn't have sealed this door with magic. Wa
anyone else with them?"

"Yeah, but she had, uh, different magic."

"What kind?"

Jekku knew exactly how Taja was going to respond to this
"She was able to drop my heart rate and knock me out. So, prob
ably not the kind that could seal a stone door."

The door finally clicked and opened with a groan. Taj
shoved it wider and stepped in, staring at Jekku in horror. "Sh
did *what*?"

"I'm fine, though, thanks for asking." Jekku crossed his arm
and leaned back against the wall. He pushed his hair behind hi
ear and made sure the bruise he knew was on the right side of hi
face was clearly visible, even in the dim light. It was petty, yes
and this was in no way Taja's fault, but at the moment Jekku di
not care.

Taja moved closer to him, then froze. His eyes widened whe
he saw the bruise and the scrape on Jekku's face. He inhale
sharply, then stepped closer with his hand raised as if to touc
Jekku's face. Jekku turned his head. Taja moved back. "Did... Di
Ellory do that to you?"

Jekku met his gaze and nodded once.

Taja fell back a few more steps and muttered another curse
"I can't believe them. What did they want?"

"They claimed they just wanted to talk." Jekku shrugged. "Yo
know them better than I do. Is this in character? Do they ofte

drag their guests down to this creepy cellar? You know, between the crowd this morning and now this, I feel so welcomed in this town."

Taja winced. He studied the floor for a second, then gradually raised his head to meet Jekku's eyes again. *For gods' sakes*, Jekku thought, *just apologize so we can move on.*

But instead Taja said, "This was a power play. They want to intimidate you. Just... don't listen to Ellory. They're a bully and always have been. The last thing we need is to let them get under our skin. That's exactly what they want, but words are one thing. Trapping you down here and hurting you is a step too far."

"I'm fine," Jekku snapped. "You don't have to look after me."

"I'm not trying to." Taja kept his voice soft, and for some reason that made Jekku angrier. Was he just going to pretend that conversation at his cottage didn't happen? He started to reach for his hand and Jekku started to pull away, but Taja caught himself first. He hovered his hand in midair, clenched a fist, then let it fall. "Jekku, I'm sorry." He sighed and met his eyes. "What I said earlier was uncalled for, and— I'm sorry. You do belong here, and though you didn't grow up as one of us, you could still be one with us if that's what you want."

Jekku watched the torch flicker in the corner of the room. For a second he debated not replying at all, but it was time to shrug off the pettiness. Jekku wanted an apology, and he was getting one. The least he could offer in return was the truth. "I don't know if that's what I want."

Out of the corner of his eye, he saw Taja drift backward. "Oh."

Jekku clenched his jaw. He could elaborate, explain that it

wasn't Taja, it was this godsdamned town. Maybe it was true that Jekku didn't belong in Båthälla. He had history to uncover here, but that didn't mean he wished to stay.

Taja, though... Jekku wanted to stay with Taja. Even though things were weird and fraught and the tension between them was pulled so tight it was about to snap. Jekku's feelings for Taja hadn't changed, but now everything about it was more difficult.

He could have explained all of this, but he let his words hang in the air. *Distance is good, right? That's what I need?* Yes, but if this was what it felt like, Jekku didn't like it. He just wanted what he and Taja had before — an easy friendship, some casual flirting, and something unspoken in the air. It was so much easier to exist around him before they had to put a name to whatever this was.

Taja spoke again before Jekku could conjure any words. "Do you want to be here?"

That made Jekku finally look at him. His anger fizzled out. He let his walls drop. "What?"

Taja searched his eyes, but Jekku couldn't fathom what he was looking for. "Do you actually want to be here?"

"Of course I—"

"Why?" Taja's voice had an edge to it now. "What is here that you're staying for?"

Jekku blinked, stunned. Taja really didn't know? Oh, gods, and Jekku was going to have to say it?

"You." He forced himself to hold Taja's gaze, but in truth he wanted to sink through the floor. He was not at all ready for this kind of confession, but clearly it needed to be said.

Taja's anger bled from his expression. He went to say something, but Jekku placed his hand on his arm. "You're here, and 'm staying for you. Because I made a promise to you, and you old me you would wait for me. That was only a few days ago. Is t still true?"

Taja blinked a few times, then nodded.

Jekku smiled. "Then I'm here. And I'm also here because I vant to support you. I want to see you win. And if that means kicking Ellory out of Båthälla, I'm first in line."

Taja cracked a smile, but he still looked hesitant. "This isn't going to be easy."

"No one ever said it would be. That doesn't change a thing." ekku brought him into a hug, which apparently startled him because he froze like a statue. Jekku breathed a laugh and drew back. "Hey. You know I'm still me, right?"

Taja looked away and fiddled with one of his curls. "It feels like you're a stranger."

"Why?"

"I mean— Look at us, Jekku." He gestured at the dim room surrounding them. "Everything is different. It's not easy anymore. Until a few days ago, all we had to care about was staying alive and keeping the Oracle Stone safe. We had a plan, and we knew what we had to do. Now I— It's like starting over. And I feel like I don't know you."

Jekku let his hands fall from Taja's arms and drew back a step.

"But that's not a bad thing." Taja closed the space between them again, reaching for Jekku's hands. This time, Jekku let him. He wouldn't say it, but he did long for the touch. He appreciated that Taja respected his boundaries, but it was startling to realize how much he enjoyed Taja's gentle affections only after they had been revoked.

"It's not a bad thing," Taja repeated, quieter. His thumb traced over the backs of Jekku's hands. "I'm not saying that you've changed so much you're unrecognizable. I know you're still you. But we can't deny that both of us have changed. Before, we came together and learned to trust each other because we had to. Now we don't. You could have chosen to leave and carry on with your life somewhere else. But you made a choice to come here with me, and I'm making the choice to know you as you truly are. So in a way, you are a stranger. There's so much more to you than what I know, and I can't wait to meet the real Jekku."

Jekku just stared at him, at a loss for words. He didn't know what to do with any of that, but it sounded something like a confession, and Jekku was historically terrible at handling those. His first instinct was to simply leave, but he'd already turned his back on Taja today. He didn't want to do it again. But the other option that the reckless part of his brain swung toward involved forgetting his efforts of emotional recovery and kissing Taja right here in this cellar.

That, too, was a terrible idea.

He dropped his gaze to their clasped hands and gave Taja's a squeeze. "I feel like I met you all over again, too. You're not the same person I met at that temple in the Crowns. You're not the boy who looked at me and thought I was his Savior." Jekku looked back up at him. "And that's not a bad thing, either."

Taja pulled Jekku into another hug and set his chin on the top of his head. Jekku was slightly indignant that he was tall enough to do that, but he indulged the hug and savored the moment.

"I don't need you to be a savior," Taja murmured. "I just need you to be my friend."

"I never stopped," Jekku said.

Taja drew back and met Jekku's eyes with that tender smile that sent Jekku's heart spinning out of control. He broke his gaze and let go, heat flooding his face. *Gods, you can't look at me like that.* That unguarded longing stirred something in Jekku's chest that made him want to reduce his walls to rubble and give in. It'd be so *easy.* Taja clearly wanted him, clearly would pick up where they left off if Jekku only said the word.

Jekku wanted to. He wanted to let himself feel everything he felt for Taja instead of smothering it. It seemed foolish to let this slide through his fingers when he could have everything he wanted right now.

But Jekku also knew he shouldn't. He knew, even if he hated to admit it, that if he went ahead with Taja, his insecurity would swarm him with a vengeance and he'd bury himself in a pit of second-guessing and overthinking. What Leo had done would lurk in the back of Jekku's mind for a long time; Jekku knew that waiting to forget it entirely was a lost cause. He would never forget, but the trick was learning to silence that voice.

It was too soon. He knew it was too soon. But still... When he had someone as beautiful and kind as Taja looking at him like *that*, how could he say no? How could he distance himself?

Taja gently touched his cheek, and Jekku jumped. Taja pulled his hand back. "You okay?"

No. "Yeah. Fine." He flickered a smile. "How did you—"

His words were cut off by a deafening crack of thunder that certainly did not come from Jekku. He exchanged a look with Taja, finding his own confusion mirrored in Taja's eyes, then the two of them darted out of the cellar room.

"What the hell was that?" Jekku asked as Taja stopped at a rickety rope ladder hanging down from a trapdoor. Taja climbed on and it held, but Jekku was not thrilled at the way it creaked under his weight.

"Nothing good, that's for sure. Come on." Taja climbed up and disappeared through the opening in the ceiling, then leaned down and offered Jekku a hand.

Jekku nervously stepped onto the first rung. *It's like five feet off the ground, you're fine.* He gritted his teeth and climbed up, taking Taja's hand even though he didn't really need to. He let Taja pull him up, then dusted off his hands and swung the trapdoor shut. "Where are we? How did you even find me down here?"

"The temple study." Taja crossed the room to a set of double glass doors. "I ran into Nedra as she was coming out of the temple, and she asked if you had found me. I said no, that I was looking for you, and she said you were just here and couldn't have gotten far. I just–– I got a bad feeling about it. And Nedra confirmed it when she said she'd glimpsed Ellory coming in here. I knew if there was any place Ellory would corner you and trap you, it's in that cellar. That's where..."

A visible shudder ran through him. His eyes darted around the dark room and he absently scratched the scar on the back of his hand. "I ran in here without thinking. I..." He shook his head and flung open the glass doors.

"What?" Jekku followed him, beyond confused, but before he could ask any more questions, an eruption of voices and horns and another crack of thunder rang through the temple.

Taja halted at the end of the hallway leading into the main room. "Oh. Shit."

Jekku wished for an answer. Any answer. "What is going on?"

Taja turned to him. "Nokaldir has finally come home."

5

TAJA

"NOKALDIR?" JEKKU QUESTIONED, trailing behind Taja. "Isn't he...?"

"He's the God of the Universe," Taja said. And according to the stories Taja had heard, he was exactly as conceited as one would expect a god of the universe to be.

Taja stopped just outside the temple, at the top of the stairs. Below, a crowd once again gathered in the town square. Temple attendants made a line down the center, cutting the crowd in two, and a few held curved ram's horns. Despite the clear path, the people were so closely packed that Taja couldn't pick out Nokaldir or even Nedra.

His heart pounded. First that onslaught of flashbacks in the study, and now this; his nerves were frayed thin. A visceral reminder of having his magic stripped out of him was not what he needed to end this hellish day.

"Nokaldir hasn't made an appearance in Båthälla in years," he told Jekku. "Decades, even. I've never met him, and I believe my parents only met him once when they were both younger. He *never* comes here."

"So what's compelling him to pay a visit now?"

Taja glanced at him. "Us."

Jekku's face shifted to a vaguely panicked expression that Taja found quite relatable. "Right. Of course he is."

"And probably Ebris," Taja added. "I'm sure he's here because of that, too. But that leads back to us, as well."

He looked back out at the crowd, but still saw no glimpse of the gods. He felt a touch on his arm and turned to Jekku again.

"Hey." Jekku searched his eyes, and Taja felt a flutter in his chest that had nothing to do with his anxiety. "Listen. We can't mess this up again. I don't know how many chances your people — and the gods — will give you."

And the anxiety was back. "I don't think they'll—"

"They will give you a second chance," Jekku said. "We'll *make* them. But we have to get it right this time. *You* have to talk to them. Tell them what they want to hear, but also tell them what they *need* to hear."

Taja's pulse thundered in his ears. "How? Jekku, how? You saw what happened out there earlier. How do I make them listen to me? Especially with Ellory there... Gods, I already blew it, didn't I?"

"No." Jekku squeezed his arm. "You messed up, sure, but that doesn't mean you throw in the towel. If you want them to give you another chance, first you have to give *yourself* another chance."

Taja pressed his lips together. "I don't think I can do this alone." He wanted to say that he didn't think he could do this at all, but he had to learn to silence those doubts.

"No one ever said you had to." Jekku let go of his arm and clasped his hand instead. "I'm on your side. And, just between us, so is Nedra."

"Nedra?" Taja blinked, surprised. "You talked to her?"

"Earlier today. She's with us, Taja," said Jekku. "She knew about Ebris's lies long ago — even when it was Saevel in your shoes — and she regrets that she wasn't able to do anything earlier. But she doesn't want to see you manipulated like Saevel apparently was. She wants to see Bâthälla thrive without the gods, so whatever we have to do, she'll help us."

Taja let out a breath. A goddess on their side. Good. This was good. This was big.

"Ah!" A deep, booming voice echoed across the square. "My beloved Elshalans of Bâthälla! How I have missed this little town."

Finally, Nokaldir appeared. He sauntered across the square, grinning and waving as people sank to their knees around him. Nedra and Oridite trailed behind him; both of them looked like they'd rather be anywhere else.

"That's him?" Jekku whispered.

"That's him." Taja rubbed the back of his neck. Nokaldir's presence wasn't *bad*, but it complicated things. Unfortunately, Taja would have to go down there sooner than later and catch Nokaldir's attention before Ellory had a chance to twist the truth.

Nokaldir stopped at the bottom of the temple steps and turned to the crowd with his arms spread wide. He wore a robe

he color of midnight, complete with a scatter of tiny white
beads that glittered like stars. No crown sat on his graying black
hair, but he didn't need any decoration to make him look regal.
t radiated from him. He was a god, and unlike the others who
made themselves smaller, more human, Nokaldir did not allow
anyone to forget that he was divine.

"God of the Universe, huh?" Jekku murmured. "So, what, he's
above the rest?"

"No," Taja said. "Or at least, he's not supposed to be."

"Neither was Ebris."

Taja pursed his lips. "True. If anyone has authority here in
Ebris's absence, it's Nokaldir. And it looks like he knows he's in
charge now."

He stood before Båthälla like he already owned the place. Or
rather, like he owned the entire world. Which, Taja reasoned, he
sort of did. Nokaldir lifted his arms and beamed at the crowd,
and the people gathered immediately silenced their excited mur-
muring.

"My children." The god's voice rumbled like the thunder that
had announced his appearance. "I truly have missed you. I regret
that I have not visited in some time, and I wish I was here now
under better circumstances. I understand there is a grave problem in Båthälla."

Taja exchanged a glance with Jekku. He barely dared to
breathe. And Jekku's nervous expression certainly did not help.

"It has come to my attention," Nokaldir went on, "that Lord
Ebris has Fallen. A god cannot exactly die, of course, but sadly...
he is gone. I am sorry."

Nokaldir's words were met with dead silence. Taja's heart

beat so hard that he swore it could be heard across the square. *A god cannot exactly die.* Did that mean there was a possibility Ebris could come back? Nokaldir said he was gone, but Taja got the sense it wasn't as permanent as he wanted it to be.

"Tradition states that the god of next highest authority would step into place as leader," Nokaldir said. He smiled again, wrinkles creasing around his eyes. "Coincidentally, that would be me."

"Oh, no," Taja breathed.

"But don't worry!" Absurdly, Nokaldir sounded... cheerful. Like he was giving a speech at a wedding instead of announcing the death of a god. Like Ebris, Nokaldir had a talent for appearing friendly and nonchalant while danger lurked behind his words. "I intend to throw tradition out the door," he declared. "Times change and so do gods. We're going to do things a little differently around here."

Taja glanced at Jekku. Jekku stared at him, confusion clouding his features. He mouthed, *What?* And Taja could only shrug.

Could it be possible that... *Nokaldir* was on Taja's side as well? Had Nedra spoken to him before he came to Båthälla? Did he know everything?

Taja barely dared to hope for that.

"I don't trust him," he whispered to Jekku. "From what I've heard, his most notable trait is his arrogance. He won't just give up this position."

"I'm giving up the position," Nokaldir declared, and whatever he said next was drowned out by disgruntled murmurs from the surrounding crowd.

Taja had never been so confused in his life. He dragged his hands through his hair. "What the hell is going *on*?"

Jekku just shook his head, dumbstruck. "I— Oh, shit. Taja." He nudged his arm and nodded down at the square. Taja followed his gaze and spotted a familiar dark-haired nuisance shouldering their way through the crowd.

Taja swore under his breath.

"Taja, we have to go down there," Jekku said.

"Do we?"

"Trust me, I'd rather jump off the roof," Jekku said. "But yes, go, before they—"

"Lord Nokaldir!" Ellory's voice rang over the square and silenced the chatter of voices. "Thank the stars for your return. Our situation is worse than you think. You see, Lord Ebris did not Fall, my Lord. He was *killed* by the very same traitor who—"

No. Taja's actions moved faster than his brain, and before he knew what he was doing, he stepped off the last temple stair and strode toward Ellory.

"*Stop.*" Now *his* voice rang across the square. "Lord Nokaldir, what Ellory Ives claims is untrue. They're only trying to stir up trouble." He shot a glare at Ellory, who returned it with a scowl to match. Taja ignored them. "Lord Ebris attempted to bring about an age of war and chaos that could have led to All Death. He meant to free the Royal Sorcerers from the Oracle Stone and let them destroy our magic. An orchestrated apocalypse, just so the world would remember him as the hero. Never mind that the role of *Sawwia Setukkda* belongs to— to someone else."

Taja kicked himself even as the words came out of his mouth. *Why can't I just say that it's me?*

"*Sawwia Setukkda.*" Nokaldir drew out the words. Amusement glinted in his dark eyes and made Taja want to shrink back, as if he'd said something foolish. "Oh, yes, we all know that Lord Ebris obsessed over those Savior myths. Prophecies and all that. I admit he lucked out the first time — the Peacebringer was a force to be reckoned with, that's for sure. But a second one..."

Taja took a deep breath. He glanced over his shoulder, briefly caught Jekku's gaze, then turned back to Nokaldir. "It's me. I'm *Sawwia Setukkda.*"

His pulse thundered. He blocked out every noise around him and barreled on. "I'm the Second Savior, and Ebris knew it but refused to believe it. He denied me the chance to help my people — my family — and now I'm taking it back. If anyone's going to change things in Båthälla, Nokaldir, it's me."

Did I really just say that? Taja's heart was beating so fast he feared he might pass out. He didn't know where this confidence had come from, but he couldn't quit now. He turned away from Nokaldir and Ellory and faced his people. "Please, stand with me. Things can be better. Our magic doesn't have to die. Do you really want to live under the heel of the gods forever?"

"The gods have protected us!" Ellory shouted. They roughly grabbed Taja's arm and forced him to look at them. "It is because of our gods that we live in peace and the humans leave us alone! But is anyone surprised that *you* have never understood that?"

"It is because of your gods that the White Lily is dying and so are we," Taja retorted.

Ellory's face twisted with rage. "How *dare*—"

A clap of thunder shook the ground. "That's enough,"

Nokaldir growled. "Vaeltaja, explain yourself. What do you mean, the White Lily is dying?"

For a second, Taja was too surprised to reply. Nokaldir didn't know? Did Ebris keep secrets even from the other gods?

"Lord Ebris never told you." He meant to say it as a question, but there was nothing uncertain about it.

Nokaldir's thick brows knit together. "I think this conversation is best continued in private. Oridite?"

Several feet away, the God of Darkness lifted one thin eyebrow.

"Will you take care of our audience?" Nokaldir flashed a grin. "Nedra, perhaps you should come with us. Vaeltaja? Ellory? With me." He strode across the square without waiting for anyone to reply, and was nearly to the temple steps before Taja shook himself into action and went after the god.

"Lord Nokaldir," Taja called as he caught up, "please hear me out. Lord Ebris was going to turn on us. I know how it sounds—"

"What it sounds like, Vaeltaja, is that you had an opportunity to seek revenge on a man who hurt you and you took that opportunity." Nokaldir paused halfway up the steps and turned to him.

Taja's heart stopped. "You don't really think that."

Nokaldir arched an eyebrow. "And how would you know what I think?"

Taja broke his gaze and lowered his eyes. The back of his neck prickled with shame. "I apologize, my Lord."

He felt a hand on his shoulder and looked up. Nedra stood beside him. "Lord Nokaldir. Perhaps you're not aware due to your absence, but Lord Ebris had indeed been fretting — dare

I say obsessing — over the White Lily for quite some time. H knew our magic was weakening, but the path he chose would no have saved us."

Nokaldir pressed his lips together. "Come." He turned, robe flapping in his wake, and strode into the temple.

Before Taja could take one step, Ellory stormed past him making it a point to shove his shoulder. Taja scowled after hin and followed, Nedra at his side.

"Be patient, Taja," Nedra said softly. "Gods are notoriously re sistant to change. But he'll come around."

"Not if Ellory has anything to say about it," he muttered, an continued into the temple.

He nearly jumped out of his skin when Jekku appeared at th entrance. "Gods— I forgot you were there." But he relaxed a littl and returned Jekku's faint smile.

Ahead, near the back of the temple, Ellory stood wit Nokaldir. They glared at Taja, but he ignored them as he an Jekku and Nedra joined them.

"All right." Nokaldir pinched the bridge of his nose. Then h spotted Jekku and frowned. "Wait, who are you?"

"I'm, uh... a friend." Jekku glanced at Taja. "And I'm here be cause Ebris tried to use *me* as the Second Savior."

Nokaldir looked baffled, but shook his head and waved hand. "Fine. Explain to me what's going on, as civilly as you ca manage."

"I don't see why you need to hear a whole saga," Ellory said They jerked their head toward Taja. "Seven years ago he deepl betrayed our village, and now he's trying to wreck us entirely b turning our people against their gods."

Taja was getting sick of this. "That is— Gods above, that is not at all what I'm saying. I'm trying to *save* us, Ellory! It is not my fault that Ebris—"

"If you say *one more* word against Lord Ebris—"

"He would have driven us into the ground, Ellory!" Taja raised his voice. He didn't care anymore. "The Peacebringer is the only reason we were saved from his treachery."

Ellory went to retort, but Nokaldir brought his hand down on their shoulder. They jumped and shoved off his hand, but he spoke before Ellory had a chance. His eyes bore into Taja.

"The Peacebringer appeared to you?"

Taja nodded. "They ultimately removed Ebris from our world. They knew he couldn't be redeemed or changed. It was time for him to go."

Ellory lurched a step forward, but Nokaldir held them back. "*Enough*, Ellory," he growled. "For skies' sakes, you're acting like a child. You forget your place, Ives. You have no more right to this village than any of us."

"I have more right to it than he does!" Ellory spat.

Anger burned under Taja's skin. "Have you listened to *any-thing* I've said? I don't want to lead Båthälla! I just want us to survive!"

"You would see us to our *graves*, traitor."

"Enough!" Nokaldir clapped his hands and a crack of thunder shuddered the temple. He took a deep breath. "What part of *civil* do the two of you not understand? And correct me if I'm wrong, but it seems to me that you have similar goals. At the very least, you have similar values. So tell me, why have you not simply *talked*?"

Taja threw up his hands. "Because every time—"

"Because *he's*—"

"They won't listen!"

"*He* won't listen," Ellory snarled.

"Gods above," Jekku muttered.

"Lord Nokaldir." Nedra sighed. "Can we get back to the real issue at hand? Lord Ebris is gone, so what is our next step?"

Taja glanced at Ellory, expecting them to violently deny Nedra's words. But for the first time all day, they stood silently. Instead of angry, they actually looked... defeated. The tension bled out of their shoulders, and they glanced between Nokaldir and Nedra with something like grief in their eyes.

For just this moment, Taja felt sorry for them. Ellory had always been popular in Båthälla, and they had a flock of friends that seemed to genuinely care for them, but Ebris was the only family they had. In Båthälla, your neighbors were also your family, but a different kind. There was an unspoken understanding that blood family — the ones who brought you into the world and raised you — were *true* family, and everyone else was more distant. Taja had never truly believed that, but he knew Ellory did.

And now their only blood family was gone. Ebris might have been a lousy father, but he was the only one Ellory had.

"It's true, isn't it?" Their voice was quieter than Taja had ever heard it. No sharp edges, no malice. "He's really gone."

"Ellory, I am sorry." Nedra set her hand on their shoulder, and this time they didn't resist. "Yes, he's gone."

"It's not like we've said that a hundred times," Jekku mut-

ered. Taja nudged him — really, this was not the time — but
ekku moved a step away.

Taja tried not to let that sting.

"Nokaldir, what is your plan, if not to step into Ebris's place?"
Nedra said.

"I wish to be nothing like Lord Ebris," said Nokaldir. "So I
thought I'd leave it up to our fellow citizens of Båthälla to decide
who they want to lead them."

Taja stared at him. Jekku frowned. Ellory's eyebrows shot up.
Even Nedra looked surprised. Taja didn't know of any Elshalans
in all of history who had ever chosen their community's leaders.
It had always been the gods. Why be led by fellow mortals — im-
perfect, greed-prone, everyday people — when there were gods
among them?

But Nokaldir was right. Why *shouldn't* a village's people decide who they wanted? Just because Taja didn't know of it hap-
pening before did not mean it couldn't happen now. Wasn't that
why he was here — to usher Båthälla into a new age?

"Oh, don't look at me like that." Nokaldir chuckled softly. His
eyes crinkled at the corners when he smiled. "Isn't it time that
our people decide what is best for them? Who would know better? We may be gods, but we only chose to live among mortals.
Who ever said we also had to rule them?"

Ellory cleared their throat. "I believe, Lord Nokaldir, that you
did."

Nokaldir frowned. "Hm. Perhaps I did. But it's human nonsense that leaders are chosen by some divine hand. The tradition
shall not continue. We'll speak to the Council Eternal, gather

some candidates —— including you and I, Nedra, and Oridite i
he wishes to —— and then leave it up to Båthälla."

Nedra was the first to shake off her surprise. "We hope for
better future, do we not? If there is one thing gods understand
it is that even the universe itself demands constant change. W
may not like it, but it is inevitable. This is a start. And Ellory, i
you are worried that your ambitions will be interrupted, don'
be. In fact, we'll need the Council Eternal more than ever. You
place here will not be erased."

Ah, so Ellory wanted a spot on the Council Eternal. Of cours
they did. Of course they continued to be everything Taja's par
ents always wanted *him* to be. Taja shuddered at the idea of El
lory holding any position of power in Båthälla. That kind o
authority would surely go right to their head, and then how lon
would it be before they fell into the same trap as Ebris did, an
put themself and their reputation before their people?

Taja did not wish to live in a Båthälla led by Ellory Ives. H
silently hoped they wouldn't make a grab for the position, bu
that was a foolish wish if Taja had ever heard one. Of course the
would. Already Taja could see the plan brewing in their eyes.

Ellory scowled, then flipped their hair over their shoulder
turned on their heel, and stalked away. Taja listened for thei
footsteps to recede up the steps to the second floor of the tem
ple, then he let out a breath.

"They have always been difficult," Nokaldir sighed. "A thorn
in my side since the day they were born."

"They're grieving," Nedra said. "Of course they won't admi
it, but this loss hurts them. Ebris was all they had left after thei
mother..." She glanced at Taja and Jekku, then back to Nokaldir

"Well. You know. At any rate, I understand their stubborn loyalty. I just wish they would set aside their devotion to Ebris and see the truth in front of them."

"They won't," Taja said. Ellory was a lost cause, for all he cared. "We have to carry on without them. There's no way they'll see reason, not when they've been manipulated for all these years."

Nedra nodded sadly. "I fear it will be a long time before Båthälla is truly out of Ebris's shadow."

"There will probably always be people who revere him," Taja said. The thought left a sour taste in his mouth. "I don't think we can avoid that. But hopefully, with time..." He shrugged.

It would be so, so vindicating if one day Ebris was forgotten entirely. Taja only wished he'd live to see it.

"Hey." Jekku touched his arm. "Can we talk?"

Taja looked at him. "What? Right now?"

"Yes." Jekku nodded toward the exit. "Walk with me. I want to tell you something. It'll help." He glanced at the gods. "If you don't mind that I steal him for a minute?"

"Whatever it takes to get our Savior on his feet." Nedra smiled and waved them off. "We'll speak again. Come, Nokaldir, I have much to tell you." She headed down the hall, Nokaldir following a second later, and Taja turned to Jekku.

"What is it?" What could be so urgent that Jekku had to do this now?

Jekku only smiled and led him out of the temple. He waited at the bottom of the steps for Taja to catch up, then continued across the square — which was now free of crowds, thank the gods — and into the trees.

Taja fell into step beside him, still confused. But he let the silence stretch out as they walked into the woods. He put the chaos of this day behind him and listened to the crunch of leaves and frost under their shoes and the warble of birds overhead. The air carried a chill, but aside from a light dusting on the ground, no snow weighed down the evergreens around them. Taja inhaled the crisp forest air, and tried to scrape up a semblance of calm.

A simple walk in a familiar place with someone he cared for. If he focused on that alone, everything else could, for the moment, fade into the background.

He turned to look at Jekku at the same time Jekku looked up at him. "A few weeks ago, when we both thought I was *Sawwia Setukkda* and I was stressed to hell and back about the Oracle Stone, you told me a story. And as most stories do, it helped. It reminded me that we're not alone and never have been. But let me tell you something a little different, something about saviors and history that's too easy to forget."

Taja found himself smiling. "I'm listening."

Jekku looked away from him and up at the trees. "Did you know that there are some places in Doweth — in Aylesbury, even — that still keep statues and portraits of Queen Margravine around?"

"I... did not know that, no." That surprised him. Wasn't she the one who caused all the troubles that Saevel had to fix nine hundred years ago?

"You won't find her face in Westdenn," Jekku went on. "Even her castle was reduced to rubble, as we saw. All that's left is that wolf statue where we found a piece of the Oracle Stone. But elsewhere? She's revered as a strong and wondrous leader of Doweth along with the rest of the Rose Monarchs. Interesting, isn't it, when we know that she and the other three stood for the division of Doweth?"

"That— Yeah, no, that's not right." Taja frowned. "Didn't she send hundreds of people to their deaths in her useless war?"

"Hundreds of thousands, probably."

"And she's still respected, even in your royal city?"

Jekku nodded. "She is. But do you know who is held in even higher regard than Queen Margravine?"

Taja winced. "Don't say the Royal Sorcerers."

Jekku turned to him again and smiled. "No. The Peace-bringer."

Taja stopped walking. His heart lifted. "Saevel? Really?"

"Most of us don't know them by name." Jekku paused a few steps ahead and faced Taja. "And a thousand different artists have tried to capture their likeness in a million different ways. The real Saevel has been lost to time. But someday, Taja, I'll take you around this country and point out every single mural and icon and portrait of a young Savior with a shiny sword, and we'll be gone for at least a decade because they are *everywhere*. Even the monastery where I lived had portraits of Saevel. So yes, Margravine's influence lingers, but Saevel has and always will outshine her." He smiled. "And so will you."

Taja couldn't find words. He opened his mouth, then closed it again. His throat felt tight. That gentle smile on Jekku's face did things to Taja's heart that he was trying hard not to feel. Jekku took a step toward him, and—

Taja blinked. Jekku *vanished*. He was gone. Just— into thin air. Taja stared at the spot where he had stood a second ago and his brain refused to make sense of what he'd just seen. One second Jekku was there, the next he was gone without a trace.

Impossible. Taja hazarded a step forward, but instead of meeting soft forest floor, his foot met empty air and then he was falling.

He had no chance to scream before darkness swallowed him.

6

JEKKU

JEKKU OPENED HIS EYES and was home.

Actual home. Not Båthälla, not the monastery, and certainly not Gallien's Peak.

Ajaphere.

He recognized the room immediately: the faded wood floor and white walls he hadn't seen in eight years. The chipped yellow paint on the window shutters. Trinkets, books — so many books — wreaths of dried sunflowers, doodles and sketches on the walls and window frames, treasures his sisters had found or made. A basket of clean clothes sat in front of his wardrobe, waiting to be put away; his desk was cluttered with scattered papers, half-full notebooks, and his current read open where he'd left off.

It was all just as he'd left it eight years ago.

He stayed where he'd woken on the floor for a minute; his eyes darted around the room, searching for some flaw, some sign that this wasn't real. It had to be just an illusion, right? A moment ago he'd been standing in the woods outside Båthälla with Taja. Now he was in his bedroom in Ajaphere, and whatever had brought him here had not missed a single detail. It had to be the workings of some god, but *why?*

For one who does not believe in any gods, grumbled a disembodied voice, *you are very quick to recognize the workings of one.*

Jekku stood and looked around, but he knew he wouldn't find a physical source of the voice. "Who are you? Where am I, and why have you brought me here?"

All in good time, Jekku Aj'ere. But clearly you already know where you are. I wish to show you something.

The bedroom door creaked open, and Jekku tensed, but no one stepped in. Jekku hesitantly approached the door and opened it wider, then gasped.

Before him stood a much younger version of himself, hovering in the hallway and dressed like he was traveling somewhere: thick cloak, sturdy boots, and a bag slung over his shoulder. He did not appear to be able to see Jekku.

Oh, no. Jekku's heart plummeted. So this wasn't a vision; it was a memory, and this was the night Jekku left to go to Aylesbury.

He wasn't Jekku here, then. He was Jakob, and— Gods above, was this really what he'd looked like? Short, scrawny, swimming in his own clothes, hair still growing out from that terrible cut that'd lobbed it to his chin. Jekku cringed at the memory of existing like this.

Jakob hesitated only a minute, then crept silently down the hall and out into the main room of the house. Jekku followed. It was dark, the fire long dead, and his mother had put out the last of the candles when she went to bed. Jekku stayed in the mouth f the hallway and watched his younger self cross the room to he front door.

Don't, he mentally begged him. *You don't know what you're doing. You're going to regret everything.*

"Jakob."

Jekku startled at his mother's voice. His younger self jumped oo, and whirled around to face the kitchen doorway. "Mom?" akob's hands gripped the strap of his bag. "W-What're you doing p?"

Jekku frowned and moved so he could see into the kitchen. ure enough, his mother was there, seated at the table with the ights off so Jakob would think she was in bed.

Jekku was caught between a thousand emotions at seeing his nother's face for the first time in eight years, and utter confusion, because this was not how this had happened. "What is his?" he asked the god.

A memory.

"No, it's not. You know it's not, and I certainly know it, too. This didn't happen. She didn't stop me. If she had, I wouldn't be here now."

Hmmm... I suppose you wouldn't. Fascinating, isn't it, how a lifetime can change with one altered event. I wonder what your life would look like, Jekku Aj'ere, had the scene in front of you actually come to pass. I wonder where, indeed, you would be now?

Realistically, he probably would have never left. Before he became obsessed with the idea of presenting his theory about magic to the Masters at Gallien's Peak, he'd expected a fairly mundane path for his life. He'd finish out the last couple years of school in Ajaphere and be completely bored the whole time, and then he'd work in his mother's bookshop. Maybe he'd meet someone, maybe not. And the only glimpses of other lives and other places he'd ever see would be in the pages of a book.

And this is not the life you want, is it? asked the god.

Once, maybe it was. But Jekku had wandered the street of the royal city, been surrounded by magic at Gallien's Peak braved the Crowned Mountains, been to a hidden Elshalan city and visited the libraries in Westdenn. He could not imagine going back to live out the rest of his life in sleepy Ajaphere.

He'd go back. He had to. But he didn't think his home was there, anymore.

"No," he said softly. "The life this town could give me is not the life I want. I'm not sure that it ever was."

Jekku watched the scene play out in front of him. Marian went to Jakob and dragged him into a hug that he only resisted for a second before indulging her. She squeezed him tight and pressed a kiss to the top of his head.

Jekku couldn't tear his eyes away from his mother's face. The dim light from the kitchen cast shadows across her round face and made her look decades older than she actually was. It might have been Jekku's imagination, but he swore her eyes welled with tears. She hugged Jakob as if she'd already lost him, as if she knew that he was about to slip through her fingers and ruin his own life.

He could only imagine how she'd look at him when he worked up the courage to go home.

Marian let go of Jakob so she could see his face. "Everything you need and everything you want is right here. Don't you dare ever forget that. Go back to bed, Jakob. We'll talk in the morning."

Jekku's vision blurred, and the scene shifted around him. Dizziness swept through his head and he pressed a hand to the wall to keep on his feet. When he could see properly again, the memory had returned to how it began: Jakob stood in the hallway, packed and ready to leave, but the kitchen was dark and empty. Just as Jekku remembered.

How about this version, then?

Jakob strode across the house, opened the door, and left. No one stopped him. Jekku followed his younger self, but the door did not take him outside. It brought him somewhere else that was achingly familiar.

His heart lurched. He stood in the middle of his room at the monastery and suddenly felt as though he was sinking deeper and deeper and deeper into an endless, frigid ocean that squeezed all the air out of him.

Not here. He couldn't be here. Not even in a memory or an illusion or whatever this was. He could not be here. Why did this god think he would want to be here?

Completely at odds with his mood, the room was bright. Gold light spilled from the lanterns hanging from the ceiling and multicolored pools dappled the floor beneath the stained-glass windows high on the walls. A trio of candles flickered beneath an old oil painting of the four gods, and an open book lay beside them. At the far end of the room, thin white curtains hung from the ceiling created a chamber around a small, neatly made bed. On the opposite end of the room was a makeshift bed of cushions, pillows, and blankets that had been Jekku's cozy nest for the two years he lived here.

He went to his old bedchamber, which, in this illusion, wasn't yet sequestered off with curtains. Actually, none of his things were here. So either this vision was after he'd left, or... before he arrived?

It's not real. He tried to keep telling himself that. Whichever god was toying with him could do their worst, but they couldn't take away the logic that this was merely an illusion.

Jekku took a steadying breath, and the familiar scent of incense and dried roses caught at the back of his throat like a sob. He usually couldn't stand the sneeze-inducing smell of incense that permeated the air in every corner of this place, but this room was the exception. It was home. It was all the kindness and comfort he was shown when he arrived here. This was his space, and this was the room where he'd fallen in love.

He wished with everything in him that these memories were not tainted now. He wished he could look back on this place fondly — not without guilt, but ideally without this dreadful feeling. But no, Firune and his godsdamned curses had ruined this for him, too.

Jekku went down the two steps into the center circle of the room, which had cushions and pillows arranged around a low table. Unconventional, but far more comfortable than wooden chairs around a high table. Even the dining hall had floor seating like this instead of real tables, and Jekku remembered joking to Leo that monks had never seen a chair. The memory pierced like a thorn now; he pushed it away and sat down on one of the fluffy cushions.

"What if I hadn't left?" He wondered out loud, knowing that if there were people nearby, they wouldn't hear him anyway. "What if I'd ignored Firune's little game and just stayed here, where I was happy? Would I ever have found out, Leo? Would you have slipped up? Or would you have admitted it and then tossed me away?" His voice broke and he swallowed, then huffed a humorless laugh. "Would've made this roommate situation pretty awkward."

You're catching on, now. The god's voice returned. *Indeed, what if you had never left? What if your life here remained as perfect as you thought it was? Consider it, Jekku: no cruel sorcerer on your tail, no betrayal from your lover, no sense of urgency. Perhaps you still would have suffered the curse from the Master of Wishes, but you were happy here despite it, were you not?*

Jekku didn't wish to admit anything to this god who was undoubtedly trying to trick him, but he couldn't deny that was true. He *had* planned on staying at the monastery as long as Firune would let him. He'd gotten comfortable. He'd let himself believe that this time, Firune had given up and left him alone. Now he knew that Firune had lured him into that sense of security on purpose, and Jekku had had to tear himself away from a place he called home yet again.

But now this god had him thinking. What if Firune was removed from the picture? What if he wasn't constantly running?

He was so tired. He missed the calming comfort this place provided.

The room's door rattled. Jekku darted to his feet and turned toward it just in time for it to swing open and reveal yet another younger version of himself.

His heart stuttered. Gods above, he looked *awful*. No wonder the monks had taken pity on him. Freshly escaped from Gallien's Peak, this two-years-younger version of Jekku was deathly pale, underfed, scraped and battered from traveling, and visibly trembling. He stared at his new lodging as if it would blink out of existence if he glanced away even for a second.

Jekku's travels from Aylesbury to the Crowned Mountain were hazy in his memory — clouded by time and trauma as well as by the sickening amount of alcohol he'd consumed — but he remembered this moment. It had felt like a milestone, the start of something new. A restart to his life. He'd stepped into this room and felt a shift in the universe.

I'm free.

That was all he could think, over and over. *I'm actually free.*

It had not settled in, until this moment, that he would never return to Firune or Gallien's Peak ever again.

Looking at his past self now, Jekku wished he could hug him. "You will have to go back," he told him, knowing his younger self couldn't hear. "And I'm sorry for that. That's our own fault, too, but this time it made a difference. Then you'll be free for real."

"So what do you think?"

Jekku froze again at the voice. He muttered a curse — mostly at the god pulling the strings here, but also at the owner of that voice. He held his breath as his past self stepped fully into the room and Leo followed behind him.

He expected a stab of grief, to be hit with a harsh blow of loss. But all he felt seeing Leo now was fury. What he wouldn't give to step out of this illusion and into the actual scene and tell Leo he knew everything. *Everything.*

"I can't believe you," he muttered. "You really had the audacity to *beg me* to stay for you when I never mattered enough to you."

He stayed by the door but watched Leo cross the room with his younger self, showing him where he could keep his things and where to find extra blankets. They eventually settled in the sitting circle, and Jekku watched the last of the stress and fear lift off his younger self's shoulders. He gazed at Leo as if Leo was a gift from the gods themselves, and Jekku was tempted to roll his eyes, but he remembered this feeling. He remembered the overwhelming gratitude he felt to the very first person who was kind to him here, who let him in, who welcomed him, who offered half his room to this stranger off the street.

He remembered the spark of interest, too, that had burst to life all too soon. And he remembered how quickly that little spark had erupted into maddening feelings that, thankfully, he did not have to suffer alone for long.

"Maybe I did matter to you, once." Jekku spoke to the illusion of Leo, and maybe it didn't matter that he couldn't hear him. "Maybe I was important to you, and maybe you did love me. I believed that, you know. I never once doubted it when you said it to me. Either that makes me extremely naive, or you really meant it. Maybe you loved both me and him. But that doesn't change a thing, does it? You still lied to me. You still cheated on me. And now I've got someone else, someone I *know* loves me, but I won't dare say I love him too because now I— I don't know what's true anymore, Leo. And that's your fault. It's your fault."

Jekku had never felt for anyone what he felt for Leo. Until he saw, thanks to Firune, that Leo had never been true to him, he had been content to let Leo live in his memory as someone he loved and had to lose for his own good. But now, Jekku wished he could forget Leo entirely. He honestly, truly wished he'd never met him.

It would certainly make things easier with Taja.

Once again, I ask, what if it could have been different?

Before Jekku could reply, the scene changed. He watched days, months, years fly by in front of him just like he used to see in the time threads his curse showed him. He watched himself settle in at the monastery, finally growing comfortable and content after the initial paranoia that he'd be chased out by Firune within a matter of days. He thrived in this lifestyle of quiet academia, and while he didn't believe in the gods that these monks devoted themselves to, he found his community with them. They studied the workings of the world, and Jekku happily shared in their quests for knowledge.

Then something changed. No longer did he watch his own memories stream by; this was an alternate future. Firune's conjured crow that had tracked Jekku from Aylesbury into the Crowns never arrived. Jekku and Leo carried on their secret affair. Leo never cheated, Jekku never left. He lived and grew with the monks, and they became his family.

And one morning, he approached the abbot and requested to take his vows to formally join the Devotees of Phometia.

Jekku snapped back to reality. *What?* No. No, that wasn't right. He wouldn't. Those vows required him to express devotion and belief in a goddess he didn't believe in. He wasn't about to take back every question and doubt he'd ever expressed about the existence of gods, and he certainly wouldn't have *lied*. No, if

ekku was going to stay with the Devotees of Phometia, he would
have continued as he was: a long-term guest. And if that wasn't
possible, he would have left when the time came.

But you had such a happy life here, remarked the god. *You
wouldn't seize this for the small price of a white lie?*

"No," Jekku said. He was sick of these mind games. If this
really was one of the Elshalan gods talking to him, he could
only assume their goal was to throw him off the path of helping
Taja save Bâthälla. Of course the gods — aside from Nedra and
Nokaldir — didn't want their power usurped. There was only one
left who had yet to speak up, but judging by his stormy mood at
Nokaldir's return, Jekku reckoned the God of Darkness was not
on his side.

"Lord Oridite, then, is it?" Jekku turned his back on the visions and walked out of the room. He didn't expect to find the
god himself in the corridor, but he also couldn't stand to remain
in that room. Just because he didn't want to change the past
didn't mean he wasn't hurt by it. "Why are you doing this? What
do you want with me?"

*I am here to show you three things: What has been, what could have
been, and what could still be. That is, if you trust me.*

"Yeah, no, that's not going to work on me again." Jekku followed the twist of hallways, navigating on instinctual memory.
"You don't want me to trust you. You know I won't. You're just
trying to distract me and lure me away from Bâthälla so you can
take control. It's not going to happen. There's nothing you can
do to me or to Taja that's worse than what we've already been
through, and your little tricks won't make us quit. I don't care

how much you can bend my life; I don't want it. I want what's in my future, Oridite, not what's in my past."

The god was silent. *Did that really work?* Maybe Oridite saw that Jekku wouldn't break, and he'd decided to leave him alone.

But it couldn't be that easy, could it? Was he really more stubborn than a god?

He made it to the monastery's foyer and, with a dizzying sensation of déjà vu, shoved through the main doors. But instead of emerging into a snowy, mountainous landscape, a long, dim hallway stretched before him. Only one door waited at the very end, emitting gold light from beneath.

A low, deep laugh resounded through the hall. *Are you so sure about that?*

7

TAJA

TAJA'S HEAD SPUN with the sensation of falling, despite the solid press of a cold floor beneath him. He scrunched his eyes shut until stars danced across the blackness, then blinked them open and stared up at a plain white ceiling. The surrounding walls were light green, and cobwebs clouded the corners. Wherever he'd ended up, it was no place familiar to him.

He searched his memory, but trying to catch a thought was like trying to see through the dense dawn fog that hugged Båthälla on summer mornings. The last thing he clearly remembered was speaking to Nokaldir, Nedra, and Ellory in the temple. Then... Jekku. Yes, he'd walked out of the temple with Jekku. They were in the woods, heading out of the village, but then... what? What had brought him here, to this dusty room? And where was Jekku?

Taja blinked again and sat up. It took a second for the room to come into focus, but when it did, the air rushed out of his lungs. Oh, he recognized it now. His heart pounded. What was he doing *here*? How? Who had brought him here?

His parents had made it abundantly clear, seven years ago, that they never wanted him beneath their roof again. Yet this was unmistakably his childhood bedroom. Not a single thing had been moved, which Taja found both comforting and eerie. It was as though he'd died, and his parents had left his room untouched out of respect. For seven years, this room had collected dust when it could've been rearranged into something else. A study, maybe, a personal office for his father. Or a library for his mother's dozens of books that Taja knew she never read.

Instead they'd left it like this. Were they too ashamed to touch this space? Or had they left it as an homage to a son they considered dead to them?

This was Taja's room, but standing here now, he felt like he was looking at a stranger's living space. It was astonishing how quickly he'd stopping thinking of this room and this house as *home*. And it was similarly astonishing that the people who had raised him had so easily become strangers even as they all lived in the same town. Taja couldn't wrap his head around it. How could you look at your child and pretend you didn't know them? Didn't his parents have an *ounce* of compassion in their hearts?

He'd thought they were good, forgiving, sympathetic people. Where had he learned that from, if not from them?

During his exile, Taja had kept to himself on the edge of the village. He'd kept his head down and told himself to be grateful that he was allowed to stay near Båthälla at all. He made sure to only go into town at quiet times when there wouldn't be as many people around. He was barred from the temple unless specifically invited — which he wasn't, until Ebris had called him there almost two months ago to show him the prophecy. He rarely

vent into shops, hadn't seen the morning market at all in seven
ears. He avoided everyone — his neighbors, his former friends,
his extended family, and *especially* his parents. On the rare occa-
ions he did run into people he used to know, they strode past
him like he wasn't there. He had become a ghost in this town,
and to his parents, he had ceased to exist.

It had stopped hurting after the first year. But now Taja real-
zed that the ache hadn't healed, he'd simply learned to ignore it.

He guessed that all that unconditional love that was supposed to hold families together didn't actually exist. At least, not
n his family.

It didn't have to be like this.

Taja startled at the voice and turned, but he was still alone.
"Who are you?"

*Not important. Well, I am very important, but you don't need to
know who I am. Only that your life could be different, Vaeltaja Ievisin,
and I can make it so. You just have to trust me. I have a few things I
wish to show you.*

Taja shook his head. "No, I don't think so. My life is..."

*Just fine as it is? Come, now, we both know that's not true. Your life
never has been what you want, has it?*

The room spun. Hazy ghosts appeared around Taja; he saw
himself at various ages, his parents, his friends, even Ellory. His
life sped by in a matter of seconds, and Taja recalled each moment in vivid detail. There was every time his father compared
him to Ellory. There was his first partner, a boy Taja had had
to see in secret because his father hated the boy's family. He
saw Kierra —— the day he'd first found her in the woods outside
Bâthälla, the day he'd gone to her hometown, the day Ebris had

found out what he'd been doing. And he saw the worst day of Taja's life, when the gods and the Council Eternal — including his father — had called for his death and Ebris had shown him mercy.

Taja winced and shut his eyes so he didn't have to watch himself have his magic taken. What was the point of this? Taja knew his own life. He knew his regrets. He still wouldn't change a thing.

Oh, are you so sure about that? You try to sound so confident in yourself, Vaeltaja, but I can feel the uneasy beat of your pulse. I can hear the tremble in your voice. You're never sure of anything.

Taja whirled around, again searching in vain for the source of the voice. It seemed to come from the walls themselves. "I am sure of one thing: my life might not be ideal, but it can be better. I will make it better. And that's not going to happen as long as Båthälla stays as it is now."

Ah, so now the truth comes out. All of this Sawwia Setukkda business is just a ruse, then, to place yourself back in your people's favor?

"No," Taja said. "All of Båthälla deserves to be better. But don't I deserve to feel at home in my own hometown?"

You could have felt as much without all of this. Things could have been so different. They still could be. Look.

Again, visions of the past flooded the room. But this time they were altered. Instead of defying his father to be with the boy he liked, he agreed to stop seeing him when his father said so. Instead of offering Kierra food when she clearly needed it, he walked away from her and never saw her again. Instead of being exiled and stripped of his magic, he grew up in his father's footsteps and became an Apprentice Councilor and eventually

earned himself a seat on the Council Eternal –– right beside Ellory Ives, who, according to these visions, was his closest friend.

His parents were proud of him. The gods were proud of him.
His magic was strong, and he practically held Båthälla in the
palms of his hands. Across every glimpse of this alternate timeline, three things were consistent:

He was the person his parents wanted him to be.

He was a powerful mage.

And he was miserable.

He smiled, sure, and he laughed with his friends, but Taja
knew himself and he saw through it. There was hardly any joy in
his eyes, and in the brief moments when no one sought his attention, those fake smiles instantly vanished from his face. He
looked so *tired*. He was only an illusion, thank the gods, but still
Taja's heart broke for him. This was who everyone wanted him to
be, but it wasn't who *Taja* wanted to be.

Taja turned his back on the visions. "Do you really think this
is what I want? Also, you've forgotten something: the Prophecy
of the Second Savior."

*Had your life followed the correct path, you would have no need for
a fool's errand from Lord Ebris. He would not have had to resort to a
myth to grant you forgiveness you did not deserve.*

"The Prophecy would have come to pass regardless of whether
I knew about it," Taja argued. "Jekku and Lilya would have gone
after the Oracle Stone whether I did or not."

And they would have failed without your help.

Taja blinked. His first instinct was to refute that; two people
as stubborn as Jekku and Lilya would not give up that easily. But
then Taja remembered that two pieces of the stone — the ring

and the dagger — had been hidden here in Båthälla, under Ebris's protection. Without Taja, Jekku and Lilya would not have been able to enter Båthälla. They wouldn't know it existed. So if Taja hadn't helped Kierra, hadn't been exiled, and Ebris hadn't needed him as a pawn, the Oracle Stone would never have been put together and the Royal Sorcerers would have stayed in their prison.

"But..." Taja couldn't wrap his head around this. Was he meant to believe that the near disaster of All Death was *his* fault? But no, Ebris was the one who wanted to cause chaos so he could play the hero. Ebris had made the choice to use Taja to bring the Oracle Stone to Båthälla.

Oh, gods, had Ebris planned the whole thing from the start?

Ah, so you are cleverer than you look. It might all sound like a raving conspiracy, but you are onto something, Vaeltaja. You see, Lord Ebris never forgot about the Oracle Stone. He was not content to let it stay buried with the Peacebringer. It had saved Elshalans once, and he believed it could save us again. When you stood trial before the gods, Lord Ebris saw an opportunity. He saved your life because he knew you'd come in handy someday, when Båthälla was so desperate for a breath of magic that they'd put blind faith in the idea of a savior. And if you died before finding the stone... well, Båthälla would suffer no loss.

Taja's heart pounded. "No. No, that-- That can't be true. You're lying. If I died, Båthälla's magic would never be saved. Ebris wouldn't have-- wouldn't have sent me to die." But even as he said it, he wasn't sure. *Or would he?*

Don't you understand? murmured the god. *The Prophecy of the Second Savior is a myth. Sawwia Setukkda is not real. You are no savior. You are nothing.*

"No." Taja shook his head. He had to get this god out of his mind before they struck any more doubts. "That's not true. I'm in the prophecy. Parts of it have happened, and it's coming together. If it's not real, it means none of this has meant anything, and I refuse to believe that. Even though Ebris lied to me, even if he used me for his own plot from the very beginning, following that prophecy got me out of Båthälla. It brought me to Jekku and Lilya and Saevel, and it led me to uncover the truth about Ebris. We are safer because I followed that prophecy, and I wouldn't give back a minute of it."

Wouldn't you? Not even for this preferable life?

"It's not preferable!" Taja barked a laugh. "You saw those visions. You *made* those visions. I am clearly unhappy."

Who was this invisible god, anyway? The voice was definitely masculine, so not Nedra, and it couldn't be Ebris — it *couldn't* be Ebris — so that left Nokaldir and Oridite. And Nokaldir had never cared enough about Båthälla to involve himself like this, so that left only the God of Darkness.

But why? What did he want? Did Oridite need Taja and Jekku out of the way so *he* could seize Båthälla, or was he meddling for the sheer fun of it?

All right, so maybe I was wrong. Maybe you don't wish to take your place here like I assumed you did. How about this, then? Assume your life is what it is now. Don't you want all of this to be over? Aren't you tired of fighting?

He was. He'd never wanted this to be a fight, and he never pictured himself at the helm of it. In his mind, *Sawwia Setukkda* was still a separate entity from Taja Ievisin; the Second Savior was someone with more confidence, courage, and allies than Taja currently had. He was a hero like Vaeltaja in the myth, someone who never backed down despite the odds.

Taja *wanted* to be that person. But he didn't know how to get there. And he was so tired of feeling like he was drowning.

Thought so, said the god. *But look, it won't always be like this. It doesn't have to be hard.*

Didn't it? Taja had known, as soon as he had made Båthäll his responsibility, that it wouldn't be easy. It *was* a fight, whether he liked it or not.

But... maybe the gods could still be allies. Maybe their power and influence was what Taja needed. Maybe it wouldn't be easy, but perhaps it didn't have to be impossible.

Across the room, the door opened on its own. Foggy white light obscured whatever was beyond.

Come and see, said the god.

Hesitantly, Taja stepped through the door.

When the fog cleared, he found himself in a meadow. Fresh green grass sprawled under his feet and bright blooms of wild flowers swayed in the breeze. Warm summer sun beamed down on him, and in the distance, he glimpsed rooftops and chimneys. Beyond them, stretching toward the horizon, the sea shone brilliant and blue beneath a cerulean sky.

Taja frowned. He didn't recognize this place, but it certainly wasn't anywhere near Båthälla. That much he sensed to be true.

"What is this?" he asked Oridite. "Where have you brought me?"

Somewhere that will be familiar to you in time. Does it mean anything to you now?

"No." Taja looked around, searching for something to clue

him into this location. But he'd only been close to the sea a couple of times, and none of those places looked like this. None of them had been so... tranquil.

Wherever this place was, life was peaceful here.

He looked up at the sky, as if Oridite would be hovering up there in midair. "This is... in my future? How? Does this mean we win, and I... I leave Båthälla?"

That is not for me to say. But you like it here, yes?

Taja nodded.

You could stay.

"What?" Taja took a step back. "Now? But..."

You could return to Båthälla whenever you please, Oridite said, *but if you wish to stay in this place, where you will be happy, at peace, and free of the complicated mess that is your life in your hometown... all you need to do is ask.*

"I——" Taja shut his mouth. No. No, it couldn't be this easy. It couldn't be *over*, and he wouldn't just run away. Oridite was trying to lure him away from Båthälla, from his mission to help the village, and Taja wouldn't fall for it.

"No." He backed away across the meadow. "If this is my future, it will meet me when it's meant to. Right now, Båthälla is my priority. You can't scare me away from that."

A rumble of laughter rolled across the sky, and then a solitary door appeared in front of Taja. *We shall see about that.*

8

JEKKU

THROUGH THE DOOR, Jekku found a garden. Unlike the current landscape of Doweth, this place was warm, sunny, in the brightest throes of summer. Wildflowers surrounded him in full bloom, their sharp scents tickling his nose. Puffy white clouds hung overhead, bright against the vivid blue sky.

Jekku looked behind him, but whatever door he'd stepped through had disappeared. So far, Oridite hadn't said a word, and Jekku couldn't sense his presence. Had he actually found a way out of that place with its visions and illusions?

He made his way a few steps forward. The garden in which he stood sloped up the side of a hill; Jekku followed it to the crest, and looked out onto a quaint village nestled at the edge of the sea.

Warm wind whipped at Jekku's hair and clothes, carrying the ocean's salty brine. Jekku had been a lot of places, but he was positive he had not been here before. It wasn't a memory, then, and he couldn't think of a reason Oridite would drop him here and disappear. Unless it was a place far, far away from Båthälla, and Oridite placed him here to get him out of the way.

But if Oridite wanted to trap him, wouldn't it be somewhere unpleasant? This place was... nice. Calm. It struck familiarity in Jekku even though he *knew* he'd never been here.

I thought it might.

"Oh, there you are," Jekku deadpanned. "And here I was thinking you'd left me."

What do you think of this place, Jekku Aj'ere?

What wasn't to like? The hush of wind through the trees surrounding the town and the gentle trill of birdsong immediately put Jekku at ease, and compared to the previous visions Oridite had shown him, this was like paradise. But he couldn't *say* that.

You like it, don't you? Of course you do. This place is significant to you — just not yet. I can't tell you when you will find your way here, but if you like... you can stay here now. Perhaps you'll even find a reason to stay, if you look hard enough.

Jekku turned his head, momentarily forgetting that he couldn't actually see Oridite. "What do you mean? Have you trapped Taja here too?"

A low, grumbling laugh surrounded Jekku. *So that's what it takes? I didn't even say his name.*

"You didn't have to," Jekku murmured. It wouldn't surprise him if the gods somehow used him and Taja against each other. "If I'm going to enjoy a place like this, it can't be without him. He deserves this peace, too. I won't leave him before our fight is over."

Oridite laughed again. *Your fight? Outsider, you are barely Elshalan. What makes you think you have any place here?*

Jekku turned away from the town and started back down the hill, toward the trees bordering the garden where he'd arrived. "Yeah, I know, I don't really belong. People keep saying that, and I already know it's true, so don't rub salt in the wound. I'm not trying to save Båthälla on my own, but I want to help. For Taja."

What if he doesn't want your help? What if he doesn't want you here at all?

Jekku halted. Taja's words from earlier echoed in his mind. *You're not one of us. You don't belong here. You don't belong you don't belong you don't belong.*

He shook the memory out of his head. No. No, that wasn't true. Taja had already apologized, already said he didn't mean it.

But...he wouldn't have said it at all if the thought wasn't somewhere at the back of his mind. Part of Taja, even if it was just a small part, *did* believe that Jekku had no place in Båthälla and therefore no place with him.

"You're wrong," Jekku said to Oridite. He moved closer to the trees, but still no door appeared to bring him away from here. "He–– He does want me here. He said–– He invited me, he promised me, he said he'd–– he'd wait. He said he'd wait."

Jekku stumbled into one of the trees and caught himself breathing hard. He tried to catch his breath, tried to throw the fears and doubts out of his mind, but they'd taken hold and now refused to let go.

What the hell did promises mean anymore? The logical side of Jekku's brain insisted that he knew Taja, knew that Taja would never promise him anything if he didn't intend to keep it. Taja *wouldn't* do what Leo had done, but Jekku had thought that of

Leo too. He'd thought he knew Leo. He was probably a fool for thinking he knew Taja, too.

Well. I didn't expect you to get to that conclusion all on your own. I'm a little impressed. How about we put that blazing confidence to the test?

A door appeared in front of Jekku. At this point, he didn't care what lay ahead. He just wanted this to be over.

He wrenched open the door.

***

Jekku considered himself a fairly patient person. He could handle a lot before he became genuinely frustrated, and even more before that turned to anger. He didn't remember the last time he was actually furious — but it was probably at Gallien's Peak, and probably aimed at Firune.

Until now. Now, the anger crackling under his skin was about to cause a furious storm over Båthälla, and Jekku hoped those damned gods would get struck by lightning.

His jaw ached from clenching his teeth so hard. His skin crawled with anxiety and the knot in his stomach only clenched tighter with every door he opened and every corridor he crossed. Oridite must have gotten sick of taunting Jekku with the past and future; now he was lost in a maze and walking in circles. If the purpose of this was to piss him off, Oridite was doing a grand job of it.

Jekku reached another plain door at the end of another empty hallway and wrenched it open, expecting either another door or a room of them. But to his mild surprise, he found neither. He stood in a fully furnished parlor, complete with a crystal chandelier hanging from the center of the high ceiling. Its candles flickered with golden mage's fire.

Jekku eyed the space skeptically. It looked like a room plucked out of a palace — thick gold curtains over the tall windows, a porcelain tea set on the low table in front of a dusty loveseat, gilded furniture that had seen better days. Actually, as Jekku studied the room, he realized the whole space was in a state of disrepair, as if no one had occupied or cared for this room in a long time.

So what was he supposed to do with this? He moved a few steps further in, and at the same moment he noticed a faded cloak draped over the back of a chair, he also realized he was not alone in the room.

Someone sat on the floor in front of the loveseat, knees drawn up to their chest and head leaned forward, face buried in their arms. For a second, Jekku questioned whether they were alive. He stepped forward and his foot leaned into a creaky floorboard, and the stranger darted their head up.

Jekku didn't know what to do. He froze like a startled deer and stared at the stranger as blankly as the stranger stared back at him. Jekku saw now that he was an Elshalan man, probably in his mid-forties. His graying black hair was tied in a neat braid that ran all the way down his back, and his pointed ears glittered with gold rings. A tiny ruby glinted on his right eyebrow.

He looked just about as stunned as Jekku was, but he managed to get the words out first. "W-Who are you?"

"Uh..." Before Jekku could say anything, the Elshalan man climbed to his feet — a little stiffly — and shuffled toward him.

"Or rather, I should say... *How* did you get here?" Worry creased his brow. Something about his dark eyes, straight nose, and high cheekbones looked familiar to Jekku, but the flicker of recognition fled as soon as it arrived.

And then it hit Jekku that this Elshalan man was not speaking Elshalan. He was speaking Dowethian. Jekku's confusion doubled. "I— I don't know. I've been running in circles for hours." Or at least, it felt like hours. Could've been less. Could've been more. Jekku had no idea. "This is the first I've run into a real, actual person that's not an illusion."

The man's frown deepened. "An illusion?"

Jekku waved a hand. "Long story. The gods are messing with me. Well, one god in particular."

The man studied him. His expression softened a little. "The gods trapped you here, too?"

He sincerely hoped not. "No, I think I'm being tested. It's, uh, long story. But— But *you*! I mean, you're just *here*? How long have you been here?"

"I..." He sighed and rubbed his jaw. "I'm really not sure." He shifted on his feet, and Jekku caught a glimpse of gold in his brown eyes. *Weird*, he thought, *his eyes look like mine.*

Something clicked in his head and stole the air from his lungs.

Wait.

No, no, it couldn't be. It *couldn't* be.

But... The same black hair. The same narrow features, right down to the straight nose and thin brows. And brown eyes with gold around the pupils.

You have his name and his eyes, Marian had told him when he'd asked after his father. It was the only answer she'd ever give.

Jekku's heart pounded so hard he could barely get the words out. "W-What's your name?"

The man blinked, as if he hadn't expected the question. "Ah. Sorry." He chuckled. "No one's asked me that in a very long time. My name is Jakob Balmoor. And what is yours?"

Jekku barely heard the question. Holy *gods*. His shock must have shown clear as day on his face, because the Elshalan — Jakob, Jekku's godsdamned *father* — frowned once again and reached a hand toward Jekku. "Is something wrong? You've gone rather pale. Do you want to sit down?"

For lack of a better response, Jekku laughed. *Is something wrong?* Well, yeah, a lot of things were wrong, namely the current fact that Jekku was standing before a man who had, for the past twenty-two years, been no more than a name and a shadow in his past. A man who did not exist in Jekku's life. Surely he lived in Marian's memory, but to Jekku? He was a ghost.

And who was Jekku to him? Did Jakob even know he had a child?

Seconds ticked by. Jekku had to say something. But what the hell do you say to your father who doesn't know you exist?

Briefly, it occurred to Jekku that he could lie. His name wasn't Jakob anymore. He could introduce himself as Jekku, leave out his family name, and pretend he wasn't looking at an older, more masculine clone of himself.

But how could Jakob not see it? This had to be equally shocking for him. Gods above, Marian had told Jekku that he had his father's eyes, not his entire *face*. No wonder people back home thought Jekku was the adopted one; he didn't look a thing like his mother.

"Are— Are you sure you're all right?" Jakob asked. He set a hand on Jekku's shoulder and brought him a few steps farther into the room, then gestured at the chair adjacent to the loveseat. "Why don't you sit for a minute? I'm sure the gods have put you through a hell of an ordeal. Settle in and we can talk. Though I didn't catch your name..."

Jekku sank into the chair and felt a tug in his chest when he looked at Jakob again. This man had known him for five minutes and was already looking after him. He didn't even know who Jekku was, yet the concern in his eyes was genuine.

He would have been such a good father.

The raw shock bled out of Jekku, and all of a sudden he could breathe again. He met his father's eyes, and it struck him that a month ago, he wouldn't have dared lest he see Jakob's history unfurl in his mind. The irony was not lost on Jekku; he had promised not to see his family again until his curse was gone, yet now that it was, the first family he faced was someone he didn't know he still had. It was a little unfair that he should look his father in the eye before he had the chance to see his mother and sisters again, but it was also Jekku's own fault for following Taja to Båthälla instead of immediately heading to Ajaphere.

That, however, was a matter for later.

Jekku took a deep breath. "My name is Jekku Aj'ere." He watched Jakob's eyes widen. "And I think you're my father."

INTERLUDE I

ELLORY

ELLORY IVES WAS IN THE MIDDLE of an argument with their best friend when the god Oridite spoke in their mind.

I have news. Come to the Palace.

Ellory cut off mid-sentence as a throb of pain shot through their head. Ava, the friend with whom they'd been fighting seconds before, immediately rushed forward and set her hands firmly on their shoulders to steady them. For a second, their argument was forgotten.

Ellory squeezed their eyes shut as stars danced in their vision. *Really? Now? Is it urgent?* And did Oridite really need to inform them via headache?

Yes. You'll want to know this.

Oridite apparently was not going to take no for an answer. His presence lifted, and Ellory sighed in relief as the pressure eased from their skull. They stood up straight and removed Ava's hands from their shoulders. "I'm fine. But I have to go. And I'd better not hear that blasphemy from you ever again."

Fire burned in Ava's brown eyes. "Excuse me?"

"You heard me." Ellory turned on their heel and headed fo the door.

"You don't get to talk to me like that, Ellory! You're not m godsdamned parent. You don't get to tell me what to believe."

They spun back to her. "And you don't get to call yourself a Elshalan of Båthälla when you speak of betraying the gods."

Her glare was murderous. "Contrary to your beliefs, Ellory you are not the leader of this city. It is not up to you to decid what makes someone an Elshalan of Båthälla."

They clenched their jaw. "I might not lead Båthälla yet, bu I will. And then it *will* be up to me. And when that happens you'd better have changed your mind." They stormed out of thei study room — *their* study room, into which Ava had come t poke holes in everything Ellory was working toward — and lef before she had a chance to respond.

This had better be good.

Ellory strode down the long hallway running the length o the upper floor of the temple, then followed the spiral stair down to the first floor. A handful of people occupied the mai room of the temple when Ellory passed through, but none o them looked up. They drew out the key that hung around thei neck and went through a concealed side door into a room mean only for the gods.

Ellory had special access, of course. Not only for being Keepe of the Temple, and not only for being Ebris's son, but becaus these days it seemed like they were the only one in this damne town still loyal to the gods. That came with its privileges.

Ellory locked the door behind themself and crossed th empty stone room to the single object that occupied it: a six-foot mirror on the wall that showed no reflection. Ellory stopped before the foggy glass and set their palm on the surface. The fog rippled, and Ellory stepped through and entered the grand sitting room in the gods' Sky Palace.

Ellory had been here a few times now, but the luxurious room never failed to steal their breath. Bathed in warm light and accented with gold, the sitting room glistened with wealth and comfort. Ellory had always appreciated that; instead of a room out of a museum, it felt lived in, like the gods actually lounged here. A blanket was bunched up on the sofa. A used, empty glass sat on a side table by the bookshelf. The leafy palms and blooming flowers had recently been watered. It was humbling to see that the gods, too, had menial tasks to occupy their days.

Oridite was waiting for Ellory. He lounged on a black velvet chaise at the center of the room, swirling a glass of red wine in his hand. He regarded Ellory with indifference. They received nothing more than a slight nod in greeting.

They stood before him on the soft, intricately woven carpet and crossed their arms. Their palms burned with their restless magic; it had been jumpy lately, probably because of the turmoil in Båthälla. Probably because they were on edge all the time, paranoid that the traitor would soon do something truly unforgivable.

Not that Ellory truly worried that Taja Ievisin would successfully turn their people against the gods. He wouldn't dare. And he didn't have a scrap of the strength Ellory had. If Taja tried anything, Ellory would squash him and his blasphemy like a bug.

While Ellory was buried in their thoughts, Oridite watched them evenly. He sipped his wine, but still said nothing. Finally,

Ellory grew irritated and cleared their throat. "Lord Oridite, you summoned me, did you not?"

He took another sip of wine and arched a sharp black eyebrow. "My apologies, Ellory, do you have somewhere else you need to be?"

They narrowed their eyes. There were a bunch of places they could be at the moment. Their argument with Ava rang at the back of their mind; they'd have to settle that later, get Ava to see reason. They needed her on their side — not just because she was their best friend, but because she thought outside the box. She'd build Ellory a flawless plan to stand against Taja and anything he might start. And she was persuasive. She could turn others to Ellory's side — to Båthälla's side — and Ellory didn't want to think about her persuasive skills being used *against* them.

"You're so tense, Ellory," Oridite drawled in his deep voice. "Why don't you sit down? Let's talk. Catch me up on what you've been doing scurrying around Båthälla. Have some wine. You look like you need it." He sat forward and set his glass down, then poured another and held it up to Ellory.

They clenched their teeth. The last thing they needed was to sit and have a chat over wine with the God of Darkness. But refusing would be rude, and Ellory didn't wish to stoke Oridite's ire in any capacity.

"Very well." They took a seat in the armchair beside the chaise where Oridite lounged. He placed the glass of wine in their hand and settled back on the soft velvet.

Ellory sipped the wine and found it deliciously bitter. Not the sweet stuff the gods brought out for parties, then. Something from Oridite's personal collection. They took another sip. "What did you wish to talk to me about, Lord Oridite?"

"Did I inform you that the traitor and the false savior have been secured here in the Sky Palace?" Oridite spoke to his wine rather than to Ellory.

Here? He put them *here*? That wasn't what Ellory thought Oridite meant when he said he had a solution in mind. No wonder there hadn't been a peep from either of them in almost two days.

"No," Ellory said. "You only said to trust you."

"Hm." Oridite swirled his wine. "Well, they are here. They're in the Labyrinth. And for a while, I thought I had them trapped. But then the false savior did something... unexpected."

Ellory set down their wine. "That ridiculous fool is the most predictable person I've ever seen. What did he do that slipped your expectations?"

Oridite finally looked up, black eyes glinting in the golden light. "He found another prisoner. One who has been there for over two decades and has, until now, sat quietly in his prison. But the false savior has him rattling the bars again, so to speak, and I fear they will be each other's key out of the Labyrinth."

"What of the traitor?" Ellory questioned.

"So far, he and the false savior have not found each other. But now that the false savior has an ally... I expect finding the traitor will become his first priority. It won't be long." Oridite scowled at his wine glass. "The Labyrinth is infinitely changing. I never could have predicted that the false savior would stumble upon that old traitor."

Another traitor? Was no one in Båthälla grateful? Gods above. But Ellory didn't care who or what Taja and the false savior found in the Labyrinth as long as they didn't get out. "I'm not worried about it. The Labyrinth can't simply be broken out of Even if they find each other, they'll never free themselves."

"I plan to tempt them with a test," Oridite said. "I'll tell them that if they pass it successfully, I'll let them out." A dark sort of amusement shone in his obsidian eyes. "I'll even use the truth room to make it exceptionally convincing."

"Showing them a chance of freedom and then snatching it away..." Ellory lifted their wine and took another sip. "Master of the Labyrinth indeed, Lord Oridite."

A smile curled across his face. "I am just doing my job."

Ellory finished their wine and set the glass down. An idea took root in their mind. "You said you suspect the false savior and this other prisoner will ally with each other? I wonder..."

Oridite raised an eyebrow. "Yes?"

"I wonder if you should let them. Let them all come back together for this final test. Let them think they can win." Ellory met Oridite's eyes. "Then break them all apart and slam the door."

9

JEKKU

TIME PASSED DIFFERENTLY in the Labyrinth. If Jekku thought back to the last time he'd seen Taja, it seemed like ages. It might've been days or months or years and he wouldn't know the difference. But sitting here with Jakob, time stretched out into wondrously long hours. The painfully awkward introduction had passed, and Jekku and his father simply talked.

It was still bizarre. Jakob was basically a stranger, but now, he didn't feel like one. Irrational as it was, Jekku felt as though he'd known Jakob forever, and they'd merely been apart a couple of years rather than a whole lifetime.

Jakob laughed a little to himself, then turned to Jekku and wrapped an arm around him. "You're sitting right here, and still I can't really believe it. A child. A son. *My* son. I never knew. Your mother... I had to leave so suddenly." His smile faded. "I thought I would come back. I knew Ebris had sent people looking for me, even as far as Ajaphere. I caught glimpses of them around town, and I thought leaving for a while — just to get them off my trail — would make them give up and go back to Båthälla. But I was wrong. It was a trap. As soon as I stepped foot out of Ajaphere they ambushed me."

Jekku didn't know what to say. He stayed quiet and let Jakob go on. He hated for Jakob to relive this, but at the same time, Jekku wanted to know the whole story.

"They dragged me back to Båthälla like a prisoner, using astruylium to disable my magic. I stood trial before Ebris, Oridite, and the Council Eternal. Nokaldir was nowhere to be seen, of course, and Nedra refused to participate — and I'm still grateful to her. Not that it helped, though, because all of them unanimously decided that I should be exiled. I'd defied the gods, broken one of our most critical laws. I almost expected my sentence to be execution. At the word, exile, though, my spirits lifted. I thought, 'Perfect, send me away and I'll run straight back to Ajaphere and be with Marian.' But of course, the gods knew that was precisely my intention. Instead of casting me out of Båthälla, they imprisoned me here in the Sky Palace and made sure not one hall is the same from day to day."

Jekku's heart ached. The story was worse than anything he'd guessed. How long had Marian waited for Jakob to come back before she decided that he wasn't? Did she still glance out the front windows and hope to see him coming up the path?

Jakob turned to Jekku again. "How old are you?"

He flickered a sad smile. "Twenty-two."

"Twenty-two." Jakob rubbed his eyes, and only then did Jekku realize how weary he looked. Deep lines creased his face, aging him far beyond his years. Jekku noticed a slight tremble in his hands when he moved to clasp them together, and then his heart plummeted.

Jakob had the same Z-shaped scars on the backs of his hands that Taja did. The gods had taken his magic.

All at once, Jekku's anger returned. He bolted up from the sofa and stormed across the room, then wrenched the door open and turned back to his father. "Come with me. We're getting the hell out of here."

Jakob grimaced. "Jekku, I can't. Believe me, I've tried. There's no way out until the gods want you to leave, and for me... this sentence is permanent."

"No." Jekku had had enough of these damned gods ruining the lives of people he cared about. "Not if I have anything to say about it. Look, I didn't tell you the whole story before because it's a lot to explain, but you should know this: Lord Ebris is gone. He does not rule over this city anymore."

Jakob's eyes widened. He stood up. "Ebris is... But how? Is he...?"

"All you need to know is that he's Fallen, and he's gone."

"Then who is leading Bâthälla, if not Ebris?" He eyed Jekku skeptically.

"At the moment? No one. Long story. But listen, Jakob, Bâthälla is going to change. *Sawwia Setukkda* has arrived, and Nedra and Nokaldir both want life in Bâthälla to be different now that Ebris is out of the picture. It's not the town you remember."

That was about seventy-five percent lies, but the actual truth — that Jekku didn't know what the hell was going to happen to Bâthälla — was not about to convince Jakob to follow him.

Jakob moved a few steps toward Jekku. A hesitant sort of awe lit up his eyes. "*Sawwia Setukkda*? Is it true?"

"It's true. I'll explain everything later. Hell, I'll introduce you to him." Assuming he could even find Taja in this place. "What do you know about the Sky Palace? How close have you gotten to getting out?" He glanced down at Jakob's bare feet. "And do you need some shoes?"

Jakob looked down and sighed. "Jekku, listen, it's not that simple. I have been here for more than twenty years. You don't think I've tried to search for a way out? Just because Ebris is gone does not mean his hold on the Sky Palace — or Båthälla — has loosened. This is Oridite's labyrinth, anyway, and as long as he resides in Båthälla, his word is law here."

Jekku wasn't deterred. He was far past the point of caring what the gods said. "Then let's break some laws. Are you coming or not?"

In that moment, Jekku felt a flicker of doubt. What if his father stubbornly remained? He'd thought — assumed, hoped — that Jakob would have more determination than this. But at the same time, Jekku understood the agony of being confined to the same space year after year. He remembered how much it'd worn on him, convinced him that the dream of freedom was hopeless and it was easier to just give up.

But even four years in the dark had not made Jekku give up entirely. He would've loved someone to come bursting into his prison and literally hold the door open for him. But he'd had to get himself out, he'd had to risk the horrors — physical and psychological — in the belly of Gallien's Peak to fight his way to freedom. Jakob had spent two decades doing the same thing; he didn't need to fight anymore.

"Jakob." Jekku opened the door wider. "Please."

Please, because now that you're in my life, I don't want to leave you behind.

Please, because I've spent twenty-two years asking questions about you and getting no answers, and I want to know you.

Please, because I want to know what it's like to have a father. And I want you to know the son you never got to meet.

Jakob's shoulders slumped. He dragged a hand through his graying hair, then looked at Jekku and nodded once. "All right. One more try. And only because I don't like the thought of you running around out there alone."

Jekku grinned. "We're going to make it out. Trust me."

Jakob paused beside him and set a hand on his shoulder. "I do. You look like you're ready to fight the gods, and Jekku, I need nothing else to prove that you're my son." He smiled. "And Marian's, too."

Jekku beamed and pretended he didn't feel the sting of tears in his eyes. But then Jakob brought him into a hug, and he closed his eyes and let them fall.

Jakob let go and squeezed his shoulder again, then let Jekku lead the way out of the room.

The corridor was different now. Instead of a dark, empty hallway, this one looked like something out of a palace: bright white paneled walls framed a marble floor that echoed their steps, and brass candelabras cast deep orange light all the way down until the corridor obscured into darkness.

Jekku glanced at his father. "So... have you seen this before?"

Jakob shook his head. "No. But we should move quickly. Don't open any doors. Try to keep your eyes straight ahead." Jakob stepped ahead and took the lead. "Remember, everything in here wants to distract, trick, or break you. Don't give them the chance."

How many horrors had Jakob endured in this place? How many escape attempts had ended with Jakob sinking under some horrible twisted memory or reflection of his deepest fears? No wonder he'd given up on finding a way out. Jekku hated to put him through this again, but he *had* to believe there was a way out. This couldn't be the end.

He would find the exit. He would find Taja. And they would fix this mess in Båthälla.

***

The hallway stretched on impossibly far. All Jekku could see in either direction was the flickering candlelight reflected on the polished floor. It was absolutely silent but for his and Jakob's footsteps, and somehow that was the most unsettling thing they had yet to encounter. Nothing jumped out from behind the doors lining either side of the hall, nothing stood in their path, nothing followed behind. No disembodied voices poked doubts in Jekku's mind.

He might have preferred that to this dense silence that felt like the Labyrinth holding its breath.

It would have helped if Jakob would actually talk to him, but when Jekku had tried to raise a conversation, Jakob had shushed him. Apparently talking would only encourage attention from whatever lurked in this place, and that was enough to keep Jekku's mouth shut.

But walking in silence next to a man he wanted to know

when there was nothing else to do but chase fear out of his thoughts was easier said than done. Jekku turned his head to look at Jakob, but before he could say anything, he walked directly into a solid barrier.

"What the hell?" He stepped back, rubbing a sore spot on his head, but there was nothing in front of him. Just the hallway, carrying on into infinity. Jekku reached out his hand, and despite all appearances suggesting otherwise, he touched what was certainly a physical wall.

An *invisible* physical wall.

Tentatively, Jakob laid his hand on it as well and felt around. His hand closed around something round, like a doorknob. He frowned and glanced at Jekku, who raised his eyebrows.

"There's nowhere else to go," he pointed out. "So I guess through this invisible door is the only way forward?"

Jakob grimaced. "I don't like this." But he turned his hand and pushed in, and a dark doorway opened in midair. Jakob stepped forward, and Jekku followed close behind.

Their first steps in were into complete darkness, but as Jekku's eyes adjusted, he made out the shapes of a furnished room similar to the one in which he'd found his father. For a second he feared the gods had led them in a big circle right back to where they'd started, but Jakob didn't seem to recognize the space.

"There's someone else here." Jakob stepped around Jekku and stood in front of him. "Show yourself. Who's there?"

Jekku's heart pounded out the seconds. Footsteps shuffled into the room from the opposite corner that was too dark to see, and Jekku braced himself to see Oridite, or even Ellory.

He did not expect to see Taja.

His breath caught. His first instinct was to go to him, but he stopped himself. What if this, too, was another illusion?

But then Taja's eyes widened. "Jekku?" He rushed to him, then stopped short. "Wait. Is it really you?"

"It's me." Jekku hoped that sounded sincere. "Are *you* really you?"

Taja gathered Jekku in a hug. "It's me."

Jekku closed his eyes and let the stress lift off his shoulder for a second. Part of him remained apprehensive that this wasn' actually Taja, but he felt right and sounded right and there wa no odd detail that betrayed this as an illusion. He held Taja a lit tle tighter, but as the seconds ticked by and neither of them le go, his focus shifted from Taja's arms around him to the fact tha his father was standing right behind him.

Jakob pointedly cleared his throat.

Taja jumped back and stared at Jakob, clearly noticing him for the first time. He stammered something in Elshalan and nod ded in greeting to Jakob, then switched back to Dowethian. "I'n so sorry. I didn't mean to be rude. My name is Taja Ievisin. Um... it seems you've met my— Er, it seems you've met Jekku?"

Leave it to Taja to complicate whatever Jakob was alread thinking of that too-long hug. Jekku flicked a glance at hi father, who looked too amused for Jekku's liking. Jekku's face flooded with heat, but Taja's curious expression reminded him that he had yet to explain who this was.

"Taja, um, this is—"

"Jakob Balmoor," his father cut in. His expression softened to a gentle smile. "Happy to meet you."

So he just... wasn't going to mention the other thing? Jekku glanced at him, then back to Taja, and said, "He's also my father."

Taja's eyes went wide again. "He *what*? But I thought— But why— How are you *here*?" Horror crept across Taja's face. "You've been here all this time?"

Jakob nodded. "For almost twenty-three years."

Taja's gaze wandered back to Jekku. "So you never..."

"No," Jekku said quietly.

"I'd say it's something like a miracle that we ever found each other, given the circumstances, but I don't wish to thank the gods in this place. It's because of them that all of us are here, so forgive me that I can't muster up a scrap of gratitude."

Jekku didn't blame him. He was relieved that Jakob was leaning into his resentment of the gods; hopefully it would fuel his will to escape.

"What is the point of this, anyway?" Taja said. "I don't know about you, Jekku, but I feel like I've been running in circles. I've seen altered memories of my past and visions of possible futures, but..." A shadow of pain flickered across his face. He drifted a little closer to Jekku and their hands bumped, but Jekku wasn't sure if it was intentional.

"They showed me the same," Jekku said. "Everything was wrong, but it was like they were trying to push me toward a future that would happen if I let this whole thing drop. They want us to give up."

"They're going to have to try a little harder," Taja muttered. His hand touched Jekku's hand again, and this time Jekku caved and took it. He looked up and met Taja's eyes, and Taja smiled a little.

Off to Jekku's right, Jakob loudly cleared his throat again. Jekku suddenly wished to sink into the floor. He turned to his father, who watched with raised eyebrows and a knowing smirk. "Do you want me to leave?"

Jekku rubbed his hand over his cheek as if he could scrub away the blush he knew was painting his face scarlet. "*Anyway.* We just have to remember that nothing is real and everything is out to get us."

"As I was telling Jekku earlier, the point of this place is to break your spirits," said Jakob. "I worry that the gods intend to keep you both here until you cave. And Jekku is right, they want you to give up and forget everything that makes you who you are. That is perhaps why they separated the two of you. Had you been allowed to navigate the Labyrinth together, you would have been each other's voice of reason. Without that, it is easier for doubts to look like truths."

Jekku nodded. "So the key is to stick together."

"But why did they *let* us find each other?" Taja said in a hushed voice. "The Labyrinth allowed you to find me, Jekku, and that can't be an accident."

Jekku glanced at Jakob, who frowned. "You might have a point. I wonder if—"

Behind them, the door that had led Jekku and Jakob into this room crashed open. Jekku jumped and reflexively grabbed Taja's wrist. Cold air rushed into the room, and a deep voice vibrated the walls.

I have brought you together for your final trial. Proceed, and if you are successful, you may bargain for your freedom. One task remains. Will you be victorious?

Jekku looked up at Taja, and then at Jakob. His father looked fiercely determined, but Taja stared ahead at the open doors and the darkness beyond them as if marching toward his own death. Jekku took Taja's hand and squeezed it, then let go and stepped forward.

"One more test." He took a deep breath. "We know their games. We know what we have to do to win." He looked back over his shoulder. "Let's go."

Taja stepped up to his side. "I trust you. We can do this."

Jakob appeared on his other side and set his hand on Jekku's shoulder. "Shall we?"

Jekku led the way into the dark.

The doors crashed shut behind them, and crimson lanterns flickered to life overhead. The space was a long and narrow rectangle, empty but for a single wooden stool several feet away in the center of the floor.

"Okay... everyone else is seeing this, right?" Jekku's voice split the still silence like a thunderclap; he flinched and lowered his volume. "Mage's fire lanterns, one little stool?"

Taja nodded, eyeing the lanterns skeptically. "No voices?"

"No voices," Jekku confirmed.

"I've never seen this room before," Jakob murmured. He moved a few cautious steps forward. "Let's split, inspect the room. Look for anything that could be a door or other way out. Whatever game they've set up in here, we need to know our exits."

Jekku didn't love the idea of separating from the others, even if it was just to the other side of this room, but Jakob had already gone halfway across and Taja drifted toward the left side of the room. Jekku moved toward the right, keeping an eye on Jakob and Taja.

He ran his hand along the wall, finding it smooth and unbroken by any crack or crease that might have been an opening. He didn't get it; there was nothing *here*. "Taking suggestions of what we're meant to find here," he called to the others.

But it was neither Jakob nor Taja who answered. *Yourselves.*

A shiver ran down Jekku's spine. He turned around, but as expected, no one stood by him. Several feet away, however, Taja had also paused his search and glanced around the room.

"Taja," Jekku hissed. "Did you hear that?"

Taja nodded once. "Oridite."

One by one, the lanterns suspended overhead blinked out, casting the room in deep shadows until all that was visible beneath one remaining lantern was the wooden stool. Jekku blinked, waiting for his eyes to adjust, but he lost sight of both Taja and Jakob and couldn't see an inch in front of his nose.

They're still here, he assured himself. Taja and Jakob were still somewhere in this room, and they'd still be there when the light returned and the three of them were allowed to leave.

Not *if*. *When*. They would pass this test.

They had to.

"Okay." Jekku swallowed and stepped closer to the stool. "What do I have to do?"

Sit, came the reply.

Jekku did. Dim crimson light pooled around him, but the rest of the room was cloaked in solid darkness. Another shiver crawled up his spine at the thought of Taja and Jakob being able to see him while he couldn't see them.

For several minutes, nothing happened. Jekku sat in the suf-focating silence, alone with his thoughts and the steady thump of his pulse in his ears. The darkness began to close in around him, and it took everything in him to keep away the memories of being locked in that prison at Gallien's Peak. He tipped his head back and kept his eyes fixed on the lantern, but it wasn't long before he started to fidget. He picked at a loose thread on the hem of his shirt, then picked at his cuticles, then resorted to his old habit of twisting a strand of his hair around his fingers. Just when he thought the test was simply judging how long he could sit in a dark room without losing his mind — of which he already had four years of practice — another lantern flickered to life in front of him.

Taja stood beneath its pool of red light, only a few feet out of Jekku's reach.

Jekku's heart lurched. He went to stand, but an unseen force held him in place, as if someone had pushed him right back down. He struggled again, but whatever magic bound him to the stool held fast. He sat back with a huff and called out, "Taja! What—" But before the rest of his question was out, he knew Taja couldn't hear him. He didn't move or react in any way to Jekku's voice. He just stood there, rubbing his hands together, and anxiously glanced around the room.

It hit Jekku then that Taja couldn't see him, either.

What is this?

Then Taja spoke. "What he wants?" He did not appear to be talking to Jekku; Oridite must be speaking to him. "But..." He blinked a few times, then his eyes widened as he looked straight at Jekku. He started to move forward, but something held him back the same way Jekku was stuck in his seat. Taja looked up into the dark; Oridite must be speaking to him again. Fear flickered across Taja's face as he lowered his gaze to Jekku once more and then he reluctantly turned around.

Jekku's heart pounded. He hated that he didn't know what Taja was hearing. "Taja! Taja, please—" He knew Taja couldn't hear him, but he tried anyway. "Whatever he's telling you, it's not real! You know it's not real! You know me. Whatever Oridite tells you, you know me better. I know you do. I—"

He cut off, breathing hard. This was pointless. Taja couldn't hear him, and now that he knew Jekku was there, he wasn't allowed to see him either. If this was a test of trust, Jekku hoped to every god he could name that Taja trusted him enough.

Oh, Jekku realized, *I have to trust him, too.*

He took a deep breath and gripped the edges of the stool until his palms ached. *I trust you. You can do this.*

"Jekku..." His name in Taja's soft voice stabbed something through his chest that he chose not to dwell upon at the moment. Taja shifted on his feet and turned his head a little, but he couldn't fully look back. "I think what Jekku wants now is what he's always wanted: magic, in all its beautiful forms."

Jekku blinked. *What?*

"It's always been special to him," Taja went on. "From the moment I met him I saw his fascination with it — his love for it I... I saw my own longing for magic in him, and when he found his affinity, part of me felt like— I don't know, like if he could find his affinity after all those years, maybe I could too. But I know that dream is hopeless, so the most I can do is hope that Jekku continues to chase *his* dream. I saw the look in his eyes when we traveled through Westdenn; I know his place is there, among Scholars of Magic. Maybe even Masters of Magic. He wants greatness, and as for me... I guess the most I can do is stay out of his way and stop holding him back."

Jekku's head spun. His heart pounded sickeningly fast. "What are you *talking* about?!" he shouted. He begged Taja to hear him. *Taja! No! Gods, I don't want greatness or fame or any of that—Why would I— I—*" He cut off with a sob and pressed his hand to his mouth. He couldn't stop shaking. *You can't fail this. You can't. I trusted you.*

The lanterns overhead extinguished. Whatever force of magic holding Jekku to the stool released, and he bolted to his feet. He darted forward, searching in the dark, but he neither heard nor felt Taja anywhere. "Taja! Taja, where—"

Jekku froze as one of the lanterns flickered to life once more. When he turned, he found Taja beneath the pool of crimson light, seated in the same spot Jekku had just vacated.

Oh, no.

The light above Jekku's head blinked to life. Taja's eyes widened. His lips moved, but Jekku couldn't hear him.

Jekku looked at him helplessly. "Please."

Taja shook his head, obviously confused. He tried to stand, but the unseen force held him back. He stared back at Jekku, fear shadowing his eyes.

And now comes your test, said Oridite's smooth voice.

Jekku had had it up to here with this cowardly god who hid in shadow. "What do you want." His voice came out as growl; he didn't bother lifting his words into a question.

Don't worry, it's simple: You must tell me what it is that Vaeltaja

Ievisin wants most. Now, he can see and hear you, but you may not see or hear him. Turn around.

Jekku knew there was no point in arguing. He did as the god said.

"What he wants?" Jekku wanted nothing more than to turn around to see Taja's face. Fear coiled in his stomach when he thought of Taja's misunderstanding of what Jekku wanted; if Jekku didn't get this right, they were trapped. This was the end of the road.

He dearly hoped that Taja's mistake didn't mean he would stay while Jekku was let free.

Jekku decided then that if Oridite chose to keep Taja trapped in the Labyrinth, Jekku would stay too. They would find their own way out, even if it took years. Or decades. Or a lifetime. One way or another, Jekku refused to leave Taja behind.

Answer carefully, Jekku Aj'ere. If you are correct and what you say matches what desires lie in Vaeltaja Ievisin's heart, you pass. But if you are wrong, neither of you may walk free.

As I told Vaeltaja, the Labyrinth is a place of introspection. If you truly do not know the deepest wants of each other's hearts, why should you deserve to leave together?

Jekku took another deep breath and swallowed his fear. He could do this. He knew Taja, and he refused to let the Labyrinth's claws sink doubts into his heart.

"Taja," Jekku began. "I know that all you want is to feel at home among your own people. You see and understand the problems in Bâthälla, and I know — we both know — that you have what it takes to rebuild it. You want to make it your own, for it to be *home* again, and you want to finish what Saevel started.

He lowered his voice. "You're the one who'll be great, and I'm the one who will keep to the sidelines."

Jekku closed his eyes. He let out a slow breath and listened to his heartbeat as silent seconds slipped by. Finally, with a soft *whoosh*, all of the lanterns overhead burst back to life and bathed the room in red. Jekku spun around, heart lifting at the sight of Taja standing in front of the stool.

But that burst of hope was smothered immediately by the blank horror on Taja's face.

The air rushed out of Jekku's lungs. *No. I can't be wrong. How could I be wrong?*

Taja began to speak, but Oridite's booming voice drowned out anything he might've said.

Congratulations, the god chuckled, *you have both failed.*

IO

TAJA

NO.

Taja's heart pounded. For a second, he and Jekku stared at each other, and Taja watched the truth crash down upon both of them.

They were wrong. They failed.

Taja took a halting step forward, but before he made it any farther, the lights blinked out once more. Taja stumbled in the dark, trying to feel his way toward Jekku. The air shifted around him, and the darkness seemed to... move? It flowed and waved like a silken sheet — a physical presence rather than the absence of light. Taja watched the whorls of dark matter gather together like a storm cloud at the far end of the room until they descended toward the floor and began to take the shape of a man.

Taja's stomach plummeted. He had to get to Jekku. They had to get out of here.

He still couldn't see an inch in front of his face, but he hurried blindly across the room anyway. Jekku had to be here somewhere, and if he hadn't moved, he should be—

"*Oof.*" Taja collided with something solid. "Jekku?"

"Taja!" Jekku's hands caught his and held tight. "Oh, thank he gods. What the hell—"

"Get down!" Jakob shouted. A blinding flash of white light xploded across the room. Taja grabbed Jekku and turned, hielding his eyes, but it was as though the sun itself had crashed nto the room.

Terror washed over him. *The sun.* Oh, no. No, it couldn't be. *He's dead. He's dead. He can't be here.*

In Taja's arms, Jekku was shaking. "What the hell was that?"

When the light faded enough that Taja felt it was safe to open is eyes, he looked up and found Jakob standing before the two f them, blazing weapon in hand. He held a sword made of pure lame, and far across the room, Lord Oridite stood surrounded y tendrils of shadow.

"Shit," Jekku hissed.

Taja realized he was still holding him and abruptly let go, but ekku stayed close. Ahead, Oridite stalked toward them. Jakob aised the flaming sword higher and adjusted his grip.

"Stay behind me."

Taja was planning to. But also, did Jakob really think he could ake on the God of Darkness?

"Jakob." Jekku took a halting step forward; Taja held him ack. Jekku whirled around, jerking his arm out of Taja's grip, ut Oridite spoke first.

"Well, well. Jakob Balmoor." A snakelike grin split Oridite's ale face. The flames of Jakob's sword danced shadows across is sharp features. He paused before Jakob and lifted his hands; hadows poured like liquid down his shoulders and over his arms. "I never thought I would see my favorite prisoner out and about once again. Are you sick of sulking in your cell? You wer so much more fun when you tried to run."

Jakob's shoulders tensed and he tightened his hands on th sword's hilt, but he did not rise to the god's taunts.

Oridite raised a sharp eyebrow. "Neat trick. But you can't foo me with smoke and mirrors. Your magic is as dead as that one's. His glassy black eyes flicked to Taja. "Funny that Båthälla's two disgraces found each other.

"You must know that nothing you try is going to work. Oridite began to pace a circle around the three of them. "I gav you your chance to earn your freedom, and you failed in the bes way possible. Really, that was something. It happens this wa every time: you think you know everything about him becaus you love him, but really, what do you know? Absolutely nothing Nothing that would save you, anyway." He grinned.

Taja held his gaze. "You tricked us. The test was rigged from the start. You wouldn't have let us win anyway."

Oridite barked a laugh. "No, Vaeltaja, this test was the onl time I refrained from tricks. This room won't allow it. Lies ma not be spoken here. Your failure was your own, and the deal i the deal. So save us both the trouble and allow me to show you to the rest of your lives."

Taja stepped closer to him. "Lord Oridite, you don't have to do this. We're not a threat to you."

"Says the notorious traitor! You'd see Båthälla launched into chaos. You have no idea what you're doing, boy."

"What do you want?" Taja said. "A shot at ruling? A slice of Båthälla?"

Oridite barked a laugh. "Of course not. This town has always been Ebris's pet. Now that he's gone, there's not a chance Nokaldir would let me get my hands on it. I am fully content to sit back and watch the chaos unfold." He raised his hands. "But that doesn't mean I'll let you destroy what's left of this pathetic village. Leave the leadership to those who are capable of it, traitor."

Taja clenched his jaw. "Let us go, and I will."

Behind him, Jekku gasped sharply. "Taja."

"Let us go," Taja repeated, never taking his eyes off Oridite. "And I will never be a threat to you or the other gods again."

Taja could feel Jekku's and Jakob's eyes burning into him as he waited for Oridite's reply. The god watched him steadily, dark eyes calculating. He tipped his chin up. "You're right." Oridite lifted his hands and closed them into fists. Fluid tendrils of darkness rose up around him. "You won't."

Oridite's eyes turned solid black, and Taja watched in stunned horror as his body began to grow and shift into something monstrously inhuman. Taja knew, somewhere in the back of his mind, that as the God of Darkness Oridite could take any shape a shadow could fill, but seeing it in action felt like a fever dream.

Light burst across his vision, cutting off his view of the creature Oridite was becoming. Taja jumped back and Jakob lunged toward the god.

"No!" Jekku again went to stop his father, but Taja grabbed him. Jekku struggled. "Let go!"

Taja held him tighter. "What are you going to do?" he demanded. Flames burst and crackled as Jakob fought Oridite, whose monstrous form bled into the shadows he wielded. If not for the flaming sword, Taja would not have been able to see Jakob at all.

Jekku jerked away from Taja, lifted his hands, and a bolt of lightning shattered the air. Taja flinched and Jekku hurled the lightning at Oridite. The god released a furious roar.

"I think you forget," Jekku growled, "that I'm not helpless anymore." Red-hot light from Jakob's sword glowed in his eyes. "Stay here." And before Taja could conjure any words, Jekku leapt into the fray.

Anger burned through Taja as bright and hot as the enchanted sword. While Jekku and his father battled Oridite, Taja was supposed to— What? Stay out of the way and wait for them to win? No way in hell. Good for Jekku that he had all this powerful magic, but Taja refused to let him make him feel inferior.

He was *Sawwia Setukkda*. His whole job was to fight the gods, damn it.

While the others scuffled, filling the space with grunts and shouts, Taja circled the perimeter of the room and dragged his hand along the wall. He winced each time Jekku's magic split the air, and his heart lurched at the occasional pained cries. He hurried faster, and finally his fingers found a break in the solid stone.

Taja's heart pounded. A door. It had to be. He felt around with both hands, found the top edge, hinges, and a circular indent where a knob should've been. But Jakob had a sword made of fire, so Taja wasn't worried about the absence of a doorknob.

"Jekku!" He shouted as loud as he could over the crackle of lightning. Light was scarce, but Taja saw Jekku look up. He earched around, hurled another strike of lightning at Oridite, then sent a blinding burst of electricity scattering across the room.

Taja couldn't help a moment of awe. Violet and white sparks of lightning crackled across the ceiling overhead, illuminating the entire space in pale, cold light. Jekku's magic was beautiful as it was terrifying.

Taja snapped his attention back to Jekku himself. He pointed at the wall. "Door!"

Jekku's eyes widened. He whirled around and shouted to his father, then started toward Taja while keeping an eye over his shoulder. But Jakob didn't follow, and when Jekku noticed, he halted. Behind him, a cloud of shifting shadows rose up around him.

Taja's heart stopped. "No! Jekku!"

At the same moment Taja lunged for Jekku and he turned and spotted the shadows lurking over him, Jakob whirled on Oridite and plunged the fiery blade into the god's chest.

The room shuddered. A force of energy burst out from Oridite's body, strong enough to throw Taja, Jekku, and Jakob off their feet. Taja hit the ground hard, spots popping in his vision.

Jakob recovered first and scrambled to Jekku, dragging him up from the floor. "Go— We have to go." He grabbed Taja's arm and pulled him to his feet, then sprinted directly toward the door without stopping.

Taja didn't have time to react before Jakob slammed his shoulder into the wall, and to his surprise, the stone crumbled like sand, revealing a dark passageway beyond. Jakob swept his

hand and the sword burst to life once again. He turned to Taj
and Jekku, breathing hard but otherwise unharmed from his bat
tle with the god. "With Oridite gone, the Sky Palace will desta
bilize. If we don't hurry, it'll trap us all here forever. Who's first?

Neither Taja nor Jekku moved. Taja glanced nervously ove
his shoulder. "He's— He's really dead?"

"As much as a god can be." Jakob nodded toward the ope
passageway. "Well?"

Taja saw it, then: the spark of hope that had burst to life i
Jakob's eyes. It hadn't been there even a short time ago whe
Taja had met him, but now it burned strong. He saw a wa
out, finally, after two decades imprisoned in this place, and Taj
doubted anything would stop him now.

The room quaked again, and Taja instinctively reached out t
steady Jekku. Jekku irritably swatted his hand away. "Stop. Com
on, he's right. We don't have time." He strode ahead into the cor
ridor.

Jakob gestured urgently at the doorway. "Unless you'd rathe
stay?"

Taja shook his head and followed Jekku. Jakob darted in afte
him and held up the fiery blade to illuminate the dark tunne
Ahead, the path stretched into oblivion with no exit in sight.

All at once the air felt too thin. Taja reached out to the wal
to his right, just to feel something tangible and solid. Jekku kep
a brutal pace, far enough ahead that he was just outside the reac
of the light, but he paused and looked back when the groun
rumbled again.

Taja's head spun. Oh, gods, they were going to die here.

A hand came down on his shoulder, making him jump, but it was only Jakob. Taja let out a breath.

"We're going to make it," Jakob said. He kept his voice low and sure, but the quaking ground beneath their feet said otherwise. Jakob gently nudged Taja to get him to keep walking. Jekku surged on ahead.

"You're Jekku's friend?" Jakob asked.

Taja didn't really know how to answer that. "You could say that."

Jakob smiled a little. "He speaks highly of you. When we were talking earlier, his eyes lit up every time he so much as said your name." He chuckled. "You clearly mean a lot to him."

Taja's heart missed a beat. He looked up at Jekku, but if he could hear this conversation he didn't show it. "Jekku is... like no one I've ever met. He's unpredictable and he's curious and intelligent and stubborn as hell, and I don't know if he sees how strong he is. He's been fighting for his life since the minute he left Ajaphere. I want..." Taja swallowed. "I just want him to be able to rest. I don't want him to fight forever."

Jakob hummed. "No, but he will. Until he has what he wants, he'll keep fighting. And I think you give him something to fight for."

Not anymore. Taja looked down at his feet. *Not since I failed him.*

"Trust me," Jakob said softly. "And trust him. By the way, is it true that you're *Sawwia Setukkda*?"

Taja was grateful for the change in subject. "Yes. Assuming we've interpreted the prophecy correctly." He rubbed his hands together absently, then looked up when he heard Jakob gasp. But

Jakob's gaze was on Taja's hands, and the jagged scars that marred the backs.

"Oh, my boy." Jakob gently touched his wrist, and Taja saw the same Z-shaped scar on the back of Jakob's pale hand. "They did this to you, too?"

Taja swallowed and turned his gaze down to the floor. "It was Ebris's decision, in the end. He told me it was kinder than putting me to death."

At the time, Taja had believed him. He still remembered the cold grip of fear that had closed around his heart as he knelt, hands and ankles bound, before the gods and the Council Eternal. Any scrap of mercy was better than none. Ebris had declared his sentence, and Taja had wept with relief. He would walk away with his life.

But then he had suffered the ordeal of having his magic stripped from him, and he had wished Ebris had been kind enough to kill him.

Jakob set his hand on Taja's shoulder again. "I'm sorry. I wish we didn't have this understanding between us, but I truly feel your pain, Taja. There is nothing worse than what the gods put us through."

Taja shook his head. "No, there's not. And to think..." He scoffed. "To think that I used to believe I deserved it."

Taja glanced up in time to catch Jekku looking back at him, but he quickly turned his head and continued forward. Taja watched the light from Jakob's sword shine in waves on Jekku's hair, and wished he wasn't all the way up front, but at Taja's side.

"No." Jakob's tone sharpened. "Of course you didn't deserve it. There's no excuse for what they did."

"I know," Taja responded. Then he looked up at Jakob curiously. "How are you doing that? That's not... a real sword, is it?"

"If that's a real sword that can catch fire," Jekku said from
head, "I know someone who would give her left leg just to hold
it in her hands."

Taja smiled. It was true, Lilya Noor would salivate over a
flaming sword. But Taja wanted to know how it worked, and he
was positive Jekku was bursting with curiosity as well.

"It's not made of metal, if that's what you mean," Jakob said.
He lowered the weapon and turned it for Taja to see. The blade
emitted no heat, but burned as bright as a plume of mage's fire —
white-hot at the center and vivid orange at the edges. Mage's fire
took on a unique color to each user, often a different, brighter
hue than natural fire, but the sword appeared to be made of natural flames despite there being absolutely nothing natural about
it.

"It's made of magic," Taja guessed. "But how? If you..."

Jakob smiled, and Taja was thrown for a second at how much
of Jekku was in that expression. "It's a spell of my own inven-
tion," Jakob explained.

Up in front, Jekku abruptly turned his head.

"Since I no longer have magic of my own, I found a way to
pull from the earth's inherent power. It's quite exhausting and I'll
need a rather long nap once we're out of here — keep walking,
by the way — but it's a solution. It's a way to reconnect with my
heart's affinity for flame. I reached out and the earth listened,
and it shares its magic with me despite the power being stripped
from my blood."

Taja stared at him, heart pounding. "But— Does that

mean...?" He dared not voice the question. He couldn't bear the crushing despair if this last bit of hope was snuffed out.

Before Jakob could reply, Jekku doubled back and walked backward in front of them. The sword's flames gleamed in his eyes. "How does it work? Isn't there a cost — some kind of exchange that you must give in order to get the earth's power? can't imagine it lets you take that kind of power without anything in return." Jekku frowned. At this point, he might as well have been talking solely to himself. "Magic has no inherent cost to its user because human limitations prevent a mage from using too much at once, but what happens when you remove that limit? If *anyone* can draw magic from the earth, what happens when it falls into the wrong hands? Isn't that basically Arcane magic? Could it create another Oracle Stone?" His eyes flicked to Taja. "Why are you smiling?"

Taja hid his grin behind his hand. *Because you are so endearing when you do that.*

"Are you laughing at me?" Jekku scoffed, but a smile hid at the corner of his mouth. "This is a serious question! I don't want to deal with *another* Oracle Stone when we aren't even done with the first one."

"I am laughing at you," Taja teased. "You're very funny."

Jekku rolled his eyes and turned on his heel, facing forward once more. "I have more questions."

"I'm sure you do," Taja murmured.

"Save them for now, yeah?" Jakob said. He slipped around Taja and Jekku and took the lead. "First let's get out of here."

Taja couldn't agree more.

11

TAJA

JEKKU FELL INTO STEP beside Taja, closely enough that their shoulders occasionally bumped, but Jekku didn't say a word to him. Taja glanced at him every few minutes, trying to read his expression in the dark, but he didn't look angry or upset. He just looked kind of lost.

Taja knew the feeling well. He was tempted to take Jekku's hand, but part of him knew Jekku would reject him. Better to spare himself the sting.

They continued through the dark in silence. Jakob surged ahead, keeping a faster pace than Jekku had. He quickened his steps each time the corridor rumbled around them.

Taja didn't know how much time had passed, but it was long enough that the quakes didn't startle him anymore. *There's another one*, he thought absently when the ground shuddered. *That was a big one. Are they getting worse?* It was probably bad that he was desensitized to the Sky Palace falling apart around them, but the alternative was dwelling on the possibility of getting trapped in here, and Taja was decidedly not thinking about that.

A violent quake shook the corridor again, this time raining pieces of brick and stone down on them. Taja and Jekku halted and exchanged a glance, but up ahead, Jakob didn't miss a step. "Keep moving. This might be one of the last parts of the palace that hasn't crumbled. We're out of time."

"Can I ask a question?" Jekku started walking again. "Isn't the Sky Palace home to *all* the gods? Why is it imploding just because Oridite is dead?"

"Because it was created by him, and therefore in his control," Jakob answered. "Unless someone else seizes control before it entirely collapses, it will continue to fall apart until it is gone."

"And if we're still in here...?"

Jakob glanced back over his shoulder. "Do you really want to find out?"

As if in reply, the ground rumbled again. Something crashed close by — *too* close. Taja looked back, and far behind them, a spot of light appeared as the corridor began to collapse in on itself. The light seemed to eat away the darkness, reducing the tunnel to dust as it drew closer and closer.

Taja touched Jekku's arm and Jekku followed his gaze. His face paled.

Jakob muttered a curse. "Okay, now is not the time to freeze! Get moving. I can get us out of here."

Jekku didn't move. "How?"

"Trust me." Jakob didn't leave time to argue. He gripped the flaming sword with both hands and closed his eyes for a second. The flames burned brighter and extended the blade until it was nearly half Jakob's height. He adjusted his grip and swung the blade full force toward the wall.

Taja braced himself for the awful screech of metal against stone, but it never came. Instead, the stone crumbled to dust, just like the door out of that room. Jakob swung the blade again, burning away more of the wall until there was enough space for the three of them to step through. Foggy white light obscured whatever lay beyond.

"I don't know what we're about to find," Jakob said, breathing hard, "but go. It's our only chance."

We're going to die in here. That doorway could lead to the *Ur-dahl* forest, or back into Båthälla, or it could swallow them whole into nothingness. They could end up trapped in the collapsing Sky Palace and be reduced to restless ghosts.

Taja looked at Jekku, and with an impulse of certainty that the two of them would not walk out of here alive, Taja grabbed his face in his hands and kissed him.

He pulled back, breathless, and met Jekku's shocked eyes. In case we don't make it," Taja whispered, and then stepped through the wall.

***

When Taja next opened his eyes, he received a view of sky obscured by bright green trees. It took a second for the branches to come into focus, and another second for him to register that he was sprawled on his back, lying on something soft and uneven. The air was cool, smelling of fresh earth, and birds sang somewhere in the distance.

Taja turned his head and found Jekku sprawled a few feet

away, Jakob beside him, and everything abruptly rushed back to him. He sat up, heart pounding, and looked around.

Familiar woods. The rushing river nearby. In the distance, a glimpse of stone buildings among the trees.

Oh, gods. They were in Båthälla. They were safe.

Taja heaved a sigh of relief and flopped back on the ground. *We made it. We escaped.*

And the God of Darkness was dead.

Taja got up again and went over to Jekku. He was still unconscious, but didn't appear to be injured. Taja gently shook him and stroked his hair back from his face.

Well, they were alive. And Taja had probably screwed *every thing* up by kissing Jekku back there, but he could not say that he regretted it. Maybe Jekku wouldn't remember it.

"Jekku." Taja shook him again, and his eyelids fluttered. He made a soft groan, then turned his head and opened his eyes.

He blinked a few times, then a smile touched his lips when his eyes fell on Taja. "It's you."

"It's me. We made it, Jekku. We're alive."

Jekku abruptly sat up, nearly crashing his head into Taja's. "We are?" He looked around, then blinked rapidly. "Where's Jakob?"

"Right here," Jakob groaned, and pushed himself to his feet. His braid had all but unraveled, and deep lines scored the skin under his eyes. He swayed a little on his feet, but managed a smile.

Taja stood and offered Jekku a hand up, which he took but didn't let linger. Taja *almost* wanted to apologize, but he wasn't about to bring up the kiss without being prompted.

"So." Jakob sighed and tugged out the last of his braid. His long, gray-streaked hair fell in smooth waves down his shoulders. 'We made it. I kind of can't believe it." He gazed around at the trees, a wistful and bittersweet smile on his face. "I have a... complicated relationship with this town. But it still feels good to be home."

Taja understood the feeling.

Jekku went to his father and brought him into a hug. "We did it," he said softly. "You're free."

Jakob hugged him back fiercely. "Thanks to you, my son." Then he looked up and extended an arm toward Taja. "Come on, now. Don't be shy. We did this together."

Taja hesitated. "I don't want to in—"

"Taja, get over here." Jekku turned to him and offered an arm, and Taja caved and accepted the group hug.

They were safe. For this moment, they were okay.

***

By nightfall, they were hours away from Båthälla. Taja didn't think it was safe to stay in or near the village, even if they laid low in Taja's cottage, and both Jekku and Jakob agreed. Ellory and the remaining gods probably already knew about Oridite, and Taja was not about to show his face in Båthälla with yet another god's blood on his hands. Not until they had a plan.

Taja had stopped by his house to grab some supplies, then the three had set off into the *Urdahl* and let the forest shelter them.

Jakob, predictably, had disappeared into the tent and gone to sleep almost immediately after they'd settled. Exhaustion weighed on Taja's bones, but he couldn't bring himself to turn in yet. Instead, he sat by the dying remnants of the fire Jakob had conjured and he wallowed in every unsaid thing between himself and Jekku.

Where did he even start? Jekku sat on the other side of the fire pit, curled into himself with his arms crossed on top of his knees. He'd pulled up the hood on his cloak and he had his face buried in a scarf he'd borrowed from Taja, but he still looked cold. And tired. So, so tired.

Say something, Taja told himself. He had spent weeks at Jekku's side, had told him things he'd never confided in anyone else. He'd offered his heart to Jekku and promised to wait for him. *You have to trust him.*

Taja wanted to trust him, but he didn't see how he could after Jekku had shattered Taja's confidence in him.

He thought Jekku knew him. He thought Jekku — who once caught glimpses of each potential path of Taja's life — would know what he wanted. Taja thought Jekku of all people would be able to see that it had *nothing* to do with Båthälla and *everything* to do with Jekku.

Jekku glanced up and caught Taja watching him, and Taja darted his eyes away. Then he kicked himself for it. *Say something. This is your chance.*

"Why don't you get some rest?" Taja murmured. It was not actually what he wanted to say, but it was something. Maybe it was best that they talked once they'd both gotten some sleep.

Jekku absently shook his head. His eyes were distant as he gazed at the dying fire. Then he blinked and looked up at Taja again. "We were wrong."

Taja swallowed. There it was, the truth neither of them wanted to admit. Not only had Jekku been wrong about Taja, but Taja had been wrong about him.

"I..." Jekku sighed and rubbed his eyes. "I thought I knew, Taja. I thought..."

"I did too." Taja stood up, intending to move closer to him, but Jekku shoved to his feet and swept toward the tent. Taja hurried after him. "Jekku, wait—"

"Nope. Not now." He stopped outside the tent and looked back, shaking his head. "Not now." And he disappeared inside.

Taja stared after him, feeling distinctly like something had snapped.

Then Jekku screamed.

12

JEKKU

OH GODS. OH GODS OH GODS OH GODS. Jekku didn't know what made him see it. He didn't know what made him look twice. But in the second between stepping into the tent and tossing a glance at his sleeping father, he saw at once that something was horribly, horribly wrong.

Behind him, Taja rushed into the tent and nearly crashed into him, but Jekku hardly noticed. His eyes were fixed on Jakob, on the unnaturally pale pallor of his face, on the blackness creeping beneath his skin from fingertips to elbows.

"Jekku." Taja set his hand on his shoulder. "What's wrong?"

How did he not see it? Jekku could barely get the words out. "L-Look at his—— his hands."

His hands, which were almost entirely black now, as if they'd been charred by fire. His blood had somehow turned black as ink, and the poison appeared to spread from the Z-shaped scar on the backs of his hands.

Jekku couldn't move. He couldn't think. His mind had gone

utterly blank, and his vision tunneled until all he saw was his fa-ther's still, lifeless face.

"They cursed him." Taja's voice, deep and dripping with fury, snapped Jekku back to the present. "They took his magic, and they *cursed* him."

But how? Why? Jekku didn't understand. He unfroze his limbs and took a halting step closer to Jakob, then all at once the strength left him and he slumped to his knees. With a trembling hand, he reached out and searched for a pulse despite knowing in his bones that he wouldn't find one. Still, the cold absence of a heartbeat was no less shocking.

Jekku dropped his hand and looked up at Taja, seeking an an-swer. Any answer. Any rational explanation of why this was hap-pening. "H-How? How did this-- Why? Why would they..."

Taja absently shook his head, gaze fixed on Jakob's body. His hands trembled as he clenched and unclenched his fists. "Because Ebris doesn't leave survivors."

"T-Taja." Jekku's voice broke. His throat closed up. He looked back down at Jakob and the reality punched him all over again. "He-- He's gone. How is he-- How is he just *gone*? He was just-- I just-- He was *here*, he spoke to us, he traveled with us, he ate with us, I was t-talking to him, we were-- we were going to go home."

A sob broke out of him and he pressed his hands to his face. He heard Taja shift and move as he sat down beside Jekku, and when Taja pulled him close Jekku didn't resist. He slumped against him, conscious of how much he was shaking but unable to stop. Silence wrapped around the two of them, heavy and cold, broken only by Jekku's uneven breaths. He tried to calm them, tried to stop his mind from spiraling, but his heart was lodged in his throat and he couldn't stop seeing the blackness in Jakob's veins and he could not believe this was real.

It wasn't fair. It wasn't *fair*. For twenty-two years, Jekku hadn't known his father was alive. His mother hadn't known if she'd ever see her partner again. Jakob had lived two decades locked in the gods' Labyrinth, and just when he thought he was free... this. Here and gone in a blink.

Jekku took a deep breath and pulled away from Taja. His eyes darted in Jakob's direction, once again seeking the lines of black beneath his skin, but Taja gently turned his face away.

"Don't," he murmured. "Just look at me." He traced his thumb along Jekku's jaw and searched his eyes. "What do you want to do?"

Jekku drew back. "What?"

"We can't leave him here."

Jekku's breath hitched. Something about the softness of Taja's voice brought the reality –– the actual reality of this –– crashing down upon Jekku. His father was dead, and Taja was right, they couldn't just leave his body here for the wolves and crows.

Jekku bolted to his feet and clawed his hands through his hair. "What do I–– Shit, Taja! I want to–– I want my father to be alive! I want to know him, and I want him to know me, and I want him to go home to my mother so she knows he's alive and she doesn't have to be alone anymore! I want–– I want..." He trailed off, breathing hard. His pulse rang in his ears, and this time when he sought Jakob's face again it wasn't grief that stabbed him, but rage.

"I want justice. For him, and for you." He clenched his jaw

nd looked up at Taja. "I want everyone who decided his fate and ours to pay for what they did."

Taja stood and reached for Jekku's arm. "Ebris is gone, Jekku. There's nothing––"

"*Don't* tell me there's nothing else we can do!" Jekku snapped. "You know just as well as I do that it wasn't *just* Ebris. You told me the Council Eternal wanted you *executed*. Am I wrong?"

Taja pressed his lips together. "No."

"And I'm sure they were involved in my father's sentence, too." Jekku shook his head. "All for falling in love. All he did was fall in love." His throat tightened again and he pressed his hand to his mouth. His eyes stung, and tears spilled down his cheeks when he closed them.

He felt a steady hand on his back. "I'm so sorry, Jekku."

"We should bury him, shouldn't we?" Jekku sniffed and looked up at Taja. "I wish I could take him home, but..."

"It's up to you what you wish to do," Taja said softly. "But our custom is cremation. Instead of placing a body in the earth, we scatter their ashes in the places they loved most so their spirit rests where they were happy."

Jekku felt tears stinging his eyes again and irritably rubbed them away. "I..." He looked down at Jakob. "I think he'd want that. Wouldn't he? Even after what his people did to him, he'd still want to follow his own customs, right?" He turned to Taja. "Right? Would you? Would you keep your traditions even after your community and your family betrayed you?"

Taja blinked a few times, clearly caught off guard by Jekku's question. "I... Well, let's put it this way. I don't know how *not* to be Elshalan. No one can take this identity from me, not even the gods. Do you think Jakob would have felt the same way?"

Jekku could only guess. He didn't *know*. He didn't have chance to know his father well enough to know what to do here He didn't expect to have to *do this*.

"Hey." Taja slid his hand across Jekku's shoulders. "Come here Come here." He brought Jekku into his arms, and Jekku only hes itated a second before hugging him back with all his strength He bunched his hands around fistfuls of Taja's shirt and choked back the sob that wanted to break out of him.

"I'm so sorry," Taja murmured. He pressed his face to Jekku shoulder and held him a little tighter.

"Taja, I— I wouldn't have convinced him to leave if— if knew this would happen." Jekku's voice sounded small and far away, even in his own ears. "This is my fault, isn't it? He died be cause I brought him out of there."

"Jekku, no." Taja let go and held Jekku's shoulders. "No. Don' think like that."

"He'd be alive if he was still in the Sky Palace." Jekku's voic wobbled. "Wouldn't he?"

"Jekku."

"Wouldn't he?"

Taja clenched his jaw. "Maybe. But even if he was alive, he'e still be a prisoner. You freed him, Jekku, and more than that you gave him hope." Taja reached up and tucked a loose piec of Jekku's hair behind his ear. "You had no way of knowing thi would happen. Neither, I'm sure, did he."

Jekku looked away from him, but couldn't bring himself to

see his father's body again. He closed his eyes and leaned his head on Taja's chest. "I'm so tired."

"I know." Taja wrapped his arms around him again. "Your father will find rest in the *Urdahl*, and you will find peace, *mä aurii*."

Jekku didn't know what that meant, but the emotion behind Taja's voice told him enough. He didn't ask, and Taja didn't tell.

"Thank you." He drew back and met Taja's eyes, finding them welled with tears. "We'll make sure Jakob rests, but I will have no peace until I see justice. We need a plan, Taja, because when we go back... we're going to tear Båthälla to the ground."

Taja's eyes widened a little.

"Some things can't be fixed, Taja. Sometimes they need to be rebuilt." Jekku held his gaze. "Are you with me?"

Taja hesitated another second, then nodded once. "I'm with you. Always."

INTERLUDE II

LILYA

LILYA NOOR HAD COME TO WESTDENN for two reasons: Firstly, to find a tutor she apparently *had* to have before she could move up into the Queen's Academy in Aylesbury, and secondly, to give someone a piece of her mind regarding the absurd and discriminatory law requiring fire mages to identify themselves in this city.

She had been here for a week and she was still angry about it. When she and her friend Nesma had been stopped at the city gates and forced to prove their affinities, Lilya had been treated with scorn and unnecessary fear. They'd handed her one of those damned dragon patches to pin to her clothes and told her that if she was caught without it, she'd be arrested. If she was caught wielding her magic, she could have it stripped.

This, of course, did not apply to any other mages who entered the city of Westdenn.

"It's a good thing they can't arrest you for staring daggers at them," commented Nesma, who strode beside Lilya as the two

made their way up to the University District. They passed a tri(
of soldiers loitering by a street corner and Lilya wished she coul(
show them what her magic was really capable of. The temptatio
to give them something to truly fear grew each day.

"Bastards," Lilya muttered. She shot another glare over he
shoulder at the soldiers, but they were too busy laughing an(
shoving each other around to notice her. She put her hands i
her coat pockets and walked a little faster. Nesma's long stride
were difficult to keep up with. "I can't wait to leave this saints
damned city."

"Oh, don't be silly. You won't leave until you've turned it up
side-down, Lilya." Nesma's voice was soft with fondness.

Lilya couldn't help a smile at that.

Nesma Ryiekki used to be Lilya's rival at Gallien's Peak, bu
when Lilya had returned to the fortress and taken the school int(
her own hands, Nesma had become a hesitant acquaintance. An(
then a friend. And then, without really meaning to, they'd be
come something like best friends. Lilya was pretty sure it sur
prised Nesma as much as it surprised Lilya herself. The mor(
time she spent with Nesma, the more she realized the two o
them weren't so different, and the only reason they had ever re
sented each other was because Firune had told them they should

The truth was, Nesma was just as talented a mage as Lilya
and under Firune's rule, that made them enemies. But now Lily;
knew who Nesma really was: a kind, empathetic, intelligent di
viner who wasn't really all that competitive. She loved magic fo
its beauty and power, and she reminded Lilya why Lilya love(
studying the art.

Lilya thanked the saints once again that the days of Firun(

were over. She enjoyed Nesma as a friend much more than a rival.

Still, a very small part of Lilya was relieved that Nesma was not here to prepare for the examination for the Queen's Academy, because if it came down to the two of them competing for very limited spots, Lilya knew she would lose. Thankfully, though Nesma was an exceptionally skilled diviner, she had no interest in a "fancy title and bragging rights that require me to sit for a ten-hour portrait," as she put it.

It was more than a title for Lilya. There was no higher honor a mage could achieve in the country of Doweth than the position of Master of Magic. It showed utmost skill, impressive ambition, and deep love for the art of magic. Being awarded the title of Master after completing her schooling at the Queen's Academy would secure her spot at Gallien's Peak, and then her true work would begin.

Lilya knew she had what it took to earn that honor. She had defeated four Royal Sorcerers and a god. She'd wielded the Oracle Stone. She had been top of her class at Gallien's Peak and had a litany of her own invented spells that Firune passed down to younger students. Lilya was a damn good mage, and after she jumped through these ridiculous hoops, Gallien's Peak would be hers.

The only things in her way now were a few exams, a grouchy tutor she had to charm, and a four-year program she intended to complete in two.

One of these things would be significantly harder than the others. She had had her first meeting with her potential tutor this morning, and... Well, it could have gone better.

***

"I am very sorry, Miss Noor, but the law is the law. Fire mages must—"

"I don't give a damn about—" Lilya cut off her sentence and swallowed. Yelling at the Headmaster of the University of Westdenn (who also happened to be the Head Magistrate of Westdenn, and therefore the one who approved of and enforced the law) would get her nowhere. And telling him she didn't give a damn about the law probably wouldn't help her case, either.

She glanced up at the dusty ceiling of his stuffy little office and folded her hands together to lessen the temptation to summon her magic. The room was so packed with old books that it'd go up in flames in an instant if so much as a spark escaped from her fingers. "I understand that this city thinks differently of fire mages," she said calmly, "but I assure you that I am no threat to your academy or its students. I trained under Master Firune, sir. He demanded nothing if not control."

The short, white-haired man shifted in his leather chair and adjusted his glasses on his long nose. His brown eyes studied Lilya with scrutiny. "Phoenix Hall is no different from the rest of the Academy, Miss Noor. You will receive the same studies and training as other mages for the entire course of your internship. If you are good enough, you will graduate with your peers and be on your way to Aylesbury. I do not see how this is an issue."

This man really didn't get it, did he? If she let them place her in this hall specifically for fire mages, she'd be apart from everyone else for the entire six month period. She'd live, train, study, and compete *only* with fire mages, and that — aside from being insulting — was *boring*.

Lilya took another deep breath. "Master Riis, I did not come here to debate the nuances of your university. I have a simple request: let me carry out my internship among other mages at my skill level, regardless of affinity. You'll quickly see that I excel above my peers, and thrive best when I have competition. Fire magic is my specialty. Let me show you that I can hold my own against other magic as well."

Master Riis leaned back in his chair and raised his bushy eyebrows. "They warned me that you'd march in here looking for a fight. Lilya Noor, the one who loves a challenge."

She flickered a smile. "Historically I've never turned them down."

"And I like that in a student," Riis said. "You'd be a fine candidate for my tutelage." His eyes drifted down to her chest, and she was about to let loose her temper when she realized it was the dragon patch pinned to her coat that he was eyeing. She quickly crossed her arms to hide it. Saints, that thing caused her more shame for her magic than anything ever had. She wanted to turn it to ash.

When she'd arrived in Westdenn, she'd debated lying about her magic. *Tell them you're a diviner*, Nesma had suggested. *They can't prove that.* And Lilya almost had. But no, she finally had a chance to let her power stretch to its full size. She had a chance to challenge herself with the most rigorous instruction a mage could enroll in, and she was not about to back down because of one city's prejudices.

Lilya cleared her throat to draw the Master's attention back to her. A dozen snide remarks along the lines of *My eyes are up here* ran through her head, but she refrained herself. *Be the nice girl for once in your life. You won't get what you want by antagonizing the Headmaster.*

Master Riis grimaced and adjusted his glasses again. "Miss Noor... the best I can say is I don't know. This is a matter that is not just up to me. I will speak to the instructors and the other University administrators, but if they are not comfortable... there is nothing I can do."

Lilya balled her hands into fists. "Not comfortable?"

To his credit, Riis looked a little nervous. "Well... you know how people are. Having someone as— as talented and ambitious as you... people might get intimidated."

Lilya stepped forward and placed her hands on his cluttered desk, leaning forward until they were eye to eye. "Good."

He pursed his lips and sat back. "I admire your persistence, I'll give you that. But look at it this way, Miss Noor: If I bend the rules for one fire mage, that gives me a reputation. 'Go to Master Riis, he will let fire mages into the University if you ask him nicely.' One exception leads to dozens, Miss Noor, and too many exceptions lead to disaster. You wouldn't want to be responsible for a domino effect, now, would you?"

Lilya's pulse jumped. The acrid stench of smoke momentarily filled her nose, and she had to take a deep breath to convince herself it wasn't real. She straightened and crossed her arms again. "What do you mean by that, Master Riis?"

"Perhaps you won't set the University aflame, Miss Noor, but if another exception did..." He spread his hands. "The rules are in place for a reason. Fire magic is dangerous and destructive. If an incident were to occur, you would be at fault even if the flames did not leap out of your hands. You would be the catalyst. Is that what you want your legacy as a Master of Magic to be?"

Fury sparked through Lilya. Her hands burned, but she clenched them tight and shoved them in her pockets. How *dare* he? Magistrate or not — Headmaster or not — Lilya didn't want this man as a tutor if this was how he treated potential students.

Riis must have seen something shift in her eyes; he smiled at her in a distinctly patronizing way, like he knew he had won. "Are we understood, Miss Noor?"

She turned on her heel and stormed to the door of his stuffy, hazy office. "Quite."

She did not regret slamming it behind her.

***

After that conversation, Lilya was ready to get the hell out of Westdenn and find another way to complete the internship she needed to get into the Queen's Academy. But Nesma had talked her down, and together they had come up with a plan.

Unfortunately, the first leg of that plan involved apologizing to Master Riis.

Lilya didn't know if she'd be able to bring herself to actually say she was sorry for — what? Leaving his office in a cloud of rage after he'd insulted her? She had every right to be angry. *He* was the one who should apologize.

Yet she still needed his help, and there was not a better tutor in Westdenn. Well, maybe there was, but Lilya had heard nothing but positive things about Master Riis, and he'd mentored mages who went on to become well-known Masters of Magic. His approval was basically a golden ticket into the Queen's Academy, so *fine*, Lilya would apologize and ask again.

And she would agree to his terms.

"Did you figure out what exactly you're going to say to him?" Nesma asked, drawing Lilya out of her thoughts.

"I'm going to apologize for leaving rudely and say something like I regret that we got off on the wrong foot or whatever." She waved a hand. "And I'll thank him for saying exactly two nice things to me. And I will not mention that he's an arrogant and bigoted prick who doesn't know a damned thing about fire magic."

Nesma laughed. "No, probably leave that part out." She touched Lilya's shoulder. "Oh, but look. Do you have to go back today? It's so beautiful out. The library gardens are calling to me. Can't we go get lost in there like all the other visitors to West-denn?"

Lilya rolled her eyes, but turned her head to hide her smile. Another thing she hadn't expected about Nesma was how similar she was to Jekku. They had the same sense of wonder, that insatiable itch for knowledge. Lilya chose not to dwell on why that similarity drew her to Nesma even more.

"As much as I would also love to visit the libraries," she said, taking Nesma's arm to pull her along, "I doubt they'll let me through the doors." With her free hand she plucked at the dragon patch on her coat. She'd meant it as a joke, but the reminder of the patch sent a spark of anger through her. As did *every* reminder that she was not actually welcome in this city — all for an affinity she didn't ask for.

As if she didn't already resent her magic enough.

Nesma turned her head, thick black curls falling in waves over her shoulders. Her brows knit together, and her bottom lip jutted out a little when she frowned. "Do you really think even the libraries would turn you away?"

"Have you been under a rock this past week? Of course they would." Lilya lowered her voice as they passed two men walking hand-in-hand. They smiled politely at Lilya and Nesma, and Lilya had an inkling that if they'd seen her patch they would've crossed to the other side of the street. That had happened more than once now. Lilya shook her head. "That's the whole point. So they can decide who they want kept out."

Nesma scowled. "It's abhorrent."

"Tell me about it."

"And it doesn't make sense. What if they tried to do that with all types of magic? How would I prove I'm a diviner?"

"Exactly. The law wasn't made to single out all types of magic. It was made to single out fire magic."

"It's ridiculous. Magic is magic."

"Yeah, well, tell that to the queen." Or the Magistrate, whom Lilya suspected conducted most of the laws in Westdenn. The queen, all the way over there in Aylesbury, probably didn't give a damn what happened in Westdenn as long as it didn't go up in flames. But Westdenn was so *particular*; as home to the largest university in Doweth that offered courses of study that were precursors to the Queen's Academy in Aylesbury, Westdenn was *almost* as important as Aylesbury. Which meant the Magistrates that oversaw the city thought *they* were as important as the queen.

Lilya had had enough of them. Crusty old mages reluctant to see a new, experimental age of magic ushered in. And reluctant to get younger faces in positions like Master of Gallien's Peak. But Lilya was determined to get Master Riis on her side. It helped that he was already impressed by her, and it was *only* the issue of her being a fire mage that stood as a barrier. To reach her goals, she might just have to swallow her pride.

It's only six months, she reminded herself. She could handle it. And all that anger she felt at being separated from other mages would only fuel her flames. She'd leave a mark, all right. The University at Westdenn would remember her for a long, long time.

But first, Master Riis. Apology. Agreement. And an outrageously expensive bottle of very high quality wine from Kelum.

"Ah, here we are." Lilya stopped in front of a charming shop with ivy crawling up the storefront. The shop's name — Taste of Meridia — was painted in gold across the rectangular front window, and behind the glass, a few dozen bottles of dark red wine were arranged in an abstract rendering of Gallien's Peak.

Which made no sense. Gallien's Peak was neither in Westdenn nor in Meridia. Meridia had its own mountains; why not use one of those?

"A liquor store?" Nesma questioned. She frowned at the window, then at Lilya. "Are you *that* stressed?"

"Well, yes, but that's not why I'm here. This is what we call a last resort, and an offer of peace." She grinned and held the door open for Nesma, who gave her an incredulous look before stepping into the shop.

The place was cozy, and might've been peaceful if it wasn't for the dozen or so people huddled around the petite shopkeeper who was balancing four different bottles in her arms. The patrons all talked over each other, asking questions, asking to see different wines, asking for recommendations. Lilya hung back with Nesma by the front of the shop and idly glanced over the elegantly scripted labels on the bottles until the flock of shoppers headed out the door and left the place blessedly quiet.

The shopkeeper approached Lilya and Nesma and let out a breath. "Well! That was the busiest rush we've had in ages. Those Aylesbury folks almost know their wine better than I do! Sorry to keep you waiting. What can I do for the two of you today?"

"What do you have from Kelum?" Lilya asked. "Specifically from the Gulf region. We're buying for someone with expensive tastes. He's picky, not easily impressed, and he likes his wine dry enough to dehydrate a lake."

The woman grinned and then snapped her fingers. "One moment."

As she dashed off, Lilya turned to Nesma and slid her hands into her coat pockets. "See? I know just what I'm doing."

"What's the plan, then, get him drunk enough that he'll say yes to anything?"

"No, it's just a *gift*," Lilya said. "A very specific gift that will hopefully put him in a forgiving and generous mood."

The shopkeeper came back then, cradling a dark bottle in her hands. But then she stopped short and her freckled face paled. "Oh—"

Lilya looked around, trying to figure out the source of her discomfort. "Is something wrong?"

Nesma touched her sleeve. "Lilya, let's go."

"What?"

The shopkeeper set the wine bottle on the nearest shelf and hummed a soft tune under her breath. Beads of moisture collected in the air around her raised hands; she was a water mage. "Please. I don't want to do this the hard way. I didn't see it before, but..." Her eyes darted down to Lilya's chest, and with a jolt she remembered the dragon patch on the front of her coat.

White-hot fury boiled under her skin. "You can't be serious."

"You think I'm stupid?" The woman waved a hand at the bottles of liquor around them. "Letting a godsdamned fire mage in here with all this flammable alcohol? Get out. Now. I won't ask again."

Lilya could have burned the whole shop to the ground. One snap, one note, and it'd go up in flames. It'd be quite the explosion, too. *Let them see that cloud from here to Aylesbury.*

She felt a soft touch on her arm. Nesma. Her hand closed around Lilya's forearm, and the distraction was enough to chase those dark thoughts from Lilya's mind. *Don't become the monster these people think you are.*

She exhaled, but her hands still trembled with anger and adrenaline. "Fine. I'll go somewhere that *doesn't* discriminate. Unbelievable." She turned on her heel and stormed out the door, Nesma on her heels.

When they were outside, Nesma touched her arm again. "Lilya, I—"

"Don't." She shoved off Nesma's hand and strode across the street.

Nesma caught up with her in a few easy strides. "Lilya, I'm sorry. That—"

"Holy gods, is that—? Lilya? *Lilya!*"

She halted, confused, and turned around. It took her a second to find the source of the voice, but when she did, the air rushed from her lungs.

A little ways down the sidewalk, looking travel-weary as if they'd crawled all the way here from Båthälla, were Jekku and Taja.

13

JEKKU

JEKKU, FIRSTLY, THANKED THE GODS that he was
ight and that was, in fact, Lilya in front of him. But secondly,
e couldn't believe his eyes. What was she doing *here*? And what
vere the odds that she was here, in Westdenn, at the same time
e and Taja had arrived?

Lilya recovered from her shock first. She let out a short laugh
nd rushed toward Jekku and Taja, grinning. "I don't believe it.
Vhat are you doing here?"

"What are *you* doing here?" Taja shot back. He gathered a
ery reluctant Lilya into his arms, and though she complained
he didn't resist. Taja let go, and before Lilya could change her
nind, Jekku hugged her too.

"*Ugh*, okay, you've reached the hugging threshold today." She
vriggled out of Jekku's grasp and straightened her coat, and that
vas when Jekku noticed the patch.

His stomach sank. "Oh, gods."

Something darkened in Lilya's expression and she crossed her
rms over her chest to hide the orange dragon pinned to her

coat. "I don't want to talk about it. Really, though, what ar
you doing in Westdenn? I thought you had business in Båthäll
Messes to clean up, news to break, all that."

Jekku grimaced. "Well... Yes. It's a long story. We thought yo
were headed back to Aylesbury?"

"I was," Lilya said. "After we parted ways, I traveled back t
Aylesbury and tested out of all the prerequisites at this littl
school you need to get through before you can attend th
Queen's Academy. But then they informed me at literally the las
minute that before I could graduate, I had to complete an in
ternship at the University here. So here I am. But Westdenn i
a disaster, and part of me is just itching to cause some troubl
while I'm stuck here for six months."

Jekku smiled to himself as Taja updated her about the situ
ation in Båthälla. Though it'd only been a few weeks — mayb
more; time was weird in the Labyrinth — since he'd last seer
Lilya, she seemed different. Sure, she was still the same bold
fiery girl he knew, but some of the shadows had fled. She wasn'
weighed down anymore. With Firune gone and the Royal Sor
cerers out of her head, there was nothing left between Lilya and
the sky.

Jekku hoped she owned it.

His attention wandered around the street, and he realize
someone was waiting for Lilya a short distance away. Anothe
Meridian girl, probably about the same age, leaned gracefull
against a streetlamp and busied herself by braiding her long
silky hair. But Jekku could tell she was listening and trying no
to be obvious about it.

He waited for a break in Taja and Lilya's conversation, ther butted in. "Hey, who's your friend?" He jabbed a thumb over his shoulder.

Lilya briefly glanced at the other girl, then back to Jekku. He watched her walls go back up; clearly there was something she didn't wish to say about her companion. "That's Nesma. A former apprentice from Gallien's Peak. She's a good friend."

Jekku knew an understatement when he heard one. He waited, but Lilya did not offer more than that. Jekku wasn't satisfied; he went to ask another question, but Taja jumped in before he could get a word out.

"Well, we shouldn't hold you back. It sounds like you've got your work cut out for you. We do too, but... we're here to try and figure out our next steps."

"And also because it's a city that has shops and inns and places to sleep that are not tents in the woods," Jekku added. The five days it had taken them to walk from Båthälla to Westdenn hung in a haze of exhaustion in Jekku's mind. He missed that Sky Elk every damned day.

Lilya smiled. "If I never sleep in the woods again, it'll be too soon. But hey, don't run off so fast. Maybe I can help you."

"That sounds like you want something from us in return," Jekku teased. "No blood oaths, Lilya Noor."

She rolled her eyes. "Jekku Aj'ere, I think a blood oath with you is a worse idea than a blood oath with Firune."

"You *wound* me." He laughed. Oh, gods, he'd missed her. "But really, what's the catch? Blood oath or not, you can never resist a trade."

The humor drained from her face, leaving her looking guilty. She dropped her gaze to the ground. "I don't need anything,

Jekku. Everything I want — from this city and for myself — I can get on my own. It'll take some work and some time, but I'll get there." She nodded, mostly to herself, and looked up at him once more. "Tell me how I can help you. What you're fighting for is a much wider issue than I thought. I want to see you win, too."

Jekku blinked. "Who *are* you?"

Taja set his hand on Jekku's arm. "Shhh... Do you hear that? Is Lilya being vulnerable?"

She smacked Taja's arm. "Oh, shut up! Since when is it a big deal if I want to help my friends?"

Jekku grinned. "You admit it! We're friends!"

She punched his arm, probably harder than she needed to. But a smile hid at the corner of her mouth. "Of course we're friends. But not if you keep rubbing it in!"

He laughed and slung an arm around her. She made a disgruntled noise, then wrapped an arm around him. "I missed you," he said softly.

She playfully shoved him away from her. "Yeah, yeah. Come on, quit spilling your feelings everywhere. Nesma and I have a room at an inn a few blocks away. We can talk there."

"Or..." Jekku shot a glance down the street, where those wonderful, grand, beautiful libraries dominated the block. "We could hole up in one of the libraries and talk *there*." He raised his eyebrows, but Lilya didn't seem impressed, so he turned the pleading look to Taja.

He sighed. "I can't say no to him when he looks at me like that."

Jekku grinned.

Lilya snorted. "Yeah, I'm sure you can't. Fine, to the libraries, then. The question is: Which one?"

***

Jekku had never been happier. The Queen's Library — the biggest of the three and the one that he and the others *hadn't* stopped at when they'd hidden the pieces of the Oracle Stone — was something out of a dream. When they stepped into the lobby, Jekku's jaw hit the floor and he had yet to pick it up. The ceiling arched up high over their heads, its dome made of glass so clear it was like it wasn't there at all. Bright sunlight poured onto the marble floor, making the whole room glow. But the real beauty arrived when they stepped out of the lobby and into the actual library — seven open floors of dark wood shelves packed with thousands upon thousands of books. A grand staircase draped in a dark green velvet carpet curved up to the upper floors. Golden mage's fire housed in frosted glass lanterns illuminated the space in a pleasantly warm glow, and several polished wood tables occupied the floor among the books. By the stairs, a podium bore a giant book that Jekku guessed was an index of the entire collection.

He buzzed with excitement. They could all spare a few hours for him to get lost in here, right? Maybe he could pretend to go off looking for something and then just... wander for a bit. He wanted to stick his nose into every inch of this place. Oh, the *books* this library must have! Histories! Mythology! Plays and novels and collections of poetry written *centuries* ago! And not only books — what was kept in those upper rooms closed to the public? What kinds of artifacts of history and magic lived unde this roof?

"Look at him," Lilya murmured behind him. "He's like a ki on Saints' Day."

"You have to admit this is extraordinary," Taja replied "There's nothing like the simple joy of a library. And this one i anything but simple."

Lilya laughed softly. "You two are made for each other."

Jekku chose not to react to that comment. He led the wa across the library, Taja and Lilya and Nesma trailing behind, an found an open table among the stacks. Lilya and Nesma went of together in search of world maps, and Jekku and Taja took to th stacks in search of myths.

"Are you sure we shouldn't look among history?" Jekku said. " know it's ancient, but look at this place. There's probably book here from the first people who figured out how to write thing down. There *must* be historical texts on Elshalans."

Taja shook his head and adjusted the scarf he wore to hide hi ears. "You said yourself when we met that Elshalans were consid ered myths to most Dowethians. I do not think we'll find record among your histories. Especially not about our gods. We can fo cus on the people later. Remember, we're here to find out how t kill a god."

They found the correct section and split up. Jekku started a one end of a row and scanned each title on each shelf, search ing for anything that might contain information about Elshala gods. Taja was right, even if the historians weren't; anything hav ing to do with the gods' stories would be filed under myth. Cul tural fiction. Jekku was almost tempted to search the religion section, too.

In the aftermath of their escape from the Labyrinth, it had become clearer than ever that the gods were not going to be merciful, and the people of Båthälla were not going to listen. The gods wanted Jekku and Taja gone, and Jekku was positive that Ellory themself would kick them out of the village if given the chance. It was only a small victory that Oridite was dead; Jekku did not trust Nokaldir, and he had mixed feelings about Nedra.

How long would she remain an ally? What was her goal, and what happened if it didn't align with theirs? What did she hope to gain from helping Taja and Jekku?

They needed a real solution, fast. They needed a way to get rid of the gods for good –– even if it meant banishing Nedra, too. They couldn't afford to take any chances.

Jekku collected an armful of books that looked promising, then went back to the table. He found Lilya poring over a beautifully illustrated map of Doweth, but Nesma was missing.

"She's still looking around," Lilya said, not taking her eyes off the map. "I told her to wander. She doesn't need to be part of this."

Jekku slid into a chair across from her and leaned his elbows on the table. "Anything you'd like to tell me about Nesma?"

She didn't look up. "Nope."

"Are you *sure*?"

She met his eyes. "Anything you'd like to tell me about Taja?"

Jekku was saved from answering by the arrival of the Elshalan in question. He set a stack of leather-bound books on the table and slumped into a chair. "I don't think we're going to find anything here."

"You haven't even looked yet," Jekku said. He nudged his arm. "Come on. Let's get reading."

***

Three hours later, Jekku's brain felt like mush. He flipped yet another book shut, slid it across the table, and set his head down on the wood.

"Jekku?" Taja questioned.

"I can't read anymore. Brain hurts."

"Same here." Lilya shut a book with a *thunk*. Her chair creaked as she leaned back. "What have we found? Anything?"

Jekku reluctantly lifted his head. "Nothing we don't already know. According to the myths, the first generation of Elshalan gods who created the earth and everything on it decided to live among their creations. They left their children in charge of the heavens, and each god took charge of an Elshalan community and shared their gifts with their people."

"And that's how it's always been." Taja rubbed his eyes. "I have found nothing about gods leaving their villages, or of Elshalans kicking them out, and certainly nothing of gods being killed." He lifted one of the larger books from the stack he'd collected and slid it across the table. "This is the Cosmos book -- or rather, a copy of it. I'm a little surprised to find it here. Anyway, this is essentially a narrative of our gods and the origin of Elshalans. If the answer we need was going to be anywhere, it'd be in here. And it's not."

"There must be a way," Lilya said. "What did Saevel do to bris at Gallien's Peak?"

Taja shrugged. "Old magic. Possibly something we don't even se anymore. I don't know. Saevel is over nine hundred years old. hey're basically a god themself."

"No, they're not," Jekku said.

Taja frowned. "What exactly would you call them, then?"

"A mortal Elshalan who had too much heaped on their shoulders and died too young." Jekku met Taja's eyes. "They are no different from you."

"Except that they're dead."

Jekku blinked. "Yeah, except that they're dead. But *you're* still ere, and you still have a chance."

"But I don't have magic," Taja argued. "I don't have a *drop* of he power Saevel had. And my last hope of getting it back died vith your father."

Jekku's heart sank. He looked down at the table and clenched is hands, focusing on the bite of his nails in his palm so he lidn't have to remember that night. His father's deathly pale ace. The blackness seeping into his veins. And the fire. And very campfire since then that had reminded him vividly of ourning his father's body.

It was a blur in his memory. His brain refused to let him lwell, and thank the gods for that. But the stab of grief still hurt.

He felt a soft touch on his arm, and found Taja's hand set here. His thumb gently caressed the inside of Jekku's wrist. "I'm orry."

"You... found your father?" Lilya said. "I thought you told me e left when you were a kid."

Jekku shook his head. "He left before I was born, but not because he wanted to. Honestly, I... I didn't even consider that h might still be alive. But he was there, in Bâthälla. The gods ha him trapped in— in this enchanted labyrinth. I found him, an he helped us escape. He killed the god Oridite. But..."

Taja squeezed his wrist. "He didn't make it."

"Oh, Jekku—"

"It's fine." He cut her off before he had to hear the sympath in her voice. "It's over, and that's that. Can we get back to the ac tual issue here? We still need a way to get rid of two gods."

"I don't think we're going to find these answers in books, Taja said. He sighed and let his hand slip from Jekku's arm. " think we need to speak to other Elshalans. No one knows ou history better than us."

Jekku didn't love the implication of that. "You'd go back t Bâthälla so soon?"

"No. Bâthälla won't help us. Not yet, anyway. But if we wen to another town, we might find some friendly faces."

Jekku sat up straighter. "There's more?"

"Here?" Lilya asked simultaneously. "In Doweth?"

"If you know where to look." Taja flickered a smile. "Bu they're probably all hidden like Bâthälla is. After the war be tween the gods and the Royal Sorcerers back in Saevel's time it was agreed that Elshalan villages would be completely cut of from human settlements. We would hide, keep to ourselves, an ideally this would keep us safe. But we've seen how well tha worked out."

"So how do we find them?" Jekku asked. It took all of his sel control to restrain himself to just one question when hundred of them burst into his mind. This reminded him all over again that there was still so much about Taja and his life and his history that Jekku had yet to learn, and it made him all the more eager to hear *everything*.

"It'll be tricky without magic," Taja said, "but I know what kinds of clues to look for."

"Wait," Lilya said, "Taja, what was that thing you said about Jekku's father giving you a chance to get your magic back? How is that possible?"

"Jekku's father had had his magic taken, like I did." Taja's fingers skimmed over the back of his hand. "But he was able to manipulate his affinity in a different way. He said it had to do with connecting to the earth itself, rather than energy within you. You draw from without, not within. I don't really see how that's possible, though. I've never heard of magic being done like that."

Jekku nudged him. "Doesn't mean it's not possible."

Lilya drummed her fingers on the table, thinking. "I wonder if you could still learn to do that on your own." Her eyes flicked to Jekku.

He stared back. "Huh?"

"You're a powerful mage." She raised her eyebrows as if Jekku was supposed to read her mind.

"Um, thank you?"

She rolled her eyes. "Your power — possibly combined with mine — might be enough for Taja to at least feel something. A flicker. A spark. Something to draw from." She turned to Taja again. "What was your affinity?"

"The touch of life," he said. "You call us nature mages."

"So what is nature — and life itself — but pulses and energy?

Jekku, your magic *is* energy. You alone are probably enough for Taja to grasp the magic that surrounds you when you call your affinity.

"Magic doesn't just live in your blood," Lilya explained. "It does flow through the earth, and all a mage is, is someone who is particularly in tune with that energy."

Jekku's mind raced. He liked where Lilya was going with this, but he still didn't get how this would work in a practical sense. "So, what, I zap Taja with a bolt of lightning and he gets his magic back?"

Taja gave a nervous laugh. "I'd rather not repeat that experience."

Jekku winced. "Right, yeah, let's maybe avoid that." He sent Taja an apologetic look.

"Not what I meant, anyway." Lilya waved a hand. "It's not about the specific affinity, it's about the *power* itself. Magic has a heart, a source, from which all the world's power is drawn. It's literally like the heart of the earth. Magic flows and circulates and pumps through the planet like blood does through our bodies. It manifests differently in everyone, but magic is magic. That's why people all over the world have found unique ways of harnessing it: Dowethian magic and Kelish magic are the same power poured out in different ways."

Jekku stood up and started pacing. "So you're saying that, in theory, someone with Meridian heritage could learn magic the way Dowethians do and it would work? But what if they grow up learning magic like, I dunno, Kelish people, and then switch to another method?"

A beat of silence passed. Jekku looked up and met two sets of confused eyes. "What?"

"Jekku, I'm Kelish," Lilya said.

"...Yes?"

"You have seen me summon my magic with song." She stared at him like he was stupid.

And, indeed, he was. "Oh. Right."

Taja snorted. "So, yes, what you're saying is correct. Anyone from anywhere can learn magic however they please."

"The differences come from culture, not the magic itself," Lilya said. "Kelish people emphasize a closeness with yourself and your emotions, and therefore we learn to connect to magic through feelings. But it takes a hell of a lot of mindfulness and control, which is why I prefer the Dowethian method of singing. Something about harmonizing melodies soothes the magic, and... well, you both already know how it feels."

Jekku smiled. "There's nothing like it."

Lilya looked at Taja again and reached across the table to touch his hand. "Hey, don't give up. There's so much about magic that we don't know. There must be a way for someone born with an affinity — especially one as strong as yours — to connect to magic again. You just have to find it."

Jekku came back to the table. "And if we can find a way for Taja to reconnect with his magic, then the same principle could apply to people who *aren't* born with magic. Who's to say that anyone and everyone can't wield magic if they wish to?"

Lilya eyed him curiously. "My first instinct is to say that's impossible, but unlike the Magistrates of Westdenn, I'm trying to

keep an open mind. You're right. Why is magic only for a selec
few?"

Jekku grinned. "Precisely! Gods, this is what I agonized ove
for *years*. All I wanted when I was a child was to be a mage, to
feel that beautiful energy. I was devastated when I grew up and
didn't feel a flicker of magic. But now I don't need to prove thi
theory for me. I can prove it for— for you." He turned to Taja
"And anyone else like you who lost their magic. I really think
we're onto something, Taja. I think we can figure it out."

Lilya watched him, chin resting on the back of her hand
"Saints, it's a good thing you won't be my competition at the
Queen's Academy. The Magistrates of Aylesbury would bend
over backwards to make you a Master of Magic."

Jekku flashed her a smile. Maybe in another life, that was the
path for him. But at the moment, he was having trouble tearing
his eyes away from the expression on Taja's face. It took him a
second to put a name to it, but there was undoubtedly hope in
his eyes. It was hesitant, and it was faint, but it was *there*, and
that was what mattered.

When they'd first met, Taja had looked at Jekku as if Jekku
would be the one to fix everything, to be his savior. There was
hope in his eyes then, too, but this was different. This wasn't
blind faith. Taja trusted him, believed in him, and it made Jekku
sick with guilt.

Don't look at me like that. You can't *look at me like that. I failed
you.*

He broke Taja's gaze. *And you failed me.*

Lilya whistled, jolting Jekku out of his thoughts. Warmth
crept up the back of his neck at the sly look in Lilya's eyes. "You

two have an *exceptional* talent for reducing your surroundings to your own tension-filled bubble that makes the rest of us feel like intruders even from four feet away."

Jekku felt Taja's eyes on him and yet kept his gaze trained squarely on the table.

Lilya snorted. "What *happened*? You really expect me to believe you two *still* haven't—"

"Okay, stop." Jekku sent her a hard look. "It's complicated, okay? I'll tell you later."

Beside him, Taja abruptly stood and sent his chair scraping across the floor. "Don't bother. There's apparently nothing to tell. At least not until one of us decides what he actually wants."

Jekku froze, pulse thudding in his ears, as Taja stormed away from the table.

Shit.

"Sorry." At least Lilya had the good sense to speak quieter. "I didn't mean to pry. But... do you want to talk about it?"

"Can we not do this here?" He gathered the books he'd collected earlier into his arms. "If you're that nosy, I'll tell you while we put these back. But I can't— I can't just sit here anymore."

Lilya nodded. "Okay. Let's walk."

***

By the time Jekku finished updating Lilya on the rather messy situation with Taja, he was more confused and frustrated than he had been before. A lump had formed in his throat when he had told Lilya about Leo and it had yet to clear, making him sound like he was on the verge of tears with every word. He hated it, but if Lilya noticed she didn't comment. She walked silently behind him, hands shoved in her pockets. Not even her heeled boots made a sound on the marble floor.

Jekku let out a breath and tried to shake off the storm of feelings brewing in his chest, but all he accomplished was making himself lightheaded. He stopped walking and closed his eyes, counted to ten.

A few steps ahead, Lilya's heels clicked as she paused. "That's certainly a lot."

Jekku opened his eyes. "Like I said, it's complicated."

She shrugged. "Doesn't have to be."

"No, I really think it does."

"Listen. As a disclaimer, I only vaguely get what you're going through, because I don't feel the same type of attraction to people as you do. So I don't get all your messy yearning feelings. But what I do understand is that you are so painfully, obviously in love with that boy."

Jekku wheezed. "*What*?"

"Let me finish. I know what you're going to say. I'd throw the same question back at you: how do you know you love him when you've only known him for a couple months?"

"It— I'm— It's not—"

"It's not rational," Lilya said. "Exactly. That's the point. It's not supposed to be rational. If it was, people wouldn't spend their whole lives writing poems about it. The logic doesn't matter. What matters is that you care about him. Don't you?"

He nodded. That much was easy to admit. Of course he cared.

"And you want to give him a chance?"

"I don't want another Leo." Now Jekku couldn't get his voice

bove a whisper. "I don't want a— a fling that turns into acciden-
al feelings. I don't want to be..." He swallowed. "I want to matter
o him more than that."

Lilya took a step closer to him. "And you can't see that you
lo?"

Jekku didn't know how to answer that.

"Taja isn't Leo," Lilya said. "But I don't need to tell you that."

"I know." He rubbed his forehead. The tightness in his throat
vas starting to cause a steady throb behind his eyes. "I know he
sn't. And yeah, I know that he— I mean, that's just it, Lilya. He
ares *so much*, and I don't know what to do with that. It's— It's
oo much of what I want. It's *exactly* what I want. And that's
vhat scares the shit out of me. Because if I let myself fall for him,
— What if I screw it up?"

His voice broke and he took a breath. "There's so much to
ose. And I'm such a mess. I can't risk wrecking something that
ood."

For a second, Lilya just stared at him. Jekku didn't blame her.
He hadn't meant for all of that to pour out. This wasn't exactly
n ideal place to let his heart bleed all over the floor.

Then Lilya's eyes flicked to a spot over Jekku's shoulder, and
is blood ran cold.

Despite himself, he laughed. No, no, he *knew* he was not about
o turn his head and find the very last person he wished to see
ight now. The universe wasn't really that cruel, was it?

If there were any gods at all, that would not be Taja behind
im.

Jekku turned.

Yeah, no, there were no gods.

Taja stood about six feet away at the mouth of a connecting corridor, looking just shocked enough that Jekku believed he hadn't followed them on purpose. He stared at Jekku with— Gods, Jekku didn't know. He couldn't begin to read that expression.

"Well." Lilya cleared her throat. "Did that clarify anything?"

Jekku shot her a glare, then turned on his heel and started to flee. But he didn't make it more than two steps before a strong hand caught his arm and turned him around.

"Jekku, *no*." Taja held him by his shoulders and searched his eyes pleadingly. "Stop running away from me."

"It's not you," Jekku breathed. Really, it wasn't Taja's affections that terrified him. It was himself. It was the idea of giving too much too soon, of letting all his feelings burn out immediately like a struck match. He didn't want to overwhelm Taja or scare him away or—

"Jekku." Taja gave him a gentle shake. "Please. Talk to me."

Jekku forced himself to meet his eyes. "How much did you hear?"

"Enough to know that we're on exactly the same page."

Somehow, that made Jekku feel worse. Maybe Taja did feel the same terror at the thought of messing this up, but clearly he knew how to silence that fear. Taja was standing here, ready and waiting to give Jekku his whole heart, and Jekku was stuck.

Part of him wanted Taja to spill everything. Put it in words. Bare his heart like Jekku just had. But at the same time, Jekku didn't know how he would respond if Taja did that. He very well might just run away again. Maybe the weight of Taja's feelings would drown him and Jekku would give up and turn his back on this and everything it might have been — all for the sake of not getting hurt again.

And maybe that meant he wasn't ready to open the walls around his heart.

He hated this. He *wanted* to be ready. He wanted his stupid brain to catch up to his stupid heart and make a decision. Did he want this or not?

Well, of course he wanted it. But committing to everything after that initial yes... That was harder. That was where the walls went up.

Jekku stepped back from Taja until several feet filled the space between them. As much as he hated to do this, he met Taja's eyes and shook his head. "I'm sorry. Not yet."

He tried not to see the shattered look on Taja's face as he turned and fled down the stairs and back to the library's lobby.

14

TAJA

"DO YOU WANT to talk about it." Lilya barely phrased the words as a question. She sat sideways in the leather armchair next to Taja's, legs kicked over the arm and head tipped back. Taja found it easier to talk — or rather, to sit in mutual silence and *not* talk — when they couldn't see each other's faces.

"To be honest with you, Lilya, no." Taja rubbed his temples. "I don't want to talk about it." Even if he did, it'd be strange to confide all this in Lilya. He wasn't as close with her as Jekku was; the only serious conversation they'd ever had was in his living room in Båthälla when she'd told him how Dowethians treated fire mages. This conversation would be no more enjoyable.

"Why not?" she asked.

Wasn't that obvious? Because Jekku's words hurt, Jekku running away from him hurt, and it was easier to let the pain fester in his chest than it was to try and put it into words for someone who couldn't actually fix it.

Besides, how much did Lilya really care? "I don't want your fake sympathy, Lilya. You're only asking because you're nosy."

Lilya sat up and faced him. "You think I don't care?"

Taja turned his head toward her and raised an eyebrow. "Why would you care about my disastrous love life?"

Lilya looked like he'd slapped her. "Of course I—"

"You care about Jekku, maybe," Taja went on. "But there's always an ulterior motive with you. What do you actually want from us? Or rather, from him?"

Lilya bolted to her feet, and Taja knew he'd made a mistake. He'd take the words back if he could. "You're wrong," she snapped. "I'm not like that, Taja. I do care about you and Jekku, because you're my friends. I didn't realize that was a sign of manipulation."

Taja looked away from her. His face burned with shame. "I'm sorry."

"Yeah, so you don't get to take out your anger at Jekku on me," Lilya said. "What could I possibly be trying to get out of either of you, anyway? It was different before, with the stone. I was being manipulated, and I know that doesn't excuse it, but I was weak. I put that fantasy of immortality before the people I care about, and it nearly cost me everything. Again."

She sighed and sank back into her chair, leaning forward with her elbows on her knees. "I'm trying to be stronger. I don't want to fall into that trap again. And... I'm learning, slowly, that there's no shame in letting myself care for people." She glanced up at Taja. "Which means I want you to believe me when I say that you are my friend. And I'd appreciate if you didn't assume the worst about me."

Taja got up and set his hand on her shoulder. "Lilya, I'm sorry.

I was upset, and you're right, I shouldn't have taken it out on you. None of this is your fault. You were just trying to help."

She smiled, and for the first time he saw the softness in her that Jekku must have seen from the start. Lilya was many things — sharp as a blade, unflinchingly confident, exceptionally talented with magic — but underneath all that, she was just human. She was a strong young woman with fierce ambitions that had been bent and used against her, and Taja couldn't fault her for that. She was trying. He saw that.

"I'm not your enemy anymore," she said.

"I know."

"You can talk to me. I know we're not as close as I am with Jekku — or as you are with Jekku — but that's... different. He's very easy to get close to because he doesn't shut up."

Taja laughed and went back to his own chair. "That's very true." And that was one of the things Taja loved about Jekku; he was easy to know, easy to be around. He acted like he was shy and introverted, but that was so far from the truth. He could fill a room with his own voice if he was excited enough.

Thoughts of Jekku, however, settled a cold, nauseous feeling in Taja's stomach. Which was ironic, in a twisted way, because he really should not feel physically ill at the thought of the person he cared for. But he guessed there was a reason they called it *lovesickness*.

He slumped back in the chair and looked up at Lilya. "I do want to talk about it. But I also know that you don't deserve to have this on your shoulders."

"It's not as heavy as you think it is," she said. "Not to me. And look at what I got out of Jekku with just a few questions. He was carrying all of that, letting it weigh him down. Now it's out of his head and floating around and it's up to both of you what you want to do with it. It's not on my shoulders."

That must be nice, to not internalize other people's problems. Sometimes Taja wished he wasn't so empathetic. His own feelings and issues were heavy enough. "I don't know what to do, Lilya. It was so much easier before either of us said anything."

"Maybe, but it was also agonizing to *watch*. I can't imagine what it was like to feel." She eyed him. "What are your options?"

That was the thing, he didn't *have* options anymore. A few hours ago he might have considered telling Jekku the truth, confessing his feelings again and seeing what Jekku said. But now, after Jekku had walked away from him, he was stuck.

Jekku obviously cared for him. A lot. The raw vulnerability in his voice when he'd spilled everything to Lilya earlier had punched Taja in the heart. He was so *close*, and clearly felt the same overwhelming tide of emotions that Taja currently drowned in. The difference was that Jekku was afraid of it, and Taja let himself drown.

"I wait." He didn't see another choice. "That's it. He said he's not ready, so all I can do is wait."

"And won't it be worth it?" Lilya asked. "You know how he feels about you. We *both* know how he feels about you. He won't make you wait forever. He's crazy for you, Taja. His feelings were never the question. But he's been through a lot these past few weeks. Give him time. He won't let you go."

Lilya was right, and Taja knew it. But that wasn't what he wanted to hear. Nothing she said would be what he wanted to hear. That could only come from Jekku, and it did not seem likely that Jekku would say the words anytime soon.

"I just wish I could talk to him," Taja murmured. "I just want a clear image of where we stand, but he keeps running away. I—I don't know how to be more approachable. It's *me*. He has never been afraid of talking to me, not like this."

"I think he's afraid *because* it's you," Lilya said. "This is different than telling you about his past. He sees his relationship with you as something that's balancing on an edge, and he thinks if he moves too quickly, it'll tip. You heard what he said: he doesn't want to mess up and lose you."

And Taja felt the same. But what bothered him was that Jekku thought Taja would just drop him at one wrong word or one mistake.

Oh. Because that was what had happened to him before, without him messing up at all. He'd been treated like he didn't matter by someone he cared for deeply, and he was terrified of it happening again.

Taja's heart ached for him. He cursed Firune and Gallien's Peak — and Leo, too — for saddling that trauma on Jekku's shoulders. He'd been so open and free with Taja before he'd learned of Leo's actions, and it would have been so much better if he'd never found out at all.

"Taja." Lilya poked his arm. "Listen. If you want to be with Jekku, and he wants to be with you, then you'll both make it happen. But like anything else, it doesn't happen overnight. Jekku needs time to rebuild his ability to trust, and you need to continue to show him that he has nothing to fear. So take your time. Take what you're feeling and nurture it. Build a stronger bond.

And... ugh, I'm going to hate myself for saying this, and if you re-peat it to anyone — *especially Jekku* — I'll haunt you forever, but others have said it and it's true: love is like magic. At its best, it's beautiful beyond description. But it won't surround you softly unless you treat it with care."

Taja bit back a smile. Those words were so unlike Lilya, but Taja resonated with them. It was true: magic was love and love was magic. And neither of them thrived without tender care.

He got up from his chair and offered a hand to Lilya. "Come here."

She let out a groan. "More hugging?"

"You know it." He held out his arms, and Lilya rolled her eyes but consented. She hugged him back tighter than he expected, then let go and punched his arm. He winced. "Yeah, that's more like you."

She grinned. "Feel better?"

"As much as I can." He touched her shoulder. "Thank you, Lilya. I'm sorry that we both poured all of this on you the mo-ment we saw you again. But we should let you get back to your fight. Where are you off to next?"

"Hey, hey, don't say your goodbyes yet, *Sawwia Setukkda*," Lilya said. "I'm coming with you."

***

Taja found Jekku in the garden outside the library. He'd cleared the snow off a marble bench and sat huddled in his cloak, looking positively miserable. His nose was red from the cold, and as Taja drew closer, he could see him shivering. But he apparently had no intention of moving.

Taja brushed off a spot beside Jekku and sat down. Jekku visibly tensed and sent a nervous glance in Taja's direction. Taja reached for his hand, expecting Jekku to refuse, but he let his hand slide into Taja's. "Gods above, you're freezing," he murmured, and rubbed some warmth into Jekku's hand.

"I'm sorry I keep pushing you away." Jekku stared down at their entwined hands. "I don't want— I'm not trying to. I just..."

"I know." Taja continued gently rubbing his hand. "Like I said, we're on exactly the same page. I don't want to push you, and I don't want to overwhelm you. I know you don't want to get hurt, Jekku, but neither do I."

Finally, Jekku looked up at him. "So... what do we do?"

"I don't know."

Jekku placed his other hand over Taja's. "I know you said you'd wait, but if you don't want to... I'd understand."

"Jekku." Taja clutched both of his hands. "I'm not going to give up on you just because things got complicated. I'm not like that."

Jekku searched his eyes, but said nothing.

"But I also need to know that you— That you're all in. I'm not asking you for immediate and unconditional commitment, Jekku, but tell me now if I should wait at all."

Jekku drew back, and Taja regretted the words. Jekku dropped his hands. "I— Taja, I can't change how you feel about me. I can't tell you what you should do. That's up to you to decide if you want to trust me. But it's a little funny that you're ask-ng me about commitment only to turn around and question whether you want this at all." He stood to go.

"Wait." Taja followed him. "Jekku, wait. You're right. I'm sorry. I didn't mean it like that."

Jekku crossed his arms. "Then what did you mean? Tell me the truth, Taja. I'm sick of games and secrets. You don't have to hide from me."

"And *you* don't have to hide from *me*."

A beat passed. Neither of them said a word.

Taja tried to string together what Jekku wanted to hear. But where did he start? How could he say any of it without scaring Jekku away again?

"What is it you want to hear from me?" he murmured.

"That's the thing, Taja." Jekku stepped closer to him. "It's not so much something I need to hear as something I need to see. I need to know that you won't— that you won't turn on me."

"I could tell you, wholeheartedly, that I would never."

"I know you could tell me. But can you show me?"

"How?"

Jekku moved closer and took his hands. "Stay with me. We'll see this whole thing through together. I'll do everything I can to help you make Båthälla what you want it to be. By then... ideally we'll understand each other better."

Taja flickered a smile. "If it's as simple as staying by your side, Jekku, you don't even need to ask. And if you wish to know me better, you could have just asked me out to dinner."

Taja received the exact response he wanted: Jekku's face turned scarlet. While he stammered for a response, Taja laughed and brought him into a hug. "That's what it takes to fluster you huh? Noted."

"I'm not saying no." Jekku drew back and smiled. "But it'd be hard to enjoy a carefree evening when there's so much hanging over our heads. Let's say I owe you one?"

Taja felt some of the weight lift off his shoulders. This was the Jekku he knew, but something was slightly altered, too. Now they were on the same page.

He brought Jekku's hand up and kissed the back of it. "It's a plan."

Jekku's expression softened. His face turned a little redder, and Taja was certain it was not from the cold. "Taja, look... this whole thing is just weird. I've never been in this kind of situation, where there's mutual feelings but no one is doing anything about it. I'm only holding back because I care about you and I care about us. This isn't what I'm used to. It's not a fling, and I don't want it to be."

Taja didn't know how to reply other than wrapping him in another hug. He held Jekku tight and pressed his face to his shoulder. *This is enough. For now, this is enough.*

"Are we still on the same page?" Jekku murmured.

"We are." Taja let go of him, a little reluctantly. "But listen, before we go, I have a request."

"What's that?"

"A shopping spree." He tugged on the front of Jekku's cloak. "This thing has seen better days."

Jekku looked down at the old, battered garment and frowned. "Yeah, I guess you're right." He fiddled with the sun-shaped button at his throat. "I don't need it anymore."

Footsteps crunched toward them. Taja looked up and found Lilya on the path leading through the garden, Nesma at her side. "Oh, there you are. Saints, I did a lap around the whole library looking for the two of you. Nesma had to use her divining affinity so we didn't spend all day circling the place. What's going on?"

"Just talking," Taja said. "Sorting some things out."

"Well, it's about damn time." Lilya set a hand on her hip. "And I meant what I said earlier, you know. I'm coming with you. What's the plan? Where's the next closest Elshalan town?"

"Is Nesma coming too?" Jekku asked.

Lilya's gaze turned murderous.

Nesma merely chuckled and shook her head. "No, not this time. I've got friends outside of Westdenn I'd like to visit while Lilya's gone."

Lilya looked at her. "I did tell you that you could go back to Aylesbury. You don't have to wait for me."

"But I want to." She smiled.

Lilya blinked, then smiled back.

Taja exchanged an identical smirk with Jekku.

"Just one thing," Lilya said, turning back to Taja and Jekku. "There's a stop I have to make before we leave, but it'll be quick."

"Actually, we wanted to pick up a few things, too," Taja said. "Do you know of any good clothing shops?"

Lilya wrinkled her nose. "You want to go *shopping*?"

"The goal is to not freeze as we travel the *Urdahl* in this gods-forsaken winter," Taja said. No wonder the gods kept Båthälla warmer than the surrounding forest. Doweth had terrible seasons.

Lilya rolled her eyes. "Fine. You two can go shopping. I'm on a mission for the best Kelish wine in this city. I'll meet you back here in an hour. Deal?"

"There's a tailor's shop four blocks from here, toward the university," Nesma said. "I know the owner; he's my friend's cousin. Tell him I sent you, and he'll probably knock down his prices."

"Perfect," Jekku said. "Thank you."

"One hour," Lilya said as she started to walk away. "Or else I'm leaving without you."

***

One hour and thirty minutes later, Taja and Jekku breathlessly found Lilya in the gardens outside the Queen's Library. She raised an eyebrow, then pointedly looked up at the giant clock on the front of the library.

"In our defense," Taja panted, "Jekku took forever."

"Me? You're the one who said you were done and then went back *three times* to look at something else!"

"You were in the fitting room for *twenty minutes*," Taja pointed out.

"I have very specific tastes, and dresses have a lot of buttons!" he shot back. Then he laughed, still catching his breath. "It doesn't matter, anyway. I told you Lilya wouldn't actually leave without us. She doesn't know where we're going."

Lilya grumbled and shoved her hands in her coat pockets. "Whatever. I see you successfully got new clothes?" She nodded at Jekku's midnight-blue cloak.

He held up the edges and spun around. "Blessedly warm,

surprisingly soft, and most importantly, did not belong to my cheating bastard of an ex-lover."

Lilya exchanged a look with Taja, then snorted. "Well. That's definitely a plus. Taja, yours looks nice, too."

"Oh— Thank you." He ran his hands down the front of the thick wool garment. His was a dark, muted forest green with gold stitching along the edges and a fur-lined hood that would keep his ears from freezing as they traveled. The inside was also lined with the same thick rabbit fur, and Taja barely felt the wind's bite.

"Very fancy," Jekku said with a wink at Taja. "Very dashing."

Taja quickly looked away from Jekku as his face flooded with heat. He cleared his throat and remembered the package in his hands. "We also got this for you." He offered the parcel to Lilya.

"For me?" She blinked, then took the package and unwrapped it. Her eyes widened when she saw the soft fur scarf Jekku had picked out for her. "Oh, wow."

"Do you like it?" Jekku asked.

"I love it." Lilya smiled and ran her fingers through the thick black fur. "You didn't have to do this. But thank you. It's beautiful." She crumpled the paper and stuffed it in her pocket, then draped the scarf around her neck. "Mmm, delightful. So warm."

"Well, now that we're all bundled up, where to, *Sawwia Setukkda*?" Jekku nudged Taja's arm.

He fiddled with the top button on his cloak. This stop in Westdenn had been a nice distraction, especially in the wake of escaping the Labyrinth, but now it was time to get back to business. There was still so much work to be done.

Taja looked at Jekku and Lilya in turn. "To the *Urdahl*."

PART II

INTERLUDE III

ELLORY

GODS WERE NOT SUPPOSED TO DIE.

Ellory knelt on the cold floor of the temple, palms pressed flat to the marble. They trembled, but whether it was with rage or sorrow, they weren't quite sure. They hung their head, letting their curls fall to hide their face as Lord Nokaldir informed everyone gathered that Lord Oridite was no more.

It's not possible, Ellory thought for the millionth time. *He is the God of Darkness. He is the night itself. He is equal in power and strength to Lord Ebris.*

And yet both of them had been killed.

And though Nokaldir and Nedra refused to say the name of their killer, Ellory knew in their bones who was responsible.

They shoved to their feet. Ignoring surprised glances from the gods and the others around them, they stormed across the temple and went upstairs. Once in their chambers, they slammed the door and then pounded their fists against it with a shriek. *"Traitor! Godkiller!"*

How *dare* he? Had seven years in exile taught him nothing? And *how* had he managed to kill a god without magic?

Ellory gasped in a breath. Could it be possible? If Taja Ievisin really was *Sawwia Setukkda*, did that mean he was granted power from the gods? Ellory knew Nedra sympathized with him, since she sympathized with everyone, but if she had lent him power and he had used that power to defeat Oridite...

It seemed there were two traitors in Båthälla.

Ellory shoved away from the door and threw off their temple robe, then strode out of their chambers and back downstairs. They burst into the private chapel and went to the dusty closet on the back wall. Within, they found a robe of bright gold silk — one of Ebris's ceremonial garments for holidays.

Ellory paused, breathing hard as their heart pounded. They ran their fingers over the fine silk. Were they really about to do this? Declare themself against the gods who had protected them all their life? Did this make them just as traitorous as Taja?

No. He wishes to destroy us. I wish to fix us.

Ellory slipped the robe over their shoulders and tied the sash. It was a little long on them — Ebris was exceptionally tall — but they could alter it later. They shut the closet and strode out of the chapel, then entered the main room of the temple with their head held high.

Nedra, who had been in the middle of a sentence, fell silent. Her brows furrowed. Nokaldir's expression darkened. Murmurs rippled across the room.

Ellory met the gods' eyes unflinchingly. "You have both disgraced your village and failed the people you vowed to protect. I serve no god but Lord Ebris. I show my respect to him alone."

They didn't wait for a response. With dead silence in their

wake, they strode across the temple and down the steps. The village square was empty; everyone was either at home for supper or in the temple to pay respects to Oridite, but Ellory went ahead and rang the bell anyway. They let it resound across the village a few times and stood halfway up the temple steps to wait.

Barely a minute had crawled by before people began to show up. A few trickled toward the square from elsewhere in the village, and then a couple dozen more poured out of the temple — Nedra and Nokaldir among them. The gods swept around Ellory and stood before them.

"What is the meaning of this?" Nokaldir demanded. He was dressed in plain black robes — mourning garments — with no jewelry or ornaments of any kind. Like this, he didn't look like a god. Only a man.

Ellory lifted their chin. "Your little popularity contest isn't going to bring the changes this village needs. I know what you're really doing, Nokaldir."

"And who are you to decide what Båthälla needs, Ellory Ives?" Nokaldir growled.

"Who are you to decide, Lord Nokaldir, when we see your face perhaps once a decade?"

Thunder cracked the sky overhead, but Ellory didn't flinch. Nedra set her hand on Nokaldir's arm, then took a step toward Ellory. "My child, listen to me. This is not the way—"

"Save your breath, Lady Nedra," they snarled. "You can't expect to win me over when you can't pick a side yourself. I know what you did to help the traitor."

Gasps and murmurs rippled across the square. Ellory saw a few people start to drift away, and without thinking they shot a burst of flame into the sky. Its explosion of sparks left silence in its wake, and Ellory raised their voice.

"People of Båthälla, it's time to put your foot down." Their voice carried strong and clear across the village. "These gods will not bring us the life we want. *Sawwia Setukkda* is not coming to save us. He is nothing but a myth and a fraud. If you want your magic saved, I am the one you must follow."

"*Lies!*" A familiar voice rang out.

Ellory looked up. Anger burst through their veins. At the other end of the square, Ava stepped out of the trees, surrounded by at least a dozen others — all armed with bows at the ready.

So this is how it's going to be, then? For a heartbeat, grief outweighed their anger. But there was no remorse in Ava's cold glare, and Ellory knew she would shoot them dead without a second thought.

And to think they had once called her their best friend. They could not believe she would betray them like this.

"Being stuck in the past is not the way to move Båthälla forward," Ava declared as she crossed the square. Most of her people hung back, but three flanked her, bows raised and arrows drawn. "I support *Sawwia Setukkda*. He is not a fraud. He has our best interest at heart." Her eyes met Ellory's. "Ellory does not."

Their hands curled into fists. "He's got you tricked. He's got all of you tricked! The boy you call *Sawwia Setukkda* is the reason two of our gods are dead!"

That did it. Outraged voices exploded across the square. Dozens of voices overlapped and shouted over each other and melded together until Ellory couldn't tell what was being said. All they knew was that the people were angry *with* them, not *at* them.

A smile crept across their face. *Good. You should be angry.*

Ellory let the arguing go on for a bit longer, then sent another burst of flame into the sky to silence the crowd. They held up their arms, letting the golden robe flow around them. "If a brighter, freer future is what you want, my people, join me. Renounce your loyalty to gods who would let the traitor see us to our graves. There is only one who loved you and cared for you and kept you safe. Declare your loyalty to me — in Ebris's name — and I will see us toward the future we need. No more cowering. No more hiding. It's time for Elshalans to take their places in history."

"Ellory." Nedra rushed toward them. "Ellory, please. You don't know what you're doing."

They lashed out with a burst of flame and sent her stumbling back. Her eyes widened. Even Nokaldir looked shocked.

Ellory's pulse thundered. They held up their hands, ready to attack again if they needed to. Gods or no gods, they could not back down now.

"Declaring war against the gods." Nokaldir's voice dropped to a dangerous tone. "That's a new low, even for you, son of Ebris." He raised his hands and thunder shook the ground. "But if it's a war you want, Ellory Ives, it's a war you'll get."

Ellory threw back their shoulders. "So be it."

They didn't give Nokaldir a chance to strike first. They strengthened the flames surrounding them, flaring them higher, brighter, hotter. With barely a flick of his hand, Nokaldir brought down a blinding lightning bolt, which Ellory dodged not a moment too soon. They gritted their teeth and lashed back.

Light and heat overtook their senses. Their pulse thundered. Their head throbbed. Magic rushed through them, freer than they ever let it flow. Every damned day was a struggle to keep their magic calm, keep the flames at bay, but now... Now they had no reason to hold back.

They pushed harder. Nokaldir had fallen back, putting a few more feet between himself and Ellory. He continued to shake the ground with white-hot bolts of lightning, but Ellory felt his magic and knew when to dodge. They wrapped themselves in a barrier of flames and hurled burst after burst at Nokaldir, but he deflected their magic easily, like swatting away a fly.

Ellory needed a different approach. They couldn't lose this fight — they *couldn't*. Båthälla was *theirs*. Ebris had promised.

He promised, he promised, he promised.

"Give it up, Ives!" Nokaldir's voice boomed over the rush of fire and lightning. "You're only going to get yourself killed. You are nothing against the strength of a god."

Ellory let out a grunt of frustration and fought their way forward, closer to Nokaldir. The throbbing in their skull grew worse. Their hands shook. Blood dripped from their nose. But they couldn't give up. They had to win.

This is my right. This is my *home.*

Ellory closed their eyes. They felt the blazing heat from their flames, felt the static in the air from Nokaldir's lightning. But beneath that, beneath the tangible effects of each of their magic, Ellory felt the power itself.

They reached, and it responded.

Power flooded them like nothing they'd ever felt. Their veins, their nerves, their bones — everything alighted with a heart-stopping burst of pure energy, and when they opened their eyes again, they saw everything through a faint golden haze.

"You're wrong, Nokaldir." Their voice sounded distant, distorted as if underwater. "I *am* a god."

They pulled on their power again, drawing every thread of it into them. Nokaldir's eyes widened. Ellory felt a tug, then a *snap*, and magic crashed into them in a deafening rush. Their head spun with the sensation of falling, then they hit something hard. Stars popped behind their eyes.

Then it all quieted. The roar of power faded, leaving them warm and trembling with adrenaline. When their vision cleared, they looked up into the wide, terrified eyes of Lady Nedra.

Nokaldir was gone.

Ellory blinked. Energy swarmed within them, restless and edgy. They lifted their hands and tiny sizzles of electricity jumped between their fingers.

"Ellory," Nedra breathed, "what have you done?"

15

TAJA

IT WAS FOUR DAYS before Taja spotted any signs of other Elshalans, and he could tell the others were getting annoyed. Jekku didn't say anything, but Taja saw the way he dragged his feet as they hiked through the snowy woods. He was quieter than usual, and hardly exchanged more than a few words with Taja before the three of them settled in to sleep. But his silence weighed nothing compared to the storm cloud that was Lilya.

Four days of travel had been slow going; they stopped often to rest, seek shelter against the snowy gales that shook the trees and to look for clues. Taja inspected the trees for carvings, studied the forest floor underfoot for signs of frequent activity, even had Jekku and Lilya reach out with their magic to see if they sensed any presence nearby. Elshalan villages radiated magic, but you had to know what to look for in order to feel it. Gods' magic felt different. That much, Taja remembered.

But it wasn't magic or broken stems that alerted him to the presence of a village. It was art.

"Look at this." Taja knelt beside a mossy, hollowed out tree with its roots halfway out of the ground. He gently brushed off some of the ice and dirt, just enough to see the carvings etched in the bark.

Jekku was beside him in an instant. "What is it? Are those symbols? Is it a language? Or just a picture? Is there a message in it? What does it say?"

Taja glanced at him and smiled, but Jekku's attention was fixed on the tree alone. Taja ran his fingers over the carving. "It's a symbol. A little faded with time, but it looks like it used to be a tree branch. See the leaves?" He traced the delicate, curved lines. "Whoever carved this did so with great care. It seems we're about to meet some Elshalans with the touch of life."

"Look over here," Lilya called from a couple trees over. She brushed frost off the bark of a giant, healthy oak whose branches were heaped with snow. "There's more carvings, but this looks more like artwork than messages."

"It could be both," Taja said, joining her. A smile crept across his face at the sight of the beautiful carvings that stretched from the ground up to where the branches split off. Trees, clouds, birds, flowers, ferns and branches and grape vines decorated the bark as if it was a canvas. Taja couldn't imagine the patience and skill it required to render this on a tree.

Jekku appeared at his side and studied the tree with rapt interest. His eyes shone brighter than they had in days. "Whoever did this has a lot of love for the natural world. There's so much care in these carvings. Do you think there's more?" He looked around. "How close are we to the village?"

Taja scanned the trees. The surrounding woods appeared empty, a natural landscape of undisturbed forest, but after a minute Taja recognized the patterns that revealed the presence of paths, buildings, and gardens among the trees.

"We're close," he said. "Let's keep going this way. I'm sure someone will notice us."

Lilya fell into step beside him. "Let's hope they're as friendly as we want them to be."

Jekku walked at Taja's other side and lightly touched his hand. "Taja, if there's nature mages here..." He raised his eyebrows.

Taja shook his head. He didn't dare let himself hope for that chance. Not again. "We'll see. Let's just focus on what we're here for."

They had not taken more than a few steps forward when Taja felt a strong barrier of magic in his path. Jekku and Lilya must have felt it too; they both halted abruptly. Jekku reached out a hand, but Taja didn't register what he was about to do until it was too late and he jumped back with a yelp. He shook out his hand. "It shocked me!"

"What the hell did you think was going to happen?" Lilya said.

"Are you okay?" Taja asked.

Jekku hissed a curse and inspected his hand. It didn't appear injured, but Jekku took several steps back from the invisible barrier.

"How are you so intelligent and yet so stupid." Lilya shook her head.

While they bickered, Taja peered into the woods ahead. The village remained hidden, but Taja heard the distinct sound of aproaching footsteps. He moved a few steps back from the barrier s two Elshalans appeared out of the trees.

Taja looked back at Jekku and Lilya and waved a hand at hem. "Hey. Shush. Look." He jerked his head toward the teadily-approaching Elshalans, and Jekku and Lilya finally qui- ted as the strangers drew close.

They approached cautiously, the taller one in the lead with a hort dagger drawn. Both wore their brown hair long, and their ingular faces were similar enough that Taja guessed they were iblings. They were dressed in thick fur tunics and knee-high oots that crunched over the snow. The one in front had a scar icross his nose that wrinkled as he scowled. "Who are you?"

Taja lifted his hands to show he meant no harm and carried to weapon. "My name is Taja Ievisin. I'm from Båthälla. These ire my friends, Jekku and Lilya. They have seen the Hidden City oefore."

The young Elshalan narrowed his blue eyes. Taja placed him it nineteen, maybe twenty years old. "Why have you come here?"

"It's a long story, and I'll be happy to tell the whole thing, but oasically... we're seeking guidance."

The boy's companion snorted. "You won't find that here."

"Don't start, Mar." He rolled his eyes and sheathed his dagger, then set a hand on his hip. "Don't mind em. Always has to com- plain about something. E's got a whole rant about it, so don't get em started. Anyway, I'll admit you have my attention, Taja of Båthälla. Any neighbor of the Peacebringer is a neighbor of mine." He bowed his head.

Relief washed over him. "Thank you."

The boy smiled. "By the way, which one of you bumped into the barrier?" He raised an eyebrow.

Taja went to translate the question, but Jekku grinned sheepishly and held up his hand. "That was me. Sorry."

Taja frowned. "Wait. You can understand them?"

"Huh?"

Taja looked at Lilya. "Can you?"

"Yes?"

He glanced at the Elshalans, who wore identical smirks. "You've got a translation spell on the village."

"Indeed. Welcome guests are invited to hear us. It seems the forest detects no ill will from the three of you, and in that case welcome to Linvalla." He waved a hand and hummed a tune and the veil lifted. Ahead, a charming town of ivy-covered stone structures wove around the trees in the same way Båthälla did, embracing the forest rather than clearing it. Snow coated the roofs of the houses and the stone paths winding around them. A large building with a domed roof at the center dominated the center of the village, but one thing above all stood out to Taja: there was no temple to the gods.

"My name is Atlas," said the Elshalan who'd greeted them. "This is my sibling, Mar. We're happy to take you to meet our Councilors."

Those words snuffed out the spark of hope Taja had felt at noticing the absence of a temple. Linvalla might not honor gods, but if they still had something like the Council Eternal, maybe it wasn't any more progressive than Båthälla was.

Although, if the Council Eternal was not chained to the will of the gods, perhaps it might actually serve the people. Taja tried not to judge so quickly.

Taja glanced to his left at Jekku, who buzzed with palpable excitement. He looked around the village with wonder, just like he had the first time he'd seen Båthälla. "Hey, can I ask a question?" He left Taja's side and fell into step beside Atlas.

Atlas glanced at him with an amused smirk. "Just one? Because it sounds like you have many but you're trying to appear only casually interested when that is very far from the truth." He laughed and Jekku's face flushed. "But yes, go ahead."

"Are, uh, you a diviner?"

Atlas quirked an eyebrow. "Was that your one question?"

"No, that's an additional question."

"I suppose I'll allow it." Atlas chuckled, and Taja was starting to dislike the way he looked at Jekku. "I am not a diviner. I have the touch of life, specializing in stone and minerals. Just like our beloved Peacebringer." He beamed.

Taja mirrored Jekku's surprise. In the little time Saevel had spent with them, Taja had never thought to ask after their affinity, and Saevel had never mentioned it. The only magic they had done was to show Jekku his history and to help capture the Royal Sorcerers. Neither instance suggested a natural affinity, but Saevel was Elshalan. Of course they had magic.

Taja made a mental note to find out what else these Elshalans of Linvalla knew about Saevel. He couldn't help but wonder if there was more to the Peacebringer's story than what the gods of Båthälla had told.

Mar took off ahead, but Atlas hung back beside Jekku, matching his pace. Taja was all too aware of the way his eyes roved over Jekku, and it settled a bad feeling in his stomach. "What was your other question?" Atlas asked.

"My—Right! My question. Um... Oh! You said you have Councilors. Does that mean— I mean, okay, I don't know a whole lot about Elshalans and I didn't know there were any communities still out there until I met Taja a couple months ago, but from what I've seen, it seems that most towns are ruled by gods with the Council being on the next step down the ladder. Do you— Is that— How does it work here, then?"

Taja wanted to sink into the ground on Jekku's behalf. He knew Jekku had a tendency to ramble when he was excited or nervous, but holy gods.

And to Taja's dismay, Atlas looked positively enamored. "Oh, you're adorable." He bumped Jekku's shoulder and briefly touched his hand to the small of his back. "Stick around for a bit and I'll get you *well* acquainted with Elshalans of Linvalla and how we do things here."

Taja halted. Jekku turned scarlet. Atlas glanced between the two of them and snickered. "Oh, so sorry. Didn't mean to step on any toes. Worth a shot, though." He grinned and gave Jekku a last once-over, then strode ahead to catch up with his sibling.

Taja's ears burned. "Does this happen often? Do you get flirted with everywhere you go?"

Jekku blinked in bewilderment, then looked at Taja and tossed his hair over his shoulder. "What can I say? I'm a catch."

"Yeah, the same kind of catch as a cold," Lilya muttered, and strolled past him to follow Atlas and Mar.

Taja hesitated, but Jekku continued on into the village square, and Taja caught up a minute later. Atlas and Mar intructed them to wait, then they disappeared through the double doors leading into the domed building.

The seconds ticked by in silence. Taja looked around at the quiet town, but his mind was too preoccupied to take in the scenery. Was it even worth it to mention to Jekku how much that had bothered him? It wasn't as though it was Jekku's fault. But why was Taja so surprised that Jekku hadn't taken Atlas's bait?

A hand touched his arm, jolting him out of his thoughts. He found Jekku beside him. "You okay?"

Taja shrugged.

"That was... weird, back there. I'm sorry."

Taja shook his head. "It wasn't your fault."

"No, but I can tell it bothered you."

"It shouldn't." Jekku wasn't even his to lose.

"You know... I kind of like that it did." Jekku glanced up at him and smiled.

Before Taja could manage a reply to that, Atlas and Mar returned. They were accompanied by an older woman with light brown skin and beautiful silver hair that fell in long braids over her shoulders. Her round, brown eyes were bright and friendly, and she beamed a brilliant smile at Taja and the others.

"Welcome! Hello!" She stood before them and folded her hands together. "My name is Ritva, Councilor of Linvalla. My other half is in the woods with her team to investigate some unusual decay patterns we've noticed in our spruces, but I'll be sure to introduce you later. Anyhow! I'm so pleased to have you in our humble little town. May I ask your names and where you come from?"

"Taja Ievisin, of Båthälla," he said. "We appreciate your warm welcome."

"Jekku Aj'ere, of— Well, that's complicated." Jekku let out nervous laugh. "Let's say Ajaphere."

"Lilya Noor, of Aylesbury," Lilya said. Jekku sent her a questioning look, which she ignored, but Taja understood. A hometown didn't necessarily make a home.

"I am so happy to meet you all!" Ritva grinned, and Taja second-guessed whether she was a god, because that smile could have melted the tundra. "What brings you to Linvalla? Atlas told me you seek guidance. What can I provide?"

"It's quite a long story," Taja said. "But we'd like to speak to you about your village. I can't help but notice that you have no temple to the gods."

Ritva nodded. "Indeed we don't. I'm surprised you haven't heard the stories of this infamous village."

Infamous? Taja had never heard of Linvalla, but he wasn't really surprised. "The gods of Båthälla are not keen to share their secrets."

"Hm. No doubt." Ritva pursed her lips. "I'm happy to share our story with you. Why don't you come inside?" She gestured toward the building behind her. "There's fresh tea, and I believe our baker paid us a visit not long ago. I admit I'm interested to hear about Båthälla as well. It has been a very long time indeed since I've spoken with anyone from there. How does the Peacebringer's village fare?"

Taja cringed. "That... is also complicated."

Ritva nodded, understanding. She waved for Taja and the others to follow her through the double doors. "I heard rumors but it's hard to know what to believe when all you hear are whispers."

"Fair enough," Taja agreed. "But whatever you heard, it's probably true."

Atlas and Mar shut the doors behind Ritva, Taja, and the others, and everyone stepped into a bright parlor kept pleasantly warm by a roaring fire. It was furnished with a small sofa, two chairs, and a low table in the middle; Taja, Jekku, and Lilya squeezed onto the couch while Atlas slumped into a chair and Mar settled on the floor next to him. Ritva offered Mar the other chair, but e shook eir head.

"Y'know," Atlas commented, "it's weird to me that the Peacebringer's hometown became the notoriously backward Elshalan village. They were a beacon of change, pretty much started a revolution. Yet Båthälla still has its gods, eh?"

Taja bristled, put off by Atlas's judgmental tone. "Båthälla has been through a lot. The gods have a strong hold on our people. It's hard to imagine what a different future would look like when all they can see is what they've always known."

"Is it true that Lord Ebris is still the patriarch?" Mar asked. "Even after what he did?"

What he did? You'll have to be more specific. "Thankfully... not anymore."

Atlas and Mar exchanged an interested look. "What happened?" he questioned.

Taja glanced at Jekku, then Lilya. *Where to start with this story?*

"The Oracle Stone happened," Jekku said. And with those words, the room silenced.

***

Three cups of tea, half a dozen tiny cakes, and one hour later Taja and the others finished their tale. Taja tried to keep it simple as possible, but the story became increasingly complex with every added layer. Taja told his side, starting with his exile and ending with his return to Båthälla with Jekku. Jekku spoke about the stone and Ebris's lies, and Lilya went into the whole ordeal with the Royal Sorcerers and what they tried to get her to do. Taja had left out all mentions of Saevel being in the picture at all, and he was relieved that Jekku and Lilya followed suit; this town seemed to be particularly reverent of the Peacebringer, and Taja didn't want Saevel's presence to distract from why they were here. Ritva, Mar, and Atlas listened intently and Taja watched the horror deepen in their eyes as the story went on.

It hit him, in the wake of recounting everything the three of them had been through, that what the people of Båthälla had experienced was neither normal nor acceptable. Taja had grown up blinded by Ebris's deceit, and he hated that he'd ever believed a word of it. Now, with everything he knew, it seemed stupid that he'd ever thought Ebris was a kind, forgiving, benevolent god.

Thank the skies Ebris had sent him away from Båthälla to find *Sawwia Setukkda*.

Ritva finished the last of her tea, set the cup down on the table, then sat back and sighed. "Heavens, my friends. I hope you hear my sincerity when I say that I am deeply sorry you've all gone through this ordeal. To be betrayed by one's gods... There's hardly anything worse. You are told to be loyal and trust them

nd they insist they will offer protection and comfort in re-
urn, but when that promise has ulterior motives, or when that
rust gets stretched too thin, you end up at a crossroads." Ritva
rought her palms together, then apart. "In one direction, you
orge your own path with no regard to what these mutinous gods
vant. But in the other direction, you continue to follow blindly.
'orgive me if I'm mistaken, but it sounds like Båthälla has fol-
owed the path of blind faith in gods who no longer serve you."

Taja nodded. "Blind faith, and a stubborn Temple Keeper
vho won't let go of their loyalty."

"I see." Ritva drew her fingers through her silver hair. "Well,
ou can't win over everyone. You will have those who resist, who
lo not wish to see your reasoning. But I can tell you with confi-
lence that banishing our gods was the best decision this village
las ever made. Instead we revere our beloved Peacebringer, who
in their time was indeed a beacon of change and of hope. The
Peacebringer showed us that just because something has always
been does not mean it always must be. And no leader should
have unchecked power over their people, especially not a god as
selfish and malicious as Lord Ebris."

Taja's knee-jerk reaction was to jump to Ebris's defense, and
he had to literally bite his tongue against that foolish reply. Then
his rationality caught up. Ritva was right. Ebris had gone too
long without consequences for smothering Båthälla's magic and
keeping his people in the dark.

"Now that we know your situation, what do you need from
us?" Ritva asked.

Atlas raised his hand. "Can I physically fight Lord Ebris?"

Ritva closed her eyes.

"No, Atlas," sighed Mar. "He's already dead."

"We hope so, anyway," Jekku said. "When we confined th
Royal Sorcerers in the stone, Ebris went with them. We're prett
confident he can't get out."

Taja glanced at him, grateful for the tiny lie but nervous i
wouldn't hold up if Ritva or the others asked any questions. "A
long as the Oracle Stone does not come together again, we'r
safe. I'm curious to know what you did, when you banished you
gods. How did you win?"

"It wasn't easy." Ritva shook her head. "You ought to accep
that right away: this will not be an easy path, but it is a worth
fight. My mother was the one to lead the revolution here in Lin
valla. She was loud, outspoken, and most importantly, she wa
stubborn. She did not give up.

"It took months, but eventually she had the majority of th
town behind her. They stood against the gods, and the combine
magic of nearly every citizen of Linvalla was just enough to de
feat them.

"But it was not merely a battle that led my mother and he
revolution to victory. She won through understanding. Our peo
ple had to see *how* life could be different before they could de
cide whether they wanted it. Change causes fear when it is to
vague or hypothetical. If you want Båthälla behind you, yo
must *show* your people the way their lives could be. Give them
hint of what life without gods looks like."

"How?" Taja didn't see how that was possible. They didn'
trust him, and that added an extra layer of difficulty. He wasn't
fearless, stubborn leader like the woman Ritva described. Unles

Taja brought his whole town here and had Ritva lecture them, he had no idea how to get them behind him.

"The Sky Palace," Jekku muttered.

Taja turned his head. "What?"

"The gods can manipulate the Sky Palace, right?"

"Y-Yes, that's how Oridite created the Labyrinth."

Jekku twisted a strand of hair around his fingers. "We still have one god on our side, don't we?"

The hints clicked together in Taja's head. "Oh! Jekku, you're brilliant. Yes, if we can convince Nedra to create a room in the Sky Palace that shows how Båthälla might be without the gods' influence, that could be the key to convincing everyone else that it's possible. We show them a concrete example. We can show them their futures —— their *real* futures, just like it tried to show us the lives it thought we wanted. That... That's it."

Jekku beamed at him. "See? You have this in you. And you don't have to do it all yourself."

"You know your people better than anyone else," Ritva said. "What are their values? What do they want that they cannot have because of the system in place?"

Taja didn't think he could answer that. He had been apart from his people for so long that he'd lost track of their values. From his angle, he'd just as soon guess that his village was content to live under the gods' heels forever. They'd all agreed with Ebris and the Council's decision to exile him, hadn't they? Taja's sentence wasn't the choice of a few; his neighbors, friends, and family had been there. They'd stood with Ebris instead of with Taja. In his eyes, that was a pretty clear tell of where their values lay.

But Taja tried to think of it objectively. What would he have thought, if the gods declared that one of his neighbors had nearly revealed Båthälla to humans who easily could have been hostile instead of friendly? He would've been terrified. He probably wouldn't have felt safe in his own home until he knew the danger had passed. And yes, he would have wanted whoever was responsible to face consequences.

Not any as harsh or violent as what Taja had faced, of course, but he would not have wanted the culprit to walk away without understanding the weight of what they had done.

Elshalans of Båthälla protected each other. They valued their community, their home, and the safety that came with supporting each other. Båthälla was ancient as the gods themselves; it was a city of history, of tradition, of strong family ties that spanned centuries. It was a city of survival.

Nine hundred years ago, Båthälla had been the heart of a revolution against the Royal Sorcerers who sought to control the world's magic. Now, that heart had to start beating again. Taja had to make his people see that they were facing the very same threat that Saevel had fought centuries ago.

History, it seemed, was on his side.

"I think I know what to do." Taja looked up at Ritva. "It'll take some planning, though. And... just in case it doesn't work, we might need allies. Båthälla's magic is weakened thanks to Ebris, so I'm not sure even our combined power would be enough against the gods."

"The magic here is strong," Lilya remarked, and Jekku nodded in agreement. "Noticeably stronger than Båthälla."

Ritva smiled. "Whatever you need, my friends, you have Linalla's support."

For the first time, Taja felt a real surge of hope. He was not alone.

Jekku set his hand on Taja's arm, and when Taja looked at him he found a fond smile on his face. "You can do this," he murmured. "Vaeltaja the hero."

This time, Taja believed it.

16

JEKKU

WHILE TAJA CHATTED WITH RITVA and met other Elshalans of Linvalla, Jekku occupied his afternoon by poking around Ritva's manor with Lilya.

"I really didn't expect you to come with us," he commented as they strolled down a long, high-ceilinged hallway. Lanterns housing blue mage's fire washed the corridor in a pale tint, as if the space was underwater. "You seemed busy in Westdenn."

Lilya shrugged. She'd left her coat with Jekku and Taja's cloaks in the front foyer of the manor, and now wore a faded burgundy tunic over a gray long-sleeved shirt. Her left hand rested on the hilt of her ever-present dagger.

"There's a lot that has to change in Westdenn," she said. "I'm foolish to think I can fix everything myself. But I'm going to be there for six months, so I might as well make some moves. One of the requirements for moving on to the Queen's Academy is pledging this thing called a Promise Project. It's basically a declaration that you're going to use your training and skills and even-ual position as a Master of Magic to actually make a difference n your community."

Jekku smiled. "Westdenn is going to be your Promise Project, sn't it?"

Lilya met his eyes. "And they're not going to like that."

"Good." Jekku looked around at the brightly lit hallway. Ritva and her partner and the others who helped govern Linvalla clearly lived in comfort here, but Jekku had noticed a row of apartments on the street perpendicular to this building that Mar explained housed visitors, travelers, and anyone else needing a roof over their head who didn't live in the village. That surprised Jekku as much as it shocked Taja; he didn't expect an Elshalan village to let just any traveler into their town.

But Linvalla wasn't Bâthälla. It was not resistant to change.

"I wish none of us had to fight for the right thing," Jekku said. "Why do people put up such resistance to a way of life that is better and happier for everyone? What is so terrifying about making a better world?"

"It's different," Lilya said. "People don't like things that are different. And that's how it's always been — wrong as it is — so rejecting those ideas scares people. You know, a lot of times I think it's because they know they're wrong and don't want to admit it."

Jekku looked at her. "How so?"

"Take Westdenn for example." Lilya gestured at the mage's fire lanterns surrounding them. "Look, that fire's not hurting anyone, is it? The potential is there, of course. If one of those were to break, the fire would grow and spread and damage this part of the building. People might get hurt." She stopped walking and faced Jekku. "But do you know what would do the exact same thing? Normal, natural fire. And you don't see that being outlawed, do you?"

Jekku nodded. "It's not about the magic."

"No." Lilya continued down the hall. "It's about controlling *people*, not magic. But no, we have to hide that truth behind something everyone can agree on. In this instance, it's that fire is dangerous. Fire hurts people. That quickly translates to 'fire *mages* hurt people,' and then there's all the reasoning you need for slapping a bright orange patch on our clothes. It was never about the flames themselves, and they know it just as well as I do. But no, doubling back on the law now would just make them look like fools, so they keep a tight hold on it even though they *know* it's horseshit."

Jekku shook his head. "I wish you didn't have to live with that for six months. Isn't there anywhere else you could do this internship?"

"Nope. Even if there was, I wouldn't want to." Lilya glanced back at him. "I want the bragging rights that come with graduating from the University of Westdenn *and* the Queen's Academy. And I'm going to shake up the foundation of both of them while I'm at it."

Jekku caught up to her and threw an arm around her shoulders. She groaned, but accepted his embrace. He set his chin on the top of her head. "You're going to change the world, Lilya Noor."

She snorted. "Damn right. But hey, so are you." She stepped back from him. "Taja sounds more confident now than he did even in Westdenn. Did you say something to him?"

"No." Jekku smiled. "He got there on his own. And honestly, he needed to. I'm happy to support him, but I can't solve everything for him."

"I don't think he wants you to," Lilya said. "But I can promise you that your support means the world to him."

"Jekku? Lilya?"

They turned simultaneously as Taja's voice echoed down the hall.

"You summoned him," Jekku said.

"As if you're complaining." Lilya elbowed him.

Jekku playfully elbowed her in return, then went to meet Taja. "So what did you learn?"

"Oh, gods, what *didn't* I learn?" Taja rubbed his forehead. "My brain feels stuffed like a pig on a feast day. But honestly, I'm grateful. They told me a lot that I think can help us."

"Taja, that's fantastic! So what's the plan?"

"Well... I still want to talk to Ritva's partner, who I wasn't able to catch when she got back from the woods," Taja said. "So I was thinking we could stay here a little longer and see what else we can learn. It might be good to speak to people who *aren't* Councilors. I want to know what everyday people think of how this town runs."

"Look, you had me at 'stay here,'" Lilya said. "I've had enough of the *Urdahl* for now."

"I've had enough of the *Urdahl* forever," Jekku said. "Did Ritva say where we can stay?"

"Well, I asked her about the apartments around the corner," Taja said. "But she insisted we stay here, in the south wing of the manor. She actually showed me where we'll be, if you want to grab your things and head that way."

"I would love to take a nap, yes," Lilya said. "Lead the way *Sawwia Setukkda*."

Taja smiled. "For the record, you pronounce that far better than Jekku ever has."

Jekku's mouth fell open. "What! That's not fair!"

Lilya punched his arm. "Ten points for Lilya. No points for Jekku."

Taja snickered and headed back the way he'd come. Jekku scrambled to catch up.

"I have pronounced *Sawwia Setukkda* correctly plenty of times! See, I just did it now. What do I have wrong?"

"Firstly, every time you say it, I can *only* hear it in the terrible way you said it when you were drunk in Båthälla that night," Taja said. "But you're too hard on the vowels. Dowethian is a lot heavier than Elshalan. Our language is lighter, more fluid. Let the words float on your tongue instead of trying to pin them down."

"*Sawwia Setukkda*," Jekku said. It didn't sound any different to him.

"Better," Taja said. "You're still strangling those vowels. "And it's *se*, not *sah*. Se-way-e-ae."

Jekku blinked. That was not at all how he'd been saying it. "*Sawwia*." He repeated it the way Taja said it, but it still sounded clunky.

"Good. *Se-tu*— and it gets tricky here, the syllable comes from your throat — *kh-de*."

Jekku tried it. And butchered it. He wheezed a laugh. "I'm

sorry. That was awful. Okay, *Se-tu*— How the hell did you make that sound?"

"And that's why I pronounce it better," Lilya chimed in. "*Sawwia Setukkda*." It came out perfectly, guttural noise and all. "Kelish has similar words. Weird how Elshalans never ventured over the sea and yet your language shares some roots with mine."

Taja shrugged. "Some Elshalans might have wandered out of Doweth. We weren't always hidden and isolated, remember. Back in Saevel's time, we interacted freely with humans."

"*Sawwia Setukkda*," Jekku said, mostly to himself.

"What?" Taja turned to him. "Oh. Oh! You did it!"

"I did?"

"Well, almost. That was close, though."

Jekku grinned. "I sound like a cat hacking up a hairball."

"You do not."

Lilya snorted. "Yeah, he does."

Jekku heaved a sigh. "Will I ever go a day without Lilya Noor being mean to me?"

"You are quite literally the most dramatic person I know."

"It's part of my charm."

"It's part of why you're annoying."

"*Annoying*?" Jekku gasped. "See, you're being mean again."

Lilya rolled her eyes. "Sure."

They returned to the front parlor where they'd met Ritva, gathered their cloaks and bags and shoes, then Taja led the way across the manor toward the south wing. On impulse, Jekku took Taja's hand, and when Taja sent him a curious look, Jekku just smiled.

Taja smiled back and gave his hand a little squeeze.

The long, curving hallway spit them into a massive ballroom that was being actively decorated and set up for some event. People dashed around and climbed up ladders to hang ribbons, banners, and paper lanterns on the stone beams that arched across the ceiling. The walls glowed with gold mage's fire, and a group of five Elshalans carried small trees in from outside.

If anyone noticed the three of them skirting the edge of the room, they didn't stop them. They exited the ballroom and went down a quieter hallway that ended in a circular lounge with four connecting doors on the walls. A fire crackled in the fireplace wedged between two of the doors, and a candelabra on the mantel flickered with blue mage's fire. Four plush chairs sat in a circle around the fireplace, and a vase of black roses decorated a round table in the middle of the circle. It was mostly quiet, save for the distant trickle of running water that Jekku couldn't figure out the source of.

"Ritva said rooms three and four are open." Taja gestured at the numbers on the doors. "She also mentioned that there's a— an indoor hot spring? Which I'm guessing is through those doors there." He nodded at the fogged glass panels to the right. "She said we're welcome to it, so..." He shrugged.

"Nap first," Lilya declared, heading toward Room Four. "Then a hot bath." She went in, tossed her stuff down, then disappeared with a wave.

"Guess that leaves us with Room Three," Jekku said, and opened the door.

His stomach dropped. Oh, of course.

"Is something wrong?" Taja asked behind him.

Jekku turned and pushed the door open wider. "See for your-
elf."

He watched about six different emotions cross Taja's face as
e took in the plain white walls, soft blue rug, and exactly one
ed. "Oh. Um." He glanced back at Jekku. "I... could sleep out
ere? In one of the chairs?"

Jekku just stared at him. "Taja."

"What?" His face turned several shades darker.

"Over the past two and a half months, we have traveled up
nd down the west coast of Doweth, slept in forests, tents, drafty
ooms in inns, a barn, and even a ship. We've been stabbed,
truck by lightning, trapped in a labyrinth of psychological tor-
ure — but sharing a bed with me is what's making you pause?"

"But—"

"I don't bite, Taja." Jekku smirked. "Unless you ask nicely."

He snickered as Taja blushed spectacularly, then slid past him
nto the room. Jekku tossed his bag and his cloak on the bed —
vhich was honestly large enough for three people, let alone two
vho didn't exactly hate each other — and then turned to Taja.
So, hot spring?"

Taja crossed the room and pushed open the curtains to let
ome light in. "I dunno."

"Oh, come on, it'll feel wonderful after freezing our asses off
n the *Urdahl* for half a week." Jekku was already heading out of
he room. "And we deserve a minute to relax. That is simply an
ndeniable fact."

He expected Taja to give in and follow him, but he still hung
·ack. Jekku paused in the doorway. "Hey. What's wrong?"

Taja just shook his head, avoiding Jekku's gaze.

"You can stay here if you want," Jekku said. "I won't make you join me."

"No, it's not that. The spring does sound nice, but..." He looked up at Jekku. "Doesn't it feel irresponsible to— to just ignore everything? Even for half a day? I just— I feel like we're wasting time. We're wasting so much time. We have no idea what's going on in Båthälla, Ellory could be wreaking havoc, they could've turned everyone against me by now, and— we don't even have a real— a real plan."

He gasped, pressing a hand to his mouth, and Jekku darted over to him. "Hey. Hey. Taja, look at me." Jekku took his hands. "Look at me. Take a deep breath."

It took him a few tries, but he managed it. Jekku had never seen him like this, clutched by a storm of anxiety, but he didn't blame him. He had so much on his shoulders. Jekku wished there was a way he could help Taja carry it.

"That's it," Jekku murmured as Taja's breathing calmed. He squeezed his hands, then let go and touched Taja's cheek. "Hey. You're okay. Remember, you're not alone in this. Right now, our focus is on *making* a plan so we can return to Båthälla ready to stand up to Ellory and the other gods. We're not wasting time. We're doing everything we can."

Taja took another deep breath and nodded. "You're right. You're right. I'm sorry."

"You don't have to apologize."

"It's just— it's so much, Jekku." He quickly wiped his cheek as a tear escaped from his eye. "I don't know how Saevel did this. It doesn't feel real that I have to do it myself. I wasn't— I'm not the right person for this."

Jekku didn't know how to tell him that he was. He didn't know how to get Taja to see that it was his humility and his optimism and his hope for a kinder world that made him the *perfect* person to lead this fight. Jekku could easily say all of that, but what would make Taja believe it?

Jekku took his arm and pulled him toward the bed, then had him sit down. Taja leaned against him and set his head on his shoulder, and Jekku wrapped an arm around him. "Do you think Saevel thought they were right for this, when it was their fight?"

Taja shook his head. "I know they didn't."

"And look at this history they made," Jekku said.

"But that's the thing, Jekku." Taja sat up and turned to him. "I don't care about making history. I'm not doing this because some prophecy said I'm a legendary savior. The only reason I'm still fighting is because a loud voice in my head is desperately begging me to put an end to the gods' cruelty. To make sure no one else suffers what I did, and what your father did. My people and my family deserve better, and I— I want to be part of that. I want to show them that I can do something good for us. But..." He sniffed. "I don't know if we can actually win."

Jekku didn't know that either, but he wasn't about to say it. He grasped Taja's hands again. "When we collected the Oracle Stone and faced Firune and the others, did you think we were going to win that?"

Taja shrugged. "I had... doubts."

"Of course you did. So did I. I was *terrified*. Even when we had our plan and knew what we had to do, I was convinced something would go wrong. That Lilya would turn on us, or the Sorcerers would be more powerful than we expected, or Firune would destroy the stone before we could steal it back. There were so many things that could have gone wrong that night, but they *didn't*. And we won. We're still here. That means something."

Taja nodded absently.

Jekku nudged him. "It does. It means that this isn't impossible, and if we can win against four Royal Sorcerers *and* a god, we can win against two gods and some grumpy Elshalans. Look at it this way: Nedra, we know, is on our side. So she's not a problem. And Nokaldir also wants Båthälla to change, just in a different way. Ebris and Oridite are out of our way, and now we just have to reason with the two remaining."

"Jekku, the gods are the least of my worries," Taja said. "It's Ellory who's going to make our lives hell."

He gripped Taja's hand tighter. "Leave Ellory to me. You focus on winning over everyone else. Now come on, that spring is calling our names. You need it, and you deserve it."

"Jekku..." Taja protested, but Jekku dragged him to his feet.

"Nope, come on." Jekku tugged his hands and Taja tripped forward; Jekku caught and steadied him just in time. He looked up at Taja's face, at his warm brown eyes, at his curled lashes that brushed the faint freckles on his cheeks. Jekku became suddenly conscious of how close they were, of his hands on Taja's arms and Taja's hands on his waist. Jekku flicked a glance down at Taja's lips, then cleared his throat and drew away.

Taja blinked and dropped his gaze to the floor. "Um— All right. I give in. Hot spring."

Jekku led the way across the circular room and through the frosted glass doors. There, he met a sudden barrier of heat. "Whoa."

"What is it?" Taja stopped behind him.

The room was stifling, the air dense with humidity and louded with steam. A large round pool, no more than three or our feet deep, occupied most of the floor. Dark wood walls kept he space hot and dim with a pleasant, soft light that glowed rom spherical lanterns spaced around the perimeter. A metal helf holding folded towels stood to Jekku's left, and to the ight, three curtained cubicles had been sectioned off as chang-ng rooms.

Jekku stepped farther into the room and immediately wished o be free of his clothes. He gathered up his hair and tied it in a un on the top of his head, then pushed up his sleeves, but it did ittle good.

"Oh, gods." Taja let the doors shut behind him. "Why would I vant to get into a hot pool when it's already sweltering in here?"

"The water's probably hotter." Jekku peeled off his socks and lipped a toe into the steaming pool. He instantly jumped back vith a hiss. "Ah. Yeah. Very hot."

"Here." Taja handed him a folded black garment that Jekku ound to be light and silky. "These were on a shelf with the tow-ls. I guess they're to wear in the pool."

Jekku held up the flowy robe. It was sleeveless, would fall to bout his knees, and folded over the chest and tied at the waist. The black material ran like liquid over his hands. "And here I hought we'd be seeing a lot more of each other." He flashed Taja grin.

Taja rolled his eyes and turned away, but not before Jekku aw his face darken. He smirked to himself and went to change.

The dressing booth was a bare square of white walls, one of

which provided a bench and another of which bore a full-siz
mirror. Jekku undressed and dropped his clothes on the bench
then slipped the light robe on and tied the sash. The robe im
mediately slid off his shoulders, but he didn't care. It wasn't th
worst thing in the world for him to show some skin in front o
Taja.

He glanced over his reflection once more, then stepped ou
of the booth. Taja was already seated by the pool with his fee
in the water, head tipped back, and eyes closed. Jekku paused
second — not to *ogle*, just to *observe*. His brown curls fell loos
over his shoulders, which were left mostly bare due to the wa
he'd tied his robe. Jekku was more than a little distracted by th
subtle muscles in his arms, but even more notable than that wa
the calm expression on his face. The worry had smoothed from
his brow, the tension had eased from his jaw. A faint smile ever
touched his lips.

Jekku made himself look away after too many silent seconds
He joined Taja by the pool and sat beside him, this time testin
the water more carefully. Instead of a harsh bite, it was pleasan
and soothing.

"You were right," Taja murmured. He turned his head towar
Jekku, a sleepy smile on his face. "I did need this."

Jekku held his gaze a little longer than was probably neces
sary; Taja was the first to look away. He rolled his shoulders, the
slid into the pool and seated himself on the bench that curve
around the inside. He set his elbows on the edge of the pool an
leaned his head back.

Jekku slid a little closer to him. He wished he could relax, bu
something about seeing Taja like this — this specific shade c

vulnerability — set him on edge. Not in a bad way, more like he was hesitant to speak too loudly or move too suddenly lest the spell break.

Besides, it was easier to sit in comfortable silence than to acknowledge the clouds hanging over their heads.

He knew they had to talk about the Labyrinth eventually, but honestly, with everything else that had happened, it almost seemed unimportant. Båthälla should be the focus, not whatever was going on between him and Taja.

But no matter how many times Jekku tried to tell himself that, his thoughts inevitably wandered back to Taja, to Westlenn, and the Labyrinth.

Maybe that was what made him hesitate to fully commit. Taja's incorrect guess during that test had shattered Jekku's trust in him. It'd been a harsh awakening that reminded Jekku that Taja didn't know him as well as he thought. And in the wake of what Leo had done, Jekku refused to lend his heart before he had trust.

But gods damn it, it was hard to wait. Especially when Taja looked at him like he did.

How will you know? questioned a voice in his mind that sounded suspiciously like Lilya. *What does trust look like? What does it feel like?*

Jekku couldn't answer that.

So maybe it wasn't about trust. If he didn't trust Taja he wouldn't be here now.

Maybe it just came down to Jekku being afraid.

But was that such a bad thing? He didn't want his heart broken again. He didn't want to dive before he knew how to swim.

Leo was the only thing close to a real partner Jekku had ever had, and even then he wasn't *really* a partner. They were lovers and it was never more serious than that. Jekku was used to the low threshold of minimal or nonexistent commitment that came with flings and one-night-stands. He did not know how to shape a real relationship.

But he wanted this. He wanted to give the two of them a chance. He— Gods, he couldn't remember the last thing he'd wanted this badly.

So maybe he didn't need to dive in. Maybe this — like the hot water before him — required slow, gradual steps to avoid getting burned.

Jekku felt a touch on the side of his leg that startled him back to the present. He found Taja smiling up at him. Moisture clung to the wispy curls around his face, and his cheeks were flushed from the heat.

"Coin for your thoughts?" Taja gently traced his finger over the soft fabric that had pooled around Jekku's legs. Jekku felt a spark under his skin each time Taja's fingers touched his thigh.

He then realized that Taja had asked him a question. "Um— Nothing."

"You look..." Taja tilted his head. "I don't know, but you're not relaxed. Come here, get in the water."

It did seem nice. Jekku slid in and sat beside Taja, submerging up to his shoulders. He let out a sigh as the warmth seeped into his skin.

Taja lifted himself out of the pool and slid over until he was behind Jekku. Jekku eyed him curiously. "What're you doing?"

"Shhh. Just relax." Taja set his hands on Jekku's shoulders. "You're so tense. Relax your shoulders."

With Taja's warm, strong hands on him, relaxing was the last thing Jekku could do. Every one of his nerves was on alert, and even when he consciously lowered his shoulders, the tension didn't ease.

"Better." Taja slid his hands closer to Jekku's neck and gently squeezed. He made a displeased noise at the knots in his muscles, then worked his hands harder.

Jekku sighed and tipped his head forward. Taja's hands made their way from the base of his neck out to the tops of his shoulders, easing out the knots and tension. But he was almost too gentle, and when his hands moved back to a stubborn knot near Jekku's neck, he gasped, "*Harder*."

Taja's breath caught. "What?"

Jekku stared at the water for a second as warmth crept up the back of his neck. "Um. I— I just mean— You don't have to be that gentle. You won't hurt me. That feels great."

Taja squeezed his shoulders, and Jekku leaned his head back with a quiet groan. "You like it a little rough, then?" Taja murmured.

Jekku had a distinct feeling they were no longer talking about shoulder massages.

Taja smoothed his hands over Jekku's skin, then pressed harder into Jekku's muscles. Jekku couldn't hold back another quiet noise. It *did* hurt, but in a good way. He felt lighter. Heat danced over his skin — and not just from the water.

"How's that?" Taja asked, working back up to Jekku's neck. He slid his fingers up to his hairline and into his hair, where he worked them across his scalp. He carefully freed Jekku's hair from its bun and let it fall, then carded his fingers through it.

Jekku could only respond with a heavy, content sigh. He let his head fall back into Taja's hands and closed his eyes while his mind wandered ever closer to that bed they were going to have to share.

Well, that wasn't going to be a problem if Jekku had anything to say about it.

Taja moved his hands to Jekku's temples and gently massaged, then drew his fingers all the way through his hair. Jekku shivered, and before he could think about what he was doing, he twisted around and pushed himself up so his face was inches from Taja's.

He let out a shaky breath. Taja's lips parted.

Then the doors burst open.

Jekku jumped back too fast and slipped, earning himself a dunk underwater. When he surfaced, coughing, he found Lilya in the doorway, looking simultaneously mortified and smug.

Several beats passed. Water dripped down Jekku's face. Taja had gone rigid. Jekku scrambled for something clever to say, but then Lilya blinked, shook her head, and took one long step out of the room.

"Carry on."

Jekku darted a glance to Taja, who was staring pointedly at the water. Jekku dragged his hands through his hair, wrung it out, then loudly cleared his throat. "So. Uh. Dinner?"

Taja raised his eyebrows. "What?"

"I'm starving, aren't you? I think it's time for dinner." Jekku climbed out of the pool and went to the towels as quickly as he could without slipping. He grabbed one, wrapped it around himself, and made for the doors.

What the hell was I thinking?

Taja stared after him. "Jekku..."

He didn't wait to hear the rest. The frosted doors shut with a click that stabbed a fresh barb of guilt through Jekku's heart.

17

TAJA

"YOU FORGOT YOUR CLOTHES." Taja dropped them on the bed, where Jekku was struggling to get a comb through his hair. He was dressed in a loose white shirt and cotton trousers he'd apparently found in this room. His cheeks reddened a little when he looked up at Taja.

"Oh. Thanks." He hissed and pulled at a stubborn knot.

"Do you...?" Taja didn't really know what to say. He was still processing what had happened in the hot spring. His heart hadn't stopped pounding.

"No." Jekku threw down the comb and tied his damp hair up in a bun. "There."

"That's just going to make the tangles worse," Taja said. "Come here." He sat beside Jekku and pulled his hair out of its bun, then gently ran his fingers through it and worked out the knots. Jekku closed his eyes and clenched his jaw, but didn't protest.

Taja picked up the comb and set to work, but after a few minutes the silence became unbearable. He wanted this simple,

omewhat intimate activity to feel normal and casual, but in
ruth it was far from it. He was conscious of his hands trembling
s he combed them through Jekku's hair, he became uncomfort-
bly aware of his pulse, and he tensed every time Jekku moved or
witched. Then Jekku looked up at him, and he forgot to breathe.

"Taja."

He blinked. "Hm?"

A smile touched the corner of his lips. "I think you got all the
angles."

Taja realized then that his fingers no longer met resistance
vhen he drew them through Jekku's hair. The black strands ran
moothly over his hands, soft as silk. Taja quickly pulled away.
'Oh. Guess I did."

Jekku's smile edged toward a smirk. His eyes shone. "Bit dis-
racted?"

Taja shook his head and got up. "Did you really want to get
something to eat? We could ask Ritva what's going on in the ballroom. At the very least they might have food."

Jekku tossed his hair over his shoulder. "Are you asking me to
a ball?"

Taja could not put up with this teasing much longer. He met
Jekku's eyes. "You know what? Yes. Yes, I am. Get dressed. We're
going to a party."

Jekku looked shocked for half a second, then beamed. "Say no
more."

* * *

It turned out that a grand dinner party in the manor's ball-

room was something Ritva and her partner hosted every week
just for fun. They invited anyone and everyone in Linvalla to join
them for a casual, friendly meal, and then musicians stole the
night away with lively tunes and energetic dances.

Taja had invited Lilya, but she'd turned him down, complain
ing of a stomach ache. So that left him and Jekku, dressed like
royalty, to enjoy the evening.

Taja had been content to wear his normal clothes to the din
ner — Ritva *had* said it was casual, after all — but Jekku refused.
His simple question of what they should wear led to Ritva ask
ing Mar to help Taja and Jekku choose something they liked, and
then thirty minutes later they stepped into the ballroom dressed
in finer threads than Taja had ever worn.

It was as if they'd found themselves guests of the queen. It
baffled him.

Nevertheless, Taja felt more confident than he had in a long
time. He wore a floor-length emerald robe with long sleeves,
gold trim, and a soft coil of gold silk around his waist. Ritva
had gifted him a new pair of earrings the same deep shade as
the robe, and he even agreed to an evergreen wreath in his hair.
Dressed like this, he almost felt invincible.

Not to mention, having Jekku on his arm was quite the boost
of confidence as well. He was stunning in a deep maroon gown
that hugged his waist and flowed behind him in a long train. Del
icate white beads decorated the top of the bodice that curved
across his chest, and he wore matching white pearls around his
neck. He'd also apparently let Mar pierce his ears while Taja was
getting ready, because he wore a tiny diamond on one lobe and

wo gold rings on the other. The whole look was more feminine han Taja had ever seen Jekku dress, but it suited him.

They'd entered the ballroom with heads held high, and then aughed and chatted their way through a plentiful meal of roasted pig and about eight different soups. At least a dozen people had brought fresh loaves of bread, and a dozen more supplied desserts.

Not to mention the wine. There was so much wine, and it cheerfully floated up and down the table all through dinner.

By the end of the meal, Taja felt like he couldn't move. He couldn't remember the last time he'd eaten so much in one sitting. But after what seemed like endless weeks of traveling on a near-empty stomach, he welcomed the indulgence. He was especially not about to turn down the desserts.

Almost as soon as everyone was done eating, the musicians started up their songs. A cheer went up across the room, and half the table leapt to the dance floor. Taja hesitated, but Jekku stood up and held out his hand.

"Come on, now. You can't invite me to a ball and not ask me to dance." He smiled, and Taja took his hand and followed him to the floor.

"You know, it's not *technically* a ball," Taja pointed out. He and Jekku lingered on the sidelines while everyone else waited for the dance to begin.

"It's close enough," Jekku said. He glanced up at Taja. "Don't you want to dance?"

"I... do, I'm just not great at it." Taja nervously watched the others on the floor begin the steps as the musicians launched into an upbeat song. "I wouldn't want to step on your toes."

Jekku rolled his eyes and tugged Taja onto the floor. "Come on, we'll figure it out as we go. Clearly you didn't have enough wine."

"Clearly you had too much." Taja laughed as Jekku spun around and then stepped close to him. He glanced around at the other dancers, then copied their positions with one hand clasped with Taja's and the other on his shoulder. Taja lightly set his other hand on Jekku's waist.

"Just follow my lead." Jekku swept them across the floor turning and spinning and stepping in perfect time with the other dancers. Taja did his best to keep up, but just when he thought he had it, he'd move his foot too fast and step on Jekku's toes again.

"Gods, I'm sorry," he muttered, watching their feet. Both of them wore soft, flat-soled slippers, so his missteps probably didn't hurt *that* much, but still.

"Don't look at your feet," Jekku said. "Look at me. If you watch your steps, you'll overthink it. Besides, the prettier view is up here." He grinned.

Taja laughed softly. He certainly agreed. "You do look stunning, Jekku."

He blinked a few times, then smiled. A warm flush colored his cheeks. "So do you."

Taja's heart skipped. "I do?"

"Oh, come on, don't be so modest." Jekku's smile softened. The lights overhead reflected in his eyes. "You're beautiful."

Taja's heart flipped over. Here was Jekku — lovely, elegant Jekku — dressed like royalty in a gorgeous gown, calling *Taja* beautiful?

Jekku gave him an odd look and swept them across the floor in a circle. "I can't tell if you're humble or genuinely oblivious."

Taja glanced down at the floor. "I don't— I mean, thank you. That— That means a lot, coming from you." He briefly met Jekku's eyes. "But it's not something I think about."

"Well, I certainly do." Jekku drew him close, sliding his hand around to Taja's back. "And I can't really believe I'm dancing with you right now." He let out a short laugh. "This is so strange, isn't it?"

Taja had a feeling that all that wine Jekku had drank was finally hitting him. "Do you want to stop?"

"Stop?" Jekku's eyes widened. "No! Do you?"

"No." In all honesty it was the last thing Taja wanted. He slid his hand up a little higher on Jekku's side. "Not at all." He glanced at the musicians as they brought the current song to a close. "In fact... let's dance another."

Jekku grinned. "Do you know this one?"

"I'm sure I can learn." Taja looked around at the others on the floor and copied their positions like Jekku had. He slid both his hands around Jekku's waist, but hesitated. "Jekku, is this okay?"

He responded by snaking his arms around Taja's shoulders. Taja stilled; his breath caught. Jekku slid one hand up the back of his neck and into his hair, and Taja had to stop himself from tipping his head down. Jekku was so *close*. Taja could all but count his eyelashes.

"Taja," Jekku breathed, "the dance has started."

"Huh?" Taja blinked and realized he was staring at Jekku's lips, and quickly darted his eyes up. His face burned. Having Jekku this close to him was dangerous as much as it was thrilling.

He longed for this, but he also knew that having this glimpse – this tease — would only make the waiting worse.

"This one is easy," Jekku said. He kept his voice soft, feather light. "Just four drifting steps. One-two, three-four."

Taja didn't know how Jekku was paying attention to any thing. Did he not also feel this— this energy? This static between them? Or maybe he did, and the dance was his way of distracting himself so he didn't give in.

Taja broke his gaze and studied the tiny beads stitched into Jekku's dress. He needed something to fill the air, *anything* to lessen the heavy tension. Hesitantly, he glanced back up to Jekku's eyes. "Can I ask you something?"

"Anything." The lights overhead shone in Jekku's eyes. A faint blush colored his cheeks, and the gentle smile on his lips pulled at Taja's heart.

Taja slid his hand down to Jekku's hip, palm skimming over soft silk. "Does this... When you dress like this, do you... feel more like yourself?"

"Sometimes." Jekku tipped his chin up. "Tonight, yes. It's not often I get to dress up like this, so when I do, it's a chance to fully present a side of me that isn't always practical. I'm not about to run all over the west coast of Doweth in a dress. But for a party? Absolutely. It's refreshing to enjoy myself like this and make everyone who looks at me do a double take." He grinned. "I want them to think, 'I'm not sure what to call that person but they are stunning.' And I want them to be jealous of the one who gets to dance with me."

Warmth bloomed across Taja's face. He pulled Jekku a little

closer and leaned close to his ear. "They should be jealous. I wouldn't trade this — or you — for the world."

He closed his eyes for a moment and took in a deep breath. Something sweet and flowery clung to Jekku's hair and filled Taja's nose, tempting him closer. While they drifted across the floor, Taja let his mind wander down every possible path this evening could take. He saw Jekku pause their dance and pull him down for a kiss. He saw himself giving up restraint at the end of this dance and pressing his lips to Jekku's with every ember of want that burned in his chest. He saw Jekku dragging him out of this room and stumbling back to theirs, closing them in while barely able to keep their hands off each other.

"Taja?"

He jolted back to the present. Heat bloomed across his face. Daydream over; Jekku was eyeing him oddly again. He cleared his throat. "Sorry. What?"

"I asked what you were thinking about," Jekku murmured. "Because you keep looking at me like that, and it's almost as intoxicating as the wine."

Taja adjusted his hands on Jekku's waist and held him a little tighter. "If either of us is intoxicating, Jekku, it's you."

"Me?" Jekku blinked. "Oh, so *I'm* what's distracting you? It's *me* who's got you so enthralled?"

Taja knew he was teasing, but all the same. "Of course it's you." He brought one hand up and touched Jekku's chin. "It always has been."

Jekku's smirk faded. His eyes flicked down Taja's face and he sighed. "Taja..."

His heart thumped. "Hmm?"

But then the music came to a close and the dance ended and everyone clapped and the world snapped back into focus. Taja darted a step back, lifting his hands from Jekku's waist, and reality rushed back.

Gods, what am I doing?

He let out a breath. "I'm sorry. That— I——"

Jekku looked surprised, a little dazed, but he blinked a few times and flickered a smile. "I think it's time to call it a night, yeah?"

Taja nodded, but he knew that no matter what either of them said, that bed was about to be entirely too small.

***

Taja couldn't sleep. Maybe because of the wine he'd drank at dinner, maybe because his heart still raced in the wake of that dance, and maybe because Jekku was, in fact, sleeping less than a foot away from him. Whatever the reason, he lay in the cloud-soft bed in a room that wasn't his and his eyes refused to stay closed. Restless energy thrummed through him, and Jekku's proximity did not help.

But mostly it was this town. Taja couldn't put his finger on it, but Linvalla *felt* different than Båthälla. It could have been his imagination, but Taja swore he felt the town's magic. It wasn't struggling to breathe here; it thrived.

Earlier, Ritva had answered every question Taja could think of and then supplied more information about her village than Taja would've thought to ask. But now he wondered something else: did every Elshalan village have a source of magic? Or was

he White Lily exclusive to Båthälla as a means of controlling its
)ower and its people?

Taja rubbed his eyes, longing for sleep. He and Jekku and
_ilya were supposed to leave tomorrow to seek out the next clos-
·st village, but the question of magic held Taja back. That would
)e the key to freeing Båthälla, and he couldn't leave without
<nowing how Linvalla's magic functioned.

Taja glanced at Jekku beside him, but he was undoubtedly
ιsleep. His shoulders steadily rose and fell with his quiet breaths,
ιnd he didn't even twitch when Taja carefully got up from the
)ed. He adjusted the blankets to cover Jekku's bare shoulder,
hen padded out of the room.

He did not expect to find Ritva in the lounge. She sat in one
)f the plush chairs, book in her lap and a steaming mug in her
wrinkled hands. She smiled at Taja and did not appear the least
)it surprised to see him. "Hello there."

"Um." Taja awkwardly cleared his throat. "Sorry, I didn't
mean to... I just needed to clear my head."

"Can't sleep?" Ritva gave a sympathetic smile. "Is there a way
[can make your stay more comfortable?"

"Oh, no." Taja shook his head. "Nothing like that. There's
just... a lot on my mind."

Ritva gestured to the chair opposite hers. "Sit, then. Let's
:alk."

Taja hesitated. "It's the middle of the night. I shouldn't im-
pose."

"Nonsense." She waved a hand. "We shall find company in
our insomnia. I can't blame you. These are troubling times, my
friend, and not just in Båthälla. I didn't wish to mention this ear-

lier, but you should know that you were not the only ones af fected by the Oracle Stone's awakening. We felt it here. Strang magical happenings. Affinities being lost, altered, and regained. She shivered, then sipped her beverage. "I am grateful that yo and your friends managed to subdue that threat. Our worl would have suffered if the Royal Sorcerers had gotten thei hands on that stone."

Taja watched the fire's embers flicker. The south wing of th manor was silent but for the gentle crackle of burning wood an soft trickle of water from the next room. "It was such a close cal If not for the Peacebringer's spell, I don't know that we would'v won."

Ritva hummed. "I am curious to know where you acquire such an ancient and powerful spell."

Maybe it was time to tell the truth. Taja looked at Ritva. "Th Peacebringer came to us. They woke with the Oracle Stone an acted as a guide — an ally." Taja would even go so far as to sa friend. "They taught us the spell that let us win."

Ritva's dark eyes widened. She sat up straighter, then set he mug down and pressed a hand to her mouth. "Truly? They ap peared to you?"

Taja nodded.

"My boy, then you are truly blessed." Ritva reached for hi hand and squeezed. "The Peacebringer chose you. That is of ut most significance. Indeed, you are *Sawwia Setukkda*."

Taja winced. "I'll feel better about that title once I hav Båthälla under control. And... actually, I wanted to ask yo something. Back home, we have—"

"—ing damn it, just what I need."

Taja startled at the familiar sharp voice, and turned his head just as Lilya wrenched her door open and stepped out of her room. She squinted in the dim light, looking like she was still half asleep, and had one hand pressed to her stomach like she was sick.

Taja stood up. "Are you okay?"

She waved a hand and slumped against the doorframe, which doubled Taja's concern. "Ritva... thank the saints. Do you have—" She groaned and squeezed her eyes shut, and Taja feared she was about to vomit. "Do you have h-honey leaf?"

Whatever that was, Ritva was apparently familiar. She got to her feet and went to Lilya. "Honey leaf? Oh, dear, I'm afraid not. It's hard to come by out here." She pressed the back of her hand to Lilya's cheek and pursed her lips. "Monthly?"

Miserably, Lilya nodded.

Taja blinked. *Oh. That.*

Ritva *tsked*. "I don't have honey leaf, but give me a moment and I'll get you something else. Have you ever tried dandetta seeds?" She scarcely waited for Lilya to shake her head no before she went on. "I've got a bunch stocked. Come sit and I'll be right back." She guided Lilya over to the chair she'd just vacated, then hurried off.

Taja occupied himself by intently studying the whorls in the wood of the table.

Lilya snorted. "I'm not going to burst into flames, you know."

He glanced at her. "Historically, you do have a habit of doing that."

She pulled a pillow out from beneath her and threw it at him.

He caught it and eyed her skeptically. "Is this why you didn't feel well earlier?"

"Ugh, yes." Lilya rubbed her belly. "I've felt weird all day, and now I know why. This is what I get for missing one dose of honey leaf tea. I blame Jekku."

Taja snorted. "Why?"

"Because I can." Lilya smirked. "And also because I can't exactly make tea while we're camped out in the *Urdahl*. So you know what? I blame you, too."

Taja smiled. "I am deeply sorry for causing you this much pain."

"You should be." She grimaced and hissed a curse. "Remember when you got struck by Jekku's magic?"

"Yes, vividly."

"Right, so this" — she pointed at her stomach — "easily hurts more than that."

Taja didn't really think that sounded right, but how would he know?

Lilya raised her eyebrows. "Don't believe me? I could stab you in the stomach, and you might get an idea."

"And I would also die," Taja said.

"Right, I said I *could*, not I *would*."

Ritva swept back into the room then, and went straight to Lilya. She dropped two tiny white seeds into Lilya's palm, then handed her a cup of water. "Make sure you chew the seeds as much as possible," she instructed. "Then drink that whole cup. The seeds are quite salty, and getting dehydrated will only make you feel worse."

Lilya tossed back the seeds. They crunched between her teeth. "Ritva, thank you."

"Of course, love. Do you need anything else? Some tea? A heat pack? Something to help you sleep?"

Lilya shook her head and sipped the water. "I'll be okay. Thank you again." She got up from the chair and headed back to her room. The door shut behind her with a soft click.

"Poor girl," Ritva murmured. "But alas, that's why we're always prepared here! Anyway..." She turned back to Taja and folded her hands together. "What were you going to ask me, my dear?"

An involuntary shudder ran through him at those words, and for a sliver of a second Taja swore it was Ebris speaking to him rather than Ritva. Her dark brown eyes flashed gold, her soft features turned hard and broad, her kind smile turned menacing. Then Taja blinked and she was herself, and he was left with a chill and a pounding heart.

He took a deep breath. *Next time, take it easy with the wine.*

"Taja? Everything all right?"

"Yeah." He shook his head. "Sorry. Um, what I was going to say is that in Båthälla, the gods teach that our magic is sourced from an enchanted flower called the White Lily. And right now, it's nearly dead." He held out his hands so Ritva could see the scars. "I haven't been able to feel magic in seven years, but I know that Båthälla feels *off*. The way my friends described it is that it feels like the whole town is under a glass dome, and soon, everyone will run out of air."

Sadness creased Ritva's face. She took Taja's hands and

smoothed her thumbs over the backs. "Dear stars above. I am s◦ sorry. This is..."

"I know." He took his hands back and clasped them betwee◦ his knees. "But I've made my peace."

Or so he told himself.

Ritva searched his eyes. "Forgive me for being so blunt, Taj◦ but if your gods did this to you, then they have no right to thei◦ divinity. They had no right to use their power against you in suc◦ a way."

You think I don't know that? Taja swallowed the retort. Sud◦ denly, he just wanted to go to bed. "Try telling that to them."

"If only I could." She pressed her lips together. "But that's u◦ to you, I'm afraid."

Taja rubbed his temples. "How do you usurp a god? Let alon◦ two?"

Ritva leaned forward in her seat and grasped Taja's hand◦ again. "One step at a time. Start with what you asked me a mo◦ ment ago. The White Lily? I don't wish to offend you, but tha◦ is a myth. If anyone is suffocating Båthälla, it is the gods, not a◦ enchanted flower. I hesitate to believe it holds any real power; a◦ most, it could be a conduit."

"That's sort of what I thought. The gods must channel ou◦ magic through the Lily and act like that's all there is." Taj◦ shrugged. "Tell a story for enough generations, and it become◦ truth."

"No." Ritva waved a finger. "It just becomes a widely-believe◦ lie. This does not make it true."

Taja rolled those words over in his head. How many fals◦

truths had the gods fed Båthälla? What even was there to believe anymore?

One step at a time.

"So what happened?" he asked. "You told me about the revolt your mother led against the gods, but you never said what led up to it. What was the final straw for Linvalla?"

"Oh... that's complicated." Ritva sat back in her chair and folded her hands together on her knee. "There was a time when our magic flourished. Our people were happy. The gods took care of us. From a distance, life in Linvalla seemed perfect. But then the gods turned careless. They took after the greed of humans and became obsessed with opulence. They wanted Linvalla to compare to the humans' royal city. They even built themselves a palace — practically on the backs of their own people. And suddenly Linvalla wasn't a community but a hierarchy, and those with less suffered at the hand of those with more. But when you kick a dog enough times, my friend, it's bound to snap and fight back."

Taja nodded, absently watching the embers die in the fireplace. Was it possible that he had more allies than he originally thought? Surely there had to be some disgruntled people in Båthälla who were sick of having weak magic. He'd gotten so used to his people being against him that he'd never considered the idea of some standing behind him. But he worried that he'd ruined all his chances with that disastrous return to Båthälla.

What went wrong that day? Why did Taja lose control of the situation?

Ellory. They might not be the entire reason, but they were part of it. Taja's real mistake was seeded in his lack of confidence, but Ellory drove it home. If Taja didn't believe what he was saying, how could his people?

Sawwia Setukkda. It was time to act the part.

18

JEKKU

JEKKU WAS WHAT ONE MIGHT CALL a fool. If there was a brain in his (currently throbbing) head, it had clearly put itself to sleep years ago and left Jekku to his own stupid, impulsive devices.

Didn't you learn your lesson last time? Or the time before that? Or every time before that? Why are you like this?

That settled it. He was not allowed to drink wine ever again.

He lay alone in the wonderfully soft bed he shared with Taja — he was not thinking about that at the moment — and pressed the heels of his palms to his eyes. His mouth felt like it was full of sand. His stomach threatened to eject itself from his body if he moved too quickly. He could not fathom the idea of leaving Linvalla today to once again hike aimlessly through the *Urdahl*. At the moment, he'd rather bury himself alive.

Jekku didn't notice the footsteps approaching until they came up right next to the bed. It was probably Taja, and he was probably judging Jekku, but Jekku couldn't quite bring himself to care. "What," he muttered.

"I'm not going to bother asking if you're okay." Taja's voice came out in a rasp; he sounded exhausted. "But I brought you some water. And bread, if you can keep it down."

The idea of eating made him want to vomit, but water sounded divine. He scrunched his eyes closed tighter, then slowly lowered his hands from his face and turned his head in the direction of Taja's voice. After a second, he cracked his eyes open.

And immediately shut them again, groaning at the awful brightness of the room.

"Rough night?" Now Taja was teasing. The bed dipped as he sat down and nudged Jekku's legs out of the way. "You'll feel better if you drink this. Here, take my hand and I'll pull you up. No eye-opening required."

Jekku made a disgruntled noise and felt around for Taja's hand. He pulled, and Taja held him upright with more strength than Jekku expected. He guided Jekku's hands around the ceramic cup and brought it to his lips. Jekku concentrated as much as his tired, dehydrated brain was able, but he still ended up spilling water down his chin.

Gods above, could he be *any* more of a mess?

"Sorry," Taja murmured. He lowered the cup and touched Jekku's chin, making him jump and flick his eyes open. He winced and shut them again as pain throbbed through his head. Taja gently brushed away the drops of water on Jekku's chin, and if Jekku's head wasn't spinning before, it certainly was now.

You need to not do that, he wanted to say. But he didn't, because part of him — a significant part of him — wanted that gentle touch as much as he wished Taja would give him another shoulder massage.

Warmth crept up the back of his neck. He turned his head and pressed his fingers to his temples, then slowly cracked his eyes open again. The light was less aggressive this time and he was able to focus on Taja's face, but the ache in his head didn't ease.

To Jekku's surprise, Taja looked just as exhausted as Jekku felt. "You look awful."

Taja let out a short laugh. "Well, good morning to you too."

Jekku shook his head. "No, I mean— You never look tired. Rough night?" He flashed a faint smirk.

Taja rolled his eyes. "Clearly not as rough as you. Here." He placed the cup in Jekku's hands. "I think you can handle it on your own from here. When you're more awake and more alive, come over to the south kitchen. It's through that gold door in the ballroom. I need you for something, if you're up for it." He smiled, then left the room.

Jekku squinted after him, baffled. Curiosity outweighed his headache, and he forced himself out of bed. He found his clothes and got dressed in a haze of exhaustion, then followed Taja's vague directions toward this kitchen.

The manor was quiet, only just waking up. Jekku didn't want to know how early it was, but the light streaming through the ballroom's tall windows was pale enough that it couldn't be long after dawn. Jekku shuffled across the polished floor and tried not to think about how little sleep he'd gotten.

The gold door indeed brought him into a bright little kitchen, where he found Lilya sitting at the island counter chatting with Ritva and Ritva's partner, whose name Jekku couldn't conjure at the moment. She turned away from the stove with a tray of fluffy biscuits and set it on the counter. Lilya didn't hesitate before snatching one, and a smile melted across her face as she took a bite.

"Jekku! Good morning." Ritva stood from her stool at the counter. "Can I get you anything? Hanne's just made biscuits!"

He eyed the fluffy rolls longingly. "I think I'll hold off on breakfast for now. But those do look delightful."

Lilya nodded, mouth full of bread. "They are."

Ritva's partner, Hanne, flashed a bright grin. "They're a favorite around here. My grandmother's recipe. I make them for all our community brunches."

"And our people *never* get sick of them," Ritva laughed.

"How could they?" Lilya said. She reached for another.

"Jekku," Ritva said, turning to him, "are you sure there's nothing we can do for you?"

He nodded. "Really, I'm okay. You've done so much already." He took a seat next to Lilya, wincing as his head throbbed. "Well... actually, would you happen to have anything to soothe a headache?"

Lilya snorted. "Rough night?"

He rubbed his temples. "I don't mix well with parties."

Ritva laughed softly. "Of course. Let me see what I can do. Hanne, will you hand me..." She trailed off as the two of them busied themselves searching for ingredients.

Lilya finished her second biscuit and dusted off her hands. "So tell me, Jekku, on a scale of one to ten, with one being 'one of us slept on the floor' and ten being 'we no longer have unresolved tension,' how was your rooming situation last night?"

Jekku heaved a sigh and got up from the counter. "Where is he?"

Lilya snickered. "Taking that as a solid six? Maybe seven? So you *didn't* sleep on the floor?"

"Lilya."

She grinned and nodded toward the sliding glass door on the other side of the room. "He went outside."

Jekku headed for the door, and Lilya tossed a biscuit at him, which he barely caught. He shot her a glare and wrapped the roll in a napkin to save for later, then went back and got another for Taja.

Hanne caught him before he reached the door. "Oh, hey, try this." She handed him a warm ceramic mug. "That should help. But also, drink some water." She winked.

Jekku gave a grateful smile and headed outside, where he stepped onto a little porch that hugged the back of the building. Taja sat on the steps, lost in his thoughts as he stared out at the gardens.

Jekku settled beside him and wordlessly offered the biscuit.

"Oh, hello." He smiled and took the roll. "Ooh, still warm. Thank you."

"According to Lilya, they're delicious." Jekku sipped the tea Hanne had given him. "But my stomach needs to settle before I try any food."

"Probably a good idea." Taja finished the biscuit, then studied Jekku's face. "How are you feeling?"

He shrugged. "Better, but not great." He drank more of the tea. "I think this is helping, but *oof*, mistakes were made."

"You may have overdone it a little." Taja smiled. "But it wa fun. I'm glad we went. I like... I like spending time with you."

Jekku snorted. "Really? I thought you loathed my existence."

"No, I'm not Lilya."

Jekku laughed, and Taja joined in. "But really," Taja said, "You know... before, it was constant motion. Running from one place to the next, not knowing how close Ebris and Firune were en croaching. I know we're still running, but it helps that the god aren't breathing down our necks. We're not running *away* this time. And you're right, we're allowed to enjoy an evening like last night and a moment like right now." A soft smile touched his lips. He leaned to the side and pressed his shoulder against Jekku's.

Jekku's first instinct was to flinch away to avoid the spike in his pulse, but he was too tired to care. He shifted over a little and set his head on Taja's shoulder.

He lost track of how long they stayed like that. Jekku stared at the gardens and forest in front of him, letting his eyes slide out of focus so he could instead concentrate on this one singular moment in time. What a change that was, after living in infinite moments for six years. He still wasn't used to his mind being so blissfully quiet, and his heart hitched at the thought of this moment being ruined by the universe's roar behind his eyes.

Jekku closed his eyes and slipped his hand into Taja's. Somewhere along the way, this simple action had become easy. He didn't fear he was sending mixed signals. His heart jumped but not with anxiety. This wasn't uncomfortable or weird. The tension in the air between them had evaporated somewhere between yesterday evening and right now, and Jekku could breathe again.

"Jekku, I wanted to ask you something," Taja said.

And just like that, the easy feeling fled. Jekku pulled away and eyed Taja warily. "What is it?"

Taja looked nervous, which made Jekku's anxiety spike higher. "When we were in Westdenn, you and Lilya spilled out all these theories about magic. I want to see if any of them work. I want to see if your magic is strong enough to help me find mine." He searched Jekku's eyes. "Will you help me?"

Jekku hesitated. The last time Taja had interacted with Jekku's magic, Jekku had nearly killed him. Jekku would never forget the blank terror on Taja's face moments before the lightning had struck him. Healer mages had done their best, but Jekku had to assume that Taja had permanent scars from the injury. And it was entirely Jekku's fault.

Taja apparently understood what Jekku was thinking. "Jekku, that was an accident. You thought you were defending yourself. I know you didn't mean to hurt me."

"But I did," Jekku whispered. "And you almost died."

"And it won't happen again." Taja squeezed his hand. "I trust you. Do you trust your own magic?"

Jekku shrugged. "I don't know."

"It wouldn't listen to you if you didn't. Look at what you were able to do against the Royal Sorcerers. You're powerful, Jekku, and I know you know how to handle your magic. I'm not asking you for a spectacle." He smiled and tucked a loose piece of hair behind Jekku's ear. "I just need to be able to feel your magic to see if I can connect to it."

Jekku nodded, but Taja had entirely shattered his concentration when he'd touched his hair. *He should stop doing that*, said one side of Jekku's brain that was really trying (and failing) to express restraint. But the other side of him was desperate for all of it — the proximity, the quick glances and lingering looks, the soft touches and affections. Taja's signals had never been clearer especially after yesterday, and it was time to stop denying that Jekku enjoyed them.

"Jekku?" Taja nudged him, and Jekku blinked out of his thoughts. How long had he just been staring blankly at Taja? Gods, he was a wreck.

"Sorry, little tired." He finished his tea, which was thankfully making his headache ebb away. His thoughts settled easier now that he didn't feel like he was being stabbed through the skull. He met Taja's eyes. "Of course I'll help you. But I don't want to push either of us too far. Can't save anyone if *Sawwia Setukkda* gets roasted."

"No, that'd be a little difficult." Taja laughed softly.

Jekku smiled back, but it quickly faded. Try as he did to make light of it, he truly feared hurting Taja again. The most he could do was hope that this time, it'd be easier to keep control in a calm situation.

"Let's give it a try, then." Taja got up and went down the steps into the garden. The small, circular space was free of the snow that coated the surrounding woods, and even had a sprinkle of pink and white flowers among the greenery. It was as though summer had left a fingerprint upon this one single pocket of forest.

"This is perfect." Taja sat down among the flowers and ran his hand over the delicate blossoms. A sad smile touched his lips.

Jekku sat facing him, and immediately sneezed when the flowers' sweet scent filled his nose.

Taja held back a laugh. "Can you still sing through your sneezes?"

"I'll be fine." He sniffed. Taja watched him expectantly, but Jekku hesitated. "Look, Taja, I have no idea how this is going to work or if it'll work at all. I have no formal training with magic."

"Jekku, you know that I trust you."

"I know. But we're going to start small." He closed his eyes and exhaled slowly, centering his focus on the ground beneath him, the smell of the flowers, the coolness of the air. He felt his magic stir within him, and he called for it with a soft hum. It took a second for his voice to smooth, but when he got the note right, a light summer rain sprinkled down on the two of them.

Jekku opened his eyes and let the song fade out, but kept his hold on his magic. Lilya was right; it was hard to control his affinity with willpower alone. And this was just rain. He couldn't imagine the strength and control required to handle a storm. He didn't know how Kelish people did this. Or Elshalans, for that matter.

That gave him an idea. He looked up at Taja. "What if you sang? It might call the magic to you. Having it float around us won't do any good if you can't control it."

Taja studied the flowers. "I never thought to try that. But I don't know the spells. How will I know what to sing?"

"I don't know the spells, either," Jekku said. "I've learned by

listening and by feeling how the magic responds to my voice.
don't know if I'm singing a real spell at all."

"And that's probably why you lost control," Taja teased. "I'
try it. But I need to feel something first. Can you do a littl
more?"

Jekku closed his eyes again. He sang louder and dipped hi
voice to a low note, then pulled on the crackle of energy that ac
companied heavy summer storms. He felt the air pressure shif
felt the hair on his arms stand up. He held his voice steady an
opened his eyes. The sky had grown dark with rain-heavy cloud
but no rain fell and no thunder rumbled. Jekku let the storm
hold its breath, pausing before that first flash of lightning.

For a second, Taja looked incredulous. He closed his eyes an
set his palms flat on the ground, then dug his fingers into the soi
and began to hum. Jekku felt a little shift; his magic responde
to Taja, just slightly. Taja sang a little louder, and this time Jekk
felt a *tug*. The energy surrounding him shifted to surround Taj
as well.

A faint smile formed on Taja's lips. A tear rolled down hi
cheek. He altered the song, switching to a softer melody tha
wasn't a storm, but something like a lullaby. Jekku fought to hol
his focus amid this discovery of how beautiful Taja's voice was.

And then the most remarkable thing happened. The flower
around Taja's hands bloomed brighter, their blossoms openin
fully, and even more pushed through the earth and uncurle
their petals right before Jekku's eyes.

Jekku let his song fade out and reached forward to place hi
hands over Taja's. Taja opened his eyes, blinking as if wakin
from a dream, and then he saw the flowers. His song cut of

abruptly and his mouth fell open. His eyes widened, and for a minute he just stared at the flowers. Then he looked up and met Jekku's eyes.

Jekku couldn't describe what he saw in Taja's gaze, but it was beautiful. It was hope and it was relief and it was confidence, and it was something clicking into place that had been gone for a long time. Jekku knew that Taja understood that he was more than his lost affinity, but that didn't change the fact that Taja must feel like his heart had started beating again.

Taja released a sob, then leapt forward and crushed Jekku in his arms, nearly toppling both of them. Jekku's focus snapped and a blinding strike of lightning crashed down somewhere nearby. Thunder cracked the sky. Rain poured down, harsh and cold this time, but Jekku didn't care and neither did Taja.

Jekku smiled and pressed his face to Taja's shoulder. "You did it, Taja. You're free."

Taja let go of him and took Jekku's face in his hands, and for a second Jekku's head spun as he expected Taja to kiss him. Jekku was about to go for it himself when another burst of lightning lashed overhead. He should probably get rid of that storm before his magic struck *both* of them. He hummed under his breath and carried the storm away; it gradually lessened to light rumbles, soft rain, and then sparse clouds.

"It–– It feels like home." Taja's voice was thick with emotion. "I thought the Oracle Stone was the magic I remembered, but no. No, this is–– this is everything I've missed. Jekku." He searched his eyes. "*Thank you*."

Jekku shook his head. "It wasn't me. This was all you, Taja.

Sawwia Setukkda." He smiled, suddenly choked up. He took one of Taja's hands and kissed it. "You're magnificent."

Taja flickered a teary smile. The way he gazed at Jekku now made his heart freeze up and melt all at once. Taja swallowed and his next words were so quiet that if it had still been storming, Jekku wouldn't have heard him.

But he did. And the words shot straight through him like an arrow.

"I really do love you."

Jekku froze. His first instinct was, again, to run away. *No, you don't love me. You can't.* But he stayed put. He met Taja's eyes. This was *Taja*, who had wholeheartedly believed in Jekku even before he really knew him, who had taught him to keep fighting, who had stayed by his side all this time and helped him through grief and doubt instead of leaving him behind.

But I...

But he...

No. Stop it. Jekku halted the invasive thoughts before they could riddle him with doubt. He blinked a few times and took Taja's trembling hands. He didn't know where to start.

It's too complicated.

But no. No, it wasn't.

"I love you," Jekku murmured. He clutched Taja's hands tighter and met his eyes. "I care about you, I care *for* you, and want you and I want to be with you and I love you. And I wish it was that simple. But I need..." He closed his eyes for a second and swallowed. The words stuck in his throat.

Taja freed one of his hands from Jekku's grip and softly

ouched his cheek. "You were hurt, and you need time. I under-
tand."

"No." Jekku looked up. "No, I— I'm sick of waiting. Time
sn't going to fix anything. It— It's trust. I need trust. And I do
rust you, Taja. Despite what happened in the Labyrinth. Despite
vhat happened with Leo, too. I trust you, and that's enough."

But Taja shook his head a little. "Tell me, Jekku, are you truly
eady to give me a chance? To give *us* a chance? I know that you
rust me. I know that you care for me. But how strong is that
ogic at the worst moments of insecurity?"

Jekku winced, a little stung, but it was a valid question. Taja
lidn't deserve to be hurt by Jekku's indecisiveness. Jekku might
rust him, but did he trust Jekku?

"My insecurities are mine to deal with," he said. "I know you
vouldn't hurt me like Leo did, not after everything we've been
:hrough. I am willing to give my heart to you, Taja, because I
<now you'll handle it gently."

Taja searched his eyes, as if looking for something unspoken.
But for once in his life, Jekku didn't hide anything. He had no
secrets to be kept from Taja.

Just this once, he decided to make the first move. He admired
Taja's restraint, but for gods' sakes. The want was clear as day on
his face. Jekku slid one hand around the back of Taja's neck, drew
him close, and kissed him with every ounce of longing that had
filled him since the last time their lips had met.

Somehow, it meant more now.

Taja abandoned his hesitation. He wrapped one arm around
Jekku and placed his other hand on his cheek, and kissed him
harder. Again and again, scarcely giving Jekku time to draw a

breath. Jekku was admittedly a little surprised; he hadn't realize how much Taja wanted this.

Foolish. He should have seen it. Well... he *had* seen it, but he' learned not to look.

That was foolish, too.

Jekku started to slow down as their desperation ebbed. H savored each kiss, each soft, tender press of Taja's lips to his. H gently drew his free hand through Taja's curls, and was about t pull back when a sharp whistle cut across the garden.

Jekku jumped and Taja jerked back. Their heads turned si multaneously toward the manor, where Lilya stood on the porc with a positively evil grin on her face.

"We have *got* to stop running into each other like this." Sh cackled. "Sorry to *interrupt*, but while you two were canoodling I figured out our next stop. So whenever you're done, let's hit th road. Some of us have schooling to finish and a stupid law t break."

She disappeared back into the house, but not before throw ing another wicked smirk over her shoulder.

Jekku's face burned. "She is *never*—"

"Going to let us hear the end of that," Taja agreed. But h laughed, and pulled Jekku close to him again. He pressed his fac to his hair. "I don't care. Let her tease."

Jekku closed his eyes and let Taja hold him for a second. "I re ally do want to give us a chance," he murmured. "I don't want t let this go."

Taja drew back just enough to kiss Jekku again. "Then don't.

19

TAJA

TAJA WAS RELUCTANT to leave the comfort of Linvalla behind, but admittedly it was time for him, Jekku, and Lilya to continue on their way. While Taja and Jekku had been in the garden, Lilya had heard from Ritva of another nearby Elshalan town with which Linvalla regularly communicated. Thankfully it wasn't far, but a fresh snow had fallen upon the *Urdahl* overnight, making their trek through the forest even slower.

It was almost like old times, with Jekku on one side and Lilya on the other. Like before, they traveled mostly in silence; the hours dragged by with only the crunch of snow underfoot and rustle of branches overhead filling the air. Occasionally a wolf howled or an elk brayed, the eerie sounds sending shivers down Taja's spine. It made him miss the Sky Elk he'd taken when he left Båthälla the first time; the animal's six legs and high endurance made for quick, easy travel. The three of them could have been up and down the coast of Doweth twice by now if they'd taken an elk, but in the scramble to get away from Båthälla after the Labyrinth, the thought hadn't crossed Taja's mind.

Now, he dearly wished for that elk. Or a horse. Or some faster means of travel that wouldn't exhaust him or take two days to get them across a distance a Sky Elk could cover in a few hours. He admired Jekku and Lilya's patience; he was unspeakably sick of hiking.

But hopefully this would be worth it. In Linvalla, Taja had seen that it was possible for Elshalans to thrive without their gods. He had an example to follow. And in this next town, Strykivik, he hoped to learn just how exactly one led a revolution against divine beings.

At the very least, it would be an interesting conversation.

***

The town of Strykivik used to be a community of exclusively Elshalans with the gift of mind — diviners, in human terms. Non-mages called them "fortune tellers," but that, Taja thought, was a vast understatement of what diviners could do. They were more in tune with the earth — and the universe — than any other type of mage, and some confidence in the future was exactly what Taja hoped to find in Strykivik.

He had been here once before, years ago, on a small pilgrimage in honor of the Peacebringer. Ebris and Nedra had led the modest group of Båthälla citizens, and Taja remembered being fascinated with the way the hidden runes indicated directions. The clues began in the *Urdahl*, carved in boulders rather than trees, and led toward the sea. Out here, the trees thinned, giving way to sprawling meadows that gradually sloped downward until the land reached the edge of a cliff that had to be a severalundred-foot drop to the water. Massive boulders and crumbling rock formations dotted the snowy meadow, and Taja used he familiar landmarks to lead the group closer to the cliff's edge.

Gusts of icy wind whipped across the open land, biting right hrough Taja's clothes despite the thick fur lining in his cloak. Without the cover of the forest, the elements were brutal, and aja knew it'd only be worse when they were on the edge of the ea.

"Are we getting close?" Jekku fell into step beside Taja, visibly hivering. He had his cloak's hood up and his arms tucked across is chest, but still his teeth chattered.

Taja put his arm around him and tried to rub some warmth nto him. "Once we reach the edge up ahead, I'll know where the ntrance is. Last time, there were two stone pillars that marked he border of the city, but even those might be invisible to us."

"How long has it been since you were here?" Lilya asked.

"At least ten years," Taja said. "We're lucky I mostly remembered how to get here."

"What b-brought you all the way out here f-from Båthälla?" ekku asked.

Lilya shot him an amused look. "You all right?"

"It's f-freezing, Lilya!"

"How are you *from* this country and can't handle the cold?"

"How are *you* from a t-tropical country and *c-can* handle it?"

She scoffed. "Kelum isn't tropical. Far from it. Our winters ren't much nicer."

"Literally anything would be n-nicer than this." Jekku shudered. "Except maybe Nalum or Qeya. When we're done in

Båthälla, Taja, I'm running away to the t-tropical islands i
Pheosa."

He laughed. "I might just have to come with you."

Lilya pulled her fur scarf a little tighter, then raised her hand
and sang a loud, strong note. Flames burst to life in her hand
soaring upwards and spiraling around the three of them in
bright coil of warmth. The wind still roared, but the cold didn
break through the barrier of Lilya's magic.

Jekku let out a relieved sigh. "Oh, gods, thank you."

Taja rubbed his freezing hands together. "Why didn't w
think of this sooner?"

"Because of the three of us, I easily have the most brains,
Lilya said. "And you never asked." She continued to hum as the
walked, keeping the flames alive.

Taja was too grateful for the warmth to be offended. "Wel
anyway, I came here with Ebris, Nedra, my parents, and a fev
neighbors when I was about twelve. It was in memory of th
Peacebringer, because apparently this place was important t
them. But if Strykivik cast out its gods, Ebris did an exceptiona
job of hiding that from us."

"It must be strange coming back here now," Jekku said qui
etly.

It was. It'd been a decade since he'd last made this trek towar
Strykivik, and it felt like a different lifetime. At the same time
though, he swore he was just here, listening to Ebris lecture hir
about leadership and strength and all those skills Taja's fathe
wanted him to have. Apparently a visit to the place where th
Peacebringer had found their destiny was supposed to make Taj
alter his entire personality to his father's wishes.

It wasn't a *bad* memory. Taja certainly had worse. But it wasn't pleasant, either.

Lilya abruptly cut off her song, and the flames flickered out. Tekku started to complain, but Lilya shushed him. "We've got company." Her hand dropped to the dagger on her belt.

Taja followed her gaze, squinting through the snow stirred up by the wind. Sure enough, a short distance ahead, four armed Elshalans strode toward them. The tall woman in the lead kept her hand on a sheathed sword at her hip, while the other three had bows drawn at the ready.

Taja held up his hand to tell the others to stop, then he stepped forward and lowered his hood so the other Elshalans saw his ears. But apparently they didn't care that he was one of them; they did not lower their weapons.

"Who are you?" The leading woman approached Taja. She was perhaps in her fifties, with ginger hair pulled back in a neat braid. A scar marked the right side of her jaw, and despite the cold, she wore no cloak over her leather armor and simple tunic. The harsh glare she leveled at Taja rivaled the wind's chill.

"My name is Taja Ievisin," he said, bowing his head. "I am an Elshalan of Båthälla. My friends and I were sent here by Ritva of Linvalla. She gave us a message for someone named Maelyrra Balsye."

He held his breath while the Elshalan woman mulled over his words. She continued to eye him suspiciously, then let her hand fall from the hilt of her sword. "Very well, Taja of Båthälla. What message does the matriarch of Linvalla have for me?"

Relief washed over him. "She says that the sun has eclipsed and the Savior's dream will come to pass."

Taja didn't need the gift of mind to divine what that meant.

All at once, the suspicion fled from Maelyrra's face. Her eyebrows shot up, green eyes widening, and she stared at Taja with something close to awe. "Oh... My stars, I didn't see it before but... it's you, isn't it?" She held up a hand as a signal to the archers behind her. "Stand down, ladies. You're in the presence of *Sawwia Setukkda*."

Taja's heart twisted with dread.

Maelyrra looked close to tears. "He has come to us at last."

20

JEKKU

STRYKIVIK WAS NOT WHAT JEKKU EXPECTED. He was used to associating Elshalan towns with forest settings: densely packed trees, rich greenery, ivy- and moss-covered buildings. But Strykivik sprawled among seaside cliffs — not *near* them, but built *into* them. Jekku couldn't focus on appreciating the quaint stone houses and castle ruins at the center of the town because he was too busy fearing for his life. The precarious hike down to the lower streets of the town was hard enough, but the only way to get from the ground to the upper parts was via this death-trap system of platforms and pulleys that nearly gave Jekku a heart attack on sight.

"Nope." He halted while the others stepped up onto one of the platforms. His eyes traced the ropes up and up and *up* the cliff towering over them, and when he spotted the little dock built into the rock face that was apparently their destination, his head spun.

This was Howl Hills all over again, but worse. This was so much worse. Jekku dug his heels into the gravel road and refused.

"Absolutely not. You all have fun plummeting to your death when one of those ropes inevitably snaps. I'm staying right here.

"Come on, Jekku." Taja extended a hand. He and Lilya and the Elshalan woman, Maelyrra, were already settled on the platform, and Maelyrra looked ready to start moving them upward. "You'll be fine. It's sturdy enough." Taja jumped a little, making the whole thing swing and creak.

Jekku's stomach flung itself up his throat.

Lilya grabbed Taja's arm. "Maybe don't do that."

"It is perfectly safe," Maelyrra said. Her voice was edged with exasperation. "We haul boulders with these pulleys. They can handle the weight of four average-sized people."

Jekku adamantly shook his head. "No. Seriously, no. Anything you learn, you can tell me later. Or, you know, we could talk somewhere else that does not require this." He gestured at the platform. "I am not getting on that thing."

Lilya glanced at Taja, then Maelyrra, then stepped off the platform. "You go on ahead, Taja. I'll stay with Jekku."

"I don't need a chaperone," he muttered.

"Good, because I'm not here to look after you." She waved at Taja. "We'll catch up later."

Taja looked nervous at the idea of being left alone, but as much as Jekku cared about him and wanted to support him, he honestly and truly could not make himself get on that platform. He'd probably throw up, at best, or pass out, at worst.

"All right," Taja agreed. "I'll find you. Just— don't get lost. And no catastrophes, okay?"

Jekku exchanged a look with Lilya. "So little faith in us."

She snorted. "I wonder why that is."

"Suit yourselves." Maelyrra checked the ropes again, then grabbed onto the wheel fixed to the center of the platform — it reminded Jekku of the helm of a ship — and gave it a hard turn. The contraption lurched upward, and Jekku's stomach lurched with it. He watched it climb higher and higher until it stopped, swinging, by one of the docks built into the cliff.

"Absolutely no way in hell," he muttered, and looked away.

Lilya nudged his arm. "Come on, stop making yourself ill by looking at that, and let's go explore. Maybe we can dig up some secrets, too."

She walked off, but Jekku hesitated. "Do you think he'll be all right? Should we have gone with him?"

"He'll be fine, Jekku. You said yourself in Linvalla that he has to do this alone. Give him a chance to believe that he can."

Jekku caught up with her. She was right. Taja was *Sawwia Setukkda*. Jekku couldn't hold his hand forever, no matter how much he wanted to.

Even the ground level of Strykivik was precarious, with steep hills and labyrinthine streets, but it was charming. The doorways and windows on all the houses and buildings were round instead of rectangular, and many of them were painted bright colors to offset the plain gray stone. Jekku and Lilya made their way down toward the sea, where the heart of the town gathered along the edge. A series of bridges — most made of stone but some, to Jekku's dismay, of planks and ropes — carried them all over the town, but Lilya showed no interest in going into any buildings and Jekku didn't ask.

But then he saw a bookshop, and he decided that was somewhere they absolutely needed to visit.

He grabbed Lilya's arm and dragged her back from yet another godsdamned suspension bridge. "This way, come with me."

She pried his hand off her arm. "Where are you taking me?"

He stopped in front of the little shop and looked back at her with a grin. "I can't resist."

Lilya tried to smother the smile that crept across her face, but it broke through. She shook her head and led the way into the shop. A bell clinked over the door when they entered. "All right, fine. Twist my arm. But you realize we won't be able to read any of the books in here, right? I don't think the translation spell applies to written words."

Jekku froze in his tracks. "Oh. Damn it." He continued into the shop anyway. The door shut behind him, closing out the wind and frigid sea air, and Jekku could finally breathe. The familiar, friendly smell of leather and ink and paper filled his nose, and he smiled. The libraries in Westdenn were incredible, but this place was *homey*. This was a place for people like him — book people, like his mother used to say.

He beamed at Lilya. "I don't even care that we can't read the language. Lilya, *look* at this place!" He gazed at the shelves upon shelves of books. It took everything in him to keep his voice down. "A whole shop packed with Elshalan books! That no one outside of their communities has ever seen!"

Lilya smiled in a way that said she was making fun of him, but he didn't care. "Yes, because we can't read them."

Jekku turned on his heel. "You're no fun. I thought you'd be excited."

"What do you want me to do? Jump up and down and squeal?"

Jekku snickered. "I would pay unbelievable amounts of coin to see that."

"In your dreams, Aj'ere." She went off toward a row of shelves beneath the windows on the wall to the left of the entrance.

Only a few others wandered around the bookshop, and Jekku had yet to see the shopkeeper, so he felt less like he was invading as he started at the back of the shop and worked his way up and down every aisle. The shop was laid out in perfectly neat rows of wood shelves that towered about a foot over Jekku's head, and though they were packed to capacity, not a single volume was out of place or stacked on the floor or crammed into an ill-fitting space, and this pleased Jekku immensely. Chaotic bookshops had their charm, but they overwhelmed him. How could anyone find anything when nothing was organized?

Jekku lost track of time — and of Lilya — as he scanned the titles on each spine. He tried to figure out what the Elshalan words said, but he didn't know nearly enough of the language to put any pieces together. He knew — what? Two words? Three? And only spoken, not read. But still, it was remarkable enough to be here with all these stories and all this history that had been carefully and lovingly kept over the years.

Could some of these books be from Saevel's time? Did they stand in this same shop? How much history had these books seen? How much history had this *town* seen?

That almost made Jekku go back to join Taja for his conversation with Maelyrra. He'd loved hearing about Linvalla and how it had survived resisting its gods, and now he wanted to know every scrap about Strykivik too.

But he slowed those thoughts and focused on the books in

front of him. Running after all the answers had not worked out for him before, and he was not about to make that mistake again. He did not have to know *everything*.

...But that didn't mean he wouldn't leave with some of these books and then ask Taja for help translating them. Maybe Jekku could even convince him to read to him. He smiled at the idea of the two of them curled up together beneath a warm blanket in front of a blazing fire, surrounded by books and Jekku's notes. He could almost hear the soft tone of Taja's voice as he read.

Jekku hoped, when all this was over, that soft moments like those in his daydreams became a regular occurrence.

He turned around a corner to go down the next aisle of shelves, already carrying a pile of three books that looked interesting solely based on the images on the covers, but stopped short when his foot came down on something soft. He jumped at the same time a black cat bolted away from him with a yowl.

"Oh no! Wait, come back, I'm sorry." Jekku tucked his books under his arm and went after the cat, which had leapt up on the back of a chair in the lounge at the back of the shop. "Did I step on your tail? I'm sorry. What were you doing under my feet?"

The cat arched its back and hissed at him.

"Aw, come on. Don't be like that." Jekku held out his free hand, hoping that universally translated to a gesture of peace. "I promise it was an accident. But I won't be offended if you bite me."

The cat batted his hand with its paw, but if it meant to scratch him, it missed. Jekku darted his hand back. "Okay, fair enough."

He went and curled up in the other chair across from the

one the cat had claimed, and set his stack of books on the table
in front of him. He grabbed the one on top and opened it, de-
lighted at once to find illustrations. Maybe these would help him
figure out what else was going on.

Then he realized, as he studied the pictures, that they were
moving.

He dropped the book in his lap and blinked rapidly. No.
He had to be hallucinating. He must be tired, or dehydrated,
or maybe he should eat something. That— That hadn't *actually*
moved, had it?

"Ah, you found one of the enchanted ones."

Jekku startled and looked up, only to find that he wasn't
alone. An older Elshalan man stood with his arm resting on the
back of the other chair and gently stroked his hand down the
cat's back. Jekku could hear it purring from where he sat.

"Enchanted?" Jekku echoed. "So the picture really is moving?"

The man smiled. Wrinkles formed around his kind eyes. He
was older, with long white hair and light brown skin. His nails
were painted midnight blue, and his pointed ears had more silver
rings than should be able to fit on one person's ears. "You are not
very familiar with magic, are you?"

Jekku almost laughed. "I thought I was. But maybe not. My
name is Jekku. Are you the shopkeeper?"

He nodded, still petting the cat. "I am. Everyone calls me Pepper. I am glad to meet a new face in here. It's not often we receive
outside guests."

Jekku resisted the impulse to cover his ears. He wished, not
for the first time, that he had some physical indicator that he
was half Elshalan. Maybe then he wouldn't feel quite so out of

place among them. "Your shop is wonderful," he said, hoping his admiration showed in his voice. "I could spend all day in here. Except... I don't know if your cat likes me."

As if in reply, it meowed.

Pepper chuckled. "Ah, she is grumpy around strangers, even after six years living in this shop. Give her some time, and she'll want to follow you home. Where would that be, for you?"

"That's... a good question," Jekku said. He flickered a smile. "Right now, nowhere."

Pepper lifted the cat into his arms and took a seat in the chair across from Jekku. "Then what brings you to Strykivik, Jekku from nowhere?"

The words hurt, even though Pepper probably didn't intend them to. He *was* from somewhere, but Ajaphere hadn't been home in a long time. It always would be, in a way, but it was not his current idea of home. He looked down at the enchanted book in his lap. "It's a long story. I'm here with my fri— Uhhmm... Partner?" That was weird to say aloud. "He's from Bāthälla, and we're trying to make some changes there."

Pepper sat up straighter and leaned forward. His dark eyes bore into Jekku with sudden intensity. "My friend... A savior is not what you need. Nor a hero, nor a god. But you do need their words — not to guide you, since the heroes of old always fell in blood, but to deter you. Your lives are not written as theirs were."

Jekku blinked, heart pounding. *What?*

Pepper blinked back at him, then eased to his feet with a light grunt. "Let me know if you need help finding anything else. Enjoy the books." He smiled as if nothing at all had happened, and then shuffled away, carrying his cat with him.

Jekku stared after him, baffled. Had that been... some kind of prophecy? Taja had said that Strykivik used to be a town of all diviners, so maybe they continued to linger here. Jekku had never heard a diviner directly reveal a vision, but that sure as hell seemed like one.

The question was, what on earth did it mean?

Jekku got up, set his books down, and paced up and down the back of the shop. He ran over Pepper's words in his head. "A savior is not what you need... I dunno about that. Isn't the whole point that the Second Savior— Wait." He pivoted and went back the other way, walking a little faster. "But we need their words – the prophecy. We need the prophecy. Okay. So what's in the prophecy that can help us? Oh, but he said the prophecy should deter us, not guide us, otherwise — what, we'll die? So we're *not* supposed to follow the prophecy even though most of it has been correct so far? Because if we..." Jekku ran his hands through his hair. "If we let the whole thing come to pass, then... we end up like Saevel?"

He paused and frowned at the floor. "But Saevel *won*. They saved their people. Hell, they saved the whole world. They just... died in the process." He sighed and looked up at the nearest row of books, but his mind was miles away. "Yeah, we don't want that, do we? So the prophecy isn't meant to guide us, but to *warn* us. That last part... 'Your lives are not written as theirs were.' So we're not written in stone. Our fates are not written in stone. Anything could happen."

Jekku blinked. His surroundings came back into focus, and a sense of peace surrounded him. "I think that's exactly what I needed to hear. We don't need to be like Saevel."

"Does that mean you're giving up?"

Jekku jumped at the voice behind him. He turned, and the ai
rushed from his lungs. *No. How?*

Ellory Ives smirked at him, mismatched eyes glinting in th
dim lantern light. "Hello, false savior."

21

TAJA

TAJA QUICKLY AND FULLY FELL IN LOVE with the city of Strykivik. He'd only seen a glimpse so far, but it was already apparent that the town never stopped moving. The rumble and creak of platforms traveling up and down the cliffs filled the air with a backdrop of ocean waves meeting the shore, and even all the way up here in Maelyrra's cliffside home, Taja could hear sounds of travel and activity below.

He loved it. The fresh ocean air, the cliffs, the view of the open sea — Taja could get used to a place like this. Båthälla, in all its messiness, would always be something like home in Taja's heart, but this was not the first time he considered starting over somewhere new. It was, however, the first time that seemed possible. So maybe that somewhere was here.

Or maybe not, since most of the homes in this town were built directly into the cliffs, easily a hundred feet off the ground, and Jekku would absolutely hate it up here.

Despite being so high up, Maelyrra's home was cozy, and bigger than Taja expected. They had stepped off the platform onto a dock, which brought them to a narrow lip of road that wrapped around the cliff and provided an alternate — albeit treacherous — way down. Taja and Maelyrra both had to duck through the doorway into her home, but the space inside opened up into a round entranceway with a high ceiling and enough lanterns to make up for the lack of windows. A rounded doorway led them further into the house, where narrow hallways branched toward various rooms. Maelyrra had invited Taja into a small sitting room off the foyer, and here they sat with tea and a crackling fire and fragrant candles placed throughout.

To Taja's relief, Maelyrra didn't treat him like some kind of god. She seemed particularly fascinated with the prophecy and him being *Sawwia Setukkda*, but after her initial shock, she treated him normally. And she was all too happy to tell him how Strykivik shook off its gods.

"Honestly, what kept us going when we kicked out the gods was a strong sense of our history — where we came from and how we started — and a clear vision of our future. As you know, Strykivik was once a village of all diviners and a couple of healers, with only one goddess among us. I do believe she was always on our side, and the people of Strykivik lived happily with her for about a century... and then other gods moved in. And they took complete power, and the people had absolutely no say."

Taja wondered if Båthälla ever enjoyed a time of genuine peace and equality between gods and Elshalans. But knowing that Ebris had manipulated Saevel just like he'd tried to manipulate Taja... he doubted it. A town under the control of Lord Ebris was never a free town.

Maelyrra settled back in her chair and set down her empty

eacup. "That system stuck around until...hmm, about twenty
ears ago, when I led a movement to get the corrupt gods out of
trykivik. It wasn't pretty, but it was necessary. And it was long
verdue.

"Alas, people still resisted. To the end, there was a solid group
ho remained loyal to the gods. But I won the majority because
reminded them that Strykivik was not always fragile and bleak.

"When those gods came in, they seized nearly all of the city's
esources and controlled everything. People starved when there
hould have been plenty of food. People slept on the streets when
here were plenty of vacant buildings. People were poor when
he gods hoarded coin. It was a mess, and it was so obvious that
he gods were the root of the problem, yet still people denied it.

"The key to my success was making them remember that our
ves had become like this because of a few greedy immortals, and
e were not always like this. We changed once, for worse, and
e could change again for the better. That promise — that *vision*
— was what secured my allies' loyalty."

Taja studied his tea. That was essentially what Ritva had told
im about Linvalla, but he still didn't know how to win that loy-
lty. He still planned to use the Sky Palace to show his people
hat they could have, but what if it didn't work? What if they
ere too blinded by their distrust of him to see past it to a bet-
er future?

Once again, he was reminded that this whole ordeal would be
o much easier if *he* wasn't the one who had to handle it.

He looked up at Maelyrra. "Was there any particular vision
hat won them over?"

She thought for a minute. "In the end, it came down to two things: their children, and freedom of magic."

"Freedom of magic?" Taja questioned. "Did the gods control that too?"

"Oh, they certainly did. They hoarded it, choked it, and only let Strykivik feel a flicker of its natural power. Only certain citizens were allowed their full abilities — a select number of healers, and one or two diviners. Everyone else slogged along with little or no magic at all."

That was entirely too similar to what was happening in Båthälla. Already their magic was weak; with the gods hoarding the power among themselves, it made a much shallower pool to be shared among everyone else. If it was allowed to continue, would Båthälla reach the point Strykivik had? Was that Ebris' ultimate plan — to take magic completely away?

Taja shuddered. He wouldn't put it past him. And he hoped to the stars that Nokaldir hadn't gotten a similar idea.

"Having our magic returned was one of the most rewarding parts of our victory," Maelyrra went on. "It was as though the city came back to life. I never realized how ill you feel when you lack magic until I felt its return."

Taja looked away. A ghost of pain prickled on his hands. He wasn't hopelessly without magic anymore — connecting to it through Jekku's affinity had felt like a gulp of air after years of drowning — but still, the reminder hurt. He might find his own way back to magic someday, but that didn't change the history that permanently set him apart from most other Elshalans. Any magic he managed to reconnect to would never be the magic he lost.

"The return of our magic confirmed to my supporters that we had done the right thing," Maelyrra continued, oblivious to Taja's mood. "It even won over a few people who were against me or most of the movement. So magic was a huge part of it, and then I pulled on their heartstrings by telling them to act not for themselves, but for their children."

Taja nodded. "You encouraged them to make a better life for the next generation."

"It takes a particularly cruel heart to look at a child and reject something that will make their life happier," Maelyrra said. "I asked them to look at the youngest ones among us, who would be the ones to either thank their ancestors or curse them. I said, 'Do you really want to be the ones to ruin it for your children when you had a chance to change their lives?' And they couldn't say anything but no in response." She looked down at her hands where they rested on her knee. Taja noticed that half her left pinkie was missing, a remnant of a long-ago injury. "The best a good parent can hope for is that their child has an easier life than they did. In Strykivik we don't believe in passing down suffering from one generation to the next. We all strive to be better than those who came before us. And in this case, that meant fighting back against corrupt gods. Eventually, enough people understood that for it to help us win."

Taja hoped to the stars that his people would see the same logic. He struggled to imagine them being empathetic, but he tried to give them the benefit of the doubt.

He finished his tea and set the cup on the table with Maelyrra's. "So, after you won your supporters, how did you actually... How did the gods leave? I can't imagine them agreeing to give up their power just because you demanded it. What did you have to do?"

Maelyrra met his eyes, and there was something dark in her gaze. "Gods cannot die. Not the way mortals do. But they can be erased from our world and confined to their unknown realms. This does not mean they can't appear as apparitions — sort of like spirits — but they can't return in physical form or access their powers."

"Is that... permanent?" Taja asked. "They can *never* return?"

"In truth, I don't know. Perhaps in a few millennia, the forces we used to expel them will wear thin and they can break through. They are gods, after all. I doubt anything can truly eliminate them."

Taja shivered. Why did these gods need to interact with the mortal world at all? They should live in mystery, relying on their followers' faith. What gave them the right to appoint themselves as infallible leaders just because they supposedly created this world? Should it not be left to the mortals they made to care for the world?

He met Maelyrra's eyes again. "What was the spell you used to— to kill the gods?"

It felt like a deep betrayal of everything he'd been taught to believe, but if this was the way, so be it. Difficult as it was to accept, Taja knew that showing the gods mercy would only come back to bite him. Even Nedra, who claimed to ally with him, should not be trusted. If she truly wanted a different future for Båthälla, she could have changed things a long time ago. She could have stopped Ebris and the Council Eternal when they

ook Taja's magic. When they banished him. When they killed
Kierra in front of him.

But she didn't, because even though she posed herself as a
friend, she still benefited from having Båthälla under her heel.

"I can have a copy made for you," Maelyrra said. "It's actually
based on the one the Peacebringer used to seal the Oracle Stone.
I trust you know that story?"

Taja let out a short laugh. "A little too well."

Maelyrra tipped her head to the side. "What do—"

Before she could finish her question, footsteps pounded toward the room and Lilya burst in, another Elshalan on her heels.
Their faces were flushed, their eyes wide.

Taja stood. "Lilya? What's wrong?"

"We— We have a situation," she panted.

"What is it?" Maelyrra bolted to her feet.

"Unauthorized visitors," the Elshalan girl said. "I— I don't
know how they got in. Three of them, and they're— they're creating a scene on Seaview Street."

Maelyrra was already fastening her cloak and on her way out
of the sitting room. "Who are they? Humans?" She whirled back
toward Taja. "Are they with you?"

He hurried after her, Lilya on his heels. "No. There was no one
else with us."

"And there's no way we were followed," Lilya added, then,
quieter, "Right?"

Taja's heart pounded. What if they *had* been followed? What
if one of the gods had tracked them all the way from Båthälla?
Taja should've anticipated this. Of course the gods wouldn't just
let them run.

Maelyrra burst outside and onto the waiting platform. The younger Elshalan girl followed her, then Lilya, but Taja stopped short before he stepped on.

"Lilya, where's Jekku?"

The look on her face told him all he needed to know. He hissed a curse and got on the platform. "I know who they are. Let us handle this. They're here because of me."

"Taja, there was nothing I could do," Lilya said as they began their long descent. "I didn't see what happened, I just saw that they had him. Who are they?"

Taja gripped the ropes until his hands hurt. "I'm sure they brought backup, but the one I'm worried about is Ellory Ives. They used to be my friend when we were children, but now they're making a claim for Båthälla, which is why they've decided I'm their enemy. They want the town to remain controlled by gods, because they think that as Ebris's son they're entitled to rule Båthälla."

Lilya stared at him. "They're *Ebris's son?*"

Taja nodded.

"So they're half-god."

Taja didn't love the sound of it when put like that. "Yes, but they have no divine powers. They're a powerful fire mage, but there's not enough of Ebris in them for them to be a true god."

And thank the skies for that.

The platform reached the ground, and Taja leapt off before it had fully stopped moving. He took off down the uneven road following the noise rising up from the center of the city. A bright burst of light beamed from a spot near the water, beckoning him forward even as his anxiety turned to fear. How had Ellory tracked them? What were they doing with Jekku? How had they captured Jekku when he was every bit as powerful as they were — and so was Lilya?

Maelyrra quickly caught up and surged ahead of Taja, flanked by half a dozen armed Elshalans. Taja ran faster, struggling to keep up with the women as they pivoted around corners and navigated the rocky streets with practiced ease. Finally they burst onto a long, wide main road sloping toward the sea, and Taja halted.

At the bottom of the hill, in the middle of a circle of castle-like buildings, Ellory stood upon an overturned crate and held a sphere of golden flames around themself. Two other Elshalans Taja recognized from home stood guard on either side of Ellory, blades raised. And at their feet, Jekku knelt, hunched over with his hands bound behind him and mouth gagged. Powerless, unable to summon his magic.

Taja's pulse rang in his ears. He started forward, but Lilya stopped him. "Wait."

He wrenched his arm out of her grip. "Lilya—"

"No, *listen*." She gripped his arm again, nails digging through his sleeve. "Do you know what's going to happen if you rush down there exactly like Ellory wants you to?"

Taja exhaled and forced himself to be reasonable. "I'm going to walk into their trap, and they'll gain the upper hand."

"Ya." Lilya raised her eyebrows. "Don't be stupid just because Jekku's in danger. Ellory is using him against you because they think he's your weakness." She pressed his arm, a little gentler this time. "Don't prove them right."

Taja glanced at Ellory, then Jekku, then back to Lilya. "You don't understand."

"I understand enough!" Lilya snapped. "Don't you dare tell me what I feel, Taja. *Focus*. What are you going to do?"

He started to turn away from her. "I'm going to talk to them."

Lilya scoffed. "And they're going to wear you down, break your confidence, and make you doubt and doubt and doubt until you slink away." Lilya darted in front of him and met his eyes. "No. Don't even give them the chance. Do you know why the Royal Sorcerers were able to manipulate me? Do you know why Ebris was able to convince Jekku he was *Sawwia Setukkda* even when both of them knew he wasn't?"

Taja saw her logic, and he appreciated it, but the clock was ticking. He didn't have time for this. *Jekku* didn't have time for this. "No, Lilya— Look, just—" He tried to get around her, but she just stood in his way again.

"Because we let them talk! We let them get into our heads. You're not a fool, Taja. Don't let that petty bully convince you otherwise." Finally, she let him go.

He nodded. "Right. No talking. No fighting. Get Jekku, get out. If Ellory wants a fight, they can bring it back to Båthälla."

Lilya fell into stride beside him as he stormed ahead down the long street. "And the best part? We've got backup. Look." She gestured over her shoulder.

Taja looked back. At least thirty Elshalans stood at the ready along the top of the hill, bows and swords drawn. Taja looked around and spotted Maelyrra perched on a rooftop a short distance away, flanked by two more guards. More archers waited on ooftops all the way down the street, and a group fanned in an rc around Ellory and their people.

Taja glanced at Lilya, who grinned. "See? We're not fighting lone."

Taja clenched his jaw and kept moving. "Let's hope it doesn't ome to that."

Hold your ground. Don't fight back. Don't give in to their taunts.

He had one goal: Walk away with Jekku safe.

When Taja was close enough, Ellory stepped to the edge of he crate and grinned. They moved their hands and their flames hifted, creating just enough of a space that Taja could see El- ory's face. The force of the fire whirling around them whipped heir black curls around their head and snapped the edge of their :loak. "Well, well. Took you long enough. I had a feeling the dog vould come running when I threatened his bitch."

Taja ground his teeth. "Let him go."

Ellory raised an eyebrow and set a hand on their hip. "So de- nanding, and we haven't even had a chance to chat. Don't you vant to know why I'm here? Don't you want to know how I oh- ;o-cleverly found you?"

"To be honest, Ellory, no." Taja shrugged, trying to appear in- lifferent even as his heart thundered. "I don't care. I'm not play- ng games. Let Jekku go."

Ellory scowled and stepped closer to Jekku, who leaned away from them as far as he could. He glared up at Ellory and mum- bled something that got muffled by the cloth stuffed in his mouth. Ellory regarded him for a second, then — in less than a blink — grabbed a fistful of Jekku's hair, yanked his head back, and pressed a blade to his throat.

"*No!*" Taja lunged forward, but reached the barrier of flame and jumped back with a hiss.

"Do I have your attention now, traitor?" Ellory's voice was strained, close to hysterics. Something wild gleamed in their eyes. "No more empty threats. No more games. Give up your crusade, rescind everything you have said against the gods, and leave Båthälla for good. Or I swear on my father's life I will end him." He pulled Jekku's hair harder, and Jekku winced.

Taja looked at Jekku. His chest heaved with each forceful breath. His terrified eyes found Taja's, and ever so slightly he shook his head. Taja shook his back. No, *no* he was not going to let Jekku get killed for the sake of a fight Taja didn't even know he'd win. He refused to let Jekku sacrifice himself like his father had done. Båthälla did not matter to him more than Jekku did. It wasn't right, and it wasn't logical, but it was the truth.

He'd save Jekku a hundred times before he saved Båthälla.

He refused to let it end like this.

"I'm getting impatient," Ellory called in a mocking tone. "My hand might slip if you don't make up your mind soon."

A sudden flash of movement tore Taja's attention away from Jekku, and he had no chance to protest when Lilya jumped in front of him, whipped out her dagger, and hurled it at Ellory. Their golden flames flickered and vanished, and Taja heard a scream — *Jekku? Ellory?*

Lilya burst into a loud, strong note, and her own crimson flames wrapped in a whirlwind around Ellory, Jekku, and the two Elshalans. A few of Maelyrra's people rushed in, and the clamor of metal against metal filled the air.

Taja was frozen. He watched, caught between shock and ter-

or, as Maelyrra's warriors fought Ellory's allies from Båthälla. Lilya wielded her magic, and between the flames Taja caught glimpses of Ellory themself, and Jekku. Both were slumped on top of the crate, but Ellory was upright, face contorted with pain and fury as they gripped their leg, and Jekku lay unmoving. Taja caught a glimpse of blood on Jekku's clothes, and his head spun.

No. No, no. Taja scrambled forward, Jekku's name on his lips. He darted straight through Lilya's flames, uncaring if they hurt him, and reached for Jekku. But in the second between one step and the next, someone slammed into him and an excruciating burst of pain shot through his body.

His vision tilted. He saw the glint of a blade, caught a whiff of blood and a glimpse of black hair. His ears started to ring. His eyes went foggy. Then everything blinked out.

22

JEKKU

JEKKU'S HEAD SWAM. He couldn't hear anything, couldn't really see straight, but what he could see was enough to force him to his feet. But he forgot he was on top of a crate and toppled over, landing hard on the ground. He groaned as stars popped into his vision, and before he could get up again, someone grabbed him by the shoulders.

He jolted back, heart pounding, but even with his head spinning he recognized Lilya in front of him. She was talking, he could hear the undertone of her voice, but he couldn't make out any words. The pressure around his wrists released, and then she untied the cloth gagging him. He coughed and pressed a hand to his mouth. "T-Thank you," he croaked.

She said something again, and he just shook his head. She urgently smacked his shoulder and dragged him to his feet. He stumbled, leaning most of his weight on her, and then his eyes fell on Taja.

Taja.

Jekku's heart lurched and he darted forward, forgetting his

292

own battered state as he took in the deep, dark blood soaking Taja's clothes and pooling on the ground around him. Jekku blinked in and out of consciousness like a flame in a blizzard, but he made it to Taja, collapsed beside him, and grabbed his shoulders. He repeated Taja's name over and over, unable to hear his own voice but desperate for Taja to hear him. *Wake up. Wake up. Wake up. You can't die. You can't die.*

"*ENOUGH.*" The voice boomed over the street, loud enough to break through the fog and ringing in Jekku's head. He looked up, and the world came back into focus, but he couldn't make sense of anything. Lilya stood beside him, hands raised. A couple Elshalans lay unmoving on the ground. More gathered around Ellory, who still crouched on top of the crate. Maelyrra stood at the center of it all.

Jekku's head started to spin again. He closed his eyes, and when he next opened them, he was fully slumped on the ground. Something warm and wet seeped through his clothes. The world tilted around him. Pain burned across his face, sending a sharp throb through his skull. Someone was shaking him, shouting at him, but he closed his eyes and the sounds faded to nothing.

He dragged his hand across the ground until it bumped warm skin. He held on to Taja's hand with the last of his strength, and let his mind slip away.

***

When Jekku next woke up, he didn't know where he was. The air was thick with salt and brine, so he must not be far from

Strykivik, but no magic hummed around him. He was no longer amid the chaos that went down in the center of the city.

That was great, but where *was* he, and how on earth was h alive?

Memories came back in pieces: Ellory cornering him in th bookstore, overpowering him with magic and a knife that mus have been made of astruylium or something like it because i burned like hell; Ellory and their allies dragging him out to th middle of the street; then Taja, Lilya, and a whole slew of Elsha lans behind them, and then just pain. Sharp, blinding pain, anc the smell of blood.

Jekku remembered all at once. *Taja.* He was hurt. Jekku hac seen him bleeding on the ground. He had to—

Pain lanced through him and he groaned, abandoning his ef fort to sit up. He slumped back on the soft bed, but hissed curse as his head hit the pillows too hard. The right side of hi face throbbed with each pulsing heartbeat; he carefully lifted hand and touched his cheek, finding a thick, greasy substance smeared on his skin. A sharp burst of pain responded to the touch. He grimaced and cracked open his eyes.

It took a second for his vision to focus, and it was still a little fuzzy around the edges, but at least the soft light in this room didn't send pain shooting through his head. He lay on a small bed in a square room with a ceiling, floor, and walls all made of the same dark wood. Two circular windows were built into the wall across from Jekku, but it was dark and he couldn't see what was outside. A trio of lanterns of varying sizes hung on chains from the ceiling in one far corner; only one was lit, casting a warm or ange glow over the room.

And beside the bed, sound asleep in a wood chair, Taja snored.

Relief hit Jekku like an ocean wave. "Taja." He didn't care that he was asleep. "*Taja.*"

Taja jolted and snapped his head up, eyes flying wide. He blinked once, then his gaze found Jekku and he exhaled. "Jekku. Oh, gods." He got up and sat on the bed instead, grasping Jekku's hands. "Thank the skies. How are you feeling?"

Jekku met his eyes and something tightened in his chest. How long had Taja been sitting there, waiting for Jekku to wake? And had Jekku imagined him being injured? Had that just been a dream? "H-How did you...? I thought— I thought you were dead."

Taja shook his head and gently stroked his fingers across the uninjured side of Jekku's face. "No, no, I'm okay. But you... When you— You didn't wake up, you were totally unresponsive..." He swallowed and closed his eyes. "I thought I'd lost you."

Jekku leaned forward and tipped his forehead against Taja's. The wound on his face throbbed, but he ignored it. "You didn't. I'm here."

It must have been a close call, though. Jekku didn't remember what happened, but judging by the empty feeling inside him and the ache in his body from lying still for too long, it had to have been at least a couple days since the fight in Strykivik. And with his injury being on his head, he was sure he gave Taja and Lilya a scare.

Lilya. She'd been there, too, in the throng of that scuffle. Jekku drew back and looked at Taja. "Where is Lilya?"

"She's here, and she's okay." Taja squeezed his hand again. "A bit scraped up and a little rattled, I think, but she insists she's fine."

"Sounds about right." Jekku sighed, suddenly exhausted. The room began to tilt again, and Jekku focused on the lanterns across the room to keep his stomach from revolting.

Then he realized, as he watched the lanterns swing on their chains, that his *head* wasn't tilting; the *room* was. He blinked and looked at Taja. "Are we on a boat?"

Taja frowned. "You don't remember anything?"

Jekku shook his head. How much had he missed?

"We are on a ship," Taja said, a little hesitantly. It was a second before he added, "We're on Kalle's ship."

Jekku's confusion doubled. "What?"

"Kalle Niska, that sailor you and Saevel—"

"Yeah, I know who he is, but... *How*?"

"I don't know. It... it's too much of a coincidence to be an accident." Taja ran a hand through his hair, and Jekku caught a glimpse of clean white bandages beneath his loose shirt. So he *had* gotten hurt; Jekku hadn't dreamed that. But clearly he was in better shape than Jekku was.

But that thought was only faintly at the back of his mind. He did not understand a single thing about this Kalle situation. "Where did he come from? How did he find— Wait, how did he find a hidden Elshalan village?"

Taja looked just about as baffled as Jekku felt. "Maelyrra and her guards were able to subdue Ellory's people, and Lilya took down Ellory themself. While the guards handled that, Maelyrra and Lilya got you and me down to the harbor. I guess the plan was to get us on one of Strykivik's ships, get us a healer, and keep

s on the ship so we could be easily guarded in the event El-
ory had more backup. But when we reached the docks — and I
m not exaggerating at all — Kalle appeared out of nowhere and
ushered us onto his ship. I was barely conscious at this point, and
n a lot of pain, but I've since seen that he's got a full crew plus a
whole village's worth of healers." He paused and pressed his lips
ogether. "*Elshalan* healers."

Jekku didn't even have a response to that.

"I know." Taja shrugged. "It's strange. It's *too* strange. But Kalle
von't tell us anything more than that he knew we needed help. I
lon't know how he found us, or what he was doing in Strykivik...
out we can ask him later." He smoothed his hand through Jekku's
hair. "You should rest. You've been through a lot."

"So have you," Jekku said. He set his hand on Taja's leg. "What
happened?"

Taja grimaced. "I don't remember a lot. Lilya could tell you
more than me, but allegedly I had an unfortunate encounter
with a sword."

"You're lucky to be alive." Jekku touched his face and kissed
him. "I'm glad you're okay."

"Me too." Taja kissed him again, then moved to get up, but
Jekku caught his hand.

"We can talk to Lilya later," he said. "Stay." He moved over
as much as he could and looked up at Taja in that pleading way
he knew Taja would not refuse. Sure enough, he sighed and gave
Jekku a knowing look, then settled next to him. The bed was far
too small for two people, but Jekku did not care. He tucked himself against Taja's side, set his head on his chest, and closed his
eyes.

"Okay, you win," Taja murmured against Jekku's hair. "This is a better use of our time."

Jekku smiled and snuggled closer to him. Taja pressed a kiss to the top of his head, and between his steady warmth and the gentle rock of the ship, Jekku nearly fell right back to sleep.

Long, quiet minutes slipped by. Sleep tugged Jekku deeper and deeper until he nodded out, and it was some time later when he woke again to the sound of a door opening and shutting.

"Oh. Yeah, they're fine." Lilya's voice. Jekku opened one eye and Taja stirred, lifting his head.

Lilya flashed a smirk, but it failed to hide her concern. "How are you both feeling?"

Jekku dragged himself up and rubbed his eyes. His head felt foggy again, but not so much from his injury as from the impromptu nap that had somehow made him more tired. He mumbled something that might have resembled Lilya's name, but even he didn't know what he was trying to say.

"A little stiff," Taja mumbled, "but otherwise fine." His voice was heavy with sleep. He eased Jekku off his body, which Jekku was too tired to protest, and slid off the bed. "I think we'll live."

Jekku slumped back on the pillows and pressed his hands to his eyes. "We just woke up. How are you speaking so much."

The bed dipped again as someone sat down, and Jekku assumed it was Taja until he felt a playful smack on his knee. "Hey."

Jekku grumbled. "What?"

"Look at me."

He reluctantly opened his eyes and lifted his head. "What?"

Lilya leaned over him and grabbed his chin somewha

roughly in her hand. Her silver eyes bore into his. "Don't ever do that again. You're not allowed to fucking die."

Jekku blinked. "I— I'll do my best."

"You'd better." She smiled, softer this time, then let go of his face and stood up. "Really, though, how's that big head?"

Jekku snorted and sat up, leaning back against the wall. "It's hard to find sympathy in your words when you're insulting me."

"That's how we know she cares," Taja said.

Lilya just smiled.

Jekku took the lull in the conversation as his opportunity to redirect it. "Lilya, what happened back in Strykivik?"

Her smile faded. "I was hoping you could answer that for me, too. You know, since you're the one who got himself captured."

"It's not like I meant to!" he retorted.

"But how did Ellory manage to get you that easily?" Lilya said. "You're a storm mage. Couldn't you have, I dunno, zapped them?" She wiggled her fingers.

"Lilya, would you have brought your magic out full force in a tiny room full of very flammable paper? Especially when that paper contains one-of-a-kind texts?"

She went to reply, then shut her mouth and shook her head.

"Exactly. I wasn't about to rain hell down on that shop," Jekku said. "I tried to reason with them, but it was useless. They didn't care that I wasn't *Sawwia Setukkda*, didn't care that I promised I wasn't a threat to them. They wanted me to get to you, Taja. And... it worked."

And that stabbed a fresh thorn of guilt into him. If he'd done or said something different, if he'd fought back, he wouldn't have needed Taja to get involved. Taja wouldn't have gotten hurt.

"I wasn't about to let them hurt you," Taja said softly. "And the bookstore wasn't the only reason you didn't use magic, is it?"

Jekku hesitated, then shook his head.

Lilya glanced between the two of them. "What?"

"Show her, Jekku."

He pulled up his shirt so Lilya could see the cut across his ribs where Ellory had struck him with the astruylium blade. It still stung a little, but the healers on the ship had mostly patched it up. "When Ellory found me, they immediately disabled my magic. I get it now, why Kalle gave Saevel an astruylium knife to use against Firune. That hurt like hell."

"Saints," Lilya hissed. "Let's just hope it didn't permanently damage your magic."

"Lilya, where were you when this happened?" Taja asked. Jekku was pretty sure he didn't imagine the slightly accusatory edge to his tone.

She stood up straighter and flicked him a glare that told Jekku he had not, in fact, imagined that tone. "I was outside. I'd gone out of the shop literally moments after Ellory must have come in. I didn't see them or their people. I only knew something was wrong when I saw them drag Jekku outside."

Taja narrowed his eyes. "And instead of helping, say, with that impressively powerful fire affinity you have, you just—"

"*Taja*," Jekku interrupted. He couldn't believe what he was hearing. Lilya was the reason the two of them were alive at all.

"I went to get help," Lilya snapped. "I went to get *you*, because I knew you'd be pissed if Ellory got away with that and you didn't know about it. Also, why would I try to take on a fire mage who's half-god and two additional Elshalans *by myself* when we had a whole village of warriors within reach?"

"What if they had killed him?" Taja challenged. "When you ran away, what if they had—"

"Taja!"

"What would you have done differently?" Lilya argued. "Stayed and fought them? With what, your bare hands?"

"That's not the point!"

"Then what is?"

"He could've died! You—"

"*I am sitting right here!*"

The room fell silent save for Jekku's thundering pulse. Pain throbbed through his head again, but he ignored it and stood up. He turned to Taja first. "It is not Lilya's fault that we got hurt, and you know it. She saved our lives, Taja, for gods' sakes."

He clenched his jaw and said nothing.

Jekku turned to Lilya. "Lilya, thank you. If you hadn't gone to get help, we'd all be dead. You did the right thing. I don't blame you for what happened." His gaze flicked back to Taja for the last part. "I don't appreciate being talked about as if I'm invisible."

Taja looked down at the floor, then sheepishly met Jekku's eyes. "I'm sorry."

He stepped aside and held up his hands toward Lilya. "I'm not the one who needs an apology."

Taja looked uncomfortable, but he managed to meet Lilya's gaze. "He's right. I'm sorry, Lilya. I... I didn't mean to imply that you let this happen. If anyone is to blame, it's Ellory, and it's not you I'm angry at, it's them. So I'm sorry, and... thank you. Truly. You are the reason we're alive."

She nodded. "I know this isn't my fight, but I became part c it when they threatened you. I stand up for my friends. I wasn' about to stand by and let Ellory slit Jekku's throat. If anyone' going to do that, it's me."

The tension in the room lifted. Jekku let out a relieved laugl and sat down on the bed. "Lilya Noor, I wouldn't let anyone els slit my throat."

"Let's maybe keep the throat-slitting to a minimum?" Taja suggested.

"No promises." She glanced at Jekku with a wink, then her ex pression sobered. "So after I went to get help, what happened?"

"It gets fuzzy," Jekku said. "There was all that chaos — you magic, Ellory's magic, some kind of scuffle between Ellory's peo ple and Maelyrra's. Did anyone else get hurt?"

Lilya shook her head. "Not on our side, anyway."

"What about Ellory?"

"If I remember correctly," Taja said, "Lilya stabbed them ir the leg."

Jekku stared at her. "Is that what happened?" He had seer Lilya throw her knife, but Ellory had struck him at the same mo ment, and all he heard after that was a scream.

Lilya nodded, grinning. "I indeed stabbed them in the thigh But if they got attention from a healer, they'll be fine. That's why Maelyrra wanted to get us onto a ship: As soon as Ellory's or their feet again, they're going to make another move. At least ou here on the sea, it won't be as easy."

Taja ran a hand through his hair. "We can't let them do this again. Like I said the other day, if they want a fight, I'll take it tc Båthälla. So... that's our next stop."

Jekku looked at him, surprised. "Are you sure?"

"Yes. It has to be. I need to know what's going on back there. I need to see what damage Ellory has done, and start undoing it." He glanced at Lilya. "I'm sure Kalle can make a stop in Westdenn so you can go home."

She looked like she wanted to argue, but then she nodded. "As much as I want to stay and help, I do need to go back."

"Taja, are we ready for Båthälla again?" Jekku asked.

He hesitated, then picked up his cloak from the back of the chair next to the bed and rifled through it. He drew out a parchment scroll. "Maelyrra gave me a spell that will... subdue the gods. It's what she used in Strykivik when they led their revolt. It's the only way to ensure the gods are gone for good."

"When you say 'subdue,'" Lilya said, "do you really mean 'kill?'"

A beat passed. Taja nodded. "As much as a god can be killed."

Jekku didn't know what to say. Even as Taja held the gods' death sentence in his hands, he looked conflicted. Jekku couldn't imagine the internal battle raging in his mind at the thought of doing this to the people who had protected him and his neighbors for his whole life. He had been raised to love those gods, and Jekku knew a part of him still did. Or rather, a part of him still loved the gods who had genuinely cared for him, before things went south.

Jekku got up and took Taja's hand, pulling his attention away from the scroll. "It's okay to mourn what you're losing," he murmured. "And what you've already lost. You can be sorry that you have to do this at all while also understanding that it's the right thing."

Taja blinked a few times, and the worry gradually smoothed from his face. Confidence hardened in his eyes. "It's the right thing to do."

"It's the *only* thing to do." Jekku squeezed his hand. "And we're going to win."

They *had* to win.

"Kalle said we've got at least three days to get to Båthälla, and that's not including a stop in Westdenn," Taja said. "We need time to recover, but this also gives us time to plan our move. I don't want to march into Båthälla like we're there to start a war. If we're going to break the city, I want to do it quietly. Strykivik and Linvalla had bloody revolutions. It doesn't have to be that way for us."

"What if it does?" Lilya murmured.

"I don't want to have to hurt my own people," Taja said.

"Then we won't let it get to that point," Jekku jumped in before Lilya could say anything else. "We keep it peaceful as long as possible."

"You know... this isn't going to happen overnight," Taja said. "We might defeat the gods, but Båthälla will take time to change. We might be looking at several months, if not years, before anything we do makes a real difference."

Jekku nodded. "I know. And I'm there. As long as you need me and want me, I'm there."

A smile melted across his face. "All right. We can worry about Båthälla later. For now, you should rest."

"I've been resting for, what, three days?" Jekku frowned. "I'm fine."

"You have a head injury," Taja said. He started to go, and Lilya ollowed. "Rest. I'll wake you up later for dinner."

Jekku grumbled and got back in bed, but only because his .ead was starting to hurt again. "I also want to talk to Kalle," he alled after Taja.

Taja waved a hand, and then was gone.

Jekku sighed and lay back on the pillows. His head throbbed, »ut he knew he wouldn't sleep. Anxiety coiled in his chest, stir- ing up worries about Ellory, about the situation in Båthälla, and vhat they'd find when they returned. Jekku realized he wasn't eady to see Båthälla again. He knew it was inevitable, but he .idn't think it would be so soon.

But if this was how he was feeling about a place he barely had connection to, he could not imagine what Taja was feeling. So ekku had to be there. Taja was plenty strong enough to win his own on his own, but Jekku would never leave him like that. Not fter everything they'd been through. Jekku wanted to be there – for Taja, but also for his father. At the very least, he owed akob some closure. He owed him a part in the fight he was never ble to win.

Jekku turned his head and watched the lanterns gently sway n their chains. When Taja had said it could be years before his vork was done in Båthälla, Jekku had agreed without a second hought. But now here came the doubts — not because he didn't vant to stay with Taja, but because he didn't know if he could tay in Båthälla. Would he feel like an outsider for all that time? Would he ever be welcomed, even if he helped turn the place round?

Båthälla was Taja's home. It was all he knew. And while it

might not be *all* that Taja wanted — Jekku's incorrect guess i
the Labyrinth had proven that — it was part of it. In some sma
way, Taja would always belong there. And once again, Jekku ha
no idea where he belonged.

Did he fit into the picture with Taja? In Båthälla, or some
where else? If Jekku chose to wander until he found somewher
to land, would Taja come with him? Was it even fair to ask?

He shut his eyes and dragged his hands through his hair, care
ful to avoid the healing wound on the side of his face. Why wa
he even worrying about this? It was too soon. He wasn't about t
make a lifelong declaration. He shouldn't assume anything. Bu
gods above, if this wasn't a sign of doom, he didn't know wha
was.

Jekku loved him. Of course he loved him. He'd fought fo
weeks to inch instead of leap, to walk instead of sprint, to catc
himself instead of fall. But it was hopeless and he knew it. H
couldn't break his fall, but he hoped to the gods he didn't brea
himself in the process.

23

TAJA

TAJA HADN'T INTERACTED MUCH with Kalle the last time they had met, but Kalle treated him, Jekku, and Lilya as if they'd all known each other for years. He burst into the cramped cabin, beaming, and threw his arms wide.

"I have said it before and I will say it again –– I am *ecstatic* to see you both again." His grin lit up his whole freckled face. "Really, I'm so happy I found you! Jekku, how are you feeling? Lilya and Taja caught me up on all of the, you know, *everything* since the last time we met, which–– whew! Busy busy bees, eh? Guess I should thank you for, you know, stopping a magical catastrophe." He spun on his heel to face Taja. "Do you *ever* slow down?"

Taja flickered a smile. "It doesn't feel like it."

"Unless one or both of us gets stabbed, hit in the head, or struck by lightning," Jekku added, "nope."

Kalle laughed. "Well, hopefully our cheery little trip up the coast will give you a chance to rest, lie low, and heal. My wonderful crew has taken great care of you, yes? Oh! And our lead healer, Iona, wants to talk to you both." Kalle pointed a finger at Taja and Jekku. "But first I understand you have questions for me?"

Taja could barely keep up with his chatter as he bounced from one subject to another. He didn't recall the sailor being like this before, and when he'd woken up on the ship a couple of days ago, he'd only seen Kalle for a few minutes at a time and he wasn't all that talkative. Apparently he'd been holding back.

"First question." Lilya plopped down on the end of Jekku's bed. "Tell me, for real — no dodging — how you found us. Why were you in Strykivik with a team of Elshalan healers at the exact moment we needed just that? How did you even know Strykivik was there?"

"Can you *see* Strykivik?" Taja asked. "Elshalan towns appear only to those with express permission. Do you know Maelyrra?"

"I can understand maybe *one* of these coincidences." Jekku pushed himself up and leaned back against the wall. "But not all of them at once." He squinted at Kalle. "Who *are* you?"

Kalle's eyes flicked between the three of them. He pursed his lips and set his hands on his hips. "Well, then... you all jump right at the difficult questions, eh?"

"We understand why you left Aylesbury," Taja said quietly. "When we were there, we saw flyers. Don't feel pressured to tell us your whole story. We're just trying to understand this piece of it."

Kalle tipped his head to the side. "Flyers? About me?"

Jekku shot Taja a confused look. "Um... I think so? The illustration *mostly* looked like you, just with longer hair. And they used a different name."

"Oh." Kalle ruffled his hair. "Yes, I suppose they would have.

hey didn't know otherwise. Huh." His eyes turned distant for moment, then he blinked and waved a hand. "The posters you aw were likely several months old, back from when I first... er, .isappeared. My mother had her guards turn the city upsideown hunting for me, but by the time they found me, it was too ate."

"You mean you were gone already?" Jekku said.

Taja eyed Kalle suspiciously. He'd almost wondered it before, ut wrote off the thought as a grim joke rather than a true possibility.

Kalle grinned. "You could say that."

"Jekku," Taja murmured, "I think..."

"No way." Lilya snorted. "You're messing with us."

Jekku stared at her, clueless. "Huh?"

Kalle batted his eyes, feigning innocence. "Don't believe me, o you?"

"But–– But you have a whole ship and crew," Taja stammered. People have seen and interacted with you. Jekku said he and aevel met you in a healer's clinic. And don't you have a reputation? Thunderstorm of the Scarlet Sea? How can you be that ell known, if...?"

"If what?" Jekku exclaimed.

Taja waited for Kalle to answer, but he only met Taja's eyes ith a cheeky smirk. Taja shook his head. "He's... He's dead, ekku."

Jekku burst out laughing. "He's what? He–– You're saying e're looking at a ghost? How can he be dead?"

Kalle sighed and, with an exasperated roll of his eyes, vanshed into thin air.

Taja's jaw dropped. Okay, he hadn't expected that. He knew spirits lingered, of course, especially if they died restlessly, but he didn't think they were so... tangible.

Jekku turned white as, well, a ghost. Kalle reappeared on the other side of the bed, and Jekku nearly jumped out of his skin. Lilya barked a laugh.

Kalle raised an eyebrow. "Boo."

"*How*?" Jekku stared at him. "How are you–– I thought––"

"That spirits are just myths? Of course not." Kalle paced back to the other side of the room, looking more like he was floating rather than walking. Taja wasn't sure if he'd always moved like that, or if he was doing it now because the secret was out. Now that Taja really looked, Kalle did seem to have an unusually pale pallor to him. Like he wasn't fully here.

But then what of his windswept hair, and the redness in his cheeks from the winter air? Could he change his appearance to appear more... alive? Or was this how he looked when he died –– and therefore how he would appear forever?

Myths didn't touch upon details like that.

"I may not be the vengeful specter you hear about in stories," Kalle went on, "but it's no myth that spirits linger. They're all around us. You may not always see them — we only appear when we wish to be seen — but chances are you have seen us and not realized you were looking at a spirit at all. Some return to places they've always known and loved, others drift around to places they wished to see but never did. I am particularly fond of this ship and this sea, so I tend to stay here. And since this is where my mortal life ended, my spirit is attached to the Scarlet Sea."

Taja's heart sank. "You died here?"

Kalle nodded, then looked away. "Precisely where I wanted to."

"...Oh."

"And before you judge a dead man, understand this: I might have been a prince, but it was by title alone. I was the runt of the Niskala family, the annoying youngest child who had absolutely nothing going for him. In truth, I was probably an accident, and there's even rumors I'm a bastard. But we can't have those rumors flying, oh no, so I was told to be quiet, be nice, and stay out of the way. When I asked to live somewhere else, to be given some kind of purpose, I was told to grow up and accept my life as it was. Wasn't this enough? Wasn't I grateful? How could I be so selfish?"

He swallowed hard and stared down at the floor. "I was miserable. I had nothing to look forward to in my life but endless days of boring balls and impossible standards set by my siblings."

Taja's heart ached for him. Kalle's situation seemed much more desperate than Taja's own life was, but he understood that feeling of hopelessness. He vividly remembered feeling like there would never be anything better than the same dreary days. He knew what it was like to feel trapped in a meaningless circle of time, and he sympathized.

"You will hear no judgment from us," Taja said softly.

"And... if you believe in this sort of thing, I hope the saints — or whoever — bring your soul comfort," Lilya murmured.

Jekku wordlessly got up from the bed and approached Kalle. He held out his arms, and Kalle only hesitated a second before accepting a hug.

He smiled when he drew back, holding Jekku at arm's length.

"Jekku, thank you. I can't tell you the last time I was offered the simple kindness of a hug."

"What? Well, we can't have that, can we?" Taja went to them and threw his arms around both of them.

"Get over here, Lilya," Jekku called.

She shot him a look, but came over and joined in.

Kalle sniffed. "My friends, anything you need during your stay with me, you need only ask. I'm here to help. You've been so kind to me, so the least I can do in return is make this an enjoy-able journey."

"It's enough that you're here at all," Taja said, drawing back. The group hug dispersed. "We wouldn't have made it without you."

"By the way, you still didn't answer our questions," Lilya pointed out with a wink.

Kalle shrugged. "The cat's out the bag. I'm a spirit. I sensed that someone desperately needed help, and I rushed in."

"But what about the healers?" Jekku said. "How did you know to have Elshalan healers ready to help if you didn't know who you were rescuing?"

"That," Kalle said, "is the most miraculous coincidence of all. The healers have been on the *Rogue* for some time now. They, too, needed my help. I only regret that... I couldn't provide it while they still breathed."

Taja frowned. "They're spirits, too?"

Kalle nodded. "They're from a town way down on the south tip of the continent. Apparently their village suffered a severe flood after their dams and bridges failed to hold. A hospital took most of the damage, and several healers were killed along with

heir patients. That's all I know. They aren't keen to talk about
t, and I doubt they remember everything. Traumatic deaths are
roubling to spirits, and our minds do their best to save us from
aving to remember."

Horror coiled in Taja's stomach. "Kalle, in a town inhabited
by talented Elshalans with strong magic, and perhaps at least one
god, how did their infrastructure fail?"

"That's just the thing," Kalle said. "Their magic failed first,
and everything else fell apart after that."

Jekku exchanged a look with Taja. "Their magic *failed*?"

"I think this is why Iona wishes to speak with you," Kalle said.
"Why don't you come up to the deck and we'll chat?"

They let Kalle lead the way outside. A bright, glittering canvas of stars swept across the sky, and the moon's sliver of light re-
lected on the ocean waves. Taja nearly crashed into Jekku, who
had stopped at the top of the steps with his head tipped back
and eyes fixed on the sky.

Taja set his hand on Jekku's back and dipped his head to press
a kiss to his shoulder. Kalle and Lilya stepped around the two of
them and crossed the deck to where a group of Kalle's crewmates
was gathered around a violet fire contained in a metal pot. Others milled about the deck, checking the rigging and adjusting the
giant sails that flapped overhead. All of them — save Kalle himself, of course — were Elshalan, and the group around the fire
wore matching red cloaks that identified them as healers.

As Taja watched, one of them vanished. He gasped, drawing
Jekku's attention, but by the time Jekku looked, the healer had
reappeared. But now Taja couldn't stop seeing it; every few seconds, the spirits flickered in and out of sight.

"Unbelievable," Jekku breathed. "I didn't think this was possi ble."

"I could fill a book with things I thought were impossibl until I stumbled upon you and that damned stone," Taja said pulling Jekku close to his side. "Nothing should surprise me any more."

"Are you two coming?" Lilya waved them over to the fire.

Kalle grinned when Taja and Jekku joined the group. "Her they are! Miss Iona, I don't believe you've met our guests sinc they've been less dead to the world." He cackled. "Pun absolutel intended. Hear that? That was ghost humor."

An Elshalan woman with gray-streaked black curls stoo from her seat around the fire and flashed a bright smile. Her eye were kind; Taja thought one of them might be lighter than th other, but it was hard to tell in the harsh light from the fir "Hello, my friends! I'm glad to meet you properly. My name i Iona. I'm pleased to see you both back on your feet. Gave us quit a scare, didn't you!"

Taja smiled and bowed his head, then accepted her hand when she reached for them. Hers were warm and soft, an gripped Taja's tightly. "It's very nice to meet you, Iona. Thank yo for taking care of us."

"It's what I do, my boy." She gave his hands another squeez and Taja realized she spoke in Elshalan to him, yet Jekku and th others seemed to be able to understand her. Then again, Iona wa a spirit, so perhaps language didn't matter so much on the othe side of the veil.

She then turned to greet Jekku, and that's when Taja saw i The pale violet light from the fire illuminated her features jus enough to clearly show the resemblance, and Taja's heart missed a beat. Her tight black curls, the rounded shape of her eyes, the soft curve of her jaw... Her features were shockingly familiar, and Taja might've written it off as coincidence if not for the colors of her eyes.

One green, and one blue.

Ellory resembled her as much as they resembled Ebris.

Taja tuned back into the conversation as Iona let go of Jekku's hands. "And I can't let any harm befall the ones who will save Båthälla!" Her smile turned wistful. "The change I hope to see you bring to that town is long overdue. I only wish..." She shook her head. "Ah, it doesn't matter. But know that you have my support, even if it is not quite mortal."

"You're... familiar with Båthälla, then?" Taja asked, treading carefully.

She hummed a soft laugh. "All too well. But it is...far behind me."

Taja glanced at Jekku, who met his gaze with the same question Taja itched to ask. Jekku flicked his eyes at Iona, then back to Taja, and subtly touched the corner of his eye. Taja nodded, then turned to Iona again.

"Iona? I–– I'm sorry if this is forward," he said, "but... is your family name Ives?"

She eyed Taja skeptically, then nodded once. "It was. But that name has not been mine in many years."

"Since you left Båthälla?" Taja asked. "How long has it been?"

Iona met Taja's gaze. "How old is my son, whom you clearly know? There is your answer."

So it was true. Taja almost couldn't believe it. What was Ellory's mother doing with a bunch of healers in southern Doweth? Why had she left Båthälla?

"Ellory will be twenty-four this spring," Taja said quietly.

"Twenty-four..." Iona looked down at her hands and shook her head. "Skies. I'm sure he doesn't even remember me."

"I'm sorry," Taja set his hand on her arm and squeezed. "I grew up with Ellory. My family looked after them often, and the two of us were like cousins. They were — and are — well cared for, I can assure you that much."

"Why did you leave?" Jekku asked.

Iona sat up straighter and her shoulders tensed. "I did not *leave*. I would never abandon my child. *Never*. Ellory was— Ellory was everything I ever dreamed of. Such a sweet, happy little child. They smiled... Oh, that smile could melt even the gods' old hearts. And it did. Perhaps too much. Because do you know the thing about a thing that melts? Eventually it cools, and all too often it solidifies into something twisted and deformed."

She gazed at the fire. "I did not leave Båthälla of my own volition. After Ellory was born, Ebris cast me out and forbid me from ever returning. He said he would raise our son on his own and give them the life a god's child deserves.

"I tried, of course, to go back. But each attempt I made to locate Båthälla after it was hidden from me left me weaker and frailer. Outwardly I appear my age, but inwardly... Some days I feel as though I've been leaning on these bones for centuries. I would have wasted away to dust if I'd kept trying to get into Båthälla. I wish I could say I persisted, but after a while, I couldn't bear it. So I left. I put it behind me and went south, where I found these lovely ladies." She flickered a smile as her companions placed their hands on her shoulders and back.

"I don't know what he told Ellory," Iona went on. "Even as a baby, they were inquisitive and curious, so I'm sure they asked questions. I'm sure they wondered where their mother was. Wondered why they didn't have someone to fill that role in their life." She scoffed. "Or maybe they did. Maybe Ebris picked up another and then banished her, too, when the guilt settled in."

"That's what happened?" Jekku exclaimed. "He cast you out because he couldn't handle his own feelings?"

Taja felt ill. He couldn't take a full breath. Anger stirred hot under his skin. At this point, Ebris's cruelty shouldn't surprise him anymore, but this was a particular punch. How different would Ellory be –– how much less damaged –– if they'd had this kind and level-headed woman as a mother? And how *dare* Ebris? How dare he?

"I think he was afraid," Iona said. Her lip curled. "I think he started to feel what love truly is, and it terrified him. Skies forbid the almighty Lord Ebris experience a scrap of humanity."

Taja clenched his hands until it hurt. He could barely look at Iona. He muttered an Elshalan curse to the gods that would be grounds for banishment back home, but he didn't care. Damn the gods. Fucking *damn* them.

A smirk curled at the corner of Iona's lips. "Be careful what you invoke in your curses, boy. You may not wish to see the gods, but they listen."

"Good." Taja's voice dipped low. "Let them."

Beside him, Jekku shifted in his seat and set his hand on Taja's arm. Taja's first instinct was to shake it off, but he took a deep breath and allowed the small, grounding comfort. He'd never felt this kind of bone-deep fury. He didn't know what to do with it.

But he was sure of one thing: Båthälla could not go on like this.

They didn't *deserve* to go on like this.

"Ah, don't waste your anger on me, my friends," said Iona. "Yes, my banishment from Båthälla was the worst thing that had ever happened to me. But I have to remind myself that when you love a god, you are bound to be burned."

"You can't possibly believe this was your fault." Taja spoke as softly as possible, but he still heard a sharp edge in his words.

"Of course not." Iona lifted her chin. "It was not my fault at all. But what am I to do? The past cannot be changed. And now my mortal life is done."

"You're right," Jekku murmured. "The past can't be changed, but the future can be."

"Come with us," Taja said. "Seriously," he added when Iona looked incredulous. "Come to Båthälla with us. Tell your story. Let Ellory see and hear what their father did. It's one thing for the harsh truth to come from us, whom they don't trust, but from you... it could turn the tide for us."

Jekku reached over and set his hand on Taja's knee. "But don't feel obligated, if you don't want to relive all of that," he said to Iona. "We're not asking you to be a pawn or anything like that. We're just asking for your voice."

Iona glanced between the two of them, brow furrowed. Then she nodded once. "I can't come with you, exactly, but I can make an appearance. I've been holding my tongue for twenty-four years. If you need my voice, it's yours."

Taja stood and pulled her into a hug. "Thank you, Iona. Thank you."

INTERLUDE IV

ELLORY

"YOU'RE A FOOL, ELLORY IVES."

They cracked their eyes open, flinching at the sudden assault of bright light. Their mind crawled out of unconsciousness, and as their senses returned so did the steady throb of pain through their body. With a groan, they turned their head toward the source of the voice.

Ava Lake sat in a chair beside the bed where they lay, ankle crossed over her knee. She was dressed for travel, knee-high boots and thick cloak included. Ellory couldn't tell whether she was about to leave or just recently arrived.

They turned away from her and closed their eyes once more. "Where am I?"

"Home." Her tone was clipped, betraying no emotion. Ellory understood that they didn't see eye-to-eye these days, but they would've thought their lifelong best friend would show some sympathy seeing them like this.

It came back to them in pieces. Strykivik. Successfully luring the traitor into their trap. Fighting him and those other traitor ous Elshalans. From there, it blurred. They remembered a burst of excruciating pain; the steady throb in their bones now con firmed that they'd been injured, but by whom? Certainly not the traitor, and certainly not his pathetic friend.

Ellory glanced at Ava again. "What happened?" They frowned. "And what are you doing here?"

She shifted in her chair, letting her foot fall to the floor with a *thump* that made Ellory's headache marginally worse. "I knew you were up to something when I hadn't heard a peep from you for almost a full day. I asked Nedra, and she told me she let you use the Sky Palace to find Taja and then follow him to Strykivik.

Ellory scoffed. They should've known Nedra wasn't to be trusted. They hated asking for her help at all, but following the traitor on foot or even Sky Elk would've taken too long. Ellory had needed him gone, out of their way, as soon as possible. And frankly it was insulting that they didn't have their *own* access to the Palace, and still had to be invited.

"I figured you were up to something extreme," Ava continued. "So I followed you. Saw everything. But I knew it'd only make you angrier if I tried to talk you out of it, so I stayed hidden until things got out of hand." She leaned forward, resting her elbow on her knees. "Although I have to say, I am a little jealous that that pretty fire mage got to stab you before I did."

Ellory frowned. "I can't believe this is what we've come to. What happened to you, Ava?"

She scowled. "You did." She shoved to her feet. "You're wel come, by the way. I brought you back here, healed your leg as much as I could. You'll have to use that for a couple months, but you'll be fine." She nodded toward a wooden cane leaning against the end of the bed, then started toward the door.

Ellory sat up, wincing as their body protested. "Wait. Ava."

She paused but only slightly turned her head over her shoulder. "What?"

"Why?" they asked. "Why did you help me, if you're so adamantly against me? What do you want from me?"

Ava turned abruptly. "What I want, Ellory, is for you to see the madness behind this crusade of yours. I want for you to listen to reason, to listen to the gods you keep insisting we need. I want you to wake the hell up and remember who has been by your side for all these years. You've always trusted me, Ellory. Even through disagreements, you have always looked up to me and respected my judgment. When did that change?"

"It changed," they said, "when you chose a delusional traitor over your best friend."

Ava once again turned her back on them. "No, Ellory. He's not the one who's delusional. So if you won't repay me with any of the things I just said, I'll settle for this." She opened the door and looked back. Her eyes softened. "Hope. That someday, you'll understand. And you'll be better."

Anger sparked through them, rousing their magic. Damn their injuries for keeping them off their feet. "I don't need––"

"I'm giving you another chance, Ellory," Ava barreled on. She stepped out of the room. "Don't waste it."

It might have been their imagination, but they thought they heard her whisper a soft, *Please.*

Ellory growled in frustration and shoved up from the bed. Their injured leg immediately buckled and they grabbed the bedpost for support, then limped over to grab the cane Ava had left. Gods damn her. Now they owed her –– literally for their life –– and they had no choice but to be grateful for it.

She didn't have to do that. She could have ignored their absence from Båthälla. She could have opted to leave them to die in Strykivik, where surely those other blasphemous Elshalans would not have shown them mercy.

But no. She saved Ellory and brought them home.

But was it really because she cared? Or did she want exactly this: a way to bend them toward her? Now she had them in her debt, and if Ellory was a magnanimous person, they might at least listen to what she had to say.

But Ellory was so godsdamned sick of being silenced. They couldn't back down now. It was far too late to let go of this fight. Ebris had *promised* that Båthälla would belong to Ellory someday, as long as they believed in him.

And Ebris needed Ellory to believe in him now more than ever. This was a test, that was all. Their strength and loyalty were being tested, and they had to remain strong.

Eyes on the prize. Taja Ievisin had gotten away this time, but Ellory could not allow it to happen again. So fine, let him stride back into Båthälla and think he could do it right this time. Let him think Ellory was no longer a threat.

When he returned, they'd be waiting.

24

JEKKU

AS THE NIGHT WORE ON, THE SPIRITS DISPERSED. Kalle told Jekku that in order to sleep and refresh their energy, spirits had to temporarily disappear from the mortal world. When Jekku had asked where exactly they went when they weren't here, Kalle had waved a hand and changed the subject. Jekku accepted that he wouldn't understand, and bid Kalle good-night.

He found Taja up on the ship's highest deck. Jekku went up the steps and eyed the water far below with disdain; even the waist-high railing wrapping around the perimeter of the deck didn't settle his stomach. Why Taja would choose to linger up here was beyond him, but he could ignore his phobia for a few minutes for the sake of offering some comfort.

Jekku knew that Iona's story had rattled Taja. He'd been quiet for the hour or so the three of them had spent with the heal-ers; as usual, Jekku and Lilya had been the inquisitive ones. They traded stories and laughs and memories, and through it all Taja barely said a word. Jekku noticed every time his gaze flicked to ward Iona.

Now, he stood at the farthest edge of the deck, elbows on the railing, and stared out at the sea receding behind the ship. The stars overhead made the water sparkle, but the darkness was ab solute; Jekku couldn't tell where the sea ended and the sky began or if there was land anywhere out there. They might as well have been sailing through a dark, dreamless void.

Jekku went to Taja and leaned his back against the rail so he didn't have to look down at the water. Taja turned his head and studied Jekku for a second, then flickered a smile. "Hey."

"Hey." Jekku moved his hand closer to Taja's arm, then placed it on top. Taja set his hand over Jekku's. "What's on your mind all the way up here?"

Taja hummed and looked down at the water again. "Nothing pleasant."

"Same here. Do you know what I'm thinking about?"

"I can't say I do."

"I'm thinking that it's at least fifty feet down to that water and it's probably ice cold, and hitting that water from way up here would probably kill me instantly, so I'd better hope to what ever gods still like me that this railing holds up."

And with that in mind, Jekku stood up straight and took few steps away from the rail. It *did* feel sturdy, but he couldn't b too careful.

Taja turned to him, obviously trying not to look amused. " think you'll be okay, Jekku."

"Oh, so do I, but you never know."

Taja chuckled softly. "Come here. I'll make sure you don

fly overboard." He held out his hands, and Jekku went to him. To be fair, this wasn't as bad as those awful pulley platforms in Strykivik, and wasn't nearly as bad as hiking up Howl Hills, but the crash of waves against the hull and the steady rock of the ship that still made Jekku stumble now and then did not do anything good for his nerves. He found his gaze wandering toward the sea once more, and grimaced.

"You're making yourself suffer," Taja said. "Stop looking at it. Look at me instead. I'm much nicer to see than the cold ocean."

Jekku laughed. Admittedly that got his attention off the water. He smiled up at Taja, letting the lightness in his chest chase away his anxiety. In truth, his phobia hadn't flared up too badly when he stepped up here. But he wanted Taja's mind off Iona's story and Ebris and Båthälla, and thankfully the distraction worked.

Taja slid one arm around Jekku and reached up to touch his face with his other hand. Jekku leaned into his palm and then stepped closer to him, wrapping his arms around him. He set his head on Taja's chest and closed his eyes. Taja stroked his fingers through Jekku's hair, down the back of his head, and all the way down his spine. A pleasant shiver ran through him, but then Taja stopped.

"There's something I've been meaning to say."

And just like that, the warm feeling fled and Jekku's anxiety returned. He knew he should move so he could see Taja's face, but maybe it was easier like this. "What is it?"

"It's... about the Labyrinth." Taja sighed. "Jekku, I'm sorry. I've been at a loss as to what I could possibly say after what happened in there, and I know an apology isn't quite right, but I don't know what else to do. I was wrong. I failed you. You believed in me so strongly, and I— It was as though, in that moment, I didn't know you at all."

Jekku held him a little tighter. "I failed you, too. I was wrong too. And I've been spinning all these possibilities in my head of what went wrong, how the Sky Palace could've been working against us, how it was an unfair test, and so on. But I don't think any of that is true. Maybe the harsh truth is that we really didn't understand what we wanted — for ourselves, or each other."

Now Jekku drew back to look at him, but didn't let go, didn't move from the circle of his arms. "I think that was something we needed more time to find."

"Did you?" Taja asked.

"I think so." Jekku studied Taja's eyes. Maybe it was his imagination or his lack of sleep or both, but he swore the stars were reflected there. "I think I know how to find what I want, and I know I don't need to find it immediately. It will come to me when it will. I've had quite enough of trying to grasp the future before it's ready to meet me."

Taja smiled and leaned back against the railing. Jekku eyed it warily, but tucked himself against Taja's side and tried not to think about it. "You know, I've always been the opposite," Taja said. "My father used to scold me that I didn't care enough about my future, that I couldn't see an inch past my own nose. That was one of his favorite criticisms, that I never thought about my future and was surely going to ruin it. But how can you ruin something that hasn't happened yet? A future will always be there, even if it's unexpected. Even if it's one you weren't 'meant to have. I don't believe all things are written in the stars." He eached up and touched Jekku's face, stroking his thumb across is cheek. "But some things certainly are."

Jekku's heart pounded; he swore Taja must be able to hear it.)h, gods, he was in love. This was something out of a dream, nd every word out of Taja's mouth battled Jekku's rationality. he flock of doubts that had taken up long-term residence in ie back of his mind started to voice their ugly cries, but Jekku lenced them. *No. Not a word from you. Not now.* He could not nagine anything more genuine than the bare affection he saw 1 Taja's eyes.

There would still be much to talk about and work out. There ould be hiccups, there would be wrinkles to smooth out, there ould be bumps in the road. Jekku knew that. Nothing would be awless, and that was okay. What mattered to him was that Taja ared for him, and Jekku hoped Taja continued to look at him ke this even after this phase of flurried excitement was over.

How can you ruin something that hasn't happened yet? The future ould bring what it would bring. Very few things were forever, ut this wasn't the time to dwell on it. This was the time to live 1 the present, for once in his life.

Taja's fingers gently skimmed over the healing wound on the de of Jekku's head as he tucked his hair behind his ear. "What is ?" he murmured. "What's running around up there?" He play- illy tapped Jekku's temple. "I can tell when you get lost in there. our eyes get that same distant look they did when you still had iat curse. Whatever it is, you can tell me."

Jekku smiled. "I love you." It simply came down to that. Jekku elieved in the weight of those words; he believed in every feel- ig, every memory, and every hope that went behind them. He

could spill all these messy thoughts to Taja, but then they'd b
here forever. All of it — even the doubts — amounted to thre
simple words that Jekku spoke as a promise.

Taja beamed at him in a way that lit up his whole face, an
now Jekku was sure there were stars shining in his eyes. H
pulled Jekku close and held tight, pressing his face to his shoul
der. Jekku hugged him back just as fiercely, then let go only t
pull him back for a kiss. And then another. And then many
He held Taja's face in his hands and smiled against his lips, an
Taja kissed him harder and pushed him against the deck's railing
Jekku broke the kiss with a gasp and glanced over his shoulder
but Taja gently touched his cheek and turned his face back t
him.

"Don't worry," he murmured, pressing a kiss to Jekku's neck
"I won't let you fall."

***

"Westdenn is in sight!" Kalle announced — loud enough t
jolt Jekku out of sleep even from two levels below the main deck
He groaned and turned over, then startled so suddenly that h
nearly fell right off the bed when he discovered and remembered
all at once that he wasn't alone. It took his groggy mind a second
to catch up, then he smiled to himself and settled back down beside Taja — who, somehow, was still sound asleep. Jekku snuggled close to him and closed his eyes. Five more minutes.

He enjoyed maybe two before pounding footsteps approached the door to his cabin. Jekku waited, listening, but there
was a pause, and then a series of loud knocks.

Taja stirred, mumbling something incoherent, and blinked at Jekku. A smile melted across his sleepy face. "Oh. Hello."

Jekku snorted. "Good morning to you too."

Taja turned over to face him and kissed him once, softly. But then the knocks sounded again.

Jekku groaned. "Ugh, okay, fine, I heard you the first time." He flung off the blankets and got up, yawning as he went to the door. He didn't bother with a shirt; it was probably just Lilya, anyway.

"Wait. Jekku."

He paused with his hand on the knob and looked back at Taja. "What?"

Taja's face had turned a shade darker. He touched his throat. "You, um. Your neck."

Jekku glanced at the mirror on the wall next to the door, then raised his eyebrows at Taja as he moved his hair to hide the love bites on his neck as best he could. Taja looked a little guilty, but then he winked.

As expected, Jekku found Lilya at the door. She mirrored Jekku's position with her hand on her hip and a somewhat exasperated look on her face. She glanced over him, then was not subtle about darting her gaze over his shoulder.

Jekku cleared his throat to get her attention back. "Thank you for knocking."

"Thank you for not being entirely unclothed," she shot back. A smirk danced across her face, but faded quickly. She looked down at the floor. "We're sailing into the Westdenn harbor. I... wanted to make sure I said goodbye before I go, so come upstairs when you're ready. I have something for you."

"We'll be there." Jekku smiled and watched her disappear down the hall and up the steps. He shut the door once she was gone and leaned back against it.

"What's wrong?" Taja asked.

He shook his head. "Nothing. It's just... that went by fast."

Taja smiled and got up from the bed, then came over and wrapped Jekku in his arms. "It's not like we'll never see her again."

"I know. And I know she has her work to do." But he would still miss her. Maybe someday Gallien's Peak would be in Jekku's future again — this time with Lilya as its Master. Maybe Jekku could learn from her, earn the title of Master of Magic from the most talented mage he knew.

But not today. Jekku wasn't ready to see Gallien's Peak quite yet.

Once he and Taja were properly dressed, they went up to the main deck, where Jekku spotted Lilya at the railing where Kalle would let down the gangplank when the ship was docked. Lilya stood facing the city, hair flying in the wind. She didn't react when Jekku approached her.

He leaned against her shoulder. "Looking for someone?"

She jumped. "Saints! Oh, it's just you."

"Well, don't sound so excited." He grinned and leaned on the rail next to her. This was a slightly less terrifying distance above the water, but still not ideal. Especially not with the shore steadily approaching. Jekku studied Lilya instead. "You look... melancholy."

She gave him a look. "I think that's just my resting face."

"Nah, your resting face is pissed off." Jekku nudged her. "What's on your mind?"

She rolled her eyes and looked away from him. "Nothing. I'm fine. Just thinking."

"About?"

"My next steps." Her gaze lingered on the docks drifting closer below. "It's time to make some real moves. Hearing your plans to fix Båthälla made me see that Westdenn *can* be changed. I was worried at first that running off with you two would distract me, but if anything it's... centered me. I know what to do now. But I don't think 'Nice' Lilya is the right one for the job."

"There's a '*Nice*' Lilya?" Jekku feigned shock. "Why have I never met her?"

She punched his arm. "Those who deserve to meet 'Nice' Lilya will meet 'Nice' Lilya."

Jekku pouted. "Why do you hate me, Lilya Noor?"

"Saints, because you're annoying." She looked at him and smirked. "Of course I don't hate you. And trust me, you'd know if you ever met 'Not-Nice' Lilya."

Jekku rubbed his arm where she'd punched him. "I'm pretty sure I have. Like just now. Or maybe when you stabbed me."

He'd meant it as a joke, but she winced. "I hardly believe that was even me."

Jekku set his hand on her arm. "It wasn't."

"But it was." She met his eyes. "It was, and I can't pretend it wasn't. I hurt you, badly, and I could have killed you. I almost *did*."

"It's water under the bridge, Lilya. I forgive you." He smiled. "I forgave you a while ago."

She looked like she didn't believe him. "How are you so..."

"Charming? Hilarious? Gorgeous?" He grinned. "I've bee called worse."

Lilya rolled her eyes. "I was going to say *kind*, but I'm rethink ing that adjective. How about *irritating*? That's fitting."

Jekku laughed and pulled her into a hug. To his surprise she didn't protest or resist, but hugged him back fiercely. Jekk squeezed her tighter. "I'm going to miss you, Lilya Noor."

"I'll miss you like a thorn in my side, Jekku Aj'ere." She drev back, grinning. "Really, though, you and Taja will be fine. I be lieve in you. Change the world."

Jekku met her eyes, thankful that he could do so without see ing that odd gray fog his curse had shown him. He still didn' know what that meant, but it didn't matter. He didn't need t see Lilya's future to know she would do great things. "I'll see yo around, Master Noor."

She beamed. "Yeah, you will."

The ship lurched as it glided up against the dock, and Kall shouted orders to the crew to get it tethered and get the plank lowered. Jekku looked around and spotted Taja, and waved hir over. "Were you going to wait until she was already gone to say goodbye?" Jekku teased.

"I wanted to let you have a minute," he said, then brought Lilya into a hug. "We'll see you soon, Lilya." He let go and helc her at arm's length. "I'm proud of you. Go win. You can do this."

It might have been Jekku's imagination, but he swore he saw a glimmer of tears in her eyes. "I'll do my best, *Sawwia Se- tukkda*. And I know you will, too. Oh! And one more thing."

She shrugged her bag off her shoulder, flipped over the flap, and brought out a sheathed dagger. "You should have this."

"A knife?" Jekku grinned. "That's very in-character for you."

"Just take it," Lilya said. "But don't open it here."

Jekku eyed her skeptically and took the knife. He started to slide it out, but Lilya caught his wrist.

"What did I literally just say?"

"You can't just hand me a mysterious knife and expect me *not* to look at it!"

Lilya pursed her lips. "I can't even argue with that, because I'd do the same thing."

Taja gently took the knife from Jekku. "I trust we'll understand later?"

Lilya nodded. "It might even come in handy."

A few feet away, the gangplank creaked into place, and Kalle waved to Lilya to tell her it was ready. He flashed a grin, then sauntered off to the other end of the deck.

Lilya stared down at the dock. "Well... guess that's my cue."

Jekku found himself a little choked up. But like Taja said, it wasn't as though they'd never see Lilya again. He managed a somewhat teary smile and waved as Lilya stepped onto the plank.

She looked back, grinned — genuinely, brightly — and then strode ahead and disappeared into the crowd milling around the docks.

Taja slipped his arm around Jekku. "We'll see her again."

He sniffed. "I know."

"Are you crying?"

"No."

"I wouldn't judge you if you are."

"...Yes." He breathed a short laugh and leaned his head on Taja's shoulder. "I'm just... I'm proud of her. After everything she's been through, she deserves a victory. She deserves so many victories."

Taja chuckled and kissed the side of Jekku's head. "If I didn't know any better, I'd be jealous."

Jekku snorted. "Why?"

"Oh, come on. It's no secret that you've always been a little enchanted with Lilya."

Well... *enchanted* wasn't quite the right word, but... "She pulled a knife on me and pinned me to a wall seconds after we met. She's exactly my type. But— No. Gods, that would be.. chaos." He looked up at Taja. "So it's a good thing you're my type, too."

"Even without a knife?"

"Even then." Jekku kissed him. "But speaking of knives, why did Lilya give us that one?"

Taja held it up and traced his fingers over the hilt, which Jekku now realized was wrapped in thick cloth. "I have a feeling..." He inched it out of the casing just enough to see the blade, and he grimaced. Jekku's eyes widened.

"Oh."

Taja shook his head. "Why did she give us this? She said she could protect it." He snapped the Oracle dagger back in its case, eyeing the weapon as if expecting it to burst into flames.

"She said it might come in handy," Jekku said. "But why?"

Taja glanced at Jekku. "She brought this from Aylesbury to Westdenn without knowing she'd run into us."

"She wouldn't leave it in Aylesbury while she's gone for six

nonths," Jekku pointed out. "And she's friends with a diviner. I
wonder if Nesma hinted at something."

"Jekku, do you think something happened?" Taja searched his
eyes. "With the stone and Lilya?"

He drew back. "No."

"I know how it sounds, but if she tried to reactivate this—"

"She wouldn't." Jekku shook his head. She *wouldn't*. Right?
Lilya wasn't the same person who'd made a blood oath and ran
after the stone without a care for the consequences. Jekku had
seen the change in her; he recognized how different she was
without impossible expectations heaped on her shoulders. He
refused to believe that Lilya had intentionally messed with the
stone, and he resented that Taja had jumped to that conclusion.

"If anything happened," Jekku said, "it was not her fault.
Maybe it had something to do with the stone being at Gallien's
Peak. Gods know that place is crawling with bad magic. But
look." He wrapped his hands around the scabbard. "Do you feel
anything? Because I don't. It's dead. Lilya did not touch it."

Taja still didn't look convinced. "I hope not," he murmured.

Jekku looked away from him and back at Westdenn. The ship
made its steady way back into the sea, and the city drifted farther and farther away. Jekku trusted Lilya, but he couldn't help
fearing that, even without the Oracle Stone tempting her, she
might still find the dark power of Gallien's Peak irresistible.

She'll be fine. She was strong and rational and no longer
blinded by her ambitions. She no longer had an overbearing
Master of Magic to impress. Her fight wasn't impossible anymore.

And neither was theirs. Jekku turned back to Taja. "Are yo
ready to do this?"

He looked up and took a deep breath. "I think so."

"Well, then, Båthälla... here we come."

25

TAJA

TAJA DIDN'T KNOW WHAT to expect when he and Jekku arrived in Båthälla, but part of him thought they'd be struck down on sight. He followed the river toward the outskirts of town, anticipating a patrol of guards or a magic barrier to keep them out. A very small, irrational part of him almost expected to encounter Ebris himself.

To his relief, they did not encounter a single Elshalan — neither guard nor god — as they stepped beneath the cover of trees and entered through the back of town. Taja stopped at his cottage so they could drop off their bags, and then, holding tight to Jekku's hand, they made their way toward the town square.

Flashes from the last time he'd done this plagued his memories. The instant rejection. Ellory's harsh words. The entire town, united against him because of one mistake from the past.

Taja had never denied that he'd been wrong to share his magic with Kierra and bring her to Båthälla. He admitted that he'd put his neighbors in danger. But he also knew how to forgive, something that many of these people clearly did not grasp.

Please be able to change, he prayed now. *Please hear us out.*

He stopped at the edge of the town square. The temple loomed directly across from him, illuminated with golden torches. Taja's stomach turned over. He wasn't sure if the flames were natural, or if they were lit by a certain fire mage, but he shuddered to think what it would mean if Ellory had claimed the temple as their own.

Taja shook the thought away and started to cross the square, but halted. A man with brown skin, black hair, and wearing a gold robe stepped out of the temple and paused at the top of the steps, and for a second Taja swore—

But no. That was impossible. The man continued down the steps and turned up the path toward the north end of town. Taja recognized him; he sold books and pamphlets up by the school.

Lord Ebris was gone. *Gone.* He was not coming back.

Taja let out a breath. Jekku squeezed his hand. "You can do this," he murmured.

"I know."

"I'm with you."

Taja looked at him. "I know." He raised Jekku's hand and kissed it, then let go. "Let's find Nedra and get our plan rolling before Ellory catches wind that we're here."

Taja was tempted to pull up the hood on his cloak and hide his face until he reached the temple, but he resisted and crossed the square with his chin tipped up. No more hiding. No more running. This was his home, and he was *Sawwia Setukkda,* and this was his fight.

He carried that energy up the steps and into the temple, but his confidence faltered when he found it occupied by at least

wenty Elshalans, all dressed in the same gold robes the book-
eller had been wearing. Taja eyed them skeptically, searching
or Ellory's face among the crowd, but as the seconds passed and
o one moved or said a word, Taja concluded that Ellory wasn't
ere.

He felt their eyes on him like burning embers, but he kept his
ead up and shoulders back and he strode straight down the cen-
er of the room. The silence was broken only by the soft thump
f his and Jekku's shoes.

As soon as he passed through the doorway into the back hall,
e slumped against the wall and let out the breath he'd held all
he way across the temple. Jekku paused a few feet away and
oked back. "What's with the gold robes?" he whispered.

"I don't know, but I don't like it." Taja pushed off the wall and
ubbed his hands. "I have a feeling Ellory has something to do
ith it."

Taja brought Jekku into the sanctuary where the White Lily
as housed, then slid the door shut behind them. He flicked a
lance at the prophecy, and then jumped when he realized some-
ne was standing in front of the wall.

"*Sawwia Setukkda*," Lady Nedra said, "you've returned." She
urned and smiled, calm and graceful as always. "And just in
me, it seems." She nodded toward the White Lily, and the air
ushed out of Taja's lungs.

The flower had entirely lost its pigment; instead of a brilliant
inkish white, the one remaining petal was gray and shriveled,
anging onto the stem by a hair. The rest of the fallen petals lay
rumpled on the table around the dried-out stem.

Taja understood, rationally, that his people's magic was not actually tied to this flower, but to see this lifelong symbol of his home's magic wither and die before his eyes... He felt something within him die with it.

The White Lily might not contain Båthälla's magic, but it was connected to it. Taja didn't want to think about what would happen if the flower fully died. If he could figure out a way to free it, to release all that pent up power like—

Like Saevel had done, when they made the Oracle Stone.

Taja set his hand on the sheathed dagger on his belt. Was that the answer? Really, after everything, was the Oracle Stone the solution he needed?

He glanced up at the prophecy. His eyes drifted back to the one line he had yet to understand. *In flame, in thorn, in heart of stone, Second Savior, awaken, find home.*

Taja thought he knew what that meant now. Lilya was the flame. He was the thorn. Jekku was the heart of stone. With them, Taja would find his way home. All of them would.

Saevel's fate was written in stone from the start. They were one person, and though they might not have done everything alone, in the end, it was them alone who had created the Oracle Stone and sacrificed themself for it.

Taja was not Saevel, and he was never meant to be. Saevel had found their power in metals and stones, and thus the Oracle Stone was their solution. But it was not Taja's.

He wasn't made of steel and sharp edges like they were. He didn't have the cleverness or the bravery of a legendary hero. But that didn't mean Taja lacked the strength Saevel had. Stone might withstand storms, but so did forests.

And that was the difference between that Savior and this one. Mountains stood alone. Forests had strength in numbers.

Taja turned to Jekku and Nedra. Jekku looked amused, probably because he'd been trying to get Taja's attention and Taja had been buried in his thoughts, but there was a spark of pride in his eyes as well.

"I think I know what to do about our magic," Taja said. "But I'm going to need your help, Jekku."

"Whatever you need," Jekku said. "I'm there."

Taja smiled. "Thank you. But that comes later." He turned to Nedra. "First, I'd like to ask for your help, too, Lady Nedra. If... you're still on our side."

Nedra nodded. "You have my support now and always, *Sawwia Setukkda*."

We'll see about that once you're asked to leave, Taja thought. Nedra might be on his side now, but she was still a goddess, and that meant Båthälla was not hers to keep. Taja wasn't looking forward to finding out how she reacted when her power was threatened.

But that was for later. For now, he had to let her believe that he trusted her without question. Maybe she'd leave more gracefully than he expected.

Or... maybe he was utterly unprepared for her wrath.

He'd find out soon enough.

"Okay." Taja looked once more at the Prophecy of the Second Savior, then met Nedra's eyes and gathered his thoughts. "Here's our plan."

***

Taja jittered with nerves. He stood with Jekku on the steps of the temple, but while Taja could barely keep still, Jekku leaned against a column and somehow looked totally calm. Did he have that much confidence that this would work? Taja tried to be optimistic, but there was too much at stake if this only made people angrier.

Also, where the hell was Ellory? Taja did not trust their absence. He understood that they'd been badly injured — *thank you, Lilya* — but if Jekku could recover from a blow to the head and Taja could bounce back from a stab wound with the help of Elshalan healers, surely Ellory must be back on their feet by now.

Taja had a sense of being watched, as if by a predator concealed just out of sight. Ellory would strike; it was a question of *when*, not *if*.

He tried to put Ellory out of mind and focus on this next task. Ellory was a problem for later. Now, all of Taja's focus needed to be directed to making this vision of the future as believable as possible.

Footsteps approached behind him. He turned and found Nedra dressed in her ceremonial attire — a pristine white robe woven with silver around the collar, sleeves, and hem, and accessorized with a string of pearls around her neck and silver bracelets glinting on her wrists. Instead of her usual half-moon crown, she wore Ebris's brilliant gold sun on her head.

The sight of the crown made Taja's heart drop like a stone. For half a beat it *was* Ebris standing there, and instead of a gentle smile he wore a sadistic look of victory.

Did you truly think you could win?

And then Taja blinked, and it was Nedra. Her smile was kind, confident, and she touched Taja's arm fondly. The cold shock of her rings against his skin grounded him in reality. Taja relaxed a little.

"Are you ready, *Sawwia Setukkda*?"

He nodded, and Jekku joined him at his side as Nedra descended the temple steps to the square below. The few people in the midst of crossing the village paused and watched. Nedra went and rang the bell, calling the rest of Båthälla to attention. Taja waited, heart pounding, as old friends, neighbors, friends of friends, distant relatives, close relatives, and acquaintances gradually drifted into the square. He spotted his parents in the crowd and his heart seized.

For a second he was tempted to hide behind one of the pillars and wait out Nedra's speech. He could keep his head down and stay out of sight until it was his turn to talk. It'd be so easy to let someone else take the lead.

But no. *No.* This was not the time to succumb to his fear. If he couldn't stand up to his people by now, then he didn't deserve to at all.

So he held his ground and let his gaze wander over people with whom he'd once laughed and hunted and shared meals and told stories. He still knew their names, but had they bothered to remember his? Did they still think of those days, or had their love for him been erased and his name replaced with *traitor*?

Please be forgiving, Taja prayed. *Please be better than Ebris told me you are.*

Taja felt a nudge on his hand and surfaced from his thoughts. He looked down and found Jekku's hand sliding into his, squeez-

ing tight as he twined their fingers together. Taja exhaled an
squeezed back.

There were a million things he could have said, but befor
Taja could find the words, Nedra began her speech and th
courtyard fell silent.

"Hello, my friends." Her voice carried strongly over the vil
lage, but she kept her tone friendly, soft around the edge.
"Thank you all for joining me so promptly. I know that there ha
been uncertainty and unrest here lately, but I'm here today wit
something I hope will soothe our anxiety. There is a way forwar
out of these troubling times. The night does not last eternall
and even as it persists there is always a beacon of light."

She paused, and Taja's heart thundered. Quiet, curious mur
murs rippled through the crowd below. Good. This was a goo
start. Taja took mental notes for when his time to talk to ther
came later.

Jekku lightly touched Taja's wrist with his free hand, and Taj
realized he was crushing Jekku's other hand. He loosened hi
grip. "Sorry."

"Breathe," Jekku murmured.

Taja did his best.

Nedra made her way to the center of the square and turne
in a slow circle, taking in as many faces as she could. "Trouble
such as the ones we are facing occur when we fall too easily int
a pattern. We have lived comfortably like this for centuries, an
to me, the message could not be clearer. It is time for a chang
And today I ask you to trust me to help lead you through th
change. Let me show you, personally, what life would be like in
brighter, newer Båthälla."

The murmurs grew louder, but not angry. Taja scanned the crowd, again searching for Ellory, waiting for them to burst out of nowhere and start shouting. But despite the presence of several gold robes in the crowd, no one spoke out. Everyone waited, caught between interest and apprehension.

They trust Nedra, Taja realized. *They still have faith in her.*

"Are you ready?" Jekku whispered.

"Not in the slightest," Taja replied.

At first, Taja hadn't wanted to participate in the visions he planned to show his neighbors. He was terrified of the Sky Palace and what it might plant in his mind, and he didn't want to subject Jekku to it, either. But in the end, Jekku had convinced him. With Oridite gone and the Palace in Nedra's hands, Taja wouldn't be run in circles and forced to relive painful memories. He wouldn't be tormented with visions of a life in someone else's control.

Hopefully, he would see what his life could be like in his *own* hands.

Now, what terrified him as he faced the threshold with Jekku was precisely one thought: *What if I don't see the future I want?*

He forced the thought out of mind as Nedra continued her speech. "In a moment, the temple will connect to a place only the gods have seen. I invite you to step into the Sky Palace, where you will see a version of your future that, with some overdue changes in Båthälla, very well might come to pass. You will see the life you most desire, my friends, and with that knowledge I hope you will find your path forward."

Curious murmurs loudened to a mix of excited and yet still apprehensive voices. A few questions rang over the crowd, which

Nedra patiently answered. No, this was not a trick. No, they were not being led to their deaths. Yes, they could choose not to participate. *No, this is not a trick.*

The frequency of that question showed Taja how his people truly felt about the gods.

Nedra came up the steps and gave her signal for Taja and Jekku to go inside. Taja hesitated, glancing over the crowd once more for any glimpse of Ellory. Still he found no sign of them.

"Taja." Jekku tugged his hand, and Taja followed him into the oblivion of the Sky Palace once more.

***

He walked through a forest. The *Urdahl*, of course; what else would it be? He recognized the bright leafy canopies, the chorus of birds within the branches, the moss crawling up trunks and taking over fallen logs. These sights and sounds had once been all he knew.

Flowers bloomed at his feet, encroaching upon the nearly-buried stone path beneath his shoes. Taja did his best to avoid stepping on them — and the butterflies that danced on the breeze — as he made his way forward.

He didn't know where he was going, but he wasn't afraid. He breathed easy and his heart beat steadily. The air was crisp and fresh, carrying a faint scent of rain. He didn't know what had brought him to this moment, and he didn't know what lay ahead, but he was happy. He recognized that. He carried it like a soft sheet on his shoulders. A weight had lifted off him; he felt its absence, and for once, nothing came down to rest in its place.

He continued walking. Soon, the trees opened to a small clearing where he found a cottage tucked against a cliff. It was surrounded by plants and greenery, as if a piece of the forest had followed Taja here and made a nest around the little wood-sided house. Moss crawled across the roof, ivy crept up the walls, and purple flowers burst from boxes beneath the front windows. The door was painted a bright sky blue, welcoming him in. Taja felt an overwhelming sense of ease as he approached.

Was this home? He looked around, but beyond the cliff and the cottage and the trees in which he stood, everything was shrouded. He couldn't place this location, and he was fairly sure he'd never seen it before. It was both unfamiliar *and* familiar; he'd never been here, but he *would* be. And he was certain that when he saw it again, he'd know that things had fallen into place.

Taja tried to move closer, but something held him back. *Just a glimpse,* an unknown sense told him. *For now, only a sliver of what might be.*

So Taja held back. He sat down in the grass among the wildflowers and let the sun warm him. He breathed in the scent of greenery and spring blossoms, and even when a warm rain began to fall, he didn't move. This place relaxed him, and it made his heart ache with longing. He wanted this to be his life *now,* with all the obstacles removed.

But if he wanted this, he had to fight for it. And he would.

"So this is it." He lay back in the grass and spoke to the pale sky above. "This is the life you can see that I want. It's... easy. Quaint. Quiet but not isolated, simple but not lacking. I can already feel how much I'll love this. I can feel the peace that'll settle in my heart when, someday, this future is my present. I know

what I have to do to get here, and I think... I think it means leav
ing."

He had assumed the woods surrounding him were the *Urdah*
but after seeing this cottage, he knew they weren't. The tree
were similar, so maybe this place wasn't far from what he knew
but this was not Båthälla.

And maybe that was good. If Taja was going to find peac
anywhere, it wasn't going to be in Båthälla, no matter how muc
it changed.

It was still his home, though. It was his to fight for, and his t
reclaim. But it was not his future. There were too many ghosts –
and not of the friendly, helpful variety. He would never rest eas
in Båthälla again, and he regretted it. He wished it didn't hav
to be like that. But there was nothing he could do, and he didn'
want to waste emotional energy on trying to find his place i
Båthälla again when he could just as easily start over somewher
he actually wanted to be.

When the fight was done, he would say his goodbyes, an
then it was time for a new path.

Taja smiled up at the sky. "So let's get started, then, shall we?

He got up from the grass and looked upon the cottage onc
more. Fog began to creep in. The Sky Palace was closing th
doors on this vision, but Taja didn't try to fight it. He wasn
afraid of losing this. Now the future he was fighting for had
tangible shape, and he swore he wouldn't quit until he stood her
in real time.

Maybe — just maybe — someone would be standing wit
him.

The thought had scarcely crossed his mind when he notice

a flicker of movement to his right. He turned his head, and through the thickening haze, he made out the shape of two people, one a bit taller than the other, strolling side by side toward the cottage. Taja couldn't see their faces or any distinguishing features, but he once again felt something click into place.

**

When Taja opened his eyes again, he was on the floor of the temple with his back against one of the front columns. Jekku was slumped against him, head on his shoulder and eyes still closed. Taja smiled and slid an arm around him, letting his head rest against Jekku's.

The temple was silent. Scattered around the main room, Taja's neighbors slumbered as the Sky Palace led them through pleasant dreams. Their faces were calm, some with gentle smiles on their lips. Some cuddled in twos or threes or entire families, others lay against the walls and columns on their own, arms crossed and heads bowed. Nedra stood in the center of them all, looking pleased. Her gaze wandered over to Taja and Jekku, and she smiled.

Taja smiled back.

Beside him, Jekku stirred. He released a startled noise, as if he'd forgotten where he was, but after a second of blinking up at Taja, a smile melted across his face. He closed his eyes again and tipped his forehead against Taja's. "You're here."

You were there. Taja knew it like he knew the scene he'd just seen was his future. Even though he hadn't seen any faces, he knew in his bones that Jekku would share that place with him —

share that *future* with him. And that, on its own, was something to fight for.

He wanted to tell Jekku what he'd seen, but that was another thing they'd agreed upon: Whatever they saw in the Sky Palace was to be kept to themselves. Futures were fragile things, always shifting and changing and sliding a little to the side. They were not written in stone, or even in the stars, but still... Taja did not dare tempt fate. Not when he was so close to getting this life he desperately wanted.

Why worry about the future, anyway, when he could enjoy the present?

Around him, the others gradually began to wake. Taja's anxiety spiked again as he searched their faces, expecting anger and outrage and distrust. He almost expected them to leap up and chase him out of Båthälla once and for all.

But...

Gods, could it be true? Taja saw no trace of anger on his neighbors' faces. Some were crying. Some clutched their loved ones' hands, others brought their children or partners or friends into crushing hugs. Taja saw hope in their eyes — *real* hope, the kind that burned in Taja's own chest.

"Jekku," he murmured, "it worked. Gods above, it worked."

Jekku pulled him close and kissed him. "You're brilliant."

"Lady Nedra..." A young woman a few feet away from Taja stood up and hesitantly approached the goddess. "How... How might these visions come true? Is the future I saw really possible?"

Nedra nodded and clutched the woman's hands. "It is. Each of you has what it takes to reach the life you saw just now. The alace of the Gods hears what your hearts want. None of it is abricated, only brought into focus. If what you saw is what you vant, then you will have it. The trick, however, is to remove one arge obstacle."

More people got to their feet and surrounded Nedra. A few f them still looked nervous, but any distrust that had been in heir eyes before was gone. Another, older woman stepped forvard. "What do we have to do?"

"Yes, tell us, Lady Nedra!" called someone else. More murnurs of approval filled the room. Taja heard hopes and dreams ise to the vaulted ceiling of the temple in the same way prayers o Ebris used to echo off the marble walls. His neighbors clamred for solutions, bursting with ideas and ways they could bring hemselves closer to the lives they had glimpsed.

Taja listened, shocked, as their dreams shifted from personal goals to bigger goals. They spoke of ways Båthälla itself could be a better, kinder, more progressive society. Without the gods smothering their magic, the possibilities were endless. They could expand the village, make space for their growing population. They could renew Båthälla's dedication to the practice and study of magic. Taja even heard a suggestion to lift the shroud on the village and quit hiding from the rest of the world.

Laws could be changed, the gods' ways could be altered. Taja heard the renewed confidence in his neighbors' voices; Båthälla could flourish. It could bloom. It was time to grow.

Nedra's gaze found him again, only briefly. She squared her shoulders and lifted her hands, and the voices quieted. Nedra smiled. "I love your enthusiasm, my friends. I've never been prouder to be a part of this village. We've always been strong,

haven't we? Elshalans of Båthälla are fighters. We survive because
we adapt. I implore you to keep what you have seen today in the
front of your minds. Let it lead you into the future until your
present matches what your heart desires. My work here is done.
It is up to you."

Silence stretched in the wake of her words. Taja held his
breath and glanced around, mainly at the people in gold robes.
He watched the truth dawn on everyone; they looked around at
each other, at first confused, a little nervous, then... accepting.

A few still frowned, still looked hesitant to trust. But most
people were smiling and nodding and clutching each other's
hands.

Taja brought his hands to his face, hardly able to believe what
he was seeing. They understood, then, that this meant an absence
of gods, and... they accepted that?

His relief turned into shame. He should have thought better
of his people, who hadn't always seen him as their enemy. Apparently most of Båthälla *was* ready for this change. But who could
blame him, after the way he'd been treated? Would he ever really
trust these people again?

If he did, it wouldn't be for a long time. And by then, Båthälla
would be entirely in his past.

"Lady Nedra!" A teenage boy hopped to his feet and carefully
stepped his way toward Nedra, tugging his partner by her hand.
"Is it true, then, what Taja Ievisin said? Is he really *Sawwia Se-tukkda*? Are the gods really hindering us?"

"Is that why our magic is dying?" asked an older man.

"I thought Lord Ebris said—"

"Lord Ebris lied to us."

"— the White Lily?"

"Why would the gods take our magic?"

At that, Taja nearly laughed. *To control you. Obviously.* His neighbors might be having a gradual change of heart, but they had so much to learn.

This was a start, though. They were no longer blind to the injustices they'd been dealt. Now that they recognized one, they would see the others.

Steeling himself, Taja stood up and left his safe corner of the temple. It was time to be seen. Jekku started to come with him, but Taja looked back and shook his head. No, he had to do this alone. Jekku sat back against the column and smiled at him in that proud, encouraging way that made Taja's heart beat a little stronger.

He joined Nedra in the center of the room, rattling with nerves. But when he looked around at the faces before him, they weren't twisted with distrust and hatred like he had become accustomed to seeing. There was some hesitance, sure, but his neighbors looked at him more openly now.

He took a deep breath. "Did you all like what you saw?"

In reply, he received affirmative murmurs and nods. A few smiles. Taja returned these with a smile of his own. "I did too. It's hard to imagine what you want your life to be when you can't actually see it, isn't it? It's too abstract, too... hypothetical. These glimpses you saw, painted from your deepest wishes, gave physical form to things you might've always wanted but didn't know how to reach. I don't know about you all, but now that I've seen what I can have, I feel a lot better about the steps I have to take to get there."

Once again, he received a chorus of agreements. A few people began excitedly whispering to each other, casting glances and smiles around the room and toward Taja.

"I have never tried to say that our gods haven't served us," Taja went on. The whispers quieted. "They have. There was a time when they let Båthälla flourish. When they truly did love and protect us. But that time, I'm afraid, has come to an end. Lady Nedra, would you agree?"

She nodded once. "We have failed our duty to you, people of Båthälla. And that means our time is done. It is time for Båthälla to stand strong on its own legs."

Murmurs scattered. Fears jumped out. Doubts crept in. Taja let it happen. It was good to question, to let concerns be heard.

When the voices lessened, he went on. "This is not a change that will happen overnight. If we're to make it to the futures we want, I'm going to need your help. And your trust. I know that isn't easy, given what I did that put us all in danger. I accept that mistake. I accept the blame. But there is one thing I must ask of you."

He paused, heart pounding once again. He scanned the room and his eyes found Jekku, briefly, seeking that burst of confidence. He didn't expect to see Jekku's eyes welled with tears.

"Forgiveness," Taja finished. His voice choked up around the word. He didn't realize, before, how much this would mean to him. "What I ask of you today is forgiveness. Please... give your Second Savior a second chance."

The young woman who'd first approached Nedra now came to Taja and set her hand on his arm. Her brown eyes welled with

ears. "I am willing to leave the past in the past, *Sawwia Setukkda*.
'm with you."

Taja was now entirely choked up. He set his hand on top of
ers and squeezed. "Thank you."

She let go and stepped back, and someone else immediately
ook her place and clapped Taja on the shoulder. They were
much taller than him, a touch intimidating, but their green eyes
vere kind. "You have my forgiveness, Vaeltaja. And my apologies.
hope you might... forgive me in return. I am not proud of what
said and thought about you in recent years."

Right, so apologies don't erase seven years of hate, Taja thought,
out he appreciated the honesty, at least. He nodded in acknowledgment, and suddenly people were coming up to him from all
sides to offer their support and trust and agreement to put the
past in the past. He received a few more heartfelt apologies,
some laced with excuses, others sounding truly remorseful, and
before long his eyes blurred with tears.

Of all the directions this could have taken, Taja had not expected *this*. He'd braced himself for the worst. He'd thought less
of his people. Even now, a tiny voice in his mind reminded him
that this was a fraction of the population of Bâthälla. He might
have several dozen people's support, but what about everyone
else who hadn't agreed to step into the Sky Palace? What about
Ellory, and that group with the gold robes that Taja suspected
had sided with them?

The fight was not over just because things were turning up.

Across the temple, a door slammed. Taja jumped. Everyone
quieted. Taja exchanged a glance with Nedra, then slowly turned
as the crowd parted to make a path.

Accompanied by the steady *click* of a cane against the marble, Ellory Ives stalked down the center of the temple. They leaned heavily on the pearl-handled cane, favoring their injured leg, and wore a brilliant gold robe that Taja recognized as one of Ebris' ceremonial gowns. But Ellory had altered it, and where once a brilliant sun motif spread from collar to waist, there were now white flames.

Ellory stopped a few feet in front of Taja and lifted their chin with a scowl. Nedra moved to stand behind Taja, and everyone else gave them space. Taja stood his ground and met Ellory's eye. "I had a feeling you'd make an appearance."

"As did I." Ellory glanced around the room. "So this is it, hm? Your pack of traitors who would rather see this city crumble without its gods?"

"If only you'd come a little earlier, Ellory, you would have seen how far that is from the truth." Taja stepped closer to them. He tried to see through their glare and the hatred that burned there. He tried to find the person he'd grown up with, who'd been almost like a sibling to him. That person must be in there somewhere.

"Ellory, it doesn't have to be like this." Taja reached out his hand.

Ellory hesitated. Taja felt a small burst of hope. But then they jerked backward and called a burst of flame to their free hand. "It will *always* be like this! Båthälla is eternal. The *gods* are eternal. And so am I."

Taja didn't have a chance to react. Light flared, heat blasted, and the last thing he felt was being thrown off his feet.

26

TAJA

"TAJA. *TAJA*. WAKE UP. You— You have to get up."

His senses crawled back in a haze, and then all at once. He gasped and bolted up, but flinched at the sudden brightness when he opened his eyes. His heart pounded, and his ears still rang. "W-What—?" He blinked until his eyes focused on a familiar face. "Jekku."

"Yeah, it's me, I'm okay, but we have to move." He wrapped an arm around Taja and dragged him up with a grunt. "Come on, you've gotta help me out here."

Taja scrambled to get his feet under him and stood, coughing. The air was thick with smoke, and then he realized that his vision wasn't foggy; the temple was—

Oh, gods.

"What...?" Taja stood among rubble. Several columns had fallen, the ceiling had caved in, and smoke still billowed from the ruins. Distantly, people were screaming. He heard whimpers, cries, sobs, but all of it was muffled under the pound of his own pulse.

"Taja." Jekku shook him. "The rest of it's going to cave. We have to go."

"But— Where...?" He stumbled as Jekku dragged him by the arm toward the exit. At least that was still clear, but they had to pick their way around pieces of stone. People rushed in and out of the temple around them, darting around rubble and dragging unconscious Elshalans outside. Taja blinked away his dizziness and watched, stunned.

"Taja, please." Jekku tugged his hand. "Just come outside. We—"

The ground rumbled. A deafening crack split the air, and Taja and Jekku both flinched. Taja grabbed Jekku's arm and darted out of the temple; chunks of marble rained down around them and the remaining columns quaked.

As soon as they were outside and down a few steps, Taja rounded on Jekku and grabbed his shoulders. "What the hell is going on?"

Jekku was breathing hard and his face was stained with dust and a bit of dried blood that seemed to come from the scar above his eyebrow, but he was otherwise unharmed. "I— Everything happened so fast. Ellory—"

"Ellory did this?"

Jekku met his eyes and nodded once.

But— None of this made sense. Ellory was a fire mage. How could their magic be strong enough to do *this*?

"Taja, I think—"

"Have I made myself clear enough?" Ellory's voice carried across the square, and Taja looked down. They stood in the center of the village, golden flames whirling around them. People

cattered around, some tending to the wounded at the bottom
f the temple steps, others slowly inching away from Ellory. But
heir supporters, dressed in gold robes, moved to surround them.

Taja didn't know what to do. He didn't have magic — not
hat he could access easily, and not that would do anything
gainst Ellory. He couldn't reason with them. The only person
who could possibly fight them with magic was Jekku, and Taja
efused to let him face Ellory alone. Ellory would kill him with-
ut hesitation.

"Båthälla was never yours to protect or to change, traitor,"
Ellory went on. They stepped closer to the stairs, carrying their
lames with them. "This place belongs to me. It is my birthright
nd I am its heir. And you have no place among us. Take your
lelusions and *get. Out.*"

Taja started down the steps. He didn't know exactly what he
was going to say, had absolutely no clue what to do, but destroy-
ng the temple was the last straw. People had gotten hurt. Some
might have been killed. This was not exactly a good start to El-
ory's reign.

If that didn't work to get Båthälla on his side, he didn't know
where else to turn.

But before he reached the ground, someone touched his
shoulder and he stopped. Iona appeared beside him, still dressed
n the same tunic and cloak she'd worn on Kalle's ship. She met
Taja's eyes, nodded once, and then stomped down the temple
stairs and faced her son.

They blinked. Their flames faltered and then snuffed out.
They lowered their hand and eyed the spirit suspiciously. "Who
are you? What is this, another trick? Another illusion?"

"If only that it were," Iona said. She glanced back at Taja, the[n] over his shoulder at the ruined temple. "What have you done, El lory?"

They narrowed their eyes. "How do you know who I am?"

Taja heard the sadness in her voice. "I would know you any where, my son."

Ellory jerked back. Their eyes widened in shock, just for a sec ond, before their face twisted with rage once again. "What kin[d] of— This isn't going to work on me! I won't be swayed by th[e] traitor's silly mind games. You're not real. My mother is dead."

Iona continued toward them. "Is that what he told you? Tha[t] I died before you ever knew me?"

"The gods are the only parents I know," Ellory snarled. "Lor[d] Ebris is the only one who matters to me."

"And would you still think that if you knew the truth?" Iona stopped before them. "Would you even *believe* the truth?"

No, they won't, Taja thought. Ellory was too stubborn, too de termined to keep on believing what Ebris wanted them to be lieve. The rest of Båthälla might give Taja a chance and be willin[g] to learn, but Ellory had shown over and over that they were not

"You're a stranger to me," Ellory said. "Why should I believ[e] anything you say?"

"You won't," Iona agreed. "Which is why I'm going to sho[w] you." Before Ellory could protest, she set her hands on thei[r] shoulders and they went rigid. Their eyes widened, but Taja could tell they weren't looking at Iona. They were seeing some thing else, something she must be showing them in their mind.

Jekku came down the steps and stood beside Taja. "Start

praying that this works. Taja, I think they have Nokaldir's power."

Taja stared at him. "*What?*"

"After they threw that initial blast of magic that knocked you out — and about a dozen other people — they... they summoned lightning," Jekku said. "They wielded that and their fire together, and that's what started bringing down the temple."

"Jekku." Taja's horror deepened. "Did Nokaldir *give* them his power, or did they take it?"

"Does it matter? Either way––"

"It matters, because if they took it by force, it means they killed him." Taja clenched his teeth as Jekku's eyes widened. "And if Ellory is powerful enough to kill a god..."

Jekku dragged a hand through his hair. "It means we don't stand a godsdamned chance."

"*NO!*"

Taja and Jekku jumped at Ellory's shriek. They had leapt back from Iona, who was already fading from view, and had their hands pressed to the sides of their head. Even from here, Taja could see their chest heaving.

"It's not true!" Their voice broke on the words. "This is a trick, it— it has to be. It must be. This is— This was you." They looked up at Taja and their gaze turned murderous. They picked up their cane and started forward, raising their hand to call flames, but before they could take more than a step, a loud whistle echoed across the square and at least twenty armed Elshalans poured into the square.

Taja didn't know what the hell was going on, but these people faced Ellory and their supporters with bows raised and that was enough for now.

Ellory straightened and let their hand fall. A laugh burst out of them. "Ava? This is what you call an army?"

"This is what I call a resistance." A girl about Taja's age stepped forward and drew her blade. She glanced back once at Taja, and he was shocked to recognize her as Ellory's childhood best friend, Ava Lake. Taja had never been close with her, but she was infinitely more tolerable than Ellory. The two of them had been inseparable as children.

And now here she was, standing against them.

"What do you mean to do?" Ellory snapped. Taja could see them shaking. Whatever Iona had showed them had clearly rattled them and they were failing to hide it. But Taja knew that would only make them more dangerous, more unpredictable, more likely to lash out.

"We mean to stop you," Ava replied. "Look at what you've done, Ellory." She threw an arm back toward the temple. "You've destroyed the house of our gods. You've let innocent people get hurt. You've spent so much energy trying to get us to hate Taja and all it's done is turn us against you. Accept your loss, accept the truth, and stop this madness."

"Do you care nothing for our history?" Ellory snarled. "For our legacy? Is this what Ebris would have wanted?"

Taja could not believe that Ellory still cared what Ebris would have wanted after learning the truth about their mother. If even that wasn't enough, Taja had one more idea. A last resort before he opted to get Ellory out of Båthälla for good. It wouldn't

e pleasant, and it wouldn't be kind, but it was better than tear-
ng Ellory away from the only home they'd ever known.

Taja would offer them mercy once last time.

"Jekku," he murmured, "where's Nedra?"

"She was helping get people out of the temple," Jekku said,
but she might have gone back in looking for more survivors."

Taja turned and darted up the steps. Jekku called after him,
out he pretended not to hear and continued into the ruined tem-
ole.

Seeing it now, with a clearer head, he was struck simultaneously by grief and anger. He knew this symbol of the gods — of
Ebris — only served to keep Båthälla in the past, but still. There
had been a time when Taja came to this place for solace. It was
ust a structure of stone and metal, but to almost everyone here,
t was a second home.

And Ellory had taken that from them.

Taja wasn't going to let them get away with anything else.

He spotted Nedra toward the back of the main room, helping
another woman carry an older man with blood running down
his face. Taja's stomach twisted and he scrambled over a broken
column to get to the goddess.

She looked up as he approached. "Oh, thank the skies you're
all right. I don't know what—"

"Lady Nedra, can you still access the Sky Palace?" Taja didn't
mean to cut her off, but it wasn't his own safety he was worried
about at the moment.

She blinked. "Yes, I can place an entrance anywhere. Why?"

"I need you to open a door. A hidden one, if you can."

Nedra turned to the woman beside her and set a hand on

her shoulder, then whispered something under her breath. The woman gasped and straightened, then easily hefted the older man into her arms. "There. You have my strength. Get the both of you to our healers, quick. I'll come by later."

"Thank you, Lady Nedra." The woman made her way across the temple, then Nedra turned back to Taja.

"What is your plan?"

He swallowed. "To trap Ellory in the Sky Palace."

Nedra's face remained neutral. "Permanently?"

He started to say yes. Yes, trap them there forever. Let them live out the rest of their miserable life in solitude and run from their nightmares. Let them encounter every path their life could have taken and let them be driven mad by doubts. Let them suffer an ounce of what Taja suffered.

But then he thought of the Labyrinth, and what he had seen there. And what Jekku had seen there. And what Jakob Balmoo had endured there. If Taja put Ellory through that, did that make him any better than the gods who had made him suffer the same thing?

Taja looked at Nedra and shook his head. "No. Not permanently. I just want them to see. I need them to see something that will make them understand once and for all. I'm giving them one last chance."

And if this last chance broke them in the process? Good. Taja hoped it rattled them to their core.

Nedra nodded once. "Very well."

Taja led the way out of the temple, hoping he wasn't about to make everything worse.

Outside, chaos had erupted. Taja's stomach plummeted;

minute ago, Ellory and their supporters and Ava and her rebels had been caught in a standoff, but while Taja had fetched Nedra, someone must have struck.

Ellory remained at the center, flames and lightning blazing around them, and their gold-clad supporters formed a barrier around them, hands raised with magic in their palms. Wielding stone drawn from the bricks underfoot and deadly shards of ice, they clashed with Ava's archers in a merciless battle. Taja feared Ellory's side was fighting to kill.

Taja's heart pounded. Jekku was down there, too, violet lightning crackling around him. He circled Ellory but didn't strike; Taja didn't know if he was only there in case things got out of hand, or if he truly meant to attack Ellory. Would he really do something that reckless?

Taja turned to Nedra. "There's no time. Can you trap them now?"

She nodded. "Leave it to me, Taja." And she disappeared.

Taja waited, heart thundering. He itched to go down there and help, but he didn't know what he could do. He couldn't fight. He had no magic. But how could he just stand here and watch his only supporters fight this battle for him?

"*Sawwia Setukkda!*"

He turned at the voice. One of Ava's rebels, a girl of maybe eighteen, came up the steps toward him and offered him a bow and quiver. "I understand this is your weapon of choice?"

Taja hesitated. It was, and he'd always been a good shot, but killing an animal to eat was so, so different than killing another person.

"Never said you had to take any lives," the girl said, as if she'd read his mind. She glanced over her shoulder and then all but shoved the weapon into his hands, then nodded once and took off down the steps. A moment later she launched herself back into the fray, blade whistling through the air as she took on a much bigger man swathed in gold. He fought back mercilessly.

Taja shook off his hesitation and nocked an arrow. If Ellory's supporters weren't holding back, neither should he. He drew the bow, exhaled, and let it fly.

Someone cried out below as the arrow hit home, piercing straight through their leg. They crumpled, sword clattering to the stones, and Taja drew and aimed again. He lost count of how many arrows he fired, and one by one Ellory's supporters dropped like stones. The rebels gained the upper hand.

But then Ellory noticed.

They looked around, turning in a circle as they tried to find the source of the arrows. Jekku drew back from them a little, also glancing around, but he spotted Taja first. A smile spread across his face.

Taja replied with a wink that Jekku probably couldn't see, but it felt right.

Ellory turned and finally spotted him. Their expression darkened and their magic blazed. They gathered the flames and lightning around them and stalked straight through the ongoing battle toward the temple stairs.

Taja drew the bow. His pulse rang. *Please, Ellory, don't make me do this.*

But Ellory never made it to the steps. One second they were there, the next they vanished. And Nedra stood in their place. She faced Taja and nodded once, then disappeared again.

Taja lowered the bow and let out a breath. Below in the square, the fight gradually came to a pause. Jekku let his magic fizzle out.

For a heartbeat, silence reigned over Båthälla. Taja started to wonder if this was the beginning of the end, if victory was within reach.

But there was still one god left.

Taja set down the bow and went to Jekku, gently taking his arm. "Are you all right?"

Jekku startled, then threw his arms around Taja. "I'm fine. Are you?"

"Yeah. Jekku, listen... about Nedra."

He drew back. "Taja, you know we can't let her stay. I don't trust her. Do you?"

He probably trusted her more than Jekku did, since he'd known her all his life. But he also knew Jekku was right. Gods –– no matter how kind or forgiving –– were inherently prone to greed. Taja didn't want to have to come back here and free Båthälla all over again in ten years.

"Not enough," he said to Jekku. "But what if we don't have to kill her?"

"Taja..."

"Just because Linvalla and Strykivik did it that way, doesn't mean we have to." He searched Jekku's eyes. "There must be another way."

"What are you going to do? Politely ask her to leave? This isn't over. She could still turn on us. Where is she now?"

"Right here."

Taja gasped and whirled around. Nedra had returned, and

stood now in the center of the square with her hands folded be
hind her back. Her dark eyes bore into Taja, but he couldn't read
her.

Movement behind Nedra drew his attention, and Taja
watched in shock as Ava and her archers drew their bows upon
the goddess. If she noticed, she didn't react.

Taja held up a hand, both as an offer of peace to Nedra and
as a signal for Ava to wait. He stepped closer to the goddess, ig
noring Jekku's hand tightening on his arm in warning.

He met Nedra's eyes. "I don't want to have to do this the hard
way. You've sworn your loyalty to me, Lady Nedra, and you have
never been anything but kind to me when the other gods were
not. But you have also been compliant, and are not free of blame
for the way things are in Båthälla."

Nedra nodded once. "I know."

"I hope you also understand that simply asking you to leave
and trusting that you will not meddle, is not an option any
more."

"I know." Taja expected shock, perhaps even anger, but Nedra
just looked sad. Understanding, but sad.

It was easy to forget that this place was home to her, too.

She eyed him carefully. "What are you going to do, Sawwi
Setukkda? Have your allies stab me in the back? Pool your magic
to kill me the same way the people of Linvalla defeated my sib
lings?"

"Not if I don't have to," Taja said softly. "I have another idea."

"Do you now?" Nedra asked.

"You do?" Jekku said, failing to hide the surprise in his voice.

Taja nodded. In the two days it took to sail from Westden

to a port closer to Båthälla, Jekku had told Taja that Nedra had shown him why the White Lily couldn't simply be freed from its dome. The influx of magic –– suffocated and suppressed for so many years –– could potentially harm everyone in the village. After decades of weakened magic, they weren't strong enough to withstand all of it returning at once.

A goddess, however, could handle it.

"Lady Nedra," Taja said, "will you do the honors of freeing Båthälla's magic from the White Lily?"

She raised her eyebrows. "I've already told Jekku that it would cause––"

"I know, I know. But if someone controlled it, someone with enough strength to withstand that kind of power, it would lessen the blow."

"Even I might not survive that explosion of power," Nedra said. "It has been captive for so long..."

Taja held her gaze. "And whose fault is that?"

Nedra narrowed her eyes, then pursed her lips and lowered her gaze to the ground. "I see your point."

"If you want to be shown mercy, Lady Nedra, then help fix what you let happen. Free our magic."

"And if I don't survive?"

"Then it will have been your choice," Taja said. "Unless you'd prefer we banish you to the gods' realm ourselves?"

Nedra drew back. "Come with me." And she turned and strode toward the ruined temple.

Taja glanced at Jekku. "Come on."

He fell into step beside Taja. "That was––" He cleared his throat. "Um, unexpected."

"You gave me the idea," Taja said.

"No, I mean... I didn't expect you to talk to Nedra like that." Jekku looked up at him and quirked an eyebrow. "I like this side of you."

He snorted and took Jekku's hand. Taja himself hadn't expected to be so short with Nedra, but his patience was worn thin. He followed Nedra into the temple and crossed his fingers that she wasn't leading him straight into a trap.

They wove their way around debris and headed straight back to the sanctuary that housed the White Lily. Thankfully, the room had survived most of Ellory's damage; save for a large crack that ran a crooked line across the ceiling and down one of the walls, it was intact.

Taja realized with a thrill that the crack split the Prophecy of the Second Savior clean in half. *Good.* That prophecy and the gods who'd written it could go straight to hell.

Nedra stopped by the table and set her hand on top of the glass dome. Inside, the flower pulsed once, then dropped its second to last petal. The final one curled in on itself, rotting before Taja's eyes.

"Are you sure about this?" Nedra asked.

"Of course I am," Taja said. "Are you?"

She looked up at the prophecy, then turned her head down and gazed at the White Lily. It was another minute before she spoke. "Yes. I am. I owe this to you."

"Nedra." Taja waited for her to meet his eyes, then nodded once. "Thank you."

She nodded in return, and then lifted the dome off the Lily.

Taja didn't have time to brace himself. The immediate burst

f magic stole the air from his lungs, making him stumble backwards. Jekku cried out and doubled over, barely catching himself on the wall. Taja held onto him, but the only thing he could do was wait for the blast of power to ease and fade. It burned through his veins just like the Oracle Stone's power had done, and if it was unbearable to him, he couldn't imagine the agony Jekku felt.

Somewhere, beyond the roaring pulse in Taja's ears, he heard a scream. And then, suddenly, he could breathe.

Jekku let out a sob and slumped against Taja, breathing hard. For several minutes, only the steady rhythm of their gasps filled the air, and then Taja drew back to look at Jekku. "Are you all right?"

He nodded. "I... I think it worked. Taja..." He blinked and stood up straight, then hummed a soft tune. Lightning burst to life in his hands and crawled in faint sparks up his arms. Jekku grinned and looked up at Taja. "It's so much easier now."

Relief washed over Taja. It worked. *Skies, it worked.*

He turned around, but he didn't have to look to know that Nedra was gone. The White Lily lay alone on the table, lush and bright and *alive*.

"Taja." Jekku's voice was edged with sudden panic. "Taja, something's wrong."

"What?" Taja turned back to him. He stared in horror at his hands and shook them out. He hummed softly, then raised his voice louder.

Nothing happened.

"Shit." Taja bolted across the room and picked up the White Lily, but despite its sudden revival it didn't hold a hint of magic.

Taja wouldn't be able to feel much, but each time he'd been clos
to the flower he'd felt *something*. "No, no, come on. Come on, yo
can't die. Not now."

"Taja, it's gone." Jekku stared at him. "My magic is gone."

"No. No." Taja closed his hands around the Lily. No,
couldn't end like this. He refused.

He looked up at Jekku once more, then rushed out of th
room and sprinted across the temple. Heart pounding, he too
the steps two at a time and stumbled into the town square.

He found a spot where the white bricks had broken and fresh
rich earth burst through. He dropped to his knees and tucke
the White Lily into the earth, then closed his eyes and presse
his palms to the ground.

"*Please*," he begged. "Please, hold on. Don't give up ye
Breathe. You can breathe now."

Taja buried his hands in the soil around the flower and bega
to hum. *Please work.* Taja knew he need only ask and Jekku woul
be at his side in a second to give him a boost of magic, but Taj
wanted to obtain it himself. He needed to know he could still d
this.

It took a second, but at last he felt it. Magic crackled lik
static, emanating from the ground. Taja grasped for it, pullin
it around him like a blanket. He hummed louder and let th
melody surround him; he pictured the notes mingling and har
monizing with the streams of magic in the air, as if these in
tangible powers were made of silk threads that could be wove
together to create the fabric of the earth itself.

Tears stung his eyes. His heart was full to bursting. Seve
years without this beautiful, gentle touch of divinity... Gods, he'

missed it. He'd ached for it. This felt like coming home, like something at his core coming back to life.

Make it grow. Help it live. He took the energy around him and directed it toward the flower, and he felt it the moment the magic took hold. Roots sprouted and crept deep into the soil. Stems grew, leaves unfurled, flowers budded. Taja opened his eyes and found not a lily before him, but a sapling — a fresh, green, newborn start of a tree.

Taja marveled at it. Tears ran down his face. He'd... done that. He had made it grow, brought it back to life stronger than ever. The White Lily was no longer something that could be suffocated under a jar; now it had space to stretch its branches, breathe, and grow.

Light rain began to fall, drawing Taja out of his magic-fueled reverie. He looked up and found Jekku beside him, palms turned toward the sky. A single gray cloud hovered up above and poured a gentle shower upon the tree.

"I figured it could use a little help," Jekku said.

Taja let out a breath. Their magic was back.

He stood and went to Jekku and pulled him into a hug. He put everything else on pause, buried his face in Jekku's shoulder, and let out a sob of relief.

"We did it, Jekku. We did it." He sniffed and pulled back, taking his face in his hands. "Thank you."

"Don't thank me." Jekku took his hands. "This was all you, Taja." He grinned and raised Taja's hand high, turning toward the others scattered across the square. "*Sawwia Setukkda!*"

"Oh, gods, Jekku—" But his words were drowned under resounding cries.

"Sawwia Setukkda! Sawwia Setukkda!"

Taja stared, frozen, as stunned, battered, and exhausted Elshalans gathered around him. Some cheered, some sobbed, some prayed, and as one they brought their hands to their hearts and then knelt and pressed their palms to the broken earth beneath them. Taja felt a surge of magic, and the Lily Tree grew bigger and taller right before his eyes.

His heart pounded. Something in the back of his mind screamed that he didn't deserve this. He wasn't a god, wasn't a hero. And yet... Here he stood.

Sawwia Setukkda. He'd really done it.

In the wake of the cheers and tearful laughs, Taja heard a sob.

He turned toward the temple. At the bottom of the cracked steps, among broken pieces of the building they brought to pieces, Ellory slumped with their head in their hands.

Taja looked at Jekku. "I... need to do this alone. Will you go see if you can help the healers at all?"

He nodded, squeezed Taja's hand, then went.

Taja approached Ellory, taking a seat beside them. They immediately tensed and curled into themself. "Go. Away."

"I can't. Not until we clear some things up."

Visibly shaking, Ellory raised their head. Dried blood stained their cheek and trailed down from a cut across their eyebrow. Their mismatched eyes bore into Taja, but there was indeed something broken in them. That fiery hatred was gone, replaced by... defeat.

Taja's heart ached with sympathy for Ellory. They had been manipulated by Ebris even worse than Taja had. But he reminded himself to tread carefully; Ellory now had nothing left to lose, and that made them dangerous.

He extended a hand, palm up. "What happened, Ellory? We used to be so close. Almost like siblings, remember?"

Their lip curled. Angry tears spilled down their face, making clean tracks through the dried blood. Taja braced himself for a enormous retort, but the fire snuffed out of their eyes almost as soon as it'd sparked. Ellory deflated, exhaling a shaky breath. "I always... looked up to you."

Taja blinked. "You did?"

They nodded and looked up at the ruined temple. Fresh tears escaped their eyes. There was something distant and haunted to their gaze, and Taja dreaded to imagine what the Sky Palace had shown them. "I wanted to be like you. Confident, carefree, so... open. So free. You knew what you wanted and— and life just handed it to you. You've never had to fight."

Taja bristled, but then realized Ellory truly believed that. They had seen what Taja had wanted them and everyone else to see. He'd never let a single other person know how much he had to fight to keep his head above water. Before Kierra, before his exile, it was a constant battle with his family, to whom he was never good enough. Never confident enough. Too carefree, too open, too soft, too forgiving, just too much of everything he wasn't supposed to be.

He sighed and flicked a loose stone on one of the steps. "And all I wanted was to be like you."

Ellory looked at him. "Like me?"

"Well... my father wanted me to be like you," Taja amended. Because you were confident, you never second guessed anything, you were sure of yourself and you had ambitions more tangible than 'I want to be happy.' You fought tooth and nail for recognition, and my father wanted me to be like that." Taja pressed his lips together. "But you know what, Ellory? You should never have had to fight for any of that. You should never have had to compete for your own father's attention."

Ellory tensed, and Taja knew he'd struck a nerve. But again Ellory didn't strike back. They unclenched their jaw and turned their head down, tangled curls falling forward to hide their face. Taja barely heard them when they murmured, "I know. You're right."

Taja offered his hand again, and this time, Ellory reached over and grasped it. Taja held tight with both hands. "I don't have to be your enemy. I don't want to be."

"I know." Their voice cracked. They sniffed and looked up, finally meeting Taja's eyes. "You were right about everything, you know. Ebris, Båthälla, the other gods, our magic..." They shook their head. "And I hate you for it."

Taja didn't know how to respond to that.

"But I hate myself more," Ellory said. They blinked tears out of their eyes. "You did everything you could to try to make me see the obvious truth, but I didn't want to. I refused. And the Sky Palace—" They swallowed. "The Sky Palace knew that. So it— it did not go easy on me."

"I'm sorry," Taja whispered.

"It— I saw everything. I saw m-myself, but I was... I was alone. I had no one. Båthälla was gone and the gods were gone and everyone— everyone I love... left me. I saw everything that ever could have happened to me if just one person hadn't showed me kindness, and Taja... Taja, I had nothing. My life was... It was worthless. And I thought... Is this what I deserve?" Ellory's voice barely rose above a whisper. "Is–– Is that what it did to you?"

Taja squeezed Ellory's hands. "It tried to trick me in different ways, but... that wasn't pleasant, either. I'm sorry, Ellory."

They released a shaky breath. "So what now, *Sawwia Setukkda*?" There was still a hint of scorn in their voice, but the question was genuine. "You won. You killed the gods. Båthälla is yours."

Taja shook his head. "No, Ellory, it's not. The whole point of everything I fought for was that Båthälla does not belong to any one person. Båthälla is *all* of us. It's not a prize to be won. It's our home, and it belongs to every person who lives here."

"That's all very idyllic and utopian," Ellory said dryly, "but we still need leaders."

"I know. That's why I came to you."

Ellory blinked, lips parting in surprise. They sat up straighter and searched Taja's eyes as if trying to find the lie. Of course, they found none. Taja would not be asking if he didn't mean it; he just hoped he wouldn't regret it.

He hoped Ellory didn't *make* him regret it.

Ellory wiped at the dry blood on their cheek. "Am I hearing this right? Are you asking me to lead Båthälla in your place? In the *gods'* place?"

"Yes," Taja said, "but *only* if Båthälla agrees to it. After what they saw today, if they don't want you leading them, so be it. It is not up to you. It's up to them. And it must stay that way. Do you understand?"

Ellory nodded.

"Good. Second condition: if Båthälla does agree to your leadership, you will not lead alone. Start with Ava as a co-leader. *Not* a second in command, but equal in power to you. You might even want additional positions, a whole team. Give our people a chance to lead *themselves*."

Taja searched Ellory's eyes, afraid he'd find hesitation or even outward defiance. But Ellory nodded again, without a hint of the stubborn fury Taja was so used to seeing in their gaze.

Maybe, just maybe, Ellory wouldn't throw away this last chance. Taja had an inkling of an idea of how to keep tabs on Ellory, but they didn't need to know about it.

They grasped Taja's hand. "I will do my best. I promise. But... what about you?"

"Don't worry about me," Taja said. "I've done my part to uncover the truth that was being kept from us and to fight for our survival. It's time to pass Båthälla's future into more capable hands."

Ellory swallowed hard and glanced up at the trees again. "You trust me with this? You trust me to do it right?"

"I do." Maybe that was foolish, but Taja was confident that Båthälla wouldn't let anything or anyone interfere with the futures they had seen today. If Ellory started to veer down a path of greed or tried to crush Båthälla under their heel, Taja was almost positive they wouldn't get away with it.

"Why?" Ellory challenged. "How could you possibly trust me after— after *everything*? How are you so forgiving? How are you so trusting, after everything that's happened to you?"

Taja flickered a smile. "I haven't forgiven everything that was done and said to me. And I haven't forgiven everything *you* did

— to me and to Jekku. But Ellory, you reacted to all of this in precisely the way I expected you to. Of course you defended Ebris and the other gods when you thought they were threatened; you were raised to believe in them and trust them above all else. You thought if you jumped to their aid and fought on their side, you'd be rewarded."

Ellory looked away. "I should've known it was all a lie from the beginning. I should have been smarter."

"You had no reason not to trust them," Taja said gently. "Not then. You heard my side of the story and it didn't match yours, so of course you reacted poorly. I can't fault you for that."

Ellory rubbed their hands down their face. "I don't know if they were ever on our side at all, Taja."

"I think, if they were, it has been a very long time since."

Ellory took a deep breath and let it out slowly, then got to their feet. Their left leg buckled and they winced, and Taja reached out to help. Ellory gripped his arm and flickered a grateful smile, then straightened. "That fire mage friend of yours really knows her way around a knife."

Taja snorted. "She's... very protective."

Ellory's smile faded. They gazed ahead at Lily Tree, which had grown into a small sapling in the few minutes Taja had been talking with Ellory. "I know this won't change what's already been said and done, but I still want to apologize, Taja. The way I've treated you... it is unforgivable. The reasons for my behavior are not justified. They're just excuses. I should have listened before I made you my enemy."

"You're right," Taja said, "you should have. But it's behind us, and I want to keep it that way. The least I can do is forgive you, if only to clear the air." He set his hand on Ellory's shoulder. "But I'm also giving you my trust, and our people's trust. Don't break it."

Ellory grasped his hand. "I promise, brother."

27

JEKKU

JEKKU WAS NOT EAVESDROPPING, but he did think it wise to keep an eye *and* an ear on Taja and Ellory's conversation. Just in case. Jekku didn't trust them even a little, and when he saw Taja help Ellory to their feet and then *embrace them*, a hot burst of anger struck him. He finished tying off a bandage on a young girl's ankle, then assured her she'd be fine and went over to the temple steps.

To Jekku's delight, Ellory looked a little nervous when he approached. He stopped beside Taja and crossed his arms and waited for Ellory to say something.

They glanced between him and Taja a few times, then turned their head down. "I've already said as much to Taja, but... I owe you an apology, too. I owe you so much more than that, really."

Yeah, no, Jekku wasn't buying this. "It's a little late for that."

"Jekku," Taja murmured.

He shot Taja a glare. "You really think some empty words are enough to take back what they've said to us? After what they've *done* to us?"

"Jekku, please, just—"

"No!" He cut Ellory off. "You've done enough damage. All you've done since we came back here is insult us, get in our way, and — oh, how could I forget? — try to kill us."

"Jekku."

He ignored Taja and barreled on. "Taja could have *died*. I could have died. And that would've been on you." He stepped closer to Ellory, taking advantage of the inch or so he had on them. "So no, I won't accept your lousy apology, because what do you want me to say? That it's okay? That I forgive you like I'm sure Taja did? No. Absolutely no godsdamned way."

Ellory held his gaze, lips pressed in a thin line. Jekku saw the tension in their jaw, the flicker of anger in their eyes, and he dared them to fight back. His heart pounded with adrenaline. *Come on, give me your worst.* He could fight fire with fire. Or rather, fire with lightning.

But Ellory lowered their gaze. They took a step back from Jekku, raising their hands. "You're right."

Jekku narrowed his eyes. "Say it again."

Ellory's eye twitched. "You're right. You don't owe me forgiveness. I just want you to know that I do regret everything I said and did against you."

Jekku snarled, "Good."

"Jekku!" Now Taja sounded surprised. Maybe even a little hurt. But Jekku didn't care. He stood his ground as Ellory slunk away, limping and using the trees on the edge of the square as support until they made it over to the healers.

When they were out of earshot, Jekku looked at Taja. "You did forgive them instantly, didn't you?"

Taja frowned. "Not instantly. But I did."

"Of course you did." Jekku couldn't quite keep the bitterness out of his voice.

"Holding a grudge doesn't change the past, Jekku," Taja said. "You have every right to be angry. So do I. But I'm choosing to forgive them, because I understand why they acted this way."

"So you're telling them that they can get away with treating you that way. With treating *us* that way." Jekku shook his head. "That's surprising, Taja, even from you."

"That's not at all what I mean," he said. "Ellory knows what they did to us is unforgivable. All I said was that I was willing to move on, and that's true. That does not mean forgetting, and that doesn't mean I'm making excuses for them."

Jekku bit the inside of his cheek. He still didn't like that answer, but it seemed it was the best he was going to get.

"I don't trust them enough for us to repair the scraps of our friendship," Taja went on. "We'll never have what we did before. That bridge was burned a long time ago. But Jekku... I offered them a chance to lead Båthälla."

His mouth fell open. "You *what*?"

Taja lifted his hands. "I know, I know. But they deserve a victory, too. I trust them enough to see that they love this place." He turned his head to look at the Lily Tree, still steadily growing before their eyes. "They want Båthälla to thrive just as much as I do, but they were misled. And so was I. They are every bit a victim as I am."

Jekku's first instinct was to argue again. To take Taja by the shoulders and shake some sense into him. But he held his tongue and took a minute to think about it.

Ellory acted out of fear. Everything they knew to be tru
was turned upside-down and proven wrong. They panicked, an
their instinct was to resist. To deny. To fight for what was famil
iar because change was too intangible, too full of possibilities.

That was natural. That was human.

Jekku sought Taja's gaze. "Do you really think they'll lea
Båthälla toward the future it deserves?"

"I am willing to give them a chance to prove themself," h
said. "And if they lose sight of that promise at all, we'll know
Iona said she'd check in now and then."

"As will I."

Jekku and Taja both jumped at the new voice. Faint but un
mistakably there, Saevel stepped out from behind the tree. De
spite the cold they wore a sleeveless white gown that tied at thei
waist and fell to the ground. Their hair fell long around thei
shoulders and they smiled as they set a hand on the Lily Tre
It glowed under their touch. "Hello, Jekku. Hello, *Sawwia Se
tukkda.*"

"Saevel," Taja breathed. "I... We did it. Båthälla is free."

They beamed. "Indeed it is." They went to Taja and graspe
his hands. "All thanks to you, my friend. You have my gratitud
I can rest easier now that my home is in better hands. I'll kee
an eye on it for you." They winked, and then disappeared.

Jekku turned to Taja. "Why does that sound like you're plan
ning on leaving?"

Taja looked down at the stones and leaned back against th
tree. It was a second before he replied. "I've been thinking... it
time to put Båthälla behind me."

Jekku waited, heart pounding, for him to go on. What did that mean? Where would he go? And what about... them?

"I don't know where to go," Taja said, "and I don't know what I'll do wherever I end up, but I know there's more out there for me than this town." His eyes flicked up to meet Jekku's. "And I hope— Er, I want—" He sighed, searching for the words, then finally tossed up his hands and then gently held Jekku's face.

Jekku smiled up at him. His heart thumped in anticipation of Taja's next words. He had a guess, but he wanted to hear it from Taja.

"Jekku..." There was that gentle tone, that whisper-soft murmur of his name that made him melt. "Not too long ago, you said you wanted to be with me, wherever I go."

He did.

"If that— If that's still true, then... I want you with me." Taja swallowed. "I..."

Jekku set his hands over Taja's. "All you have to do is ask."

He took a shaky breath. "Come with me?"

Jekku beamed. "Anywhere."

Taja let out a short laugh, as if he hadn't expected that response. As if Jekku would've said no. He kissed Jekku once and then wrapped him in a fierce hug. Jekku nestled against him and closed his eyes.

For the first time in eight years, he didn't know what the future held, and he didn't want to. The only hints he had, thanks to the Sky Palace, were a view of the sea and a warm hand tightly holding his own. Accompanied by an overwhelming feeling of comfort and belonging, this was the life his heart wanted.

He didn't know where that place from the dream was, and he

didn't know whose hand he held, but he had a guess. He had a hope.

There was no one else he'd want it to be.

He opened his eyes and looked up at the magnificent tree, but didn't let go of Taja. He watched the Lily Tree grow, little by little, fueled by Båthälla's reawakened magic. Sprouts burst from the trunk, unfurling into new stems that grew new leaves and budded flowers. Its branches stretched and spread overhead, creating a canopy over the center of the village. This tree would form the new heart of Båthälla, and hopefully refresh its magic for centuries to come.

An idea occurred to him, and he finally drew back from Taja. "Do you still have the Oracle dagger?"

Taja frowned, but handed over the sheathed knife. Jekku slid it out and knelt next to the Lily Tree — which, in his head, he kept calling the *Lilya* Tree.

"What are you doing?" Taja asked.

Jekku sank the blade into the soil at the tree's roots. Immediately, it glowed from within, and the trunk began to grow around the dagger, absorbing it into the bark. It might've been Jekku's imagination, but the tree crackled and creaked and seemed to grow a little faster and stronger than before. The thrum of magic that radiated through the ground, however, was certainly real.

Jekku shivered as his affinity came to life within him. He didn't call it, but he felt it answer the earth's call. His hands warmed and the air charged, and he summoned a light rain just to relieve the tension building around him.

A smile touched his lips. Maybe the Oracle Stone was good for something, after all.

Taja slipped an arm around his waist and drew him close. "I think... I think they're going to be okay."

Jekku set his head on Taja's shoulder. "I think so, too. I think we all are."

Taja turned and kissed the side of Jekku's head. "I hope so."

"Hey, can I... make a request?" Jekku looked up at him. "Before we wander off, there's somewhere I'd like to go."

"Where's that?"

Jekku bit his lip. "Ajaphere."

"Your... hometown?" Taja blinked. "Oh, Jekku, of course. But... are you sure you want me to come? I don't want to intrude."

"You won't," Jekku assured him. "I want you with me." And admittedly, he didn't want to face his family alone.

"Okay." Taja smiled. "When we're ready, to Ajaphere we go."

28

JEKKU

JEKKU FELT LIKE HE WAS GOING TO THROW UP.

This didn't feel real. It *couldn't* be real. He was partially convinced he was in a dream, and any minute he'd wake up and instead of standing on a road overlooking his hometown, he'd be in Båthälla or Westdenn or the *Urdahl* or Gallien's Peak or the monastery.

Anywhere would be less impossible than here.

Eight years was so much longer than he thought.

Taja touched the back of Jekku's hand, jolting him out of his thoughts. "It's okay."

It was hardly okay. Jekku didn't know where to start. He and Taja stood at the top of the hill that would take them into Ajaphere; as soon as Jekku had caught the first glimpse of those familiar rooftops, he'd frozen. And now he was stuck in the center of a packed dirt road that he knew like the back of his hand. How many times had he walked this road? Had he known, the last time he'd stood here and looked back, that it would be nearly a decade before he returned?

No. He'd had no idea. All the answers in the universe could not have predicted what he would endure in those eight years.

"Can I make a comment?" Taja asked softly.

Jekku absently nodded.

"Ajaphere is adorable."

Adorable? Jekku didn't know if he'd ever described it that way. It wasn't special, wasn't really quaint. It just... *was*. Ajaphere never tried to be more than it was, and maybe that was why Jekku had always felt out of place here.

He wondered if he'd fit in now. He knew himself far better than he had the last time he'd walked these roads. Would Ajaphere welcome him back, or was he too different?

Maybe it didn't matter. He wasn't here for Ajaphere as a town, or any of those neighbors and acquaintances who probably didn't miss him. He was here for his family.

He hoped to the gods he had not changed beyond their recognition.

He took a deep breath, steadying himself. His eyes danced over the crooked chimney towers and rooftops made of red clay shingles. Farmland surrounded the town and sprawled as far as it could go until the earth turned rocky and steep as it began its trek up into the Crowns. It really wasn't the best time of year to be here; late winter left a thin coating of wet, icy snow on the ground, and where there wasn't snow there was mud. It would not be a pleasant walk through town.

Taja squeezed his hand. "What are you afraid of?"

"Afraid?" Jekku tore his eyes away from Ajaphere and looked at Taja. "I'm not afraid."

"You are." Taja flickered a smile. "Can you talk out what's running through that busy mind of yours?"

"Not in any way that's logical or straightforward." Jekku sighed and looked out at the distant mountains. "I mean, what's the worst that could happen? They're dead. They moved. They forgot me. That's it." His voice cracked on the last word.

"Your family will not have forgotten you, Jekku." Taja touched his cheek and brought his attention back to him. "And maybe you're right, maybe they did move. But in a town this small, I expect someone here could tell us where they went. If that's the case, we'll find them."

Not if they're dead, Jekku thought miserably. But he didn't dare voice that deep-seeded fear. He tried to tell himself it was entirely unlikely.

Taja took Jekku's hand and kissed it. "It's going to be fine. I'm with you."

He forced a smile. "Taja, if you do that in front of my mother, she's going to scold me for not inviting her to the wedding."

Taja's eyes widened and his face turned several shades darker. "She— But we—"

Jekku snorted, and for a second his anxiety fled. "I'm well aware that we're not married. But if Marian Aj'ere has one talent, it's jumping to conclusions. She's going to know *immediately*, so just... be ready for an interrogation."

Jekku didn't even think he was ready for that himself.

"Are you sure I won't be imposing?" Taja asked.

"I'm positive." Jekku took Taja's hand again. "It's literally impossible to intrude in the Aj'ere house. You will be very welcome."

Jekku finally unstuck his feet from the ground and started down the hill, Taja at his side. For a minute, Jekku imagined this as a regular occurrence. In another timeline, Jekku wasn't a stranger in his own hometown. This wasn't his first time back in eight years, but a happy visit after some time away. Maybe he and Taja had still crossed paths, maybe one thing had led to another, and maybe this was Jekku introducing Taja to his family because he *did* plan to—

Okay, getting ahead of ourselves. Jekku halted that train of thought in its tracks. And just as well, because when he surfaced from his mind and his surroundings came back into focus, he realized he'd led Taja straight through Ajaphere and up the north country road completely subconsciously. Now he stopped, taking in the damp smell of earth, the rustle of wind in the trees, the ambient sounds of the town behind him.

And the sight of his childhood home in front of him.

"This is it?" Taja asked.

Jekku nodded, heart in his throat. The house looked exactly the same, nothing faded, nothing out of place. Marian would never let it fall into disrepair. The red paint on the outside shutters was bright as ever, and the flower boxes beneath the windows were carefully covered with burlap for the winter. The pine behind the house slouched a bit more than it used to and had lost one of its bigger branches, but it still stood. There was the pond that Jekku had nearly drowned in when he was nine, and there was the chicken coop, and there was the oak he'd tried to climb when he was seven only to realize he was petrified of heights. And there was the old barn, where Marian offered to store extra items for neighbors if they didn't have their own

space. Jekku recalled many, many afternoons holed up in tha
barn with books he'd snuck from his mother's shop and vowe
to return unscathed.

Out of nowhere, a sob burst out of him, and then he couldn'
stop. Everything came rushing back and slammed into him all a
once. He gasped for air, and when Taja wrapped an arm aroun
him, Jekku turned and buried his face in his chest. He didn't car
that he was a mess, didn't care that this was the most vulnerab
Taja had ever seen him. He was relieved that Taja was here, tha
he was a source of stability and comfort when it all got to be to
much.

"Shhhh." Taja stroked his hand down the back of Jekku's heac
"It's okay."

Jekku struggled to catch his breath. "It's not. It's not. Nothin
is okay. I shouldn't— I can't be here. I should have never left.
should have never come back. It's better if they think I'm dead.
can't do this."

"Hey." Taja pulled him away and gently touched his tear
stained face. "You can do this. It's going to be hard, and it's goin
to hurt, but seeing your family again... it'll heal something that
been broken for eight years. You are here because something i
your heart tells you it's where you want to be. You wouldn't hav
come if you didn't need to. All of this" — he swept away Jekku
tears with his thumbs — "is just fear. It's just fear."

Jekku took a shuddering breath. "What if they haven't for
given me?"

"From what I've heard, your mother does not sound like th
type to hold onto resentment," Taja said. "She's your mothe

Jekku. If she can welcome me with open arms, she will certainly welcome you back."

Jekku looked down, blinking fresh tears out of his eyes. He knew Taja was right, but the idea of going up to that house still terrified him.

But Taja was right about that, too. It was only fear. As soon as he went down there, he'd feel better. The day would play out as it would, and it probably would not be as bad as Jekku was anticipating. The longer he stood here and agonized over it, the worse he'd feel, and if he left altogether? He'd regret it forever.

He took a deep breath and let it out slowly. "Okay." He grasped Taja's hand and turned to his mother's house.

This time, there was someone there who hadn't been a moment ago. A short, plump woman stood on the path leading up to the house, frozen as if time itself had paused her between one step and the next.

Jekku's heart pounded, but he couldn't move, either.

Taja nudged his arm. "Is that...?"

Jekku swallowed hard. "That's my mother."

Marian shook her head as if she thought she was seeing things. She came up the path, slowly at first, then at a jog. Suddenly Jekku's panic fled. Every ounce of anxiety and fear bled out of him and all of it was replaced by an overwhelming sense of peace, because for this minute, exactly one thing was okay: his mother was here, alive, healthy, and gods above she hadn't changed at all.

Marian halted again at the end of the path. Her eyes went wide and she pressed a hand to her mouth.

Jekku blinked back tears. "Mom."

"Gods. Oh gods. Oh gods, oh *gods*." Marian bolted to Jekku and crushed him in her arms, and Jekku didn't care that he couldn't really breathe because he hadn't been hugged by his mother in eight years and oh *gods*, he had missed her.

Jekku didn't know which one of them started crying first, but suddenly Marian was sobbing and then Jekku was a mess again and still neither of them let go. Jekku held onto her as tight as he could, and realizing that he hadn't been taller than her the last time he saw her made him cry harder.

He'd spent so much of his life alone. He'd cost Marian a long chunk of years that she should have been there for. Or rather that *he* should have been *here* for.

"*Jakob*," Marian gasped, and the name threw him off for a second. He hadn't been called that in a long time. She finally let go only enough to see his face. She kept a firm hold on his shoulders, as if he'd blink out of sight if she let go. Tears spilled down her flushed cheeks. "My gods, look at you. What happened to my little boy?"

He swallowed hard and brought her into another hug. He didn't have an answer to that. He just knew that he wasn't the boy she remembered –– in many ways –– and he hoped to the gods she forgave him for that.

"You know... it's almost eerie." Marian let go and looked at him again. "Gods, you look just like—"

"My father." Jekku's voice was barely there. "I know. I— I met him, Mom. I found him. That's partially why I'm here."

Marian's eyes widened. "He— How? Is he...?" She looked over Jekku's shoulder, then gasped. "Oh! Oh, gods above, I didn't even— I'm so sorry! I didn't realize my son had brought a guest."

She shot a pointed look at Jekku, then all at once the tears were gone and Marian was perfectly composed. She hurried over to Taja and skipped the greeting to go straight for a hug.

Jekku smiled at his momentarily bewildered expression. But he recovered almost instantly and returned her warm embrace.

"Forgive us for spilling tears all over the place right in front of you." Marian chuckled and smoothed back her hair. "My name is Marian Aj'ere. I'm... guessing you already know Jakob."

Jekku slightly shook his head, hoping Taja understood not to call him Jekku here. Not until he explained everything to Marian.

Taja gave a slight nod, then smiled at Marian and politely bowed his head. "Taja Ievisin. I'm so pleased to meet you."

Marian looked back at Jekku and raised her eyebrows. Jekku smiled back and pretended not to get what she was asking.

"Gods." Marian let out a short laugh. "This is so surreal. Come inside, both of you, before we get chilled to the bone out here." She waved a hand and led the way up to the house. "I was just putting a pie in the oven! And I've got fresh bread from Ella — that's our new neighbor, she moved in a couple weeks ago — and that'll go perfectly with the jam I unearthed from the cellar the other day. Isabel and I made it last summer and I completely forgot about it!"

She paused by the door and turned back. Her excitement faltered a little. "There's so much to tell you."

"I know." He didn't know where to start, either.

And there was also the issue of his sisters, which he was not at all prepared to approach. His mother, of course, would never forget him, but Isabel — the oldest of his three little sisters —

was only three when he left. The twins, Amelia and River, wer
two.

Jekku felt the truth with each step he took into the house: hi
sisters would not remember him.

He didn't make it more than a step inside before he had
to stop. Memories flooded him, an entire childhood contained
within these walls. Marian hadn't even rearranged the furniture
everything was the same, right down to the faint pine smell in the
air from the evergreen boughs hung over the doorways. A low
fire crackled in the hearth to the left, some candles burned on
the mantel, and light blue mages' fire flickered in round lanterns
mounted on the walls.

Jekku looked at Marian. "Mages' fire?"

She smiled. "Isabel. Her affinity just manifested last year."

"Mama, that you?"

Jekku's heart flipped over. He grabbed Taja's wrist, and once
again the impulse to flee filled him. But he resisted, and a second
later Isabel stepped into the room from the back hall.

Jekku waited, hoping beyond reason that he'd see a flicker of
recognition in her eyes.

Seconds passed, and Isabel continued to look bewildered. She
hovered in the doorway leading into the main room, an open
book in one hand and a jam-slathered piece of bread in the other
Though she was older, her face was the same. Her hair had darkened from light blonde to honey yellow, but her pale blue eyes
and scatter of freckles were just as Jekku remembered.

Taja nudged Jekku, and he realized he'd been staring. "Um,
Hi."

Marian bit her lip. "Isabel, this... Do you remember your brother, Jakob?"

He tried not to wince at that name.

Isabel's eyebrows shot up. "Whoa. It's you?"

Jekku managed a nod. "It's me. I... I'm sure you don't remember me, Isa. You were so little the last time I saw you."

"Mom told me stories," she said, and smiled. "I'm glad to finally meet you."

Jekku had to look away from her. It was useless to point out that they'd met before, they'd been *siblings* before, when it was too deeply buried in her memory. But Jekku remembered. He could still recall the night he'd first met her, when Marian had brought her and the twins home and told him, in the weakest voice he'd ever heard from her, that the girls' mother could no longer take care of them, and they would be part of this family now.

He had grown attached to Isabel immediately. While his mother handled the newborn twins, Jekku looked after Isabel. He told her stories, carried her around the house and all over the yard so she could meet the world. He soon found her to be just as inquisitive and curious as he was, and he loved nothing more than teaching her everything he knew.

The twins... he'd had trouble getting used to the twins. He helped, of course, but two newborns with stubborn and demanding personalities were far more trouble than Jekku had anticipated.

It hurt, looking at Isabel now. He'd missed her entire life. Gone was the little girl who'd trailed him around the house. She was eleven now, nearly a teenager, and while she was still a child it wasn't the same.

Isabel leaned her shoulder against the wall and took another bite of the bread in her hand. "Okay, so, my mysteriously long-lost brother shows up out of nowhere with a rather pretty man with funny ears and everyone's just fine with it? I have questions."

"Isa," Marian scolded, "don't be rude." But Jekku didn't miss the interest in her eyes when she looked at Taja again. "I didn't realize before. You're Elshalan?"

He nodded. "Yes, I'm from Båthälla."

"Båthälla." Marian flickered a smile. "How funny. That's where Jakob's father was from. Tell me, Jakob, how on earth did you find your way to Båthälla?"

"Let's sit," Jekku suggested with a wave toward the couch. "It's a really long story."

***

Jekku didn't tell them everything. He glazed over his time at Gallien's Peak, made sure to omit Leo entirely from the narrative, and summarized the Oracle Stone and Båthälla mess as concisely as possible. Marian and Isabel listened with rapt interest, although Isabel looked more like she was hearing an epic legend than the real events of Jekku's life. Marian's expression shifted from shock to horror to sympathy and a thousand other emotions Jekku couldn't read, but in the end she simply stared at him in disbelief.

Then came the challenging part: his father.

Jekku handled it as carefully as he could. He skimmed over the details, but made sure Marian knew that Jakob had done everything in his power to keep Jekku and Taja safe. "He's the reason we're both here," Jekku said. "I— I knew him for a matter of hours and he—"

He paused, choked up. Taja, tucked beside Jekku on the couch, slid his hand over and placed it on Jekku's knee.

"He was always like that," Marian said softly. "That's one of the things I loved about him most. He bridged the gap between stranger and friend in just a few words and could make you feel like you'd known him forever."

Jekku nodded. "Exactly that."

Marian smiled, but it faded quickly. "But he didn't make it, did he?"

Jekku blinked tears out of his eyes. "I'm sorry. We were so close. We got out of the Labyrinth and out of Båthälla, but I guess... when the Elshalan gods took his magic, they also cursed him so that if he ever tried to leave Båthälla, he would die."

Marian stared down at her hands in her lap. She nodded slowly and closed her eyes, letting the tears fall. Jekku got up and went to her, pulling her into a hug.

"I'm so sorry, Mom. I'm so sorry."

She squeezed him tight. "It's not your fault, Jakob. And it— it's all right. He's not suffering anymore. He's not alone. He's free. That's the most I can hope for him." She let go and took Jekku's face in her hands. "All I ever wanted was for us to be a family, and I regret every day that we could never have that. But you met him despite all the odds, and I'm grateful that you got to know him at all."

Jekku sniffed. "Me too."

Before either of them could say anything else, the front door opened and two freckled, redheaded girls bustled in, arms weighed down with canvas bags. Their laughs filled the room but then they stopped short.

Jekku's heart broke all over again. If Isabel didn't remember him, there wasn't a chance Amelia and River would.

Marian stood and went to hug the twins, then took a couple of the bags from them. "Perfect timing! Girls..." She held out hand toward Jekku. "Meet your brother."

***

Later, after a somewhat awkward conversation with the twins and a proper introduction of Taja to everyone, Jekku joined his mother outside for a walk. It was cold, and the sun was on its way down, but Jekku wasn't about to complain. How many times had he wished over the past eight years that he could simply walk and chat with his mom?

"Is it weird being back here after all that time?" Marian asked. She walked arm in arm with him, the end of her long cloak dragging in the snow behind her.

"It is," he said. "But at the same time, it's almost like I never left."

She squeezed his arm. "Jakob, I felt your absence every hour of every day."

He stared at the frost-coated ground. There was that name again, but even this wasn't the right time to explain. "I'm so sorry

I put you through that," he said instead. "I can't imagine what that was like."

"Was it worth it?"

He raised his head and met her eyes. *No*, was his instinctual response. The grueling months at Gallien's Peak, Firune's cruelty, his imprisonment in the dark for four years, his death-wish journey from Aylesbury up into the Crowns... No, none of that was worth leaving the comfort of home. Neither was the Oracle Stone situation, or the Båthälla situation.

What made it worth it, though, were the victories. The moments of joy. Being surrounded by magic at its most magnificent, before his time at Gallien's Peak turned sour, was one of the most exhilarating things Jekku had ever felt. Feeling welcomed at the monastery after months of aimless wandering and bad choices had saved his life. And despite all the trouble that damned Oracle Stone caused, without it, he wouldn't have Lilya and Taja in his life.

Would Jekku go back and do things differently? Absolutely. But would he *erase* the past eight years? No. He didn't think he would.

"Some of it wasn't," he replied to his mother. "But I think the lasting things were. In ten years, I won't remember the pain or the loneliness. I'll remember the people who made it worth it."

Marian smiled. "People such as your handsome friend who is likely being interrogated by your sisters as we speak?"

Jekku went red to the tips of his ears. "I mean... yes."

Marian snickered. "Anything I should know about?"

Jekku hated how perceptive she was. He'd sooner sink through the ground and be swallowed by the earth than talk to

Marian about his love life, but... "Yes, actually. He, um. He's my partner."

She beamed at him. "After seeing the way he looks at you, I certainly hoped so! I'm happy for you, Jakob. How long—"

"Okay, wait, there's something else I need to tell you." He stopped walking and turned to her. "I'll— I'll tell you more about Taja in a minute, but..." His heart pounded. He knew he had to say this, but how would she react to him throwing away the name she'd lovingly given him in memory of his father? This felt even more like a betrayal now that he knew what his father had sacrificed. And he knew Marian wouldn't take it personally or simply refuse to call him Jekku, but he also didn't want to see the disappointment he expected to find in her eyes.

Still, it needed to be said. He was not Jakob. He was Jekku, and he was everything he'd become since choosing that name. It wasn't a betrayal of his parents to do what he needed to feel like the person he wanted to be.

"I changed my name." The words spilled out, and the next ones were easier. "I'm called Jekku now. I know that you named me after my father, but I'm no longer the person Jakob was. I think I left that boy behind the night I left Ajaphere. Since then I've done nothing but change, and it felt right that my name should change with me." He held his breath and met her eyes. "I hope you understand."

Marian smiled and brought him into a hug. "I understand enough, and I respect your choice. You've been on your own for a long time, Ja— Jekku." She breathed a laugh. "You know, it's not so different. But it suits you. Jekku."

A wide smile burst across his face. The last of his anxiety fled, eaving his heart feeling full. He didn't realize how good it would feel — how *validating* it would feel — to hear his mother call him by his preferred name. His new, true name.

Marian gave him another squeeze and then let go. "What I meant to say is, you've been on your own for a long time. Of course I won't understand everything you've gone through or everything that's changed. Maybe that's only for you to understand. My job is to be here for you through all of it, and— gods, Jekku." Her voice caught. "Do you know how many days are in eight years?"

He blinked. "A lot?"

"Two thousand, nine hundred, and twenty. Give or take." Marian touched his face. "And every single one of them, I wished from sunrise to sunset to see what I saw today: you, standing on that road, ready to come home." Her green eyes searched his. "I can't describe to you how that felt, Jekku. I won't try. My grief is mine to carry, as is yours. Eight years is a lot of life to miss, but that doesn't mean we can't pick up where we left off."

Jekku hugged her again. "I love you. I missed you so much."

Marian once again squeezed the life out of him. "I'm so glad you're home." She drew back. "But I have a feeling it's not forever."

He shook his head. "I don't... I don't think my place is here anymore."

"I understand." Her eyes turned glassy and a few tears escaped. "But will you at least stay a night? Isabel stole your room, but there's the couch and I can throw something together for you."

He scoffed. "How come Taja gets the couch?"

"Because he's our guest, of course!"

Jekku heaved a playfully exasperated sigh. "I'm gone for eigh years and don't even get the couch upon my return."

Marian laughed. "Would you rather have the barn?" she teased.

"... I suppose I can handle the floor." Jekku grinned.

Marian shook her head, still laughing, and started back to ward the house. "Come on, let's get dinner going. I'll make what ever you like."

***

"Your family is wonderful."

Jekku opened his eyes and smiled up at Taja as he ap proached. He sat in a soft, fresh patch of grass behind hi mother's house, listening to the birds and enjoying the firs warm day in... entirely too long. Taja settled beside him and me him with a kiss.

"I hope my mother hasn't scared you away," Jekku said. "Sh can be... a lot."

"Are you joking? I am immensely jealous that you grew up with her cooking. I'm still thinking about that dinner she mad last night. She's lovely, Jekku." He traced his fingers through Jekku's hair and tucked it behind his ear. "Just like you."

Jekku's face warmed and he turned his head to hide a smile "Oh, stop."

"Hmm, no." Taja pulled him close and kissed his cheek, nuz zling him. "I love it when you get flustered."

Jekku playfully shoved him away, but Taja grabbed him back

peppering him with kisses while Jekku laughed. He emerged a breathless, blushing mess, and Taja didn't look sorry at all.

"You're a menace," Jekku teased. He smoothed Taja's curls back from his face and kissed him once more.

"As if you're not." Taja stole another kiss.

"Never said I wasn't." Jekku grinned. "But you love me."

Taja's eyes softened. "I do."

Jekku settled back in the grass and pulled Taja down beside him. They lay with their heads tipped together and their hands entwined, and Taja's thumb traced a soft circle on the back of Jekku's hand. Jekku closed his eyes and let the early springtime sun warm his face. Leafy stems of not-yet-open wildflowers tickled his cheeks.

"Jekku?" Taja murmured. "Have you thought any more about where we should go next?"

"Hmmm." Jekku shrugged. "A little. I mean, there's a hundred little towns around here, and there's Westdenn and Aylesbury, but..."

"Aylesbury seems like too much."

"I don't want to live with Gallien's Peak over my head," Jekku agreed.

"And I refuse to go to Westdenn again unless they change that law," Taja added.

"Right." Jekku looked up at the blue expanse of sky overhead. Staring straight up, the sky was the only thing in his field of vision. Endless. Untouched. Just like the sea.

Jekku turned his head toward Taja. "What about the islands?"

Taja met his eyes. "Which islands?"

"The ones off the coast of Aylesbury. We call them Godsteeth.

I've never been, but I've heard it's beautiful there. I know you
liked Strykivik, but I literally *refuse* to live there even if the view
of the sea was breathtaking. But maybe we could... visit the islands?"

"Sure. Sounds like it'd be worth it just to see them." Taja
smiled.

Jekku smiled back and closed his eyes once more. He
breathed in the smell of fresh grass and new earth, and listened
to the rustle of wind through the trees. A frog trilled by the
pond. The chickens scratched and cooed. Somewhere in the
woods, a chorus of birds sang.

It was all at once so natural and so surreal. These were the
sounds that made up the backdrop of Jekku's childhood, and lying here with his eyes shut, he could almost believe he'd never
left. He could be a child again, enjoying a carefree spring day.

Time didn't exist here. Jekku wondered if Ajaphere would
ever change.

There was comfort in its consistency, but Jekku couldn't stay
here. It was *too* comfortable. Too static. He didn't want his future
to be his past, or vice versa. Let his memories live in those carefree days; he wanted his life to begin somewhere new.

And *with* someone new.

Someone who felt more like home than any singular location
ever had.

"Jekku." Taja squeezed his hand. "Look."

He opened his eyes. Taja traced his free hand over the green,
unopened buds scattered throughout the grass. He hummed
softly, and Jekku watched the flowers in awe.

They bloomed.

Acknowledgments

Wow. Here we are again. I'm having a weird sense of déjà-vu as I write this page exactly a year after the release of my debut book. It kinda feels like ten years, but it also kinda feels like two seconds.

When I finished my final draft of *The Oracle Stone*, I did not expect to write a sequel a few months later. I closed the book and began preparing to toss it into the world as a standalone. Well... I was wrong. And I have my brother, Adam, to thank for that.

So let's start there. Adam, this book is dedicated to you because you essentially commanded me to write it, but you're getting a shout-out here too because you're great. So thank you, truly, for asking for a second book and then giving me the first plot nuggets I needed to get into it. You wouldn't be holding this book otherwise.

And as always a huge thank you to my parents for their endless support, encouragement to keep doing the things I love, and for bearing with me when I was like "No sorry I have revisions we'll talk later" entirely too many times. Love you past the last number!

To my friends; especially Florence, Catherine, Felix, Sam, Windy, Rae, Carolyn, and my beloved Froup –– I love you all to pieces and I couldn't ask for a better found family. Thank you a million times to Shelby and Zee, my cheerleading team and besties in crime, for being two of the sweetest people I know. Your encouragement and enthusiasm keep me going, and you friendship means everything to me.

And a zillion—nay, an infinity of thank-yous to my wonderful, lovely, fantastic beta readers: Juniper Lake Fitzgerald, Gaylen Sinclair, and Tabitha O'Connell. You guys helped shape this book into what it is now, and I can't thank you enough for your invaluable feedback, encouragement, and instances of "OH NO" commented on the manuscript. A special shout-out to Juniper, whose on-point reaction gifs and unhinged replies to certain occurrences in this book literally gave me life. Your anguish fuels me, Juni, and I'm not sorry ;)

Thank you also to my talented author friends in the beautifully chaotic LGBTQ Writers server. Being a part of such a wonderful group of writers has been an amazing boost of confidence, you all inspire me every day. I am so proud of all of you, and so happy to be able to call myself your friend. The blue bird app sucks sometimes, but it brought us all together so I guess it's not TERRIBLE. And big hugs to Juniper, Rita, Gaylen, Tabitha, and A.E., who reviewed *The Oracle Stone* and/or provided advance reviews of *The Savior's Rise*. Your kind words mean the world to me

Finally, thank *you* (yes, you! hi!) for reading and following this chaotic trio on yet another adventure. It's still kind of wild to me that people other than me have read these books, so thank you thank you, dear reader, for picking up this book and fulfilling a dream.

The last time I wrote an acknowledgments page, I ended it with "It's time for something new." That line was both a reference to the final line of *The Oracle Stone*, but also an acknowledgment that I'd be moving on from this series and these characters. Obviously, that did not happen. So I'm not fooling myself this time. This is the end, but it's also not.

I'll see you next time.

Hailing from upstate New York, Talli L. Morgan is the author of the Windermere Tales series. When they're not buried in books –– their own or someone else's –– Talli hangs out on Twitter and co-hosts a Q&A chat for writers. And if you can't find them there, they're probably hiding in the corner of a library.

You can visit Talli at tallimorgan.com, and find them on Twitter @TLM_writes and Instagram @tallimorgan.books.

CPSIA information can be obtained
at www.ICGtesting.com
Printed in the USA
BVHW011657250222
630005BV00031B/635

9 781087 873381